The Lady of Han-Gilen

Books by Judith Tarr

THE HOUND AND THE FALCON TRILOGY

The Isle of Glass
The Golden Horn
The Hounds of God

AVARYAN RISING

The Hall of the Mountain King
The Lady of Han-Gilen
*A Fall of Princes**

AVARYAN RISING

VOLUME TWO

The Lady of Han-Gilen

Judith Tarr

THE LADY OF HAN-GILEN

A Bluejay International Edition

First printing: April 1987

A TOR Book

Published by Tom Doherty Associates, Inc.
49 West 24 Street
New York, N.Y. 10010

Jacket art by Kevin Eugene Johnson
Map by John M. Ford

ISBN: 0-312-94271-0

Printed in the United States of America

0 9 8 7 6 5 4 3 2 1

To my agent, Jane Butler

For performance above and beyond

the call of duty

A Note on Pronunciation

With regard to the pronunciation of the names herein, the most useful rule is that of medieval Latin, with the addition of English *J* and *Y*. To be precise:

• Consonants are essentially as in English. *C* and *G* are always hard, as in *can* and *gold*, never soft as in *cent* and *gem*. *S* is always as in *hiss*, never as in *his*.

• Vowels are somewhat different from the English. *A* as in *father:* Vadin is VAH-deen. *E* as in French *fée:* Elian is AY-lee-ahn; Han-Gilen is hahn-gee-LAYN. *I* is much as the English *Y:* consider *hymn* and the suffix *-ly,* and the consonantal *yawn;* hence, Ianon is YAH-non, Mirain is mee-RAYN, Alidan is ah-LEE-dahn. *O* as in *oh,* never as in *toss. U* as in Latin, comparable to English *oo (look, loom);* Uveryen is oo-VER-yen, Umijan is OO-mee-jahn.

• *Y* can be either vowel or consonant, as in English; before a vowel it is a consonant (Avaryan is ah-VAHR-yan, Odiya is OH-dee-yah), but before a consonant it is a vowel (Ymin is EE-min, Yrios is EE-ree-ohss).

• *Ei* is pronounced as in *reign* (Geitan is GAY-tahn); *ai,* except in the archaic and anomalous *Mirain* (see above), is comparable to the English *bye:* Abaidan is ah-BYE-dahn. Otherwise, paired vowels are pronounced separately: Amilien is ah-MEE-lee-en.

One

"ELIAN! OH, LADY! ELIAN!"

The Hawkmaster paused in mending a hood and raised an inquiring brow. Elian laid a finger on her lips.

The voice drew nearer, a high sweet voice like a bird's. "Lady? Lady, where *have* you got to? Your lady mother—"

Elian sighed deeply. It was always her lady mother. She bound off her last stitch and smoothed the crest of feathers thus attached to the hood: feathers the color of fire or of new copper, rising above soft leather dyed a deep and luminous green. Flame and green for the ruling house of Han-Gilen: green to match her much-patched coat, flame no brighter than her hair.

She laid the hood in the box with the others she had made, and rose. The Hawkmaster watched her. Although he was not mute, he seldom spoke save to address his falcons in their own wild tongue. He did not speak now, nor did she. But his eyes held a smile for her.

In the mews beyond the workroom, the hooded falcons rested on their perches. The small russet hunters for

the ladies and the servants; the knights' grey beauties,
each with its heraldic hood; her brother's red hawk shifting restlessly in its bonds, for it was young and but newly
proven; and in solitary splendor, the white eagle which
came to no hand but that of the prince her father.

Her own falcon drowsed near her brother's. Though
smaller, it was swifter, and rarer even than the eagle: a
golden falcon from the north. Her father's gift for her
birth-feast, a season past. It had been new-caught then;
soon it would be ready for proving, that first, free hunt,
when the bird must choose to come back to its tamer's
hand or to escape into freedom.

She paused to stroke the shimmering back with a
feather. The falcon roused slightly from its dream, a
tightening of talons on the perch, an infinitesimal turning
of the blinded head.

"Lady!"

The mews erupted in a flurry of wings and fierce
hawk-screams. Only the eagle held still. The eagle, and
Elian's falcon, that opened its beak in a contemptuous
hiss and was silent.

The Hawkmaster emerged from his workroom, followed by his two lads. Wordlessly they set about soothing
their charges.

The cause of the uproar paid it no heed at all. She fit
her voice admirably well, plump and pretty, wrinkling her
delicate nose at the scents of the mews and holding her
skirts well away from the floor. "Lady, *look* at you! What
her highness will say—"

Elian had already thrust past her, nearly oversetting
her into the mud of the yard.

THE PRINCESS OF HAN-GILEN SAT AMONG HER LADIES IN A
bower of living green, her gown all green and gold, and
a circlet of gold binding her brows. A delicate embroidery
lay half finished in her lap; one of her ladies plucked a
soft melody upon a lute.

She contemplated her daughter for a long while in
silence. Elian kept her back straight and her chin up, but

she was all too painfully aware of the figure she cut. Her coat had been her brother's; it was ancient, threadbare, and much too large. Her shirt and breeches and boots fit well enough, but they stood in sore need of cleaning. She bore with her a faint but distinct odor of the stables, overlaid with the pungency of the mews. She was, in short, a disgrace.

The princess released Elian from her gaze to stitch a perfect blossom. Once the most beautiful woman in her father's princedom of Sarios, she remained the fairest lady in Han-Gilen. Her smooth skin was the color of honey; her eyes were long and dark and enchantingly tilted, with fine arching brows; her hair beneath its drift of veil was deep bronze with golden lights. Her one flaw, the chin which was a shade too pronounced, a shade too obstinate, only strengthened her beauty. Without it she would have been lovely; with it, she was breathtaking.

At last she spoke. "We have been searching for you since the morning."

"I was riding." In spite of all her efforts, Elian knew she sounded sullen. "Then I had an hour with the Hawkmaster. Will you be keeping me long, Mother? The embassy from Asanion will be arriving today, and Father has a council just before. He bade me—"

"At your insistence." The princess' voice was soft but unyielding. "He is the most indulgent of fathers. Yet even he would not be pleased to see you as you are now."

Elian battled an impulse to straighten her coat. "I would not attend council in this state, my lady."

"Let us hope that you would not," said the princess. "I have heard that you have done so in garb but little more proper. Breeched and booted, and at your side a dagger." The princess continued her embroidery, each word she spoke as careful and as minutely calculated as the movements of her needle. "When you were still a child, I suffered it, since your father seemed inclined to encourage it. There were some who even found it charming: Han-Gilen's willful Lady trailing after her brothers, insisting that she be taught as they were taught. You learned fighting and hawking and wild riding; you can read, you can write, you can speak half a dozen tongues. You have all the arts of a Gileni prince."

"And those of a princess as well!" Elian burst out. "I can sew a fine stitch. I can dance a pretty dance. I can play the small harp and the greater harp and the lute. I have a full repertoire of songs, all charming, all suitable for a lady's bower."

"And some scarcely fit for a guardroom." The princess set down her work and folded her hands over it. "My daughter, you have been a woman for three full years. When I was as old as you, I had been two years a wife and nigh three seasons a mother."

"And always," muttered Elian, "a perfect lady."

The princess smiled, startling her a little. "Nay, daughter, I had been a famous hoyden. But I had not so doting a father, nor so lax a mother. With the coming of my woman's courses, I had perforce to put on a gown and bind up my hair and accept the husband my family had found for me. I was fortunate. He was scarce a decade older than I; he was comely; and he was kind to me. The man chosen for my sister had been none of those things."

Elian's hands were fists. She kept her voice level with an effort of will, so level that it was flat. "I have another suitor."

"Indeed," said the princess with unruffled patience. "One whom you would do well to treat with something resembling courtesy."

"Have I ever done any less?"

The princess drew a slow breath: her first sign of temper. "You have been . . . polite. With utmost politeness you rode with Lord Uzian the Hunter, and brought back two stags for his every one, and slew the boar which would have destroyed him. You saved his life; he remembered an earlier betrothal and departed. When the two barons Insh'ai would have dueled for your hand, you offered most politely to engage each one and to accept the one who bested you. You defeated them both, and thus they lost you with the match. Then I call to mind your courtesy to the Prince Komorion. Lover of scholarly debate that he was, you engaged him in dispute, demolishing him so utterly that he retreated to a house of the Grey Monks and forsook all claim to his princedom."

"He was more than half a monk already," Elian said sharply. "I had no desire to wed a saint."

"Apparently you have no desire to wed at all." Elian opened her mouth to speak, but the princess said, "You are the daughter of the Red Prince, the Lady of Han-Gilen. Hitherto you have been permitted to run wild, not only because your father loves you to the point of folly; I too can understand how sweet is freedom. But you are no longer a child. It is time you became a woman in more than body."

"I will wed," said Elian, speaking with great care, "when I find a man who can stand beside me. Who will not stalk away in a temper when I best him; who will be able, on occasion, to best me. An equal, Mother. A king."

"Then it were best that you find him soon." The velvet had fallen aside at last, baring steel. "Today with the embassy of Asanion comes the High Prince Ziad-Ilarios himself, heir to the throne of the Golden Empire. He has sent word that he comes not only to propose a new and strong alliance with Han-Gilen; it would be his great pleasure to seal that alliance by a union with the Flower of the South."

Elian had never felt less like a flower, unless it were the flameflower, that consumed itself with its own fire. "And if it is not *my* pleasure?"

"I encourage you to consider it." The princess raised a slender hand. "Kieri. Escort my lady to her chamber. She will prepare herself to meet with the high prince."

ELIAN STOOD STIFF AND STILL IN A FLUTTER OF LADIES. They had bathed her and scented her. Now they arrayed her in the elaborate gown of a Gileni princess. A tall mirror cast back her image, mocking her. She had not been a comely child: awkward, gangling, all arms and legs and eyes. But suddenly, as she grew into a woman, she had changed. Her awkwardness turned to a startling grace, her thinness to slenderness, her angles to curves that caught many a man's eye. And her face—her strong-jawed, big-eyed face, with her mother's honey skin and her father's fire-bright hair—had shaped itself into something much too unusual for prettiness. People looked and called it interesting; looked again, much longer, and declared it beautiful.

She glowered at it. Her gown dragged at her; a maid weighted her with gold and jewels, while another arrayed her hair in the fashion of a maiden, falling loose and fiery to her knees. Gently, with skillful hands, a third lady began to paint her face. Rose-honey for her lips, honey-rose for her cheeks, and a shimmer of gilt about her eyes.

A low whistle brought her about sharply, winning a hiss of temper from the maid with the brushes. Elian's glare turned to laughter and back to a glare again as her brother fell to his knees before her. "Ah, fairest of ladies!" he cried extravagantly. "How my heart longs for you!"

She cuffed him; he swayed aside, laughing, and leaped to his feet. He was tall and lithe, and as like to her in face and form as any man could be. Unlike most men of the Hundred Realms, who reckoned their beards a deformity and shaved or plucked them into smoothness, he had let his own grow to frame his face. It made him look striking, rakish, and more outrageously handsome than ever.

"And all too well you know it," said Elian, tugging at it.

"*Ai*, woman! You have a hard hand. And you so fair the god himself would sigh after you. Are you setting yourself to melt the hearts of Father's whole council?"

"If Mother has her way," Elian said grimly, "I'll win a better prize than that. Prince Ziad-Ilarios is coming to have a look at the merchandise."

Halenan's laughter retreated to his eyes. "So I've heard. Is that why your anger is fierce enough to set me burning even in my lady's chamber?"

"Little help you need there," she said.

He grinned. "I find marriage more than congenial. Even after five years of it."

"Don't you?" She thought of his two sons, and of his lady in her bower awaiting in milky calm the advent of their sister. A love match, that had been, and it had startled most of Han-Gilen; for his bride was neither a great lady nor a great beauty, but the broad-hipped, sweet-faced, eminently sensible daughter of a very minor baron. That good sense had taken her quite placidly from her father's minute holding to the palace of the Red Prince's heir, and kept her there through all the murmurings of the court, as the high ones waited in vain for her handsome husband to tire of her.

With a sharp gesture Elian dismissed her ladies. As the last silken skirt vanished behind the door, she faced her brother. "You know why I can't do as Mother is asking."

"I know why you think you can't."

"I gave my word," she said.

"The word of a child."

"The word of the Lady of Han-Gilen."

He raised his hands, not quite as if he wanted to shake her. "Lia, you were eight years old."

"And he was fifteen," she finished for him, with very little patience. "And he was my brother in all but blood, and people were plenty who said he was that too, because no man could be the son of a god, least of all the son of the Sun. And whether he was half a god or all a man, he was heir by right to a barbarian kingdom, and when the time came, he went to claim his own. He had to go. I had to stay. But I promised him: My time would come. I would go to fight with him. Because his mother left him a kingdom, but his father begot him to rule the world."

Halenan opened his mouth, closed it. Once he would not have been so kind. Once he would have said what he could not keep from thinking. The thinking was cruel enough between them who were mageborn and magebred. To Mirain their foster brother, son of a priestess and a god, great mage and warrior even in his youth, Elian had been the merest infant: his sister, his shadow, trailing after him like a worshipful hound. Wherever he was, she was sure to be. It was certain proof of his parentage, a wag had said once. Who but a god's son could endure such constant adoration?

And now he was a man grown, king in distant Ianon and raising legends about his name. If he even remembered her, it would not be as a woman who kept her word; it would be as a child who had wept to lose her brother, and sworn a child's heedless oath, more threat than promise.

"What will you do?" Halenan pricked at her. "Join his harem in Han-Ianon?"

"He has slaves enough," she snapped, the sharper for that her cheeks had caught fire. "I will fight for him, and wield my magery for him, and be free."

"And if he has changed? What then, Lia? What if he has gone barbarian? Or worse, gone all strange with the god's power that is in him?"

"Then," she said with steadiness she had fought for, "I will make him remember what he was."

Halenan set his hands on her shoulders. She came perilously close to laughing. Even in the utmost of exasperation, he took care not to rumple her gown. That much, husbandhood had done for him.

He glared at her, but half of it was mirth. "Little sister, tell me the truth. You do all of this simply to drive the rest of us mad."

"I do it because I can do nothing else."

"Exactly." He let her go and sighed. "Maybe after all you should go to Mirain. He could make you see sense when no one else could."

"I will go when it is time to go."

"And meanwhile, you turn away suitor after suitor, and refuse adamantly to tell even Father why you do it."

"You don't, either."

"I keep my promises." Their eyes met; his wavered the merest fraction. He rallied with a flare of Gilen temper. "Maybe I should. Mother would see the perfect reso-

lution: a match between you and your oldest love. With
the Hundred Realms for a dowry, and Avaryan's Throne
for a marriage couch, and—"

She struck him with a lash of power. It stopped his
mouth. It did not stop his mind. He was laughing at her.
He always laughed at her, even when she pricked him to
a rage.

"It's love," he said, "and absurdity. And maybe
desperation."

"You never were a match for me."

He bowed to the stroke, utterly unoffended. "Come
now, O my conqueror. We're late for council."

Two

THE HIGH PRINCE ZIAD-ILARIOS BOWED LOW BEFORE THE Lady of Han-Gilen. When he straightened, he stood still, his eyes steady upon her, a long measuring look that warmed into approval. She returned it with no expression at all. He was fair even for a westerner, his hair like hot gold, his eyes as golden as a falcon's, his skin the color of fine ivory; though no taller than she, he was deep-chested and strong, and very good to look on.

Her stare should have disconcerted him; it made him smile, a remarkably sweet smile, like a child's. But no child ever had a voice so rich or so deep. "My lady, you are fairer even than I looked for, with but songs and painted likenesses to guide me."

She had a weakness for a fine voice. Grimly she suppressed it. "Indeed, highness, you flatter me."

He would not err so far as to bow again. Nor would he oblige her by speaking as most men did to a lovely woman, as to an idiot child. "I have an unfortunate flaw, my lady. I tend to speak my mind. You must forgive me. Should I abase myself at your surpassingly comely feet?"

Before she knew it, she was laughing. Some people

10

said that her merriment was like bells; others, that it was much too free for a maiden's. They stared now, discreetly enough, to be sure: all her father's court, even her father enthroned under his golden canopy with his princess beside him. He smiled, a softening of his dark stern face; she looked away, back to her companion. Oh yes, he was a pleasing young man. She could do far worse than he.

He was smiling again and inviting her, not quite touching her hand, walking slowly through the glittering throng. She matched his pace. No one impeded them, although everyone watched them. "Already they have us wedded," she said.

He eluded the trap as neatly as if it had never been laid. "That is the sport of lesser mortals: to make legends of their rulers. Your legend is fascinating, my lady. In Asanion, we cannot decide whether it is a wonder or a scandal. A princess, yet you have mastered all the arts of princehood; you challenge your suitors to defeat you in their own chosen skills, and send them away when you find them wanting."

"And what is your skill?" she demanded of him.

He shrugged, a minute gesture, barely visible within his golden robes. "None. Except, perhaps, that of ruling. 'Kinging it,' the common folk would say. I do it rather well."

"You speak our tongue very well indeed."

"That is part of it. So much of ruling is in the tongue. Too much, some might add."

"Especially here in the Hundred Realms."

"In the Golden Empire, fully as much. You are eloquent, I am told, and have the gift of tongues."

"I like to talk."

"Why, so do I. But wit is hard to come by, and one cannot always converse with oneself."

"I talked a philosopher into the ground once. He sought to wed me; he wedded with solitude instead."

"He made a poor choice."

"Did he? I am thinking of taking a vow, my lord. To take lovers by the dozen, but never a husband."

"Surely you would grow weary of constant variety."

"Do you think I would?" She halted in the midst of the court and fixed her eyes upon him. "Have you?"

His laughter was as sweet as his smile. "Oh, long since! Twice ninescore concubines: that is the number allotted to the heir of Asanion. One for each day of the sun's year. Alas, I am cursed with a constant nature; where I take pleasure, there do I most prefer to love. So you see, if I follow my nature, some few of my ladies are content; the rest either dissolve in tears or succumb to murderous envy. But if I strive to please them all, I fail utterly to content myself."

"So you seek a wife."

"So I seek a wife. A married man, you see, may free his concubines."

"Ah," she said in something close to delight. "Your motives are hardly pure at all. I had begun to fear that there would be no flaw in you."

"But surely perfection is most unutterably dull?"

"You are not tall. That is a flaw, but one I cannot in conscience condemn; for you are also beautiful."

"In Asanion I am reckoned a tall man."

"And fair?"

"That is not a word we like to use in speaking of men. But yes, they call me comely. We breed for it."

"My mother has Asanian blood." Elian changed tacks abruptly, fixing him with her most disconcerting stare. "Some said that you would not come to us; that your borders are beset, and that your father has need of you there."

Ilarios was not disconcerted at all. He shifted as rapidly and as smoothly as she. "He has greater need of Han-Gilen and the Hundred Realms." His eyes leveled. They were all gold, like an animal's, but the light in them was godly bright. "You know what concerns us."

"The barbarians in the north."

"Even so. We have never exerted ourselves to conquer them, reckoning them little better than savages, too deeply embroiled in their own petty feuds to unite against us. So they should have remained. But they have spawned a monster, it seems. A chieftain—he calls himself a king—who seized the throne of one of the northern provinces—"

"Ianon," she murmured.

"Ianon," he agreed, with a swift glance. "He usurped its throne, gathered its clans, and proceeded to do the same to its neighbors. It was easier than it might have been. He rode—rides still, for the matter of that—under the banner of the Sun-god; his father, so he claims, is the god himself, his mother—"

He broke off. For once, Elian could see, his ready tongue had led him farther than he liked to go.

She led him to the end of it. "His mother was a priestess, born in Ianon but raised to the greatest eminence of her order: high priestess of the Temple of Avaryan in Han-Gilen. In addition to which, she was prophet of the realm, and bound in close friendship with its prince." She smiled, closing in for the kill. "Tell me more of her son."

"But surely—" He stopped. His eyes knew what she did, and dared to guess why. They flickered as a hawk's will, veiling just perceptibly. Calmly he said, "Her son appeared in Ianon some few summers past. He was little more than a child then; he is, so they say, very young still. But he is a skilled general, for a barbarian, and he has a knack of gathering men to himself. Hindered not at all by the parentage he claims and the destiny he has revealed to any who will listen. The world is his, he proclaims. He was born to rule it."

"Simply to rule it?" asked Elian.

"Ah," said Ilarios, "he says that it is not simple at all. He is the trueborn heir of Avaryan, the emperor foretold, the Sword of the Sun; he will bring all the world under his sway, and cast down the darkness and bind it in chains, and found an imperishable empire."

"He says? Have you spoken with him?"

"Would the son of the Sun deign to speak with a mere high prince of Asanion?"

She regarded him sidelong. "If he were anywhere within reach of you, he might."

"Soon he may be. However mad his ambitions may be, his generalship is entirely sane. With an army no larger than the vanguard of our own, he has set all the north under his heel. Since winter loosed its hold, he has begun to threaten our northern satrapies. We suspect that, should he fail there, he will move east and south into the Hundred Realms."

"We in turn suspect that he will move first against us, thinking to forge an alliance, and with our strength to advance upon Asanion."

"So he might," Ilarios said. "And so I am here, rather than in the north of the empire. We have much more to fear from a barbarian allied with you than from a barbarian alone."

"That would be a deadly joining, would it not? A hundred realms, a hundred quarrels, we say here, but at need we can band together. Not easily, not for long, but long enough to drive back any enemy. The Nine Cities, the last time. I was very young, but I remember. Have you ever fought in a war?"

He seemed no more disturbed by this latest barb than by anything else she had said. "There has been no war since I was a child."

"But if there had been?"

"I would have fought in it. The heir of the empire commands its armies."

"The Sunborn has been a warrior since his childhood. He rides always in the van, with scarlet cloak and plume lest anyone fail to know him. And under him a demon in the shape of a black charger, fully as terrible in battle as its master."

For the first time, Prince Ilarios frowned. "He is a demon himself, they say, a mighty sorcerer, a shapeshifter who may choose to be seen as a giant among his northern giants, or as a dwarf no taller than a nine-days' infant. But in his own flesh he is nothing to look at, little larger than a child, with no beauty at all."

"What, none?"

"So I have heard."

Elian looked at him, head tilted. "You would be delighted if he were hideous, would you not?"

"Women sigh at the thought of him. Young, barbarian, and half a god—how wonderful. How enchanting."

"How utterly exasperating. You, after all, were born to be emperor; if you become a great conqueror, you but do as your fathers have done before you. Whereas this upstart has but to gather a handful of mountain tribes and he becomes a mighty hero."

"Who is blasphemous enough to name Avaryan his father. They call him An-Sh'Endor: God-begotten, Son of the Morning." Ilarios sighed and let his ill temper fade. "He vaunts; but more to the point, he conquers. Much to our distaste. We prefer our world as it is, and not as some young madman would have it."

"Oh, yes, he is mad. God-mad." She smiled, but not at Ilarios. "His birthname is Mirain. He was my foster brother. One morning before dawn he left us. I saw him go. I like to think I helped him, though what could a small girlchild do when her brother would leave and her father would have him stay? except follow him and get in his way and try not to cry. The last thing he did was cuff me and tell me to stop my sniffling, and promise to come back." And the last thing she had done was to swear her great oath. But that was no matter for this stranger's pondering.

This stranger had clearer eyes than any outlander should have, and he no mage nor seer, only a mortal man. They rested level upon her, and they granted no quarter. "Ah," he said, soft and deep. "You were in love with him."

She met stroke with stroke. "Of course I was. He was all that was wonderful, and I was eight summers old."

"Yet now you are a woman. I can make you an empress."

Her throat had dried. She defied it with mockery. "What, prince! A barbarian queen over the Golden Empire? Could your people endure the enormity of it?"

"They will endure whatever I bid them endure." He was all iron, saying it. Then he was all gold as he smiled at her. "Your high heart would not be content with the place of a lesser wife, however honored, however exalted. Nor would I set you so low."

"Nor would Mirain," she said, reckless. "I knew him once. You, I do not know at all."

"That can be remedied," he said.

She looked at him. She was shaking. She stiffened, angrily, and made herself toss her head. "Ah! Now I see. You are jealous of him."

He smiled with all the sweetness in the world. It was deadly, because there was no malice in it. "Perhaps. He is a dream and a memory. I am here and real and quite royal, though no god sired me. And I know that I could love you."

"I think," she said slowly, "that I could . . . very easily . . ." He waited, not daring to move. But hope shone in his eyes. Splendid eyes, all gold. He was beautiful; he was all that a woman could wish for, even a princess.

Except. *Except.* She curtsied, hardly knowing what she did, and fled blindly.

THE NIGHTLAMP WAS LIT IN HER CHAMBER. HER LADIES flocked about her; she tore herself free and bolted her door against them all.

She flung off her robes and her ornaments, scoured the paint from her face. It stared from her mirror, all eyes, with the wildness of a trapped beast.

A trap, yes. This one was most exquisitely baited. So fair a young man; he spoke to her as an equal, and looked at her with those splendid eyes, and promised her a throne.

And why not? asked a small demon-voice, deep in her mind. *Only a fool or a child would refuse it.*

"Then I am both." She met her mirrored glare. Either she would accept this prince and ride off with him to Asanion, splendid in the robes of an empress-to-be. Or—

Or.

Mirain.

Her throat ached with the effort of keeping back a

cry. It had all been so simple, all her life mapped and ordained. A childhood of training and strengthening; and when she became a woman, she would ride to take her place at Mirain's right hand. Her suitors had been a nuisance, but easy enough to dispose of: not one was her equal. Not one could make her forget her oath.

Until this one. It was not only a fair face and a sweet voice. It was the whole of him. He was perfection. He was made to be her lover.

"No," she gritted to the air. "No. I must not. I have sworn."

You have sworn. Do you intend ever to fulfill it? Behold, here you stand, a legend in your own right, acknowledged a master of the arts of princes: why have you never gone as you vowed to go?

"It was not time."

It was no vow. You will never go. It would be folly, and well you know it. Better far to take this man who offers himself so freely, and to submit as every woman must submit to the bonds of her body.

"No," she said. It was a whisper, lest she scream it. Not that Ilarios would bind her. That he could, so easily; and that her word had bound her long ago. If she lingered, she was forsworn, surely and irrevocably. If she left, she lost Ilarios. And for what? A child's dream. A man who by now had become a stranger.

Her eyes darted about. At her familiar chamber; at her gown flung upon the floor; at her mirror. At her reflection in its shift of fine linen, boy-slim but for the high small breasts. Her hair was a wild tangle, bright as fire. She gathered it in her hands, pulling it back from her face. Her features were fine but strong, like Halenan's when he was a boy. Prettiness, never. But beauty all too certainly. And wit. And royal pride. She cursed them all.

Prince Ilarios would remain for all of Brightmoon's cycle. A scant hour with him had all but overcome her. A month . . .

Her dagger lay upon the table, strange among the bottles of scent and paint, the little coffers of jewels, the brushes and combs and ointments. A man's dagger, deadly sharp, Hal's gift for her birth-feast. Freeing one hand from her hair, she drew the blade.

For the honor of her oath.

The bright bronze flashed toward her throat, and veered. One deft stroke, two, three. Her hair pooled like flame about her feet. A stranger stood in it, a boy with a wild bright mane hacked off above his shoulders.

A boy with a definite curve of breast.

She bound it tight and flat, and hid it beneath her leather riding tunic. Breeched and booted, with sword and dagger at her belt and a hunter's cap over her hair, she was the image of her brother in his youth, even to the fierce white grin and the hint of a swagger.

She swallowed sudden, wild laughter. If her mother knew what she did now, woman grown or no, she would win a royal whipping.

HAN-GILEN'S PALACE WAS LARGE, ANCIENT, AND LABYRIN-thine. When she was very young, she had managed with her brothers to find passages no one else knew of. One such opened behind an arras in her own chamber. She had used it once before, for it led almost directly to the postern gate, and near it a long-forgotten bolt-hole: when Mirain eluded the prince's guardianship to vanish into the north.

Now she followed him, lightless as he had been then, cold and shaking as she had been when she crept in his wake. In places the way was narrow, so that she had to crawl sidewise; elsewhere the ceiling dipped low, driving her to hands and knees. Dust choked her; small live things fled her advance. More than once she paused. She could not do this. It was too early. It was too late.

She must. She said it aloud, startling the echoes into flight. "I *must*."

Her shorn hair brushed her cheek. She tossed it back, set her jaw, and went on.

* * *

WITH ASANION'S PRINCE IN THE CITY, EVEN THE POSTERN gate was guarded. Elian crouched in shadow, watching the lone armed man. From where he stood with a cresset over his head, he commanded the gate and a goodly portion of the approach to it, and the hidden entrance to the bolt-hole. Despite the obscurity of his post, he was zealous. He kept himself alert, pacing up and down in the circle of light, rattling his sword in its scabbard.

Elian caught her lower lip between her teeth. What she had to do was forbidden. More than forbidden. Banned.

So was all she did on this mad night.

She drew a cautious breath. The man did not hear. Carefully she cleared her mind of all but the need to pass the gate. More carefully still, she lowered her inner shields one by one. Not so much as to lie open to any power that passed; but not so little as to bind her strength within, enclosed and useless.

Thoughts murmured on the edge of consciousness, a babel of minds, indistinguishable. But one was close, brighter than the rest. Little by little she enfolded it. *Rest,* she willed it. *Rest and see. No one will pass. All is quiet; all remains so. All danger sleeps.*

The man paused in his pacing, hand on hilt, immobile beneath the torch. His eyes scanned the circle of its light. They saw nothing. Not even the figure which left the shadows and passed him, walking softly but without stealth. Shadow took it; his mind, freed, held no memory of captivity.

AT THE END OF DARKNESS LAY STARLIGHT AND FREE AIR. But a shape barred the way.

So near to escape, and yet so far. Elian's teeth bared; she snatched her dagger.

Long strong fingers closed about her wrist, forcing the weapon back to its sheath. "Sister," said Halenan, "there's no need to murder me."

Fight him though she would, he was stronger; and he had had the same teachers as she. At length she was still.

He let her go. She made no attempt to bolt. Her eyes caught his, held. He would weaken. He would let her pass. He would—

She cried out in pain.

His voice was soft in the gloom. "You forget, Lia. Mind-tricks succeed only with the mind-blind. Which I am not."

"I won't go back," she said, low and harsh.

He drew her out of the tunnel into the starlight. Brightmoon had risen; though waning, it was bright enough for such eyes as theirs. He ran a hand over her cropped hair. "So. This time you mean it. Did the Asanian repel you as strongly as that?"

"No. He drew me." Her teeth rattled; she clenched her jaw. "I won't go back, Hal. I can't." He lifted a brow. She pressed on before he could begin anew the old battle. "Mirain is riding southward. I'll catch him before he enters the Hundred Realms. If he means us ill, I'll stop him. I won't let him bring war on our people."

"What makes you think you can sway him?"

"What makes you think I can't?"

He paused, drew a sharp breath, let it go. "Mother will be more than displeased with you. Father will grieve. Prince Ilarios—"

"Prince Ilarios will press for the alliance, because he stands in dire need of it. Let me go, Hal."

"I'm not holding you." He stepped aside. Beyond him a shadow stirred, moving into the moonlight. Warm breath caressed Elian's cheek; her own red mare whickered in her ear. She was bridled, saddled. On the saddle Elian found a familiar shape: bow and laden quiver.

Tears pricked. Fiercely she blinked them away. Halenan stood waiting; she thought of battering him down. For knowing, damn him. For helping her. She flung her arms about him.

"Give Mirain my greetings," he said, not as lightly as he would perhaps have liked. "And tell him—" His voice roughened. "Tell the damned fool that if he sets foot in my lands, it had better be as a friend; or god's son though he be, I'll have his head on my spear."

"I'll tell him," she said.

"Do that." He laced his fingers; she set her foot in them and vaulted lightly into the saddle. Even as she gathered the reins, her brother was gone, lost in the shadows of the tunnel.

Three

ONCE ELIAN HAD BEGUN, SHE DID NOT LOOK BACK. WITH Brightmoon on her right hand, she turned her face toward the north.

She kept to the road, riding swiftly, trusting to the dark and to her mare's sure feet. Lone riders were common enough in peaceful Han-Gilen: travelers, messengers, postriders of the prince. Nor yet did she look for pursuit. Halenan would see to that.

The first light of dawn found her in the wooded hills, looking down from afar upon her father's city. The night-flame burned low upon the topmost tower of the temple of the Sun. She fancied that she could hear the dawn bells, and the high pure voices of the priestesses calling to the god.

She swallowed hard. Suddenly the world was very wide, and the road was very narrow, and there was only captivity at either end of it. East, west, south—any of them would take her, set her free.

The mare fretted against a sudden tightening of the reins. Abruptly Elian wheeled her about, startling her into a canter. Northward, away from the Asanian. Northward to her oath's fulfilling.

By sunrise the mare had slowed to a walk. Hill and wood lay between Elian's eyes and the city; she drowsed in the saddle.

The mare stumbled. Elian jolted into wakefulness. For an instant, memory failed her; she looked about wildly. The senel had halted in a glade, and finding no resistance, begun to graze.

Elian slid to the ground. A great rock reared above her, with a stream leaping down the face of it and a pool at its foot. The mare stepped delicately into the water, ruffled it with her breath, and drank. After a moment Elian followed her. First she took off the mare's bit and bridle, then the saddle; then she lay on her face by the pool, drinking deep.

The mare nibbled her hair. She batted the dripping muzzle aside, and laughed as water ran down her neck. With sudden recklessness she plunged her head into the pool, rising in an icy spray. All thought of sleep had fled; hunger filled its place.

Her saddle pouches were full, every one. She found wine, cheese, new bread and journeybread, fruit and meat and a packet of honey sweets. At the last she laughed, but with a catch at the end of it. Who but Hal would have remembered that gluttonous passion of hers?

"He knows me better than I know myself." The mare, rolling in the ferns, took no notice of her. She ate sparingly and drank a little of the wine. The sun was warm upon her damp head. She lay back in the sweet-scented grass and closed her eyes.

The dream at first was sunlit, harmless. A woman walked in a garden under the sun. She wore the plain white robe of a priestess in the temple of Han-Gilen, her hair braided down her back, a torque gleaming golden at her throat. There was a flower in her hair, white upon raven.

She turned, bending with rare grace to pluck a second blossom, and Elian saw her face. It was a striking, foreign face, eagle-keen and very dark, the face of a woman from the north. On her breast lay the golden disk of the High Priestess of Avaryan.

A child ran down the path, a boy in shirt and breeches that sorely needed a washing, his hair a riot of unshorn curls. "Mother, come and see! Fleetfoot had her colt, and he's all white, and his eyes are blue, and Herdmaster says he's demon-gotten but Foster-father says nonsense. I say nonsense too. There's no dark in him, only colt-thoughts. Herdmaster wants to give him to the temple. Come and see him!"

The priestess laughed and smoothed his tangled hair. He was as dark as she, with the same striking face and the same great black eyes set level in it. "Come and claim him, you mean to say. Is it a white war-stallion you're wanting, then?"

"Not for me," he said. "For you. For the best rider in the world."

"Flatterer." Still laughing, she let him pull her to the garden's gate.

It flew open. Mother and son halted. A man flung himself at the priestess' feet. In face, garb, and bearing he was a commoner, a farmholder of Han-Gilen with the earth of his steading upon his feet. "Lady," he gasped. "Lady, great sickness—my woman, my sons—all at once, out of blue heaven—"

All laughter fled from the priestess' face. She drew taut, as one who listens to a voice on the edge of hearing. Her face twisted, smoothed. Its calm, where a moment before it had been so mobile, was terrible to see. She looked down. "Do you command me, freeman?"

The man clutched her knees. "Lady, they say you are a healer. They say—"

She raised her hand. He stiffened. For a moment he was different, a subtle difference, gone before it won a name. The priestess bowed her head. "Lead me," she said.

He leaped up. "Oh, lady! Thank all the gods I found

you here with none to keep me from you. Come now, come quickly!"

But her son held her back with all his young strength. She turned in his grip. For a moment she was herself, brows meeting, warning. "Mirain—"

He held her more tightly, his eyes wide and wild. "Don't go, Mother."

"Lady," the man said. "For the gods' sake."

She stood between them, her eyes steady upon her son. "I must go."

"No." He strove to drag her back. "It's dark. All dark."

Gently but firmly she freed herself. "You will stay here, Mirain. I am called; I cannot refuse. You will see me again. I promise you." She held out her hand to the man. "Show me where I must go."

FOR A LONG WHILE AFTER SHE WAS GONE, MIRAIN STOOD frozen. Only his eyes could move, and they blazed.

But the priestess summoned her bay stallion and a mount for the messenger, and rode from the temple. No one took undue notice of her leaving. The lady of the temple often rode out so to work her healing about the princedom, led or followed by a desperate wife or husband, kinsman or kinswoman, village priest or headman. Her miracles were famous, and justly so, gifts of the god who had taken her as his bride.

At last her son broke free from the binding. Running with unwonted awkwardness, stumbling, seeing nothing and no one, he passed the door of the prince's stable. The prince himself was there, that dark man with his bright hair, intent still upon Fleetfoot's foal. Mirain nearly fell against him; stared at him with eyes that saw him not at all; fumbled with the latch of a stall door. A black muzzle thrust through the opening; a body followed it, a wicked, dagger-horned, swift-heeled demon of a pony.

The prince braved hoofs and horns to catch Mirain's shoulders. "Mirain!" The name took shape in more than voice. "Mirain, what haunts you?"

Mirain stood very still. "Mother," he said distinctly. "Treachery. She knows it. She rides to it. They will kill her."

Prince Orsan let him go. He mounted and clapped heels to the sleek sides. Even as he burst into the sunlight, a red stallion thundered after, likewise bridleless and saddleless; but his rider bore a drawn sword.

THE FARMER'S HOLDING LAY AT A GREAT DISTANCE FROM the city; so he told the priestess, disjointedly, driving his borrowed mount with brutal urgency. Her own stallion, better bred and more lightly ridden, kept a steady pace up from the level land into the hills. They followed the wide North Road; those who passed upon it gave way swiftly before them. Some, knowing the priestess, bowed in her wake.

The road lost itself in trees. The man slowed not at all. He rode well and skillfully for one who could not often have spared time or coin for the art. She let her stallion fall back a little, for the trees were thick, raising root and branch to catch the unwary.

Her guide veered from the track up a steep narrow path treacherous with stones. His mount slid, stumbled, recovered; the priestess heard its laboring breath. "Wait!" she cried. "Will you slay your poor beast?"

His only answer was to lash it with the reins, sending it plunging up the slope. There was light beyond; he vanished into it.

Just short of the summit, the priestess checked her senel. There was fear in her eyes, here where none could see.

None but the god, and Elian dreaming. The god would not speak. Elian could not.

Need not. All this, long ago, the priestess had foreseen. She had chosen it. She must not turn back, now that it had come upon her. Her lips firmed; her eyes kindled. Lightly she touched heel to the bay's side.

The trees opened upon a greensward, a stream and a

pool, a loom of stone. By the pool her guide waited. She rode toward him.

Something hissed. Her stallion reared, suddenly wild, stretched to his full height, and toppled, convulsed upon the grass. A black arrow pierced his throat.

The priestess had sprung free and fallen, rolling. Swift though she was, warrior-trained, her long robe hampered her; before she could rise fully, the weight of many bodies bore her down.

After the first instinctive struggle, she lay still. Hard hands dragged her to her feet. Gauntleted hands; masks of woodland green and brown, with eyes glittering behind them.

Her guide had dismounted. Now that his part was ended, he carried himself not at all like a farmholder; his lip curled as he looked at her, and he swaggered, a broad dun-clad figure among the band of forest folk. She met his stare and smiled faintly. His eyes held but a moment before they slid away. "If one of your folk has need of healing," she said, "I will tend him freely, without betrayal."

"Without betrayal, say you?" This was a new voice. It raised a ripple among the reivers: a clear, cold, contemptuous voice with an accent which could only be heard in the very highest houses of Han-Gilen. Its owner advanced through the circle of armed men to stand beside the pool. A body once slender had grown gaunt with time and suffering; hair once red-gold was ashen grey, strained back from a face which even yet was beautiful, like an image cast in bronze. The eyes in it were lovely still, though terrible, black and burning cold.

The priestess regarded her in neither surprise nor fear. "My lady," she said, giving high birth its due, "you are well within the borders of Han-Gilen. It is death for you to walk here."

"Death?" The woman laughed with no hint of mirth. "What is death to the dead?" She moved closer, a tall sexless figure in mottled green, and gazed down from immeasurable heights, too high even for hatred. "Dead indeed, dead and rotted, with a curse upon my grave; for

I dared the unthinkable. High priestess of Avaryan in Han-Gilen, face to face with a wandering initiate from the north, I accepted her into my temple. She swore by all the holy things, by the god's own hand she swore that she had kept her vows. To serve the god with all her being; to Journey as he bade her, seven years of wandering, cleaving to his laws; to know no man.

"Aye, she served him well indeed in whatever task we set her, even servants' work, slaves' work, though she boasted that she was the daughter of a king. There were some who thought she might become a saint.

"But saints do not grow big with child. Nor do even common priestesses, unless they hunger after death: the sun-death, chained atop the tower of the temple, with an altar of iron beneath them and Avaryan's crystal above.

"I was slow to see. I was high lady of the temple, and she did her service in the kitchens; and a priestess' robe can hide much. But not the belly of a woman within a Brightmoon-waning of her time, as she bends over a washtub scouring a cauldron. And every priestess in the kitchens moving to conceal her, conspiring against their lady, defying the law of their order.

"I dared observe it. I held the trial. No answer did it gain me, no defense save one, that the miscreant had broken no vows. Her guilt was as clear as her body's shape, stripped now to its shift that strained to cover her. I condemned her. I commanded what by law I must command. 'I have broken no vows,' she said to me, unshakable.

"And who should come upon us but the Prince of Han-Gilen? He defied me, son of my brother though he was, lay votary of the order, bound to obedience within the walls of my temple. His men-at-arms loosed the prisoner, and my priests stood aside with sheathed swords, for she had bewitched them also. I cursed them all. In the law's name I snatched a sword to do execution. And they seized me, my own priests, and my kinsman held me to trial. I had dared to lay hands upon the god's chosen bride, and through her his true-begotten son, heir of

Avaryan and emperor that would be. My law had no
defense for me; the prince had what he called mercy.
Forbearing to put me to death, instead he stripped me of
my torque and my office, unbound and cut away my
braid, and cast me into exile. And all the while his woman
watched me with his bastard in her belly."

The words were like hammer blows, weighted with
long years of bitterness. The priestess bore them in silence.
When the exile ended at last, the younger woman spoke.
"You chose your punishment. You could have kept your
office and accepted the truth; or you could have stepped
aside in honor, setting me in your place and retiring to
the cloister."

"Honor, say you?" The exile's contempt was absolute.
"You, who would found an empire on a lie?"

"On the god's own truth."

The exile's face was a mask. "You have found the
truth here, O betrayer of your vows. All Han-Gilen lies
under your spell. But I have escaped it. I have wielded
my freedom in its guise of banishment, to gather such
men as will not succumb to sorcery, to restore the shattered law. It remains. It waits to take you."

The priestess smiled. "Not the law; the god. Can you
not hear how he calls me?"

"The god has turned his face from you."

"No. Nor has he abandoned you, greatly though you
fear it, greatly enough to turn all against him and bow at
the feet of his dark sister. When first I came to you, when
you saw me and hated me for the love you knew he bore
me, how terribly I pitied you; for you had no knowledge
at all of his love for you. Rank you had, and power, but
where you looked for him you could not find him. You
despaired; yet you had but sought him where he was not.
He waited still, calling to your deaf ears, waiting for your
eyes to turn to him. Even now he cries to you. Will you
not listen? Will you not see?"

There were tears in the priestess' eyes, tears of compassion. The exile's hands came up to her face; she thrust
them down. Her voice lashed out. "Silence her!"

Blades flashed. The priestess smiled. If she knew pain, it could not touch the heart of her joy.

Hoofs rang upon stone. A deep voice cried out: "Sanelin!" A lighter one rose above it, close to a shriek: *"Mother!"* Black pony and red charger plunged into the glade.

The priestess lay where her captors had flung her, on her back by the water. Bright blood stained the grass. Men howled, trampled under sharpened hoofs, cloven by the prince's sword. She neither heard nor saw. Above her loomed her enemy. The exile's hand rose high, with a dagger glittering in it; yet even as the blade poised to fall, the woman looked up. Hoofs struck at her, both dainty and deadly; a narrow wicked head tossed, slashing sidewise with its horns. She writhed away, about, beneath. Her knife flashed upward, past the pony, toward its rider.

Sanelin cried out. Mirain flung up his hand. Lightnings leaped from it.

The knife found flesh. But its force was feeble. Its wielder cried aloud and reeled, clawing at her eyes, and fled.

The pony stood still, snorting. Mirain wavered half stunned, his hand dangling, burning. The fire flickered in it, burning low now, a golden ember. Sanelin could not draw his gaze, could not speak. A great fist smote him to the ground.

The silence was absolute. No living enemy stood in the glade. The man who had struck Mirain had turned and found himself alone and undefended, with the black pony rearing over him; he had bolted without a sound.

Here and there on the grass huddled shapes clad in mottled green. A red stallion stood over one in green as dark as evening, with a bloodied sword clutched in the lifeless hand. The senel nuzzled the bright tumble of hair, snorting at the scent of blood upon it.

Sanelin's legs would not yield to her will. Slowly, with many pauses, she dragged herself toward her son. He had fallen in a heap, his hand outflung, a long shallow cut stretching red from elbow to wrist. The palm flamed as if it cupped molten gold. She fell beside it and pressed her lips to it. It was searing hot, molten indeed, brand and sigil of the god, with which he had marked his son. And with which he had struck down the exile. Her anguish shuddered in the earth.

ELIAN SHUDDERED WITH IT, AND GASPED. WIND WHISPERED through the grass. The red senel had dropped its head to graze; no proud stallion horns crowned its brow, no sorely wounded prince lay at its feet. No slain men, no boy and no pony, and no dying priestess. Elian was alone and awake in the place where the holy one had died; where her father had come close to death, and lived only through Mirain, who coming to his senses had given the prince what healing the god vouchsafed, and brought him back to the city.

That was Elian's earliest clear memory: the prince bloodied and unconscious upon the stallion, and the boy riding behind him to steady him, and the pony following like a hound. And bound to the pony's back with strips of mottled green, the body of Avaryan's bride.

Elian sat up, shaking. The vision fled; yet in its place grew one that made her cry out. The face of the slayer, terrible in its beauty, like a skull of bronze and silver. Its eyes were human no longer, great blind demon-eyes, pale as flawed pearls. Even in their blindness they hunted, seeking the one who had destroyed them.

"No," Elian whispered. She hardly knew what she denied. The hate, yes; the threat to Mirain, and through him to Han-Gilen and its prince. And perhaps most of all, the dream itself. Such dreams were from the god, his gift to the princes of Han-Gilen, shaped for the protection of the realm. But she had forsaken it. She could not be its prophet.

Her mouth was dust-dry. She knelt to drink from the pool, and recoiled with a gasp. Visions seethed in the clear water. Powers, prophecies; fates and fortunes and the deeds of kings. They drew her, eye and soul, down and down into depths unfathomable save by the trueborn seer. So much—so much—

Through the spell's glamour pierced a dart of rage. Gods and demons—how dared they torment her? She bent, and with her eyes tightly shut, drank long and deeply. Almost she had expected the water to taste of blood and iron, but it was pure and icy cold; it quenched her terrible thirst.

Cautiously she opened her eyes. No visions beset them. There was only the glint of sun on water, and through its ripples the pattern of stones upon the bottom of the pool.

She sat on her heels. The sun was high in a clear sky, the air warm and richly scented. Her mare grazed calmly, pausing as Elian watched, nipping a fly upon her flank. Whatever power of light or darkness had led her to this hidden meadow, it had left her unperturbed.

A small portion of Elian's mind gibbered at her to mount, to ride, to escape. But cold sanity held her still. Even at this distance from the city, any Gileni peasant would know both mare and rider for royal, and any pursuit would mark them. They were well hidden here where no one ever came; when darkness fell, they could ride.

Elian prowled the glade. Its beauty now seemed a mockery, its shelter a trap. Like Han-Gilen itself, enclosed and beset; like herself.

She made herself sit down, crouching on the grass well away from the pool. The sun crawled across the sky. "I cannot go back," she said over and over. "Let Father see visions, or Hal. I cannot go back!"

The water laughed at her. *Prophet,* it said. *Prince's prophet. You have the gift. You cannot refuse it.*

"I can!" She scrambled to her feet, fumbling for bridle and saddle.

Han-Gilen has had no prophet since the priestess died. Her mantle lies upon the Altar of Seeing over the living water. Go back. Forsake this child's folly. Take what is yours.

The mare skittered away from Elian's hands, eyeing the bridle in mock alarm. It was an old game; but Elian had no patience to spare for it. She snapped a thought like the lash of a whip. The mare stopped as if struck.

So too must you. The soft voice was a water-voice no longer. Deep, quiet, hauntingly familiar. *You play at duty. Yet what is it but flight from the path ordained for you?*

Elian slipped the bridle over the mare's ears, smoothing the long forelock. Her hands were trembling, but her smile mocked them all. "It is not," she said. "It is anything but that."

Is it?

She knew that voice. Oh, yes, she knew it. She hated it.

Hated? Or loved?

She flung pad and saddle over the mare's back, and after them the bags of her belongings, and last of all herself.

Elian.

The voice crept through all her barriers, throbbing to the heart of her.

Elian.

She struck at it. "*You* sent the vision. You tried to trap me. But I won't be held. Not by a lie."

It is no lie, and well you know it. The god has stretched out his hand to you and laid you open to me.

Hands reached for her. She kicked her senel into a jolting trot. The shadows were black under the trees, the sky blood-red beyond the branches.

Elian, come. Come back. Behind her eyelids a figure stood, tall, dark, crowned with fire. *Daughter, it is madness, this that you do. Come back to us.*

"To my oath's betrayal."

To those who love you.

"I cannot."

His thought had borne a hint of sorrow and a promise of forgiveness. Now it hardened. Whatever her mother might say, Prince Orsan of Han-Gilen was far from besotted with his daughter. He had raised her as she wished, as a boy, not only in the freedom but in the punishments, meted out to her precisely as to her brothers. *Elian.* She trembled in the saddle, but urged her mare onward. *This is no child's game. Will you come back, or must I compel you?*

Walls closed in upon her mind. There was but one escape, and her father filled it. Even yet, his eyes held more sorrow than wrath. He held out his hands. *Daughter. Come home.*

With a soft wordless cry she backed away. Her body rode at breakneck pace through a darkening wood. But in her mind she huddled within a fortress made of defiance, and her father towered over her, clothed in the red-golden fire of his magery. He was far stronger than she. *You are of Han-Gilen, blood and bone. This venture is a bitter mockery of both your lineage and your power. So might a child do, or a coward. Not the Lady of Han-Gilen.*

"No." There was no force in the word. Yet somewhere deep within her, a spark kindled. "No. I have sworn an oath. I will keep it, or die in the trying."

You will come home.

His will was as strong as a chain, its links of tempered steel, drawing her to him. In a madness of resistance she clung to the stronghold of her mind. Earth; three walls of will; her father. But above her the open sky. She hurled herself into it.

The mare shied. Elian clutched blindly at the saddle. Her body ached; her fingers could barely unclench from the pommel to take up the reins, to guide her mount. She could not see. For an instant she wavered on the edge of panic; but her eyes, straining, found the shadowy shapes of trees, and through the woven branches a twilit sky.

The mare had settled into a running walk, smooth and swift as water. The footing was good, soft leafmold upon the level surface of a road. Without guidance, the mare had found the northward way through the wood.

Elian tensed to quicken the senel's pace, but did not complete the movement. Her father knew surely where she was and where she went. The forest should have been alive with searchers, the realm with pursuit. But none followed her. Han-Gilen was quiescent about her.

As if, she thought when at last she took time to think, as if, after all, her father was minded to let her go.

She had a brief, striking vision: a hawk, freed to hunt for its master or to escape his will. And far beneath it in its flight, her father, watching, waiting for it to return to his hand.

Anger blurred the image and scattered it. He was so certain; so splendidly, utterly confident that in the end she would yield.

"I'll die first!" she cried.

Four

THE NORTHERN BORDER OF HAN-GILEN WAS CALLED THE Rampart of the North, its pass the Eye of the Realm. There the hills rose to a lofty ridge and fell sheer, down and down to the rolling green levels of Iban.

Because Iban's lord was tributary and kinsman to the Prince of Han-Gilen, the fortress that guarded the Eye was lightly manned, watchful but not suspicious even of one who rode alone by night. Although Elian's neck prickled and her heart thudded, certain that her father had laid his trap here where she had no escape, no challenge rang from the gate; no armed company barred her way. She was free to go or to stay.

In the high center of the Eye, she halted the mare. Han-Gilen lay behind her. Iban was a shadow ahead, moonlit and starlit, deep in its midnight sleep. Above her loomed the tower, dark and silent. If she called out, named herself, demanded lodging, she would have it, and in the morning an armed escort to bring her to her father.

Her back stiffened. Had she come so far, to turn back now? With high head and set face, she sent her mare down into Iban.

*   *   *

WHEN ELIAN WAS YOUNG, SHE HAD LEARNED BY ROTE THE names of all the Hundred Realms. Some were tiny, little more than a walled town and its fields; some were kingdom-wide. Most owed friendship or tribute to the Red Prince of Han-Gilen.

As she rode across sleeping Iban, she called to mind the realms between Han-Gilen and the wild north. Green Iban; Kurion with its singing forests; Sarios where ruled her mother's father; Baian, Emari; Halion and Irion whose princes were always blood brothers; Ebros and Poros and stony Ashan. And beyond the fortress walls of Ashan, the wild lands and the wilder tribes that called Mirain king.

So close to mighty Han-Gilen and so far still from the outlands, her father's peace held firm. But there was a strangeness in the air. Mirain An-Sh'Endor: men dreaded the rumor of him with his barbarian hordes. Had not imperial Asanion itself begun to arm against him?

No, she thought, pausing before dawn to lever a stone from her mare's hoof. It was not all fear. Some of it was anticipation, some even joy at the coming of the Sun-king.

No hiding place offered itself to her with the dawn, only the open fields and a village clustered about an ancient shrine. Elian might have pressed on past, but the mare, unused to steady traveling, was stumbling with weariness. And no temple, however small, would deny a traveler shelter, whoever that traveler might be.

This shrine was small indeed, made of stone but shaped like the villagers' huts, round and peak-roofed with a door-curtain of leather. Its altar stood where the hearth should be, with the Sun's fire on it in a battered bowl, and a clutter of holy things.

Behind the shrine stood the priesthouse, a simple wattle hut with a pen for an odd assortment of animals: a lame woolbeast, a white hind, a one-eyed hound. The woolbeast blatted at mare and rider, the hound yawned, the hind watched from a far corner with eyes like blood rubies.

Elian dismounted stiffly. The village seemed asleep or deserted, but she felt the pressure of eyes upon her. Her hand went unconsciously to her head, to the cap that hid her hair, drawing it down over the bright sweep of her brows.

Someone moved within the hut. Tired though she was, the senel lifted her head, ears pricked.

This village had a priestess, a woman in late middle years, square and solid, red-brown as the earth her fathers had sprung from. Her robe was shabby but clean, her torque of red-gold dimmed with age, as if it had passed through many hands, over many years, to this latest bearer. Over her shoulders she bore a yoke and a pair of buckets.

She regarded Elian with a calm unquestioning stare. "Your senel may share the pen," she said, "but you will have to cut her fodder yourself."

For an instant Elian stood stiff, outraged. That was servants' work. And she—

She was a rankless vagabond, by her own free choice. She made herself bow her head and say the proper words. "For the hospitality of your house, my thanks."

The priestess bowed in return, as courteous as any lady in hall. "The house is open to you. Take what you will and be welcome."

First Elian saw to the mare. There was grass not far away, and her knife was sharp; she cut an ample armful. As she brought it back to the pen, she found she had companions: a handful of children, some too young for breeches, others almost old enough to be men or women. There were one or two in the enclosure itself, coaxing the mare with bits of grass. At Elian's coming they scattered, but not far, less afraid of her in her strange splendid gear than fascinated by her mount. One was even bold enough to speak to her. The priestess' dialect had been thick but clear enough, but this was like an alien tongue.

"He asks, 'Is this a real battle charger?' "

Elian started. The priestess stepped past her to dip water into the beasts' trough, saying to the children in her deep soft voice, "Yes, it is a war-mare, and a fine one too; and isn't that your father calling you to the fields?"

The children fled, with many glances over their shoulders. The priestess laid down her yoke and straightened. "Very fine indeed," she repeated, "and worn to a rag, from the look of her. Will you rest in the temple or in my house?"

"Wherever you like," Elian answered her, suddenly weary beyond telling.

"In my house then," said the woman. "Come."

THIS SLEEP WAS DEEP, UNTOUCHED BY VISIONS. ELIAN WOKE from it to firelit darkness, and a scent of herbs, and a deep sense of peace. Slowly she realized that she lay on a hard pallet; that there was a blanket over her; and that she wore only her shirt beneath it.

She sat up in alarm. The firelight fell upon metal and cloth: her clothing, her weapons, all together, all laid neatly at the foot of her bed. Beyond them knelt the priestess, tending a pot that simmered over the hearth. She looked up calmly. "Good evening," she said.

Elian clutched the blanket to her breast. "Why did you—how dared you—"

The priestess' gaze silenced her. "My name is Ani. Yours I need not know unless you choose. Here, eat."

Elian took the fragrant bowl but did not move to eat, although her stomach knotted with sudden fierce hunger. "My name is Elian," she said almost defiantly.

Ani gestured assent. Her mind was dark and impenetrable, like deep water. "Eat," she repeated. And when Elian had obeyed: "Sleep."

Power, Elian thought, even as she sank back. *This is power. A witch . . . I must . . .*

". . . go." Elian's own voice startled her. The hut was deserted, the fire quenched. Sunlight slanted through the open door-curtain. Her clothes lay as she remembered, her weapons beside them, and close to her hand a covered bowl. In it lay bread, still faintly warm from the baking, and a bit of hard yellow cheese.

She found that she was hungry. She ate; found a bucket filled with clean water to wash in; dressed and combed her hair and pulled on her cap, and ventured into the light. She felt better than she had since she left Han-Gilen; and the day matched it, a clear day of early summer, warm and bright and wild with birdsong.

The mare seemed to have sworn friendship with her odd penmates, sharing with them a mound of fresh-cut grass. For her mistress she had a glance and a flick of one ear, but no more. She was clean and well brushed, her mane and the tassel of her tail combed like silk. After a moment Elian left her, seeking the shrine.

Ani was there, sweeping the worn stone floor, brisk as any goodwife in her house. Like the mare, she greeted Elian with a glance, but she added, "Wait a bit for me."

The temple was oddly peaceful even in the midst of its cleaning. Elian sat on the altar step and watched the priestess, remembering the great temple in Han-Gilen. This place could barely have encompassed one of its lesser altars, let alone the high one with its armies of priests and priestesses devoted entirely to its tending.

Someone had brought a garland of flowers to lay beside the Sun-fire. It was fresh still, with a sweet scent: a lovers' garland, seeking the god's favor for two who were soon to wed.

Elian set her teeth. Let them have each other. She had her oath and her flight.

"Maybe I should become a priestess."

She did not know that she had spoken aloud until Ani said, "No. That, you were never made to be."

"How can you know?" demanded Elian.

The woman set her broom tidily in its niche behind the altar. "If the god had wanted you, he would have called you."

"Maybe he has."

Ani filled the nightlamp with oil from a jar, and trimmed its wick carefully, without haste. "Not to that, Lady of Han-Gilen." Elian was silent, struck dumb. "No;

he has another task for you. Are you strong enough to bear his burden?"

"I am not returning to my father. I am riding north. A geas binds me. You cannot stop me."

"Should I want to?" The priestess seemed honestly surprised.

"You *are* a witch."

Ani considered that. "Maybe," she conceded, "I am. When I was a novice they said I might make a saint, if I didn't go over to the darkness first. I know I'm far from saintly, but I like to think I've evaded the other as well. So too should you." Her eyes changed. Though no less calm, they were harder, sterner. "It lays its snares for you. Walk carefully, child."

"I try to." Elian made no effort to keep the sullenness out of her voice.

"And well you might. There is more than the Sun's son waiting across your path."

In spite of herself Elian shivered. "The—the goddess?"

The priestess brushed the altar with her fingertips, as if to gain its protection. "Not she. Not yet. But one who serves her and grows strong in her service. One who hates in love's name, and calls envy obedience, and binds her soul to an outworn law. Guard yourself against her."

Against her will, Elian saw again what she had seen in the glade by the pool: the exile who was of her own blood. But what danger could dwell in the woman, outlaw that she was, without eyes to see?

"Much," Ani said, "with the goddess beside her, and maybe other, more earthly allies."

"But who—"

"Asanion. Any prince in the Hundred Realms. The north."

"Not Mirain. Mirain would never—"

"People aren't likely to know that. And the goddess is strong among the tribes."

"No. He would never allow it. But Asanion—Asanion serves itself. If it could conquer us all . . ." Ziad-Ilarios' face gleamed ivory-pale behind her eyes. She had dealt his pride a crippling blow. If another alliance offered itself, a means to defeat Mirain, even if by treachery, would he not take it? Or if not he, then surely his father, the one they called the Spider Emperor, who spun his webs to trap all not yet bound to his empire.

Her father's peace was hard won through a long and bitter war. Mirain had fought in it, been knighted in it, he and Halenan together. Would he remember that? Or would his hordes roll over the Hundred Realms to clash with those of Asanion, crushing the princedoms between them?

She covered her face with her hands. But that only strengthened the vision. Han-Gilen's banner, flameflower burning on shadow green; Asanion's imperial gold; and one both strange and familiar, scarlet field, golden sun. With the ease of a dream they shimmered and melted, revealing faces. Hal and her father side by side, more alike than she had ever thought they could be, and Ziad-Ilarios with an old man who held a mask of gold before his face, and the exile with her terrible blind eyes. But the sun remained and seemed to kindle, to blaze up like Avaryan itself, surrounding her, overwhelming her, bringing blessed blindness.

Ani's voice was strong and quiet in her ear. "Go where you will to go. The god will guide you."

Away from it all. *Away.*

She lowered her hands. They were shaking; she made them be still. Ani looked down at her without either awe or pity. "I . . . I will go," she said. "For your welcome, for your help—"

"Give your thanks to the god. I'll saddle the mare for you."

Ani left her there alone and shaking. When she rose, she was steady; the sick fear had faded. She could make the proper obeisance, and walk away with her chin up and her feet firm.

Ani held the mare's bridle. On impulse Elian embraced

her. She was strong, calm and calming, but warm with a human warmth; she returned the clasp freely. Neither spoke. Elian mounted. She raised her hand in farewell, and rode out upon the northward road.

Five

SENT OUT FROM IBAN BY DAYLIGHT, ELIAN RODE UNDER
the sun, one of many passers through the north of the
Hundred Realms. By night she sheltered in wayside
shrines or in farmholders' byres, or, once and boldly, in
an inn in Ebros. Darkness and rain and the rumor of
highwaymen had driven her there, with some touch of
wildness that tempted her to test her disguise in close
company. None but Ani seemed to have divined the truth;
to all she met, she was the youth she looked to be, with
her cap pulled rakishly low over her eyes.

There was a goodly crowd in the inn. A party of
pilgrims journeying south to Han-Gilen; a merchant with
his armed company coming back from Asanion; sundry
folk from the town, high and low, some with painted,
bare-breasted women. Elian kept to herself in a corner,
nursing a mug of ale. In the steaming heat she had
yielded at last to discomfort and taken off her cap. The
coppery gleam of her hair, even in the dimness, drew not
a few eyes; but there were men in the merchant's party
with manes scarcely less remarkable, tawny or straw-pale.

The eyes slid away, intent on the drink or the women or the flow of speech about the common room.

An-Sh'Endor. His name was everywhere. He was riding south, they said. He had taken Cuvien without a struggle, received the homage of its chieftains and held a festival for his army. Now he looked toward Ashan. But no, tribes to the west were rising; he would deal with them first, and turn then upon Asanion.

"Now there is one fine fighter," said a man almost dark enough to be a northerner, a pilgrim's robe straining across his massive chest. "Have you heard how he took the castle of Ordian? It was impregnable, everyone said. Food and water enough for two years' siege, and no way up to it but under its gate, with the whole tribe defending it from above. So what does he do? Lines up his army just out of the gate's reach, makes all the motions of settling in for a siege—and sends a company round the back up a road a mountain goat would shrink from, with himself in the lead. So here's the tribe, laughing at the army and daring it to come closer, and shooting offal at a man in the king's armor; then the joke turns on them. A round hundred bows aimed at them from behind, and a cocky young fellow telling them they'd better surrender before he feeds them to his army."

One of the merchant's guards laughed, short and scornful. "Tribesmen's tales," he said in a thick western accent. "He has never met a proper army, nor faced Asanian steel."

"That lad is afraid of nothing," the first man said. "He'll go where no one else will go, and take his army with him."

"So?" someone asked. "Have you seen him?"

"Seen him? I've fought with him. That was before I saw the light: he was a fosterling in Han-Gilen and I was one of the prince's hired swords. Fourteen summers old, he was, and the prince knighted him in battle, with the whole army yelling his name."

The Asanian curled his lip. "If he ever knew the ways

of civilized man, he has left them far behind him. He is a mountain bandit, and he will die one."

"Not so!" cried a new voice. It was a very young one, almost painfully sweet. Elian, seeking its source, found a thin dark boy in the grey robe of a sacred singer, with his harp at his back and his eyes burning in his narrow Ashani face. "Oh, not so! He is the holy one, the god-king. He comes to claim his inheritance."

"What inheritance?" demanded a bejeweled young fellow, a local lordling by his accent, which strove to be cultivated. "He had some claim to Ianon, or so they say: his mother was its king's bastard. He murdered the king, by poison I hear, and killed the king's son in an ambush."

The pilgrim's voice boomed from end to end of the crowded room. "Begging your pardon, young sir, but that's a barefaced lie. The Sunborn's mother was heir of Ianon in her own right, being the king's daughter by his queen, who was an Asanian princess." His eye lingered for a moment on the westerner. "The old king died, true enough, and maybe poison speeded it, but it wasn't my lord who sweetened his wine. He had a son who really was a bastard, who had a hand in his killing, and who tried to claim the throne. The Sunborn fought the pretender man to man, barehanded. That was a fight to sing songs of! My lord is a great warrior and a great king, but he's not what you'd call a big man; and he was still only half grown. His uncle was a giant even for a Ianyn, and the greatest champion in the north of the world. But they fought, and my lord won, full and fair."

"And the king came forth and took his throne, and the gods bowed down before him." The singer's eyes shone; his voice thrummed like the strings of his own harp.

"If he is so divine a wonder," inquired the Asanian, "why does he march armed across the north? He need but raise his hand to bring the world to his feet." He yawned with feline delicacy. "The boy is mad. Power-mad. He will seize what he may seize, destroy what he may destroy, and set his foot upon the necks of kings. Until Asanion rises to crush him."

The singer, if dream-mad, was obstinate. "He brings Avaryan's peace to the world. But men cling to their old darknesses. Them he must conquer by force of arms, since no other force do they understand. In the end they shall all be his. Even Asanion, with its thousand demons. Its emperor shall bow down to the Lord of the Sun."

"Moonshine," drawled the westerner.

The boy looked ready to do battle for his dreams. But the pilgrim laughed, quelling them both. "Me, I walk down the middle. Yon's the best general this old world's seen in a long age. If he chases after a god and a dream, what's that to me? The fighting's good, the loot's better, and the man's well worth the service."

There was a brief silence, the pause due a subject well interred. Thereafter the talk shredded and scattered, blurring in a haze of wine.

Elian yawned and thought of bed. But a chance word froze her where she sat. "—the Exile." She could not see who spoke, but it was a new voice, and close. "Yes, Kiyali, *the Exile:* that's what they're calling her. Half the bandits on the roads are holding up travelers in her name."

"And the other half swear by the Sunborn," put in another man. "If you ask me, they're one and the same, and that's nobody at all, just a good way to shake gold out of locked purses. You know what they do in outland villages? Name a name, Outcast or Sunborn, and tell the folk to pay up and the local bandits will protect them."

"Or flatten them if they refuse. But the Sunborn exists. Maybe the other does too. I've heard tell she's a great sorceress; she rules in the woods, no one knows where, and she's as rich as an emperor. She lives on blood and fear, and she sleeps on gold."

The second man laughed. "What is she then? A dragon?"

"A woman. That's monster enough, all the gods know. My youngest wife, now—"

They spoke no more of exiles or of Sunborn kings, although Elian strained all her senses to hear them. At last she rose. She was weary and her mood had darkened;

the sour ale sat ill beneath her breastbone. She made her way through the crowd, seeking the stair to the sleeping-room and a night of formless dreams.

BEYOND EBROS THE LAND TURNED WILD, TOWNS AND VIL-lages growing fewer, hill and forest rising toward the northern mountains. The rumors here were dark, tales of marauders upon the roads, villages sacked and burned, forces moving under captains who swore allegiance to no lord, but perhaps to a young barbarian king. There was even that wild tale, that Mirain had sworn alliance with the reivers of the roads, to open the way before him into the Hundred Realms.

Elian began to meet with people fleeing south like birds before a storm. Pilgrims, most called themselves, or travelers, but none faced northward. Those who went north went for need, and they went armed.

She rode with care, but none molested her. Outlaws sought fat merchants in their caravans, where the booty might be well worth the battle; lone riders, armed and well mounted, they let be.

Perhaps her long safety lulled her into folly; perhaps she thought too much on her journey's end, which was close now, close enough to sense with the barest flicker of power. She even fancied that she had found Mirain: a rioting golden fire, center and focus of all his army.

Herself focused upon it, she rode down from the hills into a wooded valley. The sun was setting behind a veil of cloud; the wind promised rain before dawn. She was weary and hungry, beginning to think of a camp and a fire and a haunch of the wildbuck which she had shot in the morning. On the edge of thought, she took note of the silence in these woods that should have been alive with birds and beasts. The only sound was the soft thud of hoofs upon the track, the creak of leather, the jingle of the bit. Even the wind had stilled with the sun's sinking.

Uneasiness grew, rousing her from her half-dream. She looked back. Already the trees had closed in upon the path. She could see no more than a few lengths behind, a few lengths ahead.

She was not, yet, afraid. The road was clear enough even in the gloom. Mirain's army was no more than two days distant, perhaps less, camped on the fells beyond the border of Ashan.

Her mare snorted and shied. She gentled the beast and halted, stroking the bright mane, every sense alert. There was no sound at all.

Softly Elian slid from the saddle. The mare stood braced, head high, eyes and nostrils wide. At the passing of weight from her back, she shuddered once and was still.

Something rustled in the undergrowth. A small beast—a bird.

Another. The wood was coming alive. Somewhere a bird called. Elian eased her sword from its scabbard.

An insect buzzed. The mare bucked and reared. Blood stained her haunches. A second arrow sang between her ears.

Elian wheeled. "Cowards! Cravens! Come out and fight like men!"

They came at her call, more than she could count, figures swathed in green and brown, with masked faces and strung bows. The mare whirled into attack. Blades flashed through the sharp slashing hoofs; she fell kicking.

Elian hardly saw. She had her back to a tree, sword and dagger a bright blur before her.

A shadow fell from above: a net, trapping her, drawing tighter as she struggled. Steel pricked, her own sword, more deadly now to her than to her enemies. She loosed her grip upon it; it fell through the net. Hard hands tore the dagger from her fingers.

Two of her captors heaved her to their shoulders. As they began to walk, she saw her mare rigid in death, and faceless men stripping the body of its trappings. There was no room in her for grief. Only for rage.

Twilight turned to darkness. It began to rain, a light drizzle, warm and not unpleasant. One of her bearers cursed it in a tongue she knew, a dialect of northern Sarios. "Go out, she says, lay an ambush, she says, take what comes, she says. So what comes? One futtering boy on a futtering mare, and now this futtering rain, and not enough futtering loot to keep a mouse happy."

"Shut your flapping mouth," snarled the man behind him, "or she'll nail it shut."

Elian shivered, and not with the rain. *She.* Only one woman that she knew of commanded outlaws, masked men in woodland colors. After all the warnings and all the foreseeings and all of Elian's own fears, the Exile had taken her.

The men mounted a slope with much hard breathing and not a few curses. From the height of it Elian looked down into a wide clearing. Fires flickered there in despite of the rain; men moved about them. Most had shed their masks. She glimpsed a face or two: Ebran, Gileni, a dark hawk-nosed northerner.

Her captors bore her through them all in silence full of eyes, to the central and greatest fire. A shelter rose beyond it, made of stripped boughs and overlaid with oiled leather. The leather was dark, perhaps black, perhaps deep blue or violet, the standard set in the ground before it dark likewise, without device.

Elian tumbled to the ground, rolled about without mercy as her bearers freed her from the net. Dizzy, all but stunned, she let them haul her to her feet. A hand struck between her shoulders, thrusting her into the shelter.

After the bright firelight, this was nearly total darkness, the only light the ember-glow of a lamp. Slowly Elian's eyes cleared. She discerned the dim shapes of furnishings, few as they were, and simple to starkness. And in the lone chair, a woman.

She was alone. She seemed oblivious. Thin and frail, her hair white, pulled back from her face and knotted at her nape. Her eyes were lowered as if to contemplate the creature nestled in her lap. It was of cat-kind, silken-furred, purring as she stroked it.

The purring stilled. The cat's eyes opened. Elian shivered. They were white as silver, pupils slitted even in the dimness, fixing her with intensity that spoke of no dim beast-mind. It knew her; and it laughed, knowing that she knew.

"So," her tone said for her. "You turned to the Mageguild."

The Exile raised her head. She had aged little since she slew the god's bride; her beauty had deepened, the ravages of bitterness smoothed, fined, transmuted. As if she had yielded. As if she had come through cruel battle to acceptance of her suffering. "I am mageborn," she said. Her accent was Elian's own.

"Mageborn," said Elian, "and Guild-trained. I know that robe. But why do you require a familiar? Did Mirain take more from you than your eyes?"

"He gave more than he took," the Exile said with something very like serenity.

Elian looked about. Her fear had faded not at all: she was stiff with it. But scorn was a potent weapon. She wielded it with reckless extravagance. "What have you gained? I see a bandit queen with a demon in her lap. She is blind; she is old; she has no name and no country. To her kin she is as if she had never been. Even her Guild— why are you here? Did they too grow weary of your arrogance, and drive you out of the Nine Cities?"

"I cannot fault you," the Exile said without anger. "You are too young to have known the truth of it."

"I know all I need to know."

The Exile smiled. She was not gentle—she could not be that. But she could indulge a child's innocence. "Do you, O Lady of Han-Gilen? You dream that you ride in fulfillment of an oath. Yet what was that oath? What was it truly? Was it to fight beside the priestess' son? Or was it to be his queen?"

Elian bit her tongue, hard. The Exile wanted her to cry out, to deny the twisted truth. Yes, she had sworn that she would marry none but Mirain. But not at the last. Only when she was very young, hardly more than an infant. Never when she knew what vow she was taking.

"Wise," said the Exile. "Most wise. Perhaps after all you knew. In Asanion they mate brother and sister. In Han-Gilen they shrink from it."

Still Elian held her tongue. It was a bitter battle, and it was no victory. The Exile knew what she struggled not to say. Knew everything; and toyed with her, for amusement, before the headiness of the kill.

"No," the woman said. "It need not be so. We are kin, you and I. As you are now, so was I once: the beauty and the high heart, and the reckless bravery. For them I fell. Had I held back, waited, seemed to submit to my brother's son and his northern paramour, I would have spared myself much suffering. I could have slain not only the mother but the monster which she bore."

"Mirain is no—"

Elian bit off the rest. The Exile forbore to smile. "He is comely enough, they tell me. In body. It is the spirit I speak of. I am not the seer that you will be, kinswoman, but a little of the gift is mine. I have seen what he would make of the world. No greater danger has ever beset it."

"He will save it. He will bring it to the worship of Avaryan."

"He will cast it into the Sun's fires." The Exile rose. Her familiar wove about her feet, tail high, gaze never shifting from Elian's face. The woman held up her hands, not pleading, not precisely. Her blind eyes seemed to look deep into Elian's own, with such a shimmer on them as lies in the pearlbeast's heart. This, Mirain had made. This, he had done, scarcely knowing what he did.

"He is not evil," the Exile said. "I grant him that. Perhaps truly he believes his mother's lies. But he is deadly dangerous. Mageborn as he is, bred to be king, with the soul of a conqueror, he cannot do aught but what he does. Nor in turn can I. He threatens the chains that bind the world. So I saw before ever he was born."

"You saw a threat to your own power."

"That also," the Exile admitted without shame, "and for my sin I fell. Now I am given grace to redeem myself. I live, and I am strong. I have conquered hate. I have learned to serve justice alone."

"And in the name of justice you command the reivers of the roads."

"It is necessary."

"Of course," said Elian with a curl of her lip. "How else can you buy traitors, unless you steal the wherewithal?"

"I do as I must."

Elian stilled. That was madness, that calm fixity. It turned upon her. It seized her.

"Kinswoman," the Exile said. "I have waited for you. I have prayed that you would see what for so long I have seen. If my men have handled you ill, I cry your pardon. They are men; they do not know subtlety. Come now, sit, be at ease. Grant your sufferance at least to my words."

Elian would not obey her. Could not. Must not. Not though that face spoke ever more to her of her own; though that voice entreated her ears with the accents of her own kin. "You weave me about in lies," she said tightly. "You think to seduce me. You know how strong Mirain will be, if he has me to stand beside him and fight for him and be his prophet. You dream that I can sway your enemies, even my father. Especially my father. But much though he loves me, he loves his realm more. He would never destroy it for my sake."

"You would be its salvation. Think you that his intent can be secret? He has forged alliances throughout the Hundred Realms. He toys with Asanion, to ease its suspicions. Yet his purpose is clear to any who can see. When the Hundred Realms are firm in his grasp, he will give them as a gift to the conqueror."

"If the conqueror proves worthy of them."

"By his existence he is worthy. He was bred to rule under your father's hand."

"Old lies," said Elian, "and old spite. How can I credit a word of it? You who were high priestess of Avaryan— you wear the robes of a black mage. You stink of darkness."

"It is all one," the Exile said. "Light and dark, all one. That is truth, kinswoman. To that, your father is blind; and with him the one whom he wrought for empire."

"So then must I be. I am no slave of the goddess. I will not yield to you."

"I did not speak of yielding. I spoke of taking arms

for the truth." The Exile sighed as if weariness had overcome her. "Time will be your teacher. Time, and your
clear sight, which in the end you cannot deny."

TORMENT, ELIAN COULD HAVE BORNE. THERE WAS NO AMBI-
guity in it. This was subtler. She had a tent to herself.
She was bound, but lightly, with a tether long enough
that she could move about. Food and drink waited for her
to deign to notice them.

She refused. It would be a yielding; and she must not
yield. She crouched by the tentpole and shivered, weeping a little, child-fashion, less for fear than for humiliation.

Something watched her. She froze. The Exile's familiar sat before her where had been empty air, washing its
forepaw with perfect and oblivious innocence.

Her eyes narrowed. The beast nibbled a claw. No
stink of the hells lay on it. It seemed but a lady's pet,
harmless, absorbed in itself. Yet it was here, and it had
not come through the sealed door.

Mageborn, she had studied little of the sorcerer's art.
She needed neither spell nor familiar. Her power ran
deeper, closer to instinct. But her father had taught her
enough, or tried to teach her, if she could but remember.

It came to her in a flicker of vision: three magelings
before the master, and two were red Gileni and one was
Ianyn-dark, and the youngest was small enough to sit on
the master's knee as he spoke, and set her ear against his
chest, and fill her head with the drum-deep cadences of
his voice. "A familiar," he said, speaking as much to her
as to her brothers, "like a staff or a grimoire, is a vessel of
power. It need have none in itself. It can be eyes and ears
and feet, and it can guard what the mage wishes it to
guard."

"Useful," said Halenan. His voice, which was breaking, wavered even on the single word; Elian was too
interested to laugh at him.

"Useful," Mirain agreed, "but cumbersome, and maybe
dangerous. What if the familiar is captured by another
mage? Or killed? What happens to its master then?"

"That depends upon the depth of the bond," answered the Red Prince. He stroked Elian's hair, idly. It was pleasant; she let him do it, slitting her eyes to make the world go strange. Mirain's face blurred into a shadow.

"I would never so divide my power," he said.

"You need not," said the Red Prince. "It is born in you. But if you were a simple man, and you had come to magic through spells and long art, a familiar would not lessen your power: it would focus it, and nurture it, and make it strong."

"But I would always be vulnerable," said Mirain.

ELIAN DREW A SLOW BREATH. THE FAMILIAR COILED BONE-lessly upon itself, scouring the base of its tail. She tugged at the thongs that bound her wrists. The creature raised its head, turned its eyes upon her. She set teeth to her tether.

White pain flung her back. Her cheek burned and throbbed. Blood spattered her coat.

The cat sat erect, vigilant. She bared her teeth. It yawned. Its fangs were white needles. She crouched, and would not think of pain. Surely those claws had raked her to the bone. The bleeding would not stop, even for her hands pressed to it, an awkward knot of leather and flesh.

She struggled to gather her power. It kept scattering, eluding her grasp, mocking her with a spit of feline laughter. Grimly she kept her temper. Rage would fell her. Despair would cast her into her enemy's hands.

She had it. Not all of it, but perhaps, by the god's will, enough. It writhed and fought as if it were no part of her at all but an alien thing. She set upon it the full force of her will.

Her hands were free. The tent's door was open, a guard blank-eyed before it. She stepped toward him.

The cat yowled. She whirled. Claws raked her tender breast; teeth snapped at her throat. She tore the thing away, flung it with all her trained strength.

Silence. Stillness. She backed away. Nothing. She spun, leaped past the motionless guard.

Her power was quiet in her center, obedient at last. She let it lead her round the edge of the camp. No one saw her. No one would see her. The forest waited beyond with its promise of safety.

It came without warning, springing out of the night, swift and silent and terrible. Its claws stretched to seize her, to rend her. She flung up all her shields.

The shadows rippled with cold cat-mirth. For she stood full in the light of a watchfire, clear for any mortal eyes to see.

Someone shouted.

Left was night, and the green gleam of eyes. She darted right, round the flames. Voices cried out. Fire seared her face. With the strength of desperation she dropped her mind-shield, thrusting all her power into the fire. Her body sprang after it. Flames roared high, engulfing her. The shadow-beast veered away.

In the instant of confusion, she reached from the very core of her.

The fire vanished. Darkness swathed her, the darkness of earthly night, with a shimmer of stars and a whisper of wind in leaves.

Later she would begin to shake. She had gone—otherwhere. But where or how far, she could not tell, although the air tasted still of the woodlands of Ashan. Her power, unguided, had served her far better than she had any right to expect. Or perhaps it was luck, or fate. Or the god.

Her knees buckled. Power, strength, she had none. All gone. All spent. If men or sorcery found her now, she had no defense. "Avaryan," she breathed as if he could hear, or would. "Help—protect—"

The night opened its arms. She let it take her.

Six

IGHT WOKE HER FIRST. SHE TURNED HER HEAD AWAY from it, waking pain. With a groan she burrowed into her bed.

And sneezed. Her bed was no bed at all, but deep leafmold; her face was pillowed in it. She levered herself up on her hands. Trees loomed all about her, evergreens with but little growth between them. Their sharp fine needles matted in her hair, pricked her skin. She worked her knees beneath her and brushed at the clinging fragments.

At the sight of herself she made a small sound, part pain, part disgust. She was filthy, spattered with blood, with her garments hanging open like a harlot's. Cheek and breast were raked with thin deep scratches, bleeding no longer, but burning fiercely. She managed with some fumbling to fasten her coat; enough remained of buttons and lacings for that. She was ravenously hungry and parched with thirst. And no water within sight or scent, nor enough of power left to find any.

The sun slanted through branches almost full before her. Left and perhaps north the ground sloped downward, broken with stones and hollows. Downward, her masters had taught her, water runs downward always, and many a hillside boasts a stream at its foot.

She was safe, uncaught, unbound. She would not think of the rest: that she was alone, afoot, and wounded, without water or food or weapon, and sorely worn from her battle of power; and that she had no knowledge of this place into which her waning witchery had cast her. For all she knew, she was but returning the way she had come. It was enough now that she set one foot before the other, and that if she stumbled she did not often fall.

Once she fell badly. The slope was steep; she rolled, bruising herself on root and stone, stopped at last by the solid strength of a tree. For a long while she could not move at all, nor even breathe.

Little by little she gathered herself together. Nothing had broken. But ah, she hurt. She made herself stand, take one limping step, then another.

She scented it before she heard it, an awareness far below the conscious, a blind turning of the body toward its greatest need. Water, a trickle over moss and stone, pausing in a pool little bigger than her hand. She collapsed beside it, to drink until she could drink no more. Every muscle cried then for rest, but she took off her garments one by one, slowly, like a very old woman, and washed herself a hand's breadth at a time. Only when she was clean would she lie back with the sun's warmth seeping into her bones.

Food. That, she needed still, and sorely. But the sun lay like a healer's hand upon her skin. She let it lull her into a doze.

Wake! It was not a voice, not precisely. *Wake and move. Sleep after power—sleep is deadly. Wake!*

Feebly she tried to close it out, to sink back into her stupor. Yet her body stirred and rose and fumbled into its filthy coverings. They were stiff; they itched and they stank. Her clean skin shrank from them.

Food. Here, green, and a white root, crisp and succulent. There in an open space, a tangle of brambles with fruit nestled within their thorns. Beyond, a widening of the stream; a small silver fish, now leaping in her hand, now cold and sweet upon her tongue.

She gagged, but the fish had found her stomach, and she was herself again, weak and still hungry but clear enough in mind. She found a further handful of thornfruit, and a clump of greens, root and top. Time enough later to fashion a snare for the meat she needed.

She drank from the stream and knelt for a time beside it, laving her face. Her father had warned her often and often. All power had its price. Used lightly, it asked no more of the body than any other exercise. Expended to its limit, it drained all the body's strength, could even kill unless its wielder moved to master it. And even with mastery one needed long sleep after, and ample food and drink, and a day or more of rest. She had never gone so far, but she had seen her father after some great feat of wizardry, building or healing or calling of the wind, borne away like an invalid, bereft of all strength.

But she had done so little. Unlocking; illusion; shielding; swift travel from place to unknown place. Yet she had come as close to dissolution as she ever cared to come.

It was still too soon to remember. She stood wavering. Only a little farther. Then she would seek shelter and set her traps. She began to walk beside the water. She felt hale enough but very weary. A little farther—a little. Where the stream, wider now, descended between steep banks and bent out of sight, she stopped. Her knees folded beneath her. Shelter—her snares—

A shadow crossed the sun. She regarded it without alarm. A voice spoke above her, strange words, yet she ought to have known them.

The shadow cast a shape. A man in kilt and cloak of shadow green, a very dark man, black indeed, with a proud arch of nose over a richly braided beard.

Fear erupted within her, and beneath it despair. She was caught again. There would be no second escape.

Another man appeared beside the other, dark likewise, and taller, and perhaps younger; his face was clean-shaven. From where she lay they seemed very giants. The newcomer stooped, reaching for her.

She fought. But her blows were feeble; the men laughed. They were handsome men, with very white teeth, and rings of copper in their ears and about their necks and upon their arms. The taller one said something; she thought it might have been, "Now, brave warrior, be still. We'll not be killing you right this moment."

No. She would die slowly, at the Exile's hands. She renewed her struggle, striking with all the strength that was left her.

"Aiee!" yelped the man who held her arms. "He's a regular wildcat. Tangled with one too, from the look of him." Her elbow caught him in the ribs; he grunted. *"Now* then, you. No more of that!"

It was less a blow than a cuff, but it half stunned her. She sagged in his grip. He slung her over his shoulder and strode forth, with his companion following.

Belatedly, and numbly, she realized that they had been speaking the tongue of Ianon.

With no more transition than a thinning of trees and a leveling of the hillside, the forest ended. Elian had come by then to herself, but she rode quiescent on the broad shoulder, only lifting her head to see what she might see. She marked the opening of land and sky, and the changing of the ground from leafmold to long grass and stones; and she heard and scented and felt the camp upon the field. Here were the voices of men and beasts; the pungency of a cookfire; an ingathering of folk to inspect the arrivals, with much curiosity and some amusement. "Hoi, Cuthan!" they called. "What luck in the hunt?"

"Better than I looked for," her bearer called back.

In the center of the gathering he halted and set Elian down. Tall though she was for a Gileni woman, as tall as many men, he stood head and shoulders above her. Yet she faced him bristling, eyes snapping, hands fisted at her sides. He grinned. "See," he said, "a wildcat."

There were not, after all, so very many people about.

A dozen, maybe. And despite their amusement, they had watchful eyes; their fire was well shielded, with little scent and no smoke, their seneldi tethered near the trees. Binding each cloak or glinting on the collar of each coat was a brooch of gold in the shape of a rayed sun.

Although no one held her, she was surrounded. Several of the men held bows, loose in their hands but strung, with arrows ready to fit to the string.

"Well, little redhead," said the man called Cuthan, "suppose you tell us who you are."

"You are Mirain's men," she said. Few of them were northerners. She marked trousered southerners, red and brown, and one Asanian clad incongruously in northern finery. "Where is he, then? Is he close by? For if he is, he trespasses. This land belongs to Ashan's prince."

"Does it now?" Cuthan gestured, no more than a flicker of the eyes. The scouts began with seeming casualness to disperse, but several stayed close by. He laid a hand on Elian's shoulder, guiding her toward the fire, seating her there.

His knife glittered as he drew it. She tensed. He barely glanced at her, cutting a collop from the haunch that roasted over the flames, bringing it to her. He did not lend her the knife to cut it. She held it gingerly, for it was searing hot, and nibbled with care.

Cuthan waited, patient. When the meat was gone, he held out a cup. She sniffed it. Water. Gratefully she drank.

A second man sat on his heels beside Cuthan: the Asanian. In that company he seemed almost a dwarf, a smooth sleek ageless man with bitter eyes. They took in Elian with neither favor nor trust. "Gileni," he said in thickly accented Ianyn. "Born liar."

"Maybe not," said Cuthan.

"Maybe so," the Asanian said. "Test it. He spoke clearly enough. This is Ashan; its prince is no more a fool than our king. He would have engaged spies."

"Redheaded Gileni spies?"

"Why not? Red mane, witch-power, they say in the south."

Cuthan frowned. "I'll question him. That's fair enough. But I'm not sure—"

"If I were spying," said Elian, "you would never have caught me. I was looking for your army. I want to fight for your king."

"Why?"

"Why not?" Elian bit her tongue. Cuthan was amused, but not entirely. She met his eyes. "Your . . . friend sees this much of the truth. I am from Han-Gilen. I heard of the Sunborn. I wanted to be free. I wanted to fight. I thought that if I joined with him I would have both. I ran away from home." Cuthan's grin came back. He believed that. She found an answering grin. "My mother would never have let me go. At night I ran away."

"You came alone? Unarmed? Afoot?"

"Alone, yes. The rest I—I lost. Back yonder. Have you heard of the woman called the Exile?"

The men within hearing tensed. Cuthan leaned forward. The Asanian's look was almost a look of triumph.

Her fist clenched at her belt where her sword had hung. "She camps a day's journey south, maybe more. She has men with her. They caught me and killed my mare and took all I had."

The Asanian's full lip curled. "They let you go."

She bared her teeth at him. "No. Not the likes of me. Red mane, witch-power. She knows that as well as you. But not well enough."

"No one escapes from that demon incarnate."

"One does if she happens to turn her mind elsewhere. She is not, yet, omniscient."

"Southern lies."

"Plain truth." Elian faced Cuthan. "Take me to the king and let him judge."

The Asanian leaped to his feet. "The Exile is Gileni. Red Gileni, witch and sorceress. What better weapon against my lord than one of her kin? Young and innocent to look at, but shaped for murder, as she murdered the god's bride."

"She is traitor and outcast, abhorred by all her kin." Elian flung back her tangled hair. "Your king will know. Take me to him."

Cuthan shifted. Shamelessly she followed his thoughts. He was commander here, but he was young, and a better judge of land than of men. An obvious spy, a grown man prowling where he ought not to be, that was easy enough to judge. But this lordly youth, pretty as a girl, found fainting by the waterside: was he truly what he seemed to be, or was he indeed a servant of the enemy?

"The king," said Elian. "He can judge."

"He can," Cuthan said slowly. "Maybe he'd better. But first we'll see to those scratches. They look nasty."

"They should. The witch's familiar gave them to me." Elian held out her hands. "Take me now. The sooner I see the king, the better."

"Not with your face like that," said Cuthan, stubborn. "Even if I could allow it, the king would have my hide."

She sighed and submitted. He himself cleaned her cheek and salved it with numbroot, clicking his tongue the while, mourning her poor marred beauty. His hands were light and skilled. Elian found herself smiling at him, crookedly, all numbed as she was.

"Bind him," snapped the Asanian, who had never taken his eyes from them. "Or should I? You're half in love with him already."

Cuthan seemed unoffended. "No need of that. I'm taking him where he wants to go."

"And if he knifes you in the back?"

"I'll chance it." Beneath Cuthan's lightness lay steel. The Asanian subsided with the swiftness of wisdom.

Elian was honored with trust. She had a senel to herself, no cord to bind her and no leadrein to bind her mount, and Cuthan's guardianship was light to invisibility. He rode beside her or ahead of her, sometimes silent, more often singing. His voice was very pleasant to hear.

In one of his silences she asked him, "Is it common

for a captain of scouts to proclaim his presence to the whole realm?"

"If the realm is his king's own," answered Cuthan, "yes."

Elian's breath shortened. She had kept herself from thinking. That she was almost there. In front of Mirain. Telling him why she had come.

I told you that I would.

I keep my promises.

I want to fight for you.

Or most shameful, and closest to the truth: *There was a man, I was as much as commanded to marry him, I could have done it in all gladness, and for the sheer terror of it I ran away.*

As far as she could, as far into her childhood as she might. Running to Mirain as she had then, to be held and rocked and maybe chided a little, maybe more than a little, but always granted his indulgence.

Truth. It burned. *I promised. My first promise. I would marry you, or I would marry no one at all.*

And *no one* could so easily, so appallingly easily, have become *someone*, a face carved in ivory, lamplight in golden eyes.

She fixed her stare on Cuthan, for distraction, for exorcism. He was singing again. She made herself think of nothing but his song.

In spite of all the tales, the army of the Sunborn was no barbarian horde. Each nation and tribe and mercenary company had its place in the encampment, even to the camp followers: merchants and artisans, women and boys, singers and dancers and talespinners. It was like a city set on the moor, a city with order and discipline under the rule of a strong king.

Elian almost turned at the edge of it and bolted southward. It was not good sense that held her. Far from it. Good sense would have kept her in Han-Gilen and wedded her to the Asanian prince.

Pride brought her into the camp, and temper steadied her within. The king would not oblige her by waiting docilely in his tent. Everyone knew where he was, and everyone named a different place. Cuthan seemed content, even pleased, to play the hunter; and why not? He was a captain of scouts.

"Is this common?" Elian demanded after the fourth guide had led them to a space full of men and arms and seneldi, but empty of the king.

Cuthan had the effrontery to laugh. "He's not easy to keep up with, is my lord." He said it lightly, but the respect behind it came very close to worship. "Come now. I know where he may be."

This city, like any other, had its market: wide enough and varied enough to rouse even Elian's respect. She found herself loitering by a stall spilling over with gaudy silks, stretched into a trot to catch Cuthan. She had matched his grin before she thought. She flushed; her grin twisted into a scowl. He laughed and led her deeper into the maze of tents and stalls and booths.

Its heart was not its center. A stall with a reek of wine about it; a clamor of men and the odd shriek of a woman's laughter; someone singing, the clatter of a drum, the sudden sweetness of a flute. The faces were all northern faces, like a gathering of black eagles. Elian saw more gold on one man than a whole band of women would flaunt in Han-Gilen. And beneath it, more bare skin than she had ever seen in one place. One of the women wore nothing but ornaments. Her nipples were gilded. Elian blushed and looked away.

At, it chanced, one of the more bedizened of the men. He was tall and he was handsome even among these tall handsome people, beautiful indeed, so that Elian's eye caught and lingered. He lounged on the bench like some long-limbed hunting cat, awkwardness transmuted into grace, and although he wore the full, barbaric, copper-clashing finery of his people, he wore it as easily as he wore his skin; one could not envision him without it.

He met her gaze with no expression that she could read, not staring as others did at her bright hair and her torn face, simply returning look for look. He was young, perhaps. Under the beard and the baubles it was hard to tell. His skin was smooth, his face unlined; but his eyes were ancient. Or newborn.

He was not a mage. He was not born to magic, nor trained to it. Yet there was power in him, on him, part of him. He would wield it as he breathed, because he could do no other. Elian had never seen anything like him.

She looked away from him. Clamor burst upon her. Only he had eyes for her. Everyone else was fixed on someone whom she could not see, a shadow in shadow, with a voice that came suddenly clear. A black-velvet voice, sweet as the honey of the southlands, saying words that mattered too little for remembrance. A question. The answer was shrill beside it, and harsh, and thick with outland consonants.

Elian's feet took her out of the sunlight. New eyes found her, widened. She took no notice. The dark sweet voice rippled into laughter. Its bearer rose out of the tall man's shadow, leaning on the glittering shoulder, glittering himself, white teeth flashing in the face she knew best of any in the world.

He had always called it ugly. It had never sunk to prettiness; it was too irregular to be handsome. All Ianon was in that bladed curve of nose, in those cheekbones carved fierce and high, in those brows set level over the deep eyes.

Why, she thought. He had hardly changed at all.

But ah, he had.

He was neither the dwarf nor the giant of his legend. He stood a little taller than she, middling for a man in Han-Gilen. His hair submitted no more tamely than ever to its priestly braid; his body was slender still, a swordsman's body or a dancer's, graceful even at rest.

The difference was not in his eyes. God's eyes; no one had ever found it easy to meet them. Nor was it his face. All northern faces were made for arrogance. Nor was it even that he had forsaken the good plain clothes of the south for the gaudy near-nakedness of the north, so that the torque of his father's priesthood seemed lost amid the extravagance of copper and gold. No; the change ran deeper than that. She had bidden farewell to a boy, her brother. This was a man and a king.

He drained his cup, still leaning lightly on his companion. Their eyes met for an instant as he lowered the cup; a spark leaped in the meeting. It was nothing as feeble as passion, nothing as shallow as love. As one's self would meet one's self; as brother to soul's brother.

Elian knew then who the tall man must be. Vadin alVadin, Lord of Asan-Geitan in the kingdom of Ianon. He, next to Mirain himself, was the heart of the legend that was An-Sh'Endor. Commanded by the old King of Ianon to serve an upstart, southern-born prince, he had obeyed with utmost reluctance. Reluctantly he had seen the prince raised to king, and continued as squire and unwilling confidant; and he had died for his master, taking the assassin's spear that had been meant for Mirain. But Mirain had brought him back, and he had discovered that his reluctance was lost, and that he loved his outland king. They had sworn the oath of brothers-in-blood; and more, people said, but that, no one had ever proven. No one needed to prove it. To the eyes of power they were like the halves of a single shining creature.

Elian did not understand why her heart constricted. It was not fear of the visible and palpable power that dwelt in the man. She was mageborn herself, and stronger than he would ever be. And if they were sworn brothers, if somewhere among the long campaigns they had been lovers, what could it matter to her?

It could matter. He stood where she had sworn to stand. He had what she had come to take.

Mirain was laughing again, refusing a new cup of wine. "No, no, I've had my fill already, and I've a pack of lords clamoring for their king. What will they say if I reel in like a drunken soldier?"

"You?" someone called out. "Drunken? Never!"

"Ah," he said, wicked. "I'll tell you a secret, Bredan: I can't hold my wine at all. I slip it to my brother."

They roared at that, but they let him go. He seemed

not to see the hands that reached as he passed, touching him as by accident, or falling short; loving him.

Elian knew the precise instant when he saw her. He checked, the merest hesitation. His face betrayed nothing. He passed her without a glance, striding into the sunlight.

Someone touched her. She wheeled, hand to hilt. Cuthan beckoned. And when she did not move, set his hand on her shoulder, light but inescapable.

Beyond the winestall was a space like an alleyway, a joining of blank walls, deserted. Mirain stood there, alone. In the glare of the Sun his father, he was no one she knew. God's son, conqueror, Ianyn king. His eyes were level upon her, and cold, and still.

His hand rose, gestured. Sun-gold blinded her. Cuthan was gone. Where he had been was the coldness of absence, and curiosity rigidly restrained, and a flicker of fear for her, melting like a mist in the sun.

She stood mute, with her chin at its most defiant angle. Let this stranger cast her out. Let him even kill her. She had gone too far to care.

Mirain's head tilted. His lips quirked, the old not-quite-smile. "Well?" he asked her. The Gileni word. In a tone she knew so well that the hearing of it was like pain.

"Well?" she countered, angry at nothing and at everything. "Now you can dispose of me. Majesty."

"So I might," he agreed. Damn him. He folded his arms, looked her up and down. "I've been waiting for you."

She clenched her jaw before it could drop. "How in the hells—"

He seemed not to have heard. "You took your time about it. I was beginning to wonder if you'd forgotten. You were very young when you swore on my hand that you would follow me to Ianon."

"I thought *you* had forgotten," she said. "With so much to think of—a world to conquer—"

His hand silenced her. She stood, awkward, on the edge between anger and flight. His eyes had stilled again.

He held out his hands. She stared at them. He smiled.

His eyes were dancing. She leaped, laughing, and spun with him in a long, breathless, delighted embrace.

At length and as one they stepped apart. Again Mirain looked at her, and now he was not cold at all. "You've grown," he said.

"So have you."

"The whole half of a handspan," he said a little wryly. He ran a lock of her hair between his fingers. "Redder than ever. And your temper?"

"Worse than ever."

"Impossible." She bared her teeth at him; he grinned, looking for a moment no older than she. "How is Foster-father? And Hal? And—"

"All well and all prospering. Hal has two strapping sons, and another child coming: a daughter, he says. He takes his dynastic duties very seriously."

Her tone must have betrayed something. His glance sharpened. "And you? You look a little the worse for wear. Were you beset upon the road?"

"I was beset," she answered steadily, and as calmly as she could. "I ran afoul of your old enemy." He frowned slightly. Of course he would have forgotten; it had been so long ago. "The one who lost her name and her eyes for denying you. My kinswoman, whom my father drove out. She caught me, but I escaped her. She hates you, Mirain."

"So," Mirain said softly, as if to himself. "It begins." He looked up, sudden enough to make her gasp. "And you have cast in your lot with me. Your father might forgive me for allowing it. Would your mother?"

Elian swallowed hard. Her mind was empty. It made her words as light as she could ever have wished them to be. "Mother is preeminently practical. Better you, she'll judge, than some of the alternatives. At least you'll see that my virtue remains intact."

"Will I?"

Her face was hot. She tried to laugh. "You had better, if you want to be forgiven."

He bent to pluck a sprig of heather, sweet and startling in this trampled place. "Then I must try, mustn't I?"

He turned the blossom in his fingers. "My regents in Ianon are waiting for you. Both are great ladies, and Alidan bears arms. You'd like one another, I think."

"No!" Her vehemence brought him about. She tried to speak more softly. "I don't want to be packed off like—like baggage. I came to see you. To fight for you. I came to be free."

"You are free." Her chin was set, stubborn; he faced her with stubbornness no less. "You vowed to come to Ianon."

"I vowed to fight for you."

"Elian," he said with mighty patience, "I can't assign you to one of my companies. Even if your disguise would outlast the first river crossing, you make far too handsome a boy to thrust among an army."

"I thought you would understand. But you're like all the rest." She thrust her hands in his face. "Tie me up then. Send me back to Han-Gilen. See me wrapped in silks till I can't move at all, and auctioned off to the highest bidder."

"Elian." He spoke quietly, but his tone was like a slap. "I do not send either women or fair-faced boys to eat and sleep and fight with my veterans, unless they are well prepared to contend with the consequences. Which you, my lady of Han-Gilen, are not." She was silent, eyes blazing; he continued implacably, "There is a place for you in Ianon; I can provide an escort to take you there, or to return you to your family, as you choose."

She could have railed at him; she could have burst into tears. She struck him with all her trained strength.

He rocked under the blow but did not fall. She stood still, shaking, beginning to be appalled. She had raised her hand against a king.

Suddenly he laughed.

She hit him again. Still laughing, he caught her hand; then the other. She hurled her weight against him.

They rolled in the trampled grass, he laughing like a madman, she kicking and spitting and cursing him in every tongue she knew. A stone caught her. She lay gasping, hating him. There were tears on his cheeks, tears of laughter. But his face had sobered; his eyes met hers, dark and bottomless. Abruptly he was gone.

She rose shakily. He stood a little apart, watching her. His face was cold and still. Either he had grown or the world had shrunk. He towered over her, lofty, unreachable, royal. "By the laws of war you are my captive, to do with as I will. I can send you back to your father as one lord returns a strayed herdbeast to another. I can dismiss you to Ianon to await my return and my pleasure. I can keep you with me, take you and use you and discard you when I tire of you."

"Not you," she said without thinking. "Not that."

The mask cracked a very little. He stood no longer quite so high. "No. I confess I have no taste for rape. What else can I do? I won't inflict you on one of my captains."

"Then," she cried recklessly, "let me do something else. Let me be your guard, your servant, anything!"

He looked at her, measuring her as if she were a stranger. She could not meet his stare. "It happens," he said at last, "that I stand in need of a squire."

She opened her mouth and closed it again. His face had softened not at all. And yet he offered her this. Esquire. Armor-bearer. Guard and servant both, yet higher than either; to ride at his right hand, sleep at his bed's foot, and serve him with life and loyalty until death or knighthood freed her.

And this lord of all lords—he had his legend. He had no squire of his body. Not since the one who had died for him, whom he had raised again, whom he had made a knight and a prince and a sworn brother. That he judged her worthy of that one's place, was a gift beyond price.

"Surely," she said, "surely there are princes vying for the honor."

"You are a princess."

She could not speak.

His lips thinned. "Yes, you do well to hesitate. Any woman who speaks to me is soon called my lover. One sleeping in my very tent, close by me always, would lose all pretense to good name."

Her voice flooded back, as strong as it had ever been. "What of a boy?"

"If that is your choice," he said, "I'll do nothing to betray you. But in the end the truth will out."

"Let that be as it will be." She knelt at his feet. "I will serve you, my lord, in all that you ask of me; even to death, if so the god wills it."

He laid his hands upon her head. "I accept your oath and your service, your heart and your hand, to hold and to guard while my life lasts. In Avaryan's name, so let it be."

She swallowed hard. She had said only what came to her; but this was ritual, the binding of the vassal to his lord, complete and irrevocable.

It was what she had come for. Perhaps. She sprang lightly up and found a grin for him. "Well, my lord? How shall I begin?"

"By walking back to my tent with me."

But as she came to his side, he paused. His eyes were fixed upon her. She looked down. The bindings of her garments had weakened in the struggle; they parted even as she moved, baring her breast and the long deep weals there.

His hand went out, but did not touch her; his breath hissed between his teeth. "You didn't tell me of that."

"It's nothing." She pulled the broken laces free, angrily. *"Damn!* Now everyone in the world will be able to see—"

Gently but firmly he set her hands aside and eased back coat and shirt. She did not resist him, at first for defiance, and after because there was nothing shameful in either his look or his touch. The wounds were red, inflamed, a steady pain which she schooled herself to ignore. Yet where his hand passed, even where she was most tender and most cruelly torn, the pain lessened, faded and shrank and was gone; the scarlet weals paled to scars and vanished.

His hand rose to her cheek. She caught it. "No," she said. He blinked, caught between power and its refusal. "Let me have my own pain."

"It will scar," he said.

"I've earned it with my foolishness."

For yet a moment he was still. Then he bowed his head. "Here," he said in the most ordinary of tones, holding out a bit of leather from his belt, "see if this will hold."

It would, admirably. With her shirt well and tightly laced and her coat belted against the world, she strode with Mirain into the clamor of the camp.

Seven

MIRAIN'S LORDS GATHERED ABOUT HIS TENT, AND their clamor sounded for all the world like the lowing of cattle. When he plunged into the midst of them with Elian at his heels, their silence was abrupt and absolute. Elian admired it; even Prince Orsan had not mastered that art as Mirain had. He stood in the center of them under the Sun-standard, and settled his arm easily, lightly, over Elian's shoulders. "See," he said, with no more greeting than that. "I have a new squire. Galan, my lords and captains."

Later she would match the faces to the names out of Mirain's legend. Now they were a blur: curiosity, hostility, haughty indifference. One or two were envious. One or two, perhaps, wished her well.

One gave her nothing at all. He stood a little aloof, glittering in his finery, meeting her gaze here as he had in the winestall. "Ho, Vadin!" Mirain called out in pure and hateful exuberance, "I've found us a new recruit; or your brother has, with a little help from his scouts. What do you think of him?"

The Lord of Geitan made his way through the clustered captains. Elian, looking up and up, knew that he would hate her.

He looked down and down. He was cool, proud, running those splendid eyes over her disheveled and travelworn figure. Pausing. Raising a brow the merest suggestion of a degree. Her probe met a wall. It was high, it was broad, and it was impenetrable. His face betrayed nothing but consummate northern arrogance. His voice was neither warm nor cold, although she knew he had a temper, a hot one; it was in all the tales. He could be as cruel as any mountain bandit, as gentle as any sheltered maiden. "So this is a red Gileni," he said. "Red indeed! I've seen fire that was paler."

"So this," said Elian, "is a Ianyn of the old breed. I've seen eagles who were humbler."

Vadin startled her speechless: he grinned, wide and white and irrepressible. He looked exactly like Cuthan his brother, no older and not a whit wiser. "By the gods, you've got a tongue on you. A temper too. What do you do for sport? Trade insults with dragons?"

"Only if they insult me first."

He laughed, undismayed. "I wasn't insulting, I was admiring. We love copper, we savages. What a wonder to grow one's own."

"Pretty, no?" Mirain's eyes glinted upon them both, and flickered round the circle of faces. "My lords, I am at your disposal." And as they bowed, he returned to the two who still faced one another, and said, "Vadin, for charity, take my squire in hand. He's had good training, but he's a stranger here; there's much that you can teach him."

The Ianyn bowed his high head. Mirain smiled his swift splendid smile and left them, striding swiftly, with his lords in a gaggle behind.

Elian watched him go, and considered hating him. He had abandoned her. She was alone, a stranger to all that was here, where everyone had his duties and his place. She had nothing but the clothes she stood in and the throbbing weals upon her cheek.

Slowly she turned to face her guide. Vadin was expressionless again, and no doubt seething. He was the right hand of An-Sh'Endor, chief of the lords and generals; for a certainty he had duties far higher and more pressing than the nursemaiding of one young foreigner.

His lips twitched. "I've done it before," he said, driving her behind her strongest shields. "Come, youngling. We'll make you one of us."

At the beginning of their progress Vadin acquired a servant, a great hulk of a man who bore with ease the weight of clothing and weapons and the odd necessity. "No kilt for you, I think," Vadin said as she contemplated one in utter dismay. "My lord likes to see his people in their own proper dress. Even," he added with a curl of his lip, "in trousers."

She kept her temper in hand. It was not easy. "Don't you sometimes find a kilt rather uncomfortable? In the saddle, for example? In the dead of winter?"

"In winter we lace our boots high and pin our cloaks tightly and laugh at the wind. In the saddle," said Vadin, and now he was certainly laughing, "which is where all of us are born, we're perfectly comfortable."

"I'll wager you cheat and wear breeches underneath."

"Would you like me to show you?" He laid a hand on his belt; his eyes danced, utterly wicked.

Elian closed her mouth and set it tight. Yes, she hated Mirain. Of all the men in all his horde, why had he thrown her on the mercy of this one?

"Southern kit," Vadin said to the quartermaster, blissfully ignorant of her fury, "in the king's colors. Dress and campaign issue both, and be quick. My lord will be waiting for it."

The quartermaster all but licked the Ianyn's feet. Likewise the armorer, who measured Elian with much commentary on her fine boyish figure, and how much growing room was the lad likely to need?

"Not overmuch," replied her insufferable guide. "We'll take a knife now, and a sword. The three longswords you forged for my lord before he found one that satisfied him—bring them out."

"But, lord, they—"

Vadin's voice did not rise, but the man stopped as if struck. "The king's body-squire must be armed as well as the king himself. Bring out the blades."

They were plain, yet perfect in their plainness: pure, unadorned, deadly beauty, forged not of bronze but of priceless steel. In the Hundred Realms, few even of princes had such weapons. Prince Orsan had two; they were the greatest treasures of his armory. Neither was as fine as these.

She tested each with the reverence it deserved. Each fit well into her hand. But one, lifted, settled as if it had grown there. "This—this one," she said unsteadily, tearing her eyes from that wondrous, shimmering edge.

When she left the armorer's tent, the sword hung scabbarded from her belt, and she walked a little the straighter for it. Even Vadin's presence seemed less of a burden; as he led her toward the cavalry lines, it slipped from her mind altogether.

The north was famous for its seneldi, and Ianon above all; and these were the cream therefrom. Even the draybeasts were fine strong creatures; the war-seneldi, horned battle-stallions and tall fierce mares, were magnificent. Elian walked down the long lines, among the penned wagonbeasts and the remounts, pausing here and there to return a whickered greeting.

Alone of them all, one son of the night wind was free to run where he would. He was as black as polished obsidian, without mark or blemish; his horns were as long as swords, his eyes as red as heart's blood. He trotted through his domain with such splendid, royal arrogance that even the stallions made no move to challenge him.

"There goes a creature worth a kingdom," Elian said.

"If any king could master him," said Vadin. "No one but Mirain has ever sat on the Mad One's back."

The senel came closer. Grooms and idlers were quick

to clear his path. Even Vadin stepped aside, without fear but with considerable respect.

Elian stood her ground. She was no less royal than the stallion; while she had no hope of becoming his master, she was certainly his equal.

She was full in his path. On either side stretched a long line of tethered mounts. He snorted and flattened his ears. "Courteously, sir," she said.

His teeth bared. He pawed the ground.

"If you harm me, my lord may not be pleased."

He seemed to ponder that, lean ears flicking forward, back. As if in sudden decision, they pricked. He stepped forward. With utmost delicacy he lowered his head and blew sweet breath upon her palm. She ran a hand over his ears, along the splendid arch of his neck. "Indeed, lord king, now you may pass. But if it would please you, is there one of your herd who would consent to carry me?"

He himself would, and gladly, but he had but one lord. Yet there were some . . . He turned, stepping softly. She laced her fingers in his mane.

As the Mad One permitted no man but Mirain on his back, likewise he suffered no other beast to do that service. Even so, Ianon's king traveled with his own stable: the nine royal mounts decreed by custom, and the mounts and remounts of his household. These held to their own guarded lines, watched over by grooms in scarlet kilts.

The Mad One paid no heed to the lesser beasts, the least of them as fine as Elian's poor lost mare. He passed them in cool disdain, seeking out the center of the line and the King's Nine tethered there. Two were stallions, a black and a grey, sleek with light work and good feeding. The rest were mares, one of each color: brown, bay, roan, grey, striped dun, and gold. The ninth, a mare likewise, grazed apart. She had been tethered; Elian saw a halter empty upon the ground.

The Mad One loosed a high, imperious cry. The mare raised her head, and Elian caught her breath. Line for line, the young senel was the Mad One's image. Save only in color: that was the precise, fiery red-gold of Elian's hair.

The stallion arched his neck. His daughter, this was: Ilhari, Firemane. She was young; she was very foolish; she had never yet been ridden. But she would carry the lady, if the lady wished it.

Ilhari flattened her ears. And what right had he to say what she would or would not do?

The same right, he responded with a toss of his head, that the Sunborn had to bring a useless filly to war. One who, moreover, could not even keep her place in the line, but would slip free at every opportunity and run wild on the grass.

Precisely like her sire.

Elian laughed, approaching the mare slowly. Indeed Ilhari was the Mad One's daughter. She had the same wild ruby eye, the same wicked temper. Yet she also had his deep and well-concealed core of perfect sanity. She watched, but she did not threaten, merely lifted a hind foot in warning.

"Princess," asked Elian, "would you consent to carry me?"

Ilhari's back quivered as if to cast off a fly. It would certainly please yon great black bully. For herself . . .

Elian touched the quivering muzzle. The mare was finer than her sire, smaller, more delicate. Elian stroked aside the long silken forelock and smoothed the star upon her forehead. "I would not bridle you, nor tether you. A saddle I would need, for battle if for naught else."

No one had ever sat upon Ilhari's back. The Sunborn had not allowed it. She was the free one, the king's ninth mount, the Mad One's daughter.

"I am royal. The Sunborn calls me his kin. The Mad One has consented to accept me."

Ilhari snorted. Ah, the Mad One! He did as he pleased.

"And might not we? Come, stand, so. Yes. Yes!" Lightly Elian swung onto her back. For a long moment Ilhari stood rigid. Cautiously she essayed a step. She felt strange, unbalanced.

"That passes," said Elian.

She reared. Elian's knees tightened; her body shifted forward; her fingers knotted in the long mane. Ilhari bucked and twisted. Elian only clung the tighter. The mare reared again, wheeling as she came down, flinging herself forward, plowing to a halt.

Elian laughed.

Ilhari snorted. Rider, nothing. This was a leech.

Elian stroked the sleek neck. "You're not angry with me. You only pretend to be."

Ilhari extended a forefoot to rub an itch from her cheek. It was not so very unpleasant. Perhaps. Once she learned the way of it.

"Well," said Elian, "shall we begin?"

Caught up in the beginnings of subtle and intricate art, with the Mad One both mocking and teaching beside them, neither noticed until very late that they had gathered an audience. Elian had her first hint of it when, glancing sidewise, she met Mirain's white smile. He had come up unseen, smooth as a partner in a dance, and found his way onto the stallion's back.

She tensed. Ilhari had halted, immobile as a carven senel. "My lord, she's yours, I know it, but—"

"Mine," he said, "she never has been. If her sire sees fit to bring you two together, should I interfere?"

"But—"

"She has made her own choice." He saluted them both with a flourish. "The singers will have a new song tonight."

"Singers? Song?" Elian looked beyond him. She had completely forgotten Vadin. He stood near the lines, foremost of a mob of watchers. Even at that distance she could see his smile and the hand he raised in salute. All about him, a cheer went up, high and exuberant.

She acknowledged them without conscious thought, a bow and a smile they could see, and words they could not hear. "Sun and stars! How long have they been there?"

"A good hour, I should think."

Elian dismounted hastily and ran her hands over

Ilhari's flanks. The mare was sweating lightly but otherwise unharmed, and scarcely weary. She danced a little,
nuzzling Elian's hair. That had been delightful. When
could they do it again?

"Tomorrow," Elian promised her.

THE KING'S COUNCIL WAS LESS AN AFFAIR OF STATE THAN A
gathering of friends. Splendid as the evening was, warm
and clear, with a sunset like a storm of fire, they sat as
they pleased before his tent, eating and drinking and
conversing at first of small things.

Elian did squire's duty for the king until the wine
went round, when he drew her down beside him. One or
two kilted chieftains looked askance. The others, Geitan's
lord conspicuous among them, took no notice.

She settled herself as comfortably as she might in her
stiff new livery, and toyed with a cup of wine, resting its
coolness against her torn cheek. The flow of speech had
shifted. Hawks and hounds and women, fine mounts and
old battles, passed and were forgotten.

"We have a choice," said a man who had once called
himself a king. He decked himself still with a circlet of
gold, although he was lavish in his homage to his conqueror. "We can strike south into the Hundred Realms.
Or we can turn west. There's a wide land between here
and Asanion, full of tribes ripe, and rich, for conquest."

"West, say I." The accent was Ianyn, and proud with
it. "Then south, with the whole force of the north behind
us."

Another man of Ianon spoke from across the fire.
"Why not head south now? We're in Ashan already, or as
close as makes no matter. There's easy pickings here by
all accounts, and easier the farther you go: fat rich southerners gone lazy with peace."

"Not that lazy," said one with the twang of Ebros and
the garb of a mercenary captain. "They can fight when
they're roused. They drove back all the armies of the
Nine Cities not so long ago, and kept them back."

"Talked them back, I hear," a northerner drawled. "Southerners and westerners, they talk. We fight."

Someone came up round the edge of the council. With a small start, Elian recognized Cuthan. He flashed her a glance that took in her place and her livery, and saluted her with a smile, even as he bent to murmur in Mirain's ear. She opened mind and ears to overhear.

"Nothing, sire," Cuthan was saying. "We found evidence of a fair-sized camp, and not an old one either, but it was completely deserted, with nothing to show where the reivers had gone."

"Might they have scattered?" Mirain asked.

"Maybe. If so, they went to all the dozen winds, and covered their tracks behind them."

"How many might there have been?"

"Hard to tell, my lord. Say, half a hundred. Maybe less, not likely more, or they'd have left some traces."

Mirain bowed his head. "You've done well. Go out again for me, and search further. If you find even the smallest thing, see that I hear of it."

"Aye, my lord. The god keep you."

Cuthan grinned at his brother, and again at Elian. With a scout's skill, he merged himself with the twilight and was gone. Mirain reclined as before, propped up on his elbow, eyes hooded as the council continued about him. Elian knew better than to think that he had missed a word of it.

Voices raised, cutting across one another. "And I say the north is enough! What do we want with a pack of barbarians, southern, western, whatever they may be?"

"What do we want? Damn you, we want to rule them! What else are barbarians good for?"

"Yes." Mirain spoke softly, but he won sudden silence. "What are we good for? For I was born in the south."

"Your mother was heir of Ianon," said the man who had spoken last, with a touch of belligerence.

"Her mother was a princess of Asanion." Mirain rose. He could use his height exactly as he chose, to tower over the seated captains, yet to make clear to them that he lacked much of the stature of Ianon. "My lords, you speak of choices. South or west; east no one seems to think of, but that's only wild lands and the sea. Well then. West are our kinsmen, tribes who serve the god as we serve him, and past these the marches of the Golden Empire. South lie the Hundred Realms. Another empire, one might say, though none of the people there would choose to call it that."

"Well, so are we," said Vadin, speaking for the first time. "The empire of the north. And hasn't your father given you the world to rule?"

Mirain's smile was wry. *"Given* is hardly the word, brother, and well you know it. Offered for my winning, rather." His eyes flashed round them. "What next, then? South or west? Who will choose?"

"You, of course," said Vadin. "Who has a better right?"

"Someone may. Galan!"

She started. Mirain faced her, suddenly a stranger, fierce and fey. "Galan, where would you have me go?"

She spoke her thought, unsoftened and unadorned. "When you're done with your jesting, you will do exactly as you always meant to do: pass the border your scouts have already pierced, and march upon the south. Halenan knew. He gave me a message for you. He called you a damned fool; he said, 'If he sets foot in my lands, it had better be as a friend, or god's son or no, I'll have his head on my spear.'"

Anger flared within the circle. But Mirain laughed, light and wild. "Did he say that? He can say it again when we meet. For southward indeed I will go, with the god before me. What of you, Red Prince's kin? Will you ride at my right hand?"

He wanted a bold brave answer. Elian gave him one; though not perhaps the one he had expected. "I will ride at your right hand," she said. "And see to it that it is indeed friendship in which you come. Or—"

"Or?" He was bright, laughing, dangerous.

She grinned back. "Or you will answer not simply to

me, or to Halenan. You will answer to the Red Prince himself."

"I think I need not fear that."

"You should," she said, surprising herself: because she believed it. "But as for me, I have given you my oath. While I live I will keep it. I will ride south with you, Mirain An-Sh'Endor."

Eight

THE SON OF THE SUN TOOK ASHAN WITHOUT A BLOW struck. For as his army passed the forest that was the northern march of the princedom and entered upon its maze of stony valleys, riders came to him under the yellow banner of the prince. They laid themselves at Mirain's feet, sued for peace, and called him king, beseeching him to receive their lord's homage in his own walled city. Themselves they offered as hostages, and with them an open-faced young fellow who, but for the distinct red-brown cast of his skin, might have been Ianyn; he was, he said, close kin to the prince.

Not the heir, Elian took note, but close enough. Old Luian, who might have waged a long and deadly war among his crags, had cast in his lot with the conqueror.

And, having made his choice, he stinted nothing. His castles lay open to the army; his folk hailed them as victors; his vassals came forth with gifts and homage. It was no invasion but a royal progress that brought Mirain to Han-Ashan where waited the prince.

He was old. Too old, his messengers said, to venture his bones upon the mountain tracks. He received Mirain

85

at the gate of his own hall, leaning on the arms of two stalwart young men, the most favored of his twoscore sons; yet he left his living props to perform the full obeisance of a vassal before his king.

Mirain received it as he had received all else in Ashan, with gracious words, royal mien, and the expressionless face of a god carved in stone. His king-face, Elian called it. His mind yielded nothing at all to her, blank and impenetrable as the walls of Luian's castle.

She served him at the feast in Prince Luian's hall, squire service much eased by the courtesy of the host; there was in fact little for her to do but stand behind Mirain's seat and see that the servants kept both his cup and his plate filled. He ate little, she noticed, and only pretended to drink.

She thought she knew why. Ashani women lived like women of the west, veiled and set apart from men, but the highborn dined in hall at festivals. Luian's chief wife shared his throne, a woman of great bulk and yet also of great and imposing beauty; many of his lords and commons kept company with wives or mistresses. Of unwedded women there were few, and those only the highest: a tall lithe woman with a priestess' torque who was the prince's daughter, and the daughters of one or two of his sons.

One of whom, child of the heir himself, had been set between Mirain and her father. This, Elian well knew, was somewhat out of the proper order. Most of the royal ladies tended to favor their grandsire: Ianyn-tall, nearly Ianyn-dark, and strikingly handsome. This one was smaller, slight and shapely, her delicate hands and her smooth brow unmarred by any taint of southern bronze, her eyes huge, round, and darkly liquid as the eyes of a doe. The rest of her face was clear enough to see beneath the veil, a delicate oval, a suggestion of perfect teeth. If she had a flaw, it was her voice: high and, though she took pains to soften it, rather sharp.

Mirain seemed captivated, leaning close to hear her murmured speech, smiling at a jest. He was splendid to see, clad in the full finery of a Ianyn king, all white and gold; his skin gleamed against it like ebony. Elian herself had braided the ropes of gold into his hair. He had turned as she struggled to tame the unruly mass of it, and ruffled her own newly subdued mane, and laughed at her flash of temper.

Her lips twisted wryly. Well; was that not what she had wanted? She walked abroad as a man, and he regarded her as one; although she shared his tent, he had never once touched her save as a brother or a friend, nor looked at her as a man might look at a woman. Even when he had seen her naked breast, he had seen only wounds that cried for healing.

The lady held his hand in hers, giggling on a high and piercing note. The god's mark fascinated her: the Sun of gold set in the flesh, fused with it, part of it.

"You can touch it," he said, warm and indulgent. "It won't hurt you."

She giggled. "No. Oh, no! I couldn't. That would be sacrilege!" But she did not let go his hand.

Elian's glance crossed Vadin's. The Ianyn lord had evaded the bonds of princely protocol by the simple expedient of commanding his brother to take his name and his place, and putting on the garb and the bearing of a guard, and setting himself to watch over Mirain. Elian had learned, not easily, that it did no good to resent him. He went where he would, did as he pleased, and answered only to his king. Elian he treated with unfailing courtesy, which some might even have taken for friendliness: the friendliness of a man toward his brother's favorite hound.

He leaned against the wall, cool and easy, smiling a little. "My lord is well entertained tonight," he observed. "They make a handsome pair, don't you think?"

Elian kept her face quiet, but her eyes glittered. "How can he endure her?"

"How does any man endure a beautiful woman?"

"She has a voice like a tortured cat."

"She has a rich dowry."

Elian drew a sharp breath.

"After all," said Vadin, "he's been king these seven years. It's time he got himself an heir."

"Strong throne, strong succession." Elian bit off the words. "I know that. Who doesn't? But this—"

"Can you offer a better candidate?"

Elian would not answer. Dared not. And Vadin did not press her. He was, inexplicably and maddeningly, amused. Yet he did not know. He could not.

Elian put on her best, boyish scowl. Vadin only grinned and wandered off on some whim of his own.

Mirain came up very late from the feasting. Later than Elian, who had left as soon as was proper, after the second passing of the wine; but the women had retired before the first.

He greeted her with his quick smile. He had been drinking deep: his eyes were bright and his breath wine-scented. Yet he was steady on his feet. As she rose from her pallet, he motioned her down again. "No, be at ease; I can undress myself."

She came in despite of him to catch his cloak and his jewels as they fell. He always turned his back on her to doff his kilt, more for her modesty's sake than for his own; in Ianon, Cuthan had told her, all the servants of his bath were women, maiden daughters of noble houses. She smiled in spite of herself as she unbound the intricate plaits of his hair, remembering the tale, a young priest from Han-Gilen forced for the first time to strip naked before a roomful of fine ladies. And knowing full well the root of the custom: the strengthening of noble lines with the blood royal, perhaps even the choosing of one favored lady to share the throne.

Mirain yawned and stretched, supple as a cat. "Hold still," Elian bade him, half annoyed, half preoccupied. He obeyed docilely enough. She continued her patient unraveling, letting each freed strand fall to his shoulders. He had battle scars in plenty, but all were on his front; his back was smooth, unmarred. Once, as by accident, she let her fingertips brush his skin. It was soft like a child's, but the muscles were steel-hard beneath.

He yawned again. "These Ashani," he said. "They seem to practice half their statecraft in a haze of wine."

"They have a maxim: Wine to begin a thought, sleep and morning light to end it. And another: Soften your opponent with wine, and mold him when he wakes from it."

"They do the same in Ianon. But not so blatantly. Once he had the company down to the serious drinkers, Prince Luian launched his attack. He would become my true and loyal liege man, faithful servant of the god's son, if only I would grant a small favor in return."

"Of course. How small?"

"Minuscule. The merest trifle. It seems that he can't agree with the Prince of Ebros as to the lordship of a certain valley. The Prince of Ebros has garrisoned it very recently with his own troops. Will I lend my army to restore the vale to its rightful master?"

"Will you?"

"I've been considering it. There's been a great deal of tumult over this bit of green with a river running through it: embassies and counterembassies, threats and counterthreats. I've a mind to see if I can uncover the rights of the matter."

His hair was free. She coiled its golden bindings in their box; when she turned back, Mirain was upright in the bed, the coverlet drawn up, wielding a comb with no patience at all. Deftly she won the comb and began to repair the damage. "Ebros and Ashan have never been fond of one another. If you march on this valley, even if you only intend to determine its possession, Ebros' prince will say you've come to start a war."

"In that event, I'll make sure I come out the victor."

"You want Ebros, don't you? However you get it."

He looked up. He was still, quiet. But the mask had gone up between his heart and the world. "Will you stop me?"

She considered it with no little care. He watched her.

She scowled at him. "You're playing with me again. Pretending that what I say can matter."

"But," he said, "it can."

Her scowl blackened. "Because I'm myself, or because I have a father who can raise the south against you?"

"Or," he continued for her, "because the High Prince of Asanion wants you for his harem?"

Her heart stilled. Her throat locked, all but strangling her voice. "I—I never—how did you—"

"Spies," he answered. He was not laughing. She could not read him at all. "They have an ill name, these royal Asanians. They are trained from the cradle in the arts of the bedchamber; they keep women like cattle; they worship all gods and none. They have three great arts: love, and sophistry, and treachery. And their greatest pride lies in the weaving of all three."

"Ilarios is not like that at all." The silence was abrupt, and somehow frightening. Elian filled it with a rush of words. "He asked for me in all honor. He promised to make me his empress."

"And you came to me."

"I came because I promised."

Mirain said nothing for a long count of breaths. When he spoke, he spoke softly, and as if Ilarios had never been. "I will have Ebros. If I must take it by force, so be it. But I will rule it in peace." He shifted, body and mind; he lightened, turned wry. "A subtle man, my host. He sweetens his conditions with purest honey: the offer of his granddaughter's hand."

Elian's hand stopped. "Did you accept it?"

He laughed. "I have a policy," he said. "When a man offers to make a marriage for me, I thank him kindly. I promise to consider the matter. And I make no further mention of it."

"And if he insists?"

"I speak of something else."

She was silent, combing the wild mane into smoothness. Many a woman might have envied it, waist-long, thick and curling as it was. At length she said, "A king should marry for the sake of his dynasty." Her lip curled a little as she said it. Wise words. Her mother had said very nearly the same thing, in very nearly the same tone.

Mirain could not see her face; he said calmly, "So a king should. So shall I."

"When you've found a woman fit to be your queen?"

"I have found her."

Elian's eyes dimmed as if she had been struck a blow. But she was royal; she had learned discipline, seldom though she chose to exercise it. "How wise of you," she said lightly, "to let your allies believe that they are free to bind you with their kinswomen. What is she like, this lady of yours?"

"Very beautiful. Very witty. Rather wild, if the truth be told; but I have a weakness for wild things."

"Well dowered, I suppose."

"Very. She is a princess."

"Of course." Elian was done, but she toyed with his hair, lingering, like a woman who frets with an aching tooth, testing again and again the intensity of the pain. "Her kinsmen must be very pleased."

"Her kin know nothing of it. I've not yet offered for her. She's shy, you see, and elusive, and wary as a young lynx. She is no man's to give, nor ever mine to compel. She must come to me of her own will, however slowly, however long the coming."

"That's not wise. What if someone takes her while you are away on your wars?"

"I think I need have no fear of that."

Slowly, carefully, Elian set the comb aside. "You are fortunate."

He lay back. His smile was a cat's, drowsy, sated, with the merest hint of irony. "Yes," he said. "I am."

She turned her back on him and sought her pallet.

"Good night," he called softly.

"Good night, my lord," she said.

Nine

ELIAN FLEXED HER SHOULDERS. HER NEW PANOPLY FIT like a skin of bronze and gold, but its weight was strange, both lighter and stronger than the Gileni armor she was used to.

Under her, Ilhari shifted. Strangeness? Maybe. Or maybe it was simple fear. She for one would be greatly pleased when her first battle lay behind her.

Ilhari's logic was as usual impeccable. Elian smoothed the battle-streamers woven into the mare's mane, green on red-gold. Mirain, she noticed, was just completing the same gesture. The Mad One's streamers were scarlet, the color of blood.

He seemed unconcerned, even lighthearted, sitting at ease in the saddle, gazing down a long gentle slope at the enemy. His army massed behind him, swelled now with Ashani troops. The field beneath it had been golden with grain, but the grain was trampled, its gold dimmed. The earth had sprouted another crop altogether, a harvest of flesh and steel.

Elian watched him consider it calmly, without haste. His forces were disposed on the ground he had chosen, a shoulder of Ashan's mountains that dwindled here to a low rolling hill, with wide lands behind and his camp settled in them.

More than a garrison faced him. The whole army of Ebros had mustered to drive back the northerners; had refused all his embassies and his offers of just and blood-less judgment; had forsaken the high-walled town whose folk tilled these fields, and come forth to open combat. They had the town and its steep hill at their backs, but their own emplacements lay perforce below Mirain's; if they charged, it must be uphill against a rain of arrows. Yet they were strong, and they had a wing of that most terrible of weapons, the scythed battle-car. Even their own men kept well away from those deadly whirling wheels.

Their commander rode up and down before them in a lesser chariot, yet one very splendid, flashing gold and crimson. Matched mares drew it, their coats bright gold, their manes flowing like white water. He himself shone in golden armor, with a coronet on his high helmet.

"Indrion of Ebros," said Prince Luian's heir from his chariot beside Mirain, with a century of bitter feuding in his voice and in the glitter of his eyes. "Now we shall settle with that cattle thief."

It was an ill word, Elian thought, for that splendid royal vision. Mirain paid its speaker no heed. The enemy had begun to fret before the massed stillness of his army. Yet that stillness was his own, the immobility of the lion before it springs.

The Ebran line could bear it no longer. With a roar it surged forward.

Still Mirain did not move.

Elian's heart thudded. The Ebrans were close, peril-ously close. She could pick out single men from among the mass: a mounted knight, a light-armed charioteer, a footsoldier in worn leather with a patch in his breeks. She saw the patch very clearly. It was ill-sewn, as if he had done it himself, and of a lighter leather than the rest, incongruously new and clean.

A hand touched her. She started and stiffened. Mirain's

hand left her, but his eyes held. No man's eyes, those, but the eyes of a god: bright, cold, alien. "Remember," he said, soft but very clear. "No heroics. You cling to me like a burr; you look after my weapons; you leave the rest to my army."

She opened her mouth to speak, perhaps to protest. But he had turned from her, and his household was watching. Some smiled. The younger ones in particular; they thought they understood. "Cheer up, lad," said the one closest. "You'll get your chance."

"Aye and aye!" agreed another. "Here's luck, and glory enough for everybody." He grinned and clapped her on the shoulder, rocking her in the saddle. She grinned back through clenched teeth.

Ebros reached the hill's foot. Bows sang. Arrows arced upward. One fell spent at the Mad One's feet.

For a long moment Mirain regarded it. Elian longed to shriek at him, to beat him into motion.

His sword swept from its scabbard. With a fierce stallion-scream, the Mad One charged.

Ilhari pounded upon his heels. Elian clung to the saddle by blind instinct. All her anger, all her impatience, even the sickness of her fear, lost itself in the thunder of the charge. There remained only startlement, and a growing exhilaration. The wind in her face; the splendid sword—when had she drawn it?—in her hand; the surge of seneldi strength beneath her. Behind her, the army; before her, always before her, the scarlet fire of the Sunborn. No target practice, this, no game of war upon a table. This was battle as the singers sang of it. She laughed and bent over the flying mane.

With a mighty shock, the armies clashed.

Alone, Elian might have run wild. But Ilhari would not leave the Mad One. That too was madness, of a sort; for there always was the press thickest, the battle hottest. Southern-trained Mirain might be, but he fought as a chieftain of the north, at the forefront of his army, guide and beacon for all the rest.

He was mad. God-mad; possessed. No arrow touched

him. No blade pierced his flashing guard. His eyes shone; his body kindled with light that waxed as he advanced. Even when a cloud dimmed the sun, he blazed forth bright golden.

Elian, tossing in his wake, carrying his spears and the shield that, like a true madman, he scorned to use, felt the last of her temper drain away. Awe rose in its place.

She fought it as she fought the enemy who massed about her, fiercely. This was her brother. She had taken her first steps clinging to his hand, shaped her first letters under his teaching, learned first how to wield a sword with his hand over hers upon the hilt. He ate and slept like any man, dreamed both well and ill, and woke blear-eyed, tousled and boylike and faintly cross-grained. He laughed at soldiers' jests, wept unashamedly when his singer lamented the sorrows of old lovers, cast admiring eyes upon a good mount or a fine hound or a handsome woman. He was human. Living, breathing, warm and solid, human.

He rode in battle like a god.

A blade leaped at her. She parried, riposted, as her weapons master had taught her. The keen steel plunged through hardened leather into flesh and grated on bone. With a wrench she freed it. She never saw the man fall. Her first man. Ilhari slashed with hoofs and teeth at a smaller, broader senel, its rider fantastically armored, whirling a sword about his head.

Heroics, thought Elian. His bravado left bare the un-armored space between arm and side. Her sword's point found it, pierced it.

" *'Ware right!*"

She wheeled. Bronze sang past her arm. Another's blade cut down her attacker; a white grin flashed at her. Vadin in barbaric splendor, his helm crowned with copper and plumed with gold, his gorget of copper set with Ianyn amber. His brother was with him, trying to echo his grin, but regarding Elian with eyes wide, level, and much too dark. Why, she thought, nettled, the boy had been terrified for her. Suddenly it all seemed wonderfully ri-

diculous. She laughed. "My thanks!" she called out to
them both.

Vadin bowed and laughed with her and spun his
mare away. Cuthan nudged his tall stallion to her side as
if he meant to stay there. He refused to see her glare.

For a moment the tide of battle had ebbed. The
vanguard could rest, catch breath, inspect one another
for wounds. Mirain's standardbearer grounded the staff
of the Sun-banner and gentled his restive mount. The
king sat still, eyes running over the field.

It was a good vantage. They had passed the hill's foot
and begun to mount the slope to the town. All over the
wide field the battle raged; but the northerners had thrust
deep, driving Ebros against the walls. The prince's banner
caught the wind before the gate. He kept to the custom of
southern generals, ruling from behind, where he could
see all that passed and escape danger to himself.

"It goes well," said Cuthan. "See, their right has fallen."

"Their left holds," another of the household pointed
out, "and they've got walls to retreat to. We're not done
yet."

"They're regrouping." Cuthan leaned forward, intent. The enemy was drawing back, gathering together,
mustered by trumpets and by the shouts of captains.
Mirain's forces pursued them hotly; they offered little
resistance.

Mirain loosed an exclamation. His trumpeter glanced
at him. His hand swept out in assent.

His army heard the sudden clear notes. *Retreat,* they
sang. *Retreat and re-form.* The companies wavered. *Retreat!*
the trumpet cried.

Slowly, then more swiftly, the army moved to obey.
But one great company was not so minded. Deaf or
obstinate, it pressed on, harrying its Ebran prey. Its captain rode behind it under the banner of Ashan.

Ebros massed now before the walls. As the last company fought its way forward, the ranks seethed. Horns
rang. Cymbals clashed.

Mirain's voice lashed out at his household. *"Stay!"* But the Mad One was in motion, springing toward the Ashani forces.

Ilhari followed. Elian urged her on. Mirain's glance blazed upon them, his will like a physical blow. Cuthan's stallion, close and dogged upon their heels, staggered and bucked to a halt, and would not advance for all of Cuthan's spurring and cursing. Ilhari stumbled, shook her head, lengthened and steadied her stride.

Glittering, deadly, the scythed chariots rolled forth from the Ebran lines.

The Mad One stretched from a gallop to his full, winged speed. He closed in upon the Ashani rearguard, veered left.

Ilhari swayed toward the right. The wind whipped into Elian's eyes, blinding her; yet she knew where they passed. Round the racing army, footmen, cavalry, chariots. Chariots foremost, the light war-cars of nobles, unscythed, all but unarmored, their strength resting wholly in the arms of the warriors who rode them.

Ilhari hurled herself across their path. Seneldi veered. Reins and wheels tangled. Men rolled under sharp cloven hoofs. "Back!" cried Elian, high and piercing. "In Avaryan's name, back!"

Sun's fire blazed, dazzling her. A deep voice echoed her own. The Ashani ground to a halt.

"Back!" roared Mirain.

Step by step, then in a rush of hoofs and feet and a clashing of bronze, they obeyed him.

Thunder rumbled behind. Indrion had loosed the scythed chariots.

Ilhari tensed to bolt. The Mad One spun on his haunches. His nostrils were wide, blood-red, his neck whitened with foam, yet Mirain seemed as calm as ever. Enspelled, perhaps, by the whirling scythes.

"No," he said. Softly though he spoke, Elian heard him distinctly. "See. They hinder one another; they fear their own fellows." He might have been on the training

field, instructing her in the arts of war. "Come now. We
have our own work yet to do."

He did not return directly to his command, but angled
right, riding swiftly yet easily. When Elian glanced over
her shoulder, the chariots were closer. Yet, terrible though
they were, still they were but a few. And Mirain's army
was drawn up in a wide crescent. At its center, the charge's
target, massed a phalanx of men on foot, shields linked
into a wall. Before them waited mounted archers, and
men in light armor on light swift mares, armed with long
lances.

Ashan's men found their place in the right wing.
Some companies might have continued their flight once it
was begun, but if the Ashani were fools, they were brave
fools. They turned again to fight at need.

As Mirain crossed the face of his army and circled
the phalanx to find his banner, a shout ran with him, deep
and jubilant. It had his name in it, and his titles, and—
Elian stiffened a little, startled—her own usename. But
she had done nothing. It was Ilhari who had refused to
leave her sire.

And Galan who brought half a charging legion to a standstill.
Stern though Mirain's face was, his mind-voice held more
approval than not. He was almost proud of her. Almost.
There was still the matter of his command and of her
flagrant disobedience.

She would pay for it later. But as she returned to the
household gathered behind the phalanx as behind a wall,
she felt the warmth of their greeting. Even Cuthan met
her with a wide white grin. Recklessly she returned it.

The chariots came on. Behind them advanced the
Ebran army. The prince's banner rode in the center now,
edging forward.

Mirain's mounted archers sprang into a gallop, fanning across the field. In the spaces between them spurred
the lancers. Their spears swung down in a long glittering
wave, and leveled, and held.

The air filled with arrows. So slow, they were, rising
in lazy arcs yet dropping with blurring speed. Seneldi

screamed. Men howled and fell. The lancers thrust in among the racing beasts, striking at them, veering away from the scythes. Arrows sought targets, men and seneldi both, harnessed beasts and unarmed charioteers.

A senel misstepped, stumbled, fell into the whirling blades. Its screams shrilled over the din of battle. Elian squeezed her eyes shut.

The screams faded; hoofs crashed upon metal. Her eyes flew open. The chariots had collided with the phalanx. It held. By Avaryan, it held.

Buckled. Swayed. Stiffened. Broke.

Mirain snatched the trumpet from its startled bearer, set it to his lips, blew a clear imperious call. A roar answered it. With a great clangor of bronze on bronze, the wings of his army closed upon the enemy.

GLORY WAS A FINE WORD IN THE MORNING WHEN ONE WAS fresh and unscathed and rode at the Sunborn's back. But glory lost its luster in hour after hour of grueling labor, dust and sweat and screaming muscles, blood and entrails, shrieks of pain, curses and gasps and the ceaseless, numbing, smithy-clamor of battle.

Elian no longer knew or cared where she went, save only that the Mad One remained in her sight, black demon spattered with bright blood. For a time she thought they might be falling back, driven before the chariots and the fierce defenders of Ebros. Then, as a wrestler musters all his strength and surges against his enemy, they thrust forward again. On, on, up the slope of the hill, under the walls.

No, she thought. *No.*

A deadly rain fell upon them: arrows, stones, sand heated in cauldrons and poured down from the walls, seeping beneath armor, searing through flesh into bone.

Mirain's voice cut across the shrieks of agony. The infantry, embattled, thrust together. Shields locked again into the moving fortress of the phalanx. Relentlessly it advanced. Ebros stood at bay with its back to the walls.

Heedless of the hail from the battlements, Mirain

sent his stallion plunging against the Ebran line. "Indrion!"
he cried, his voice rough with long shouting. "Indrion!"

The Prince of Ebros had long since forsaken either
custom or prudence to fight in the first rank of his army.
He turned now, hacking his way through Ashani troops,
striving to reach Mirain. The young king, battle-wild,
strained toward him.

Even as they came together, a chariot cut between
them. A man in Ashani armor struck wildly at his old
enemy.

Mirain's sword flashed round. The charioteer flailed
at reins that held no longer. The flat of the king's blade
caught the team across their rumps, sent them bucking
and plunging into the heart of the Ashani forces.

Freed of the obstacle, they faced one another, king
and prince. Indrion was a tall man, northern-tall, but not
so dark; his eyes beneath the plumed helmet were almost
golden, and feral as a cat's. With a single graceful movement he vaulted from his chariot and bowed in not-
quite-mockery.

Mirain laughed and sprang from the Mad One's back.
They stood a moment, poised, taking one another's measure. Without a word, they closed in combat.

Elian's breath came harsh in her throat. Oh, he was
mad, mad, mad. He all but held the victory: his shieldwall
battered at the gate; his cavalry drove that of Ebros in
rout across the field. Yet he faced this giant, this warrior
famous throughout the Hundred Realms, and he laughed,
daring death to snatch away his triumph.

She clapped heels to Ilhari's sides. The mare set her
ears back and braced her feet. Elian tensed to fling herself from the saddle, but iron hands held her fast. She
glared into Vadin's eyes. "No," he said. "This is the king-
fight. It's not for lesser folk to meddle in."

Elian cursed him, and her obstinate mare, and her
madman of a king. Not one of them would yield.

All about them the fight had cooled. Enemies stood
side by side, blades drawn and dripping, eyes upon their

lords. Even the folk upon the battlements—women, Elian saw now; boys and old men and a mere handful of warriors—had ceased their barrage.

Mirain and Indrion fought alone, gold and gold, scarlet against crimson. Mirain was a warrior in ten thousand, but he had fought unstinting from the first; god's son or no, he was made of flesh, and he was weary. Indrion, newer to the battle, met his skill with skill no less, and with greater strength.

The king was weakening. His blows were less strong, his parries less firm. The two swords locked, guard to guard; his own trembled visibly.

A dead silence held the field. In it, his breathing was hoarse, labored.

With a mighty heave, Indrion flung him back. He stumbled, half fell, recovered without grace. All his guards were down. Even his proud head drooped.

He was beaten. Beaten and waiting to fall. Indrion laughed short and sharp, and closed in for the kill.

Steel whirled in a flashing arc. Up, around, down, full upon the prince's golden helmet. Indrion reeled, incredulous, and toppled.

Mirain stood over the prone body. He was breathing hard, but not as hard as he had pretended; his sword was steady in his hand. City and armies waited for the killing stroke.

He pulled off his helmet and tossed it into the nearest hands—an Ebran's, a youth in the prince's livery, his charioteer. As the boy gaped, Mirain said, "I claim my prisoner and all that is his. Who challenges me?"

No one moved.

Mirain's sword hissed into its sheath. "So." His eyes flashed across the field. "I claim my prisoner, and I set him free. You—you—you. A litter for the prince. Who commands now for him?"

"I command for myself." Prince Indrion could barely sit up. His face was grey, his eyes glazed; but his voice was clear enough. "I yield, my lord king. On this sole condition: that neither my men nor my town be destroyed."

"I had meant it to be so," Mirain said. His hand clasped the prince's; his smile illumined the air between them. With his own hands he saw Indrion settled in a litter and borne from the field.

Ten

EBROS WAS CONQUERED. MIRAIN'S ARMY HELD THE town; Prince Indrion's camped without, under the walls. In the grey evening, men with torches moved slowly over the battlefield, heaping the dead for burning, bearing the wounded to the healers' tents on the edge of the Ebran camp. Wherever they passed, the croaking of carrion birds followed them.

Elian could hear it even in the keep. Having seen to it that Mirain doffed his armor and washed away the stains of battle, she had been banished to her bed. She had not struggled overly hard against his will. He had only gone to break bread in hall with the captains of both sides, and she was bone-weary. She had bathed long and rapturously; she had put on a clean shirt, soft over her many bruises and her few, slight wounds; she had lain as Mirain commanded her across the foot of the great bed reserved for the lord of the keep. But sleep would not come.

Her bed was soft, her body no less comfortable than it had been after many a long hunt. She was numb with exhaustion. And she lay open-eyed, hearing the harsh cries of the birds called heirs of battle, children of the goddess, eaters of the slain. Where men fought, they fed. They grew fat on slaughter.

She lay on her face deep in the feather bed. In the darkness behind her eyes, the battle unfolded itself, clearer by far in memory than it had been while she fought in it. She saw her bright sword swing up; she saw it fall and grow lurid with blood.

She was a warrior now. Her blade had been blooded. She had learned to kill.

None of the songs told of what came after the fierce joy of the charge: the blood upon the trampled grain, the scatter of limbs and entrails, the carrion stench. There was no splendor in it. Only a dull ache, a sickness in body and brain.

They called her valiant, the men of Mirain's household. After the battle they had given her their accolade, the armor of the Ebran lord whom she had slain, such a trophy as a squire could not claim save by the will of his lord's whole company. And seldom indeed could he win it in his first battle.

If they could see her now, they would despise her.

Or worse, they would know her for a woman. They would mock her, a girlchild who played at manhood, a hoyden princess who feigned the voice and manners of a boy. And there forever would be her fame: in the rude jests of soldiers, where it well deserved to be.

She rolled onto her side. Her stomach heaved; her body knotted about it. "No," she said aloud. "No!"

Abruptly she rose. She pulled on trousers and boots and snatched up the first warm garment that came to hand. Mirain's cloak; but she made no effort to exchange it for a coat of her own. It was warm; it covered her; it carried a faint, comforting scent of him.

The town was quiet, startlingly so. Mirain's army, forbidden either sack or rapine, had also found the stores of strong drink well and firmly guarded. Well fed and sparingly wined, they kept order as in camp, with discipline which many a southern general might have envied. And, Elian thought, remarkably little grumbling.

The gate-guards knew her; they let her pass unchallenged. She paused beyond them. The sky was dark, starless; a thin cold wind skittered over the field. Torches flickered there, moving to and fro like ghost-lights, rising and dipping and sometimes holding still for a long count of breaths. Among them she discerned humped shadows, mounds of the dead. There were three: Ebran, Ashani, Ianyn.

Round the curve of the wall spread the Ebran camp, a huddle of fires, a silent massing of tents. Neither voice nor song rose from them, nor the muted revelry of Mirain's men, nor even the keening of grief. Defeated, pardoned, they took no chances upon their new lord's mercy.

But one pavilion more than made up for the silence of the rest: the healers' tent between the outer wards and the battlefield. Here was clamor, such an uproar as might rise out of hell: moaning and shouting, cries and curses and shrieks of pain.

Close to it, the tumult was numbing, overlaid with a gagging stink and lit with a red demon-light. But worse than the assault upon the body's senses was that upon the mind, wave upon wave of mortal agony.

Elian staggered under it. The tent flaps gaped open; within, men lay in row upon row, lamplit, with somberclad healers bending over them. The wounded, the maimed and the dying, all mingled, friend and enemy, in a red fellowship of pain.

Someone jostled her, muttered a curse, pointed sharply toward a corner. "Walking wounded over there. We'll get to you when we get to you." Before she could speak, the man was gone, tight-drawn with the immensity of his labor.

She edged into the tent. Whatever had brought her here would not let her escape, although the manifold odors of suffering set her stomach in revolt. Battling to master it, she stumbled and fell to her knees.

A man stared at her. A northerner, dark and eagle-proud yet abject with pain. A great wound gaped in his side, roughly bound with strips torn from a cloak. He was dying; he knew it; and his terror tore at all her defenses.

She flung up both hands against it. One brushed the wound, waking agony. Her power swelled like a wave and broke.

Part of her stood aside and watched it and was grimly amused. Blessed, O blessed Lady of Han-Gilen! She who dealt wounds could also heal them; she who slew could bring new life to the dying.

No, not she. The power that dwelt in her, mark of her breeding as surely as the fire of her hair. For those were the three magics of Han-Gilen: to see what would be, to read and to master men's souls, and to heal the wounds of body and mind. Prophet, mage, and healer; by the god's will she was all three. Under her hand the flesh lay whole, marked only by a greying scar.

She looked up. Dark eyes met her own. Mirain bowed his head, equal to equal. This gift too he had, the legacy of his father.

He knelt beside a man in battered Ebran armor. She moved past him to another who waited with death at his shoulder.

THUNDER WOKE ELIAN FROM A DEEP AND DREAMLESS SLEEP. For a long moment she lay bemused. She could remember in snatches: laboring far into the night, finding at last that nothing remained for her to do; every man was dead or healed or would heal of himself. And she who had been weary when she began, had passed beyond exhaustion. She had felt light, hollow, almost drunken. So wonderful, this healing was, the only magic which left one more joyous than one began, that healed the healer as well as the one she tended.

Mirain had appeared out of the shadow of the tent, smiling. She swayed; he caught her, himself far from steady. Leaning on one another, they made their way to the keep.

They ate, she remembered that. The bread was warm,

the first of the new day's baking. The wine was rich with spices. There was fruit and new cream and a handful of honey sweets. Mirain was as gluttonous for them as she. They laughed, counting them out, half for each and one over. "You take it," he said.

"No, you."

He grinned and bit off half of the confection and fed her the rest. There remained only the wine, a whole flask of it, strong and heady. Elian, warm with it, loosened the laces of her shirt and let it fall open as it would.

He watched her, head tilted. "You should never do that where anyone can see you."

"Not even you?" she asked.

"Maybe." His finger brushed her cheek lightly, tracing the paling scars. "It must be sorcery. When you stand in armor or in my livery, I see a boy, a youth, Halenan when he was very young. But now, no one with eyes could possibly take you for aught but a woman. Even your face: it's too fine to be handsome. It's beautiful."

She snorted. "Some of the men say I'm too pretty for my own good, scars and all. And much too well aware of it."

"No. That, you aren't. I remember when you used to lament. Your eyes were too long and too wide; your chin was too stubborn; your body was too thin and too awkward. For all that anyone can say, you still believe it."

"That's the best part of this game. No one treats me the way people treat a beautiful woman. A boy is different, even a pretty boy."

He reflected on that in the way he had; but the wine had lifted his barriers. His eyes were as clear as water, with a brightness in the heart of them.

"You are *not* ugly!" she said sharply.

He laughed. That had always been the end of her complaining. He would say, "Ah, but I really am as unlovely as you think you are." And she would cry out against him, and he would laugh, because he believed himself, and she never would; and that was the way of their world.

She seized his face in her two hands and glared into his eyes. "There are plenty of handsome men in the world, brother my love. But there is only one of you."

"Thank Avaryan for that."

"Yes, for begetting you. Who else would have let me be what I want most to be?"

"But what is that?"

She let him go abruptly, filled his cup, thrust it into his hand. "Now's no time to go all cryptic and kingly. Here, drink up. To victory!"

He might have said more, but he paused. His brow lifted; he raised his cup and drank. "To victory," he agreed.

They had drunk, and drunk again. And then, what? Sleep, yes. There had been a very mild quarrel, that she would spread a pallet on the floor, with so wide a bed, and he needing so little of it.

She lay on celestial softness. He had won, then. Carefully she opened an eye. It had been good wine; the light was bearable. Mirain slept in utter and youthful abandon, with the whole long line of his side not a handspan from her own. Whatever his quarrel with his face, even he could not deny that the rest of him was well made. That was clear to see; for he slept as he always slept, as bare as he was born.

And so, this drunken night, had she.

Her breath caught. If anyone ever, ever heard of this, then there would be a scandal in truth. Who would believe that they had done nothing?

They had had wine enough and to spare, but they had not fallen to that. He had not even hinted at it. Had only looked at her long and long, smiled at last, and taken the far side of the bed, with an acre of blankets between.

Again, thunder. It had been rolling at intervals since first she woke.

This burst shook her fully out of her dreaming. Not thunder; a swordhilt upon the massive door. For an instant she froze. They knew—they all knew. They had come to denounce her. Liar, deceiver, harlot—

Idiot. She rolled out of bed, snatched the first garment that came to hand, pulled it on. Swiftly but quietly she slid back the bolt.

The man without was shaking with urgency: a big man, Ianyn, one of Mirain's household. Even as the door opened he cried, "My lord!" And stopped at the sight of her, seeing only the hair at first, and his own disappointment. Of course it would be the squire who opened the door. Face and manner shifted, and stilled again. His eyes widened.

She glanced down swiftly. She was covered. She had her shirt.

Her thin, unlaced, entirely undeceptive shirt.

It came as memory comes, swift, piercing: a vision not of what was past but of what was still to come. The man, his message delivered, returned to his companions, and he had a new and startling tale to tell. One that traveled as all such tales must, swifter than fire through a dry field.

Foresight passed. In its aftermath she knew only a weary irony. All her fears—she had shrugged them aside as folly. And they had been prescience.

Mirain's voice spoke close to her ear, shattering the impasse. "Bredan. You have news?"

The king's presence and his own training brought Bredan to attention. His eyes strove not to follow Elian as she gave Mirain the doorway. "Urgent news, sire. The Lord Cuthan sent me to wake you."

"Go on." Mirain was wide awake; and he was blocking Bredan's view of the chamber.

"Troops, sire," the man said, recalling his urgency. "South of here, across the river where Ebros and Poros meet. A whole army, thousands strong. They march under royal banners, princes' banners. The Hundred Realms have come to fight us."

Mirain did not flinch or falter. "All of them?" he asked.

"My lord counted upwards of five thousand men, and twenty-odd standards. Including . . ." Bredan paused, and swallowed. "Including Han-Gilen."

"Following? Or leading?"

Bredan swallowed again, very carefully not attempting to find the Gileni face behind his lord's back. "Leading, sire."

"Yes," Mirain said as calmly as ever, "Han-Gilen would lead. Go now, Bredan. See that my captains are told of this."

"Aye, my lord. Should we post guards?"

"See to it. And send a man to the lords of Ashan and of Ebros. I'll speak with them after I've broken my fast."

MIRAIN BATHED ALMOST LEISURELY, AND ATE WITH GOOD appetite. Her half of the bath, Elian was more than glad of, but she could not eat. She tended Mirain's hair instead, cursing to herself when it proved more than usually intractable.

"Yes," he said as if she had addressed him, "your game is over. Even if you hadn't betrayed yourself, there would still be Han-Gilen's army to face."

"And my brother." She knew that, beneath thought, as she knew that her father had not come. She doubted that it was arrogance. She wondered if it was wisdom. "Are you going to make me fight?"

"Would you?"

She breathed deep, to steady herself. "I swore an oath."

"You did." His hair was half braided; he freed the plait from her fumbling fingers and finished it much more deftly than she had begun it, and surveyed her, a swift keen glance. She wore livery as always, with her sword girded over the scarlet surcoat. "Come," he said to her.

THE KEEP'S WIDE HALL WAS FULL OF MEN AND THRUMMING with tension. Although some had come here on honest business with the king, most seemed merely to be hangers-on. Mirain's own men mingled freely enough, but there were two distinct camps set well apart and bristling at one another. Luian's heir led one. Over the other rose the tall form of Ebros' prince. He came forward as Mirain entered the hall, bowing regally, if somewhat painfully, as lord to high lord.

Mirain smiled his quick smile and clasped Indrion's hand. "You look well, lord prince. I trust that you are recovered?"

"I am well," the prince answered, smiling in return, his eyes warming to amber. "Apart from an aching head. That was a shrewd blow, my lord."

"A simple one, and an old trick."

"Ah, but it succeeded."

There was a bench nearby. Mirain sat on it. Elian, taking her place behind him, admired his art that turned the humble seat into a throne, and in the same instant invited his new vassal to share the seat but not, ever, the kingship.

Indrion hesitated no more than a heartbeat, and slowly sat. His smile was gone, but he looked on Mirain in deep respect. "My lord," he said, "I regret that I challenged your kingship. But I shall never regret the fight. It was a fine battle, and well won."

"As well lost." Mirain raised a hand. "Lord Omian."

Luian's heir left the ranks of his countrymen. To reach Mirain he had to cross before the Ebrans. He neither speeded nor slowed his progress for them, nor acknowledged that they existed. He bowed to Mirain, and without perceptible pause, to Indrion.

Mirain smiled warmly and beckoned. "Sit by me, sir."

There was space on the bench, but only beside Indrion. Ebros' prince had made certain of that. Omian sat with perfect ease, and with a smile, which was more than his enemy could muster.

Mirain seemed to see none of it, either hostility or forced amity. When Omian was settled, the king said, "The Hundred Realms have risen, my lords, and come to meet us. They are close now to the ford of Isebros."

Neither of the princes would glance at the other.

"Indeed, sire," Indrion said, "I had had word that Han-Gilen was rousing the princedoms. I had not thought they would arrive so swiftly."

"Had you not?" asked Omian. "Surely you were praying for them to overtake us and cut us down while we were still in disorder from fighting you."

Indrion shrugged slightly. "I was a fool, I grant you that. I should have held to my walls and waited and let you mount a siege, to be crushed by the advancing forces. But I thought I could stop you. I chose open battle, a day too soon. I am well paid for it."

"Aye, and now you think to catch us with your Ebran treachery."

At last Indrion's temper escaped its careful bonds. "And what of yours, dog's son? You could not but have known what Han-Gilen called for. Yet you and your hound of a father plotted to be first at the trough, to lick the king's feet and to win all his favor, and to steal my land into the bargain."

"Your land, cattle thief? You knew you claimed what was never yours; you knew the judgment would go against you. Thus you gambled. Either you would slay my king and win my valley, or he would defeat you in combat and offer you his famous clemency, which else you had no hope of."

Indrion half rose; Omian bared his teeth in a feral grin. Mirain's glance quelled them both. Ebros' prince hooded eyes gone hot gold. Ashan's heir sat still, with but the merest suggestion of a smile. Quietly the king said, "When I have done what needs doing here, I shall ride to meet the army."

"My forces are at your disposal," said Indrion a little tightly still.

"And mine," Omian said, "my lord."

"My thanks," said Mirain. "I shall take twoscore men; and you with them, sirs, if you are willing."

Omian laughed, incredulous. "Twoscore men against five thousand?"

"It will suffice." Mirain did not ask him where he had

learned their number. "If you will pardon me, my lords, I have duties."

IT SEEMED TO ELIAN AS SHE KEPT TO THE SQUIRE'S PLACE that every man in the hall watched her, and whispered, and wondered. Eyes flicked toward her, held, flicked away. They had always done that: bored, or intrigued by the brightness of her hair, or caught by the beauty of her face. Now they strained to see if it were true that the boy was indeed a woman; they peered at the slim erect form in the king's livery, searching for curves no boy could claim. Maybe they laid wagers. Surely they sniggered, recalling that she spent her every night with the king, and wondering if she would turn her eyes elsewhere. Bold as she was, how could she be aught but wanton?

In a pause between petitioners, Mirain touched her hand. "Go free," he murmured. "You'll know when it's time to ride."

Her brain blurred, shifting from her own troubles to the danger he faced. "You want me there?"

"At my right hand, you promised me." He smiled a little. "It's not a fight we go to."

No. No prince would attack a mere twoscore men, if they rode with care. Certainly Halenan would not. And he would talk to Mirain, if only for memory's sake. She bowed. "I'll ride with you, my lord."

Mirain's smile followed her from the hall. So too, and much less warmly, did the stares. She straightened her back and stalked away from them.

Eleven

IT WAS AN HOUR'S RIDE FROM THE TOWN TO THE FORD OF Isebros. The road was wide and well kept, running past villages whose folk hid in their houses, and farmsteads barricaded against invading armies. The word had spread abroad that the Sunborn had swept out of the north, and that the Hundred Realms had massed against him. And when princes struggled for mastery, it was the land and its people who suffered most.

A goodly land, this vale on the marches of Ashan between Ebros and Poros. Its fields were rich; its villages seemed prosperous even in their fear.

Where the river swept wide round the last low outrider of Ashan's mountains, its ford offered passage from Ebros into Poros. No town had grown there on either side, but walled villages stood in sight of it; somewhat upstream of it on the Poros side, a bold soul had built a watermill.

Oddly, when Elian remembered after, the mill came first to her mind: the turning and the clacking of the wheel and the washing of water through it. How foolish, she thought. Any marauder could overrun the mill, and hold it or destroy it as he chose. Yet it was built of stone and well fortified, and folk from leagues about could bring their grain to it to enrich the miller.

Perhaps she focused upon it to avoid what could not be avoided. All the green land between the mill and the village was lost to sight, overspread with the camp of a great army. The banners were banners Elian knew, every one a royal standard, sigil of a prince from the north of the Hundred Realms; and beneath each one ranged a city of tents. Not since the war on the Nine Cities had so many princes come together into a single force.

Now as then, the center and command post, first among equals, was the flameflower of Han-Gilen. Elian sat very straight on Ilhari's back. She might yet have to draw blade against her own kin; but as she rode beside Mirain to the river's bank, she knew no shame of her lineage. Han-Gilen's princes had ruled in the south before ever king or emperor rose to challenge them; kings and emperors had fallen, and they remained, stronger than ever. And they would remain, she knew with sudden certainty. Whatever befell between this hour and the sun's setting, the Halenani would endure.

Mirain raised a hand. His escort halted. The Mad One stepped delicately down the bank into the swift shallow water. There he too was still.

Their riding had been marked. A line of men had formed on the camp's edge, arrows nocked to bows. Beyond them others crowded, a manifold glitter of eyes. Mirain's banner was clear for them to see, whipped wide as the wind swept down from the north. Ebros' and Ashan's unfurled on either side of it but slightly behind, in token of subjection.

Behind the archers a horn rang. As one the bows lowered. Elian loosed a faint and involuntary sigh of relief.

A company made its way from the camp's center, mounted and yet apparently unarmored. Every man was clad as for a procession, adorned with jewels that dazzled in the sunlight, but the only metal was the gold and silver and copper worked into the embroideries of coats and trousers, into the heels of the riders' boots, into the saddles and bridles of their seneldi. Elian saw no weapon anywhere.

No banner floated over them, but they needed none. The man who rode foremost, tall on a tall grey stallion, shone in green and flame-gold; his head was bare, his hair and beard red as fire.

Without Elian's urging, Ilhari advanced to the very edge of the water.

The Mad One had reached the middle of the ford. Like Halenan, Mirain wore no armor and no weapon; only a light kilt and his scarlet war-cloak and a glitter of ornaments, gold and ruby, and the heavy torque of his priesthood about his throat. Any man of the southern army could have shot him down as he waited there.

Free at last of the press of men, Halenan's senel stretched into a gallop. The prince's eyes were fixed on Mirain, his face as stern and still as ever his father's could be.

The grey left the escort behind, leaping down the long slope of the bank, plunging into the river. The Mad One stood his ground, horns lowered slightly, but his ears pricked. In a great shower of spray the grey stallion halted. Miraculously Halenan was dry, even to the high golden heels of his boots. His gaze never left Mirain's face, searching it keenly, suffering no secrets.

It seemed that Mirain yielded none. Abruptly Halenan said, "It has been a long while. Brother." He spoke the word as if in challenge, daring Mirain to remember.

"Long years, my brother," Mirain answered.

From the sudden light in Halenan's face, Elian knew that Mirain smiled. The air between them warmed and softened; Halenan essayed a smile in return. "Will it please my lord to enter into Poros with me?"

Mirain did not move. "What if I do not enter as a friend?"

"You are my enemy then?" asked Halenan amid a great stillness.

"That depends upon your own intent."

There was a pause. At length Halenan backed his stallion and turned, leaving the way open for Mirain to pass. "Let us judge that upon dry land, under my word of honor."

Mirain bowed his head very slightly. He raised his hand to his escort; the Mad One moved forward. One by one the company followed in his wake.

North and south faced one another on the riverbank, wary, forbearing to mingle. Elian, hanging well back, saw faces she knew, noblemen all, all intent upon the two who faced one another in their center. Neither had yet dismounted; neither had touched, or ventured it, despite the growing amity between them. Perhaps it was only that their stallions would not allow it.

Again it was Halenan who broke the lengthening silence. "I see that you have won Ebros."

"Yesterday," said Mirain without either gloating or humility.

"Some might say that you should no longer be called king. That you should name yourself emperor."

"Not yet."

"Perhaps. You have only lessened the Hundred Realms by two. It could be a very long conquest, brother."

"Or very short," said Mirain. "I count a score of banners yonder. If it is battle you look for, I may win the north of the Realms at a stroke."

Halenan laughed suddenly. "Ah, kinsman! Your arrogance is as splendid as ever."

"It is not arrogance. It is certainty."

Halenan's grin lingered, bright and fierce. "Test your foresight here, King of Ianon. We have read your intent in your conquest of the north; we have seen its proof in the taking of Ashan and Ebros. This is our answer. The Great Alliance: all the Hundred Realms gathered together before you under the command of Han-Gilen. Yonder sits its vanguard, the tithe of its full strength. Is it not a fine brave number?"

"I have more, honed in my wars. But yes, it is fair to see. Have you brought it here to challenge me?"

"To challenge you?" Halenan looked back at his men with such a sheen of joy and pride and sheer boyish mischief, that Elian dared at last to understand. He leaped from the saddle, kneeling in the road, eyes shining. "No, my lord An-Sh'Endor. To lay at your feet."

For a long moment Mirain sat still, gazing down. All his life he had waited for this. Yet now that it had come, he seemed stunned, shaken to the heart of him. There before him in the hands of this bright-maned prince lay the empire he had been born to rule.

Slowly he swung his leg over the pommel and slid to the ground. "Brother," he said. "Halenan. Do you know what you have done?"

"The god's will," Halenan answered promptly. "And my father's, if it comes to that. It was easier than we thought it might be. The Realms were ready for you."

Mirain tried to speak, but no words came. He drew Halenan up and embraced him long and hard, putting into it all his love and his wonder and his joy, and even his awe of these princes who, in the purity of their pride, would choose the king whom they wished to rule over them.

Halenan's awe was deeper, but tempered with mirth. "Just for once," he said laughing, "I've rendered you speechless. Who'll ever believe I did it?"

Mirain smiled, grinned, laughed aloud. "Who will believe you did any of this? Hal—Hal, you madman, without a blow struck or a drop of blood shed, you've changed the whole shape of the world."

ELIAN HAD SEEN MIRAIN EXALTED IN BATTLE, OR BEFORE his men, or in the face of victory; but now, as he rode through this army that had come to follow him, he was more than exalted. He was touched with the high and shining splendor of a god.

Elian could be glad of his gladness, but she could not share in it. Anonymous in surcoat and helmet, well hidden between Cuthan and his silent and unreadable brother, she veiled herself from the mind as well as from the eye. But she felt Halenan's searching, passing and passing again.

His tent stood in an open circle kept clear by his guards. There were seats under a canopy, and servants with wine and ices, and grooms to tend the escort's seneldi. Halenan welcomed Mirain to it with a flourish; but still he hunted with eyes and power.

It was Vadin who betrayed her. As the two companies mingled in the tumult of dismounting, Ilhari jostled his mare. The tall grey laid back her ears. Ilhari skittered, bucked, threatened with heels and teeth.

Vadin laughed, sharp in a sudden pause. "What, little firemane! Menace your own mother, would you?"

Ilhari thought better of it. On her back, Elian sat stiff and still. Halenan had heard. He turned. His eyes met hers.

She left the saddle. All at once, her brother was there. "Elian," he said.

People were staring. Whispering. Someone laughed. *Damn them!* she thought.

And then: *Damn all of it!* For Halenan was holding her, shaking her, shouting at her; and she knew how deeply, terribly, endlessly he had feared for her. Damning himself more fiercely than she ever could, not only for letting her go, but for helping her to do it.

There were tears on her cheeks. She dashed them away. He held her, taking her in, helmet and livery and all. "Sister," he said roughly. "Little sister. I've had hell to pay in Han-Gilen."

"Were they fearfully angry?" She sounded plaintive; she scowled to make up for it.

"Not angry," he said. "Not after a while. You left Father to make some very difficult explanations."

She swallowed. "I—I thought—"

"You didn't think at all, infant. But you seem to be thriving."

That was a refuge. She snatched at it. "I am. I'm

Mirain's squire. I have a new sword; it's steel. It's a marvel. You see my mare—Ilhari. Her sire is the Mad One. We've fought our first battle together. The household gave me a trophy. You'll see it—when—"

She broke off. He was no longer looking at her but beyond her, with an expression which she labored to decipher. Greeting; respect; apprehension. And a touch—the merest inexplicable touch—of compassion.

She turned in his hands. A man stood there. A man no taller than she, clad all in golden silk, regarding her with a steady golden stare.

If Halenan had not held her, she would have staggered. Of all the people she had ever thought to see, this was the last. "But," she said stupidly, "you were supposed to go back to Asanion."

"But," he answered her, "I chose to come here."

"For me?" She flushed, twisting out of her brother's grip. "No. Of course not. You wanted to see the Sunborn. To know what, in the end, cost you the alliance with my father. You were not very wise, my lord. The High Prince of Asanion is a hostage of very great value indeed."

"Should you be the only one to gamble fate and fame and fortune on the wind from the north?"

He was more handsome even than she remembered, more witty and more gentle. She pulled off her helmet, shaking out the shorn bright hair, turning her torn cheek to the sun.

He winced at the marred loveliness, yet he smiled, finding in her a greater beauty still: that not of the hound chained in hall, but of the she-wolf running wild in the wood.

"My lord," she said to him, "your father can be no more pleased with your choice than is mine."

He shrugged. "So, lady, we pay. But the game is well worth the price."

Her eyes found Mirain. He stood near the tent in a circle of taller men, yet he stood taller than any of them. One of them was Halenan; and she had not even seen him go.

"There," said Ziad-Ilarios, "is an emperor. I was bred to rule and not to serve, but with that one . . . oh, indeed, I could be tempted."

"You mock him, surely."

"No. Not now. Not in his living presence."

"He is not a god," she said sharply.

"Only the son of one."

She turned to him. "You know what must be. The world will not suffer two emperors. And Mirain will not yield what he has gained to any mortal man."

"Then the gods be thanked that I am not my father."

Some demon made her catch at his hand. It was warm and strong, and yet it trembled. Her own was little more steady, her voice breathless, pitched a shade too high. "Come. Come and speak to him."

They were much alike, the dark man and the golden. High lords both, emperors born, each measuring the other with a long level stare. Here could be great love, or a great and lasting hate.

For a long moment the balance hung suspended. The silence spread. Even the seneldi stilled. Ilhari was watching. Thinking of stallions: horns lowered, poised, choosing, whether to suffer one another or to kill.

They moved in the same instant, to a handclasp that was like a battle. Mirain was taller, but Ilarios was broader; they were well matched.

As they had begun, they ended, within a single moment. But Ilarios' smile showed his clenched teeth. Mirain's was freer, if no warmer. "Well met, my lord high prince. My esquire has told me of you."

"Of you, lord king," said Ilarios, "my lady of Han-Gilen has had much to say. It was she who first whetted my appetite for a sight of you, if only to see at first hand what sort of creature you were."

"And what am I?" asked Mirain with a glint in his eye.

"A barbarian," Ilarios answered, "and a king. But not now, and not ever, emperor in Asanion."

Elian sucked her breath in sharply. Some even of

Halenan's men had reached for their swordhilts; Mirain's escort drew together, narrow-eyed.

Mirain laughed and pulled Ilarios into a swift half-embrace, as if he were delighted with the jest. And that, by every law and custom of the Golden Empire, was *lèse-majesté*. An upstart foreigner had dared to lay hands upon the sacred person of the high prince.

Ilarios stood rigid, outraged. Mirain grinned at him, white, fierce, and splendidly unrepentant. Ah, his eyes said, you are high prince, but I am Sunborn. Hate me if you please, but never dare to despise me.

Asanion's heir flashed back with all the pride of a thousand years of emperors. And laughed. Unwillingly, unable to help himself, caught up in the sheer absurdity of their rivalry. Laughing, he reached, completing the half-embrace, meeting the bright dark eyes. "And yet, Sunborn," he said, granting that much to Mirain's pride, "whatever comes hereafter, we are well met."

Twelve

BEFORE MIRAIN TURNED SOUTHWARD, HE RESTED HIS troops where they had won this last victory: where Ashan and Ebros and Poros met, an hour's ride from the ford. It was a great and splendid festival, and a wonder to all the lands about. People came three days' journey merely to look at the city of tents about Isebros' walled town, and at the high king over them all.

Both were well worth looking at. The mingled armies of north and south had put on their finery to enter into the revelry. And Mirain had a love of splendor and the flair to carry it off, whether it might be the kilt and the clashing ornaments of the north or the boots and trousers and richly embroidered coat of the south; or even and often the stark simplicity of his priesthood, the golden torque and the long white robe girdled with gold.

But then, thought Elian, he could put on his worn riding kilt and stroll through the camp, and still draw every eye to himself. It was the light of him; the splendor of his eyes and of his face, and the royalty of his bearing.

The army knew now who and what she was. An easy camaraderie had begun between the king's squire and his

men, in particular the knights of his household. This was
gone. No one denounced her; no one avoided her openly;
but the ease had turned to a guarded courtesy. Even
Mirain—even he was turned to a stranger.

No, she told herself when she was calmest. It was
only that, all at once, he had become lord of a great
empire. Kingship was not all silk and jewels and state
processions; there was a great deal of drudgery in it, long
hours buried in councils or in clerkery, and innumerable
and interminable audiences. He seemed to thrive on it,
but he had little leisure, and none it seemed for his
squire. There were servants now in plenty to bathe him
and dress him and tend to his needs. She slept at his bed's
foot as before, and served him at table, but more of him
she did not have.

Halenan could not help. From their first meeting at
the ford, king and prince had settled together as if they
had never been parted. Odd brothers they made, Halenan
tall and graceful and dark golden, with his fiery hair, and
Mirain Ianyn-dark, Asanian-small.

And there was a third, always a third. Halenan had
faced Vadin much as Ilarios had faced Mirain, but the
sparks had flown less fiercely and settled more swiftly.
Vadin sneered at Halenan's trousers but applauded his
beard; Halenan raised his brows at the barbarian's kilt
and braids and superfluity of ornaments, and admired his
long-legged grey mare. Out of scorn they had forged
respect, and out of respect a strong bond of amity. Now
they were inseparable, the right and left hands of the
king, and where Vadin saw to the ordering of the army
and its festival, Halenan scaled the mountain of scribework.
He kept the king's seal, and wore it on a chain of gold
about his neck. That was burden enough; Elian would
not add her own to it.

And yet there was one who had time for her. Ziad-
Ilarios was known as the king's friend, but he held himself somewhat aloof. He was a guest, and royal; there was
little that he could do and less that he must. When Elian
rode Ilhari as long and as far as they both could go, his

golden stallion valiantly kept pace; when she hung about the castle or the camp, he found occasion to hang about with her, coaxing her into smiles and even into laughter. Even when she was as close to tears as she would ever let herself come, he knew precisely how to make her forget her troubles.

Somehow, somewhere between Han-Gilen and the marches of Ashan, she had lost all her fear of him. Yet she had more reason than ever to be afraid. It was clear in his eyes, indeed in everything he did and said: He had not come so far against his father's will and command, endangering himself and his empire, only to look on the Sunborn. He had come because he loved her.

She knew it. She did not try to stop it. Perhaps she had begun to love him, a little. She found herself looking for him when he was not immediately in evidence. Sometimes she even sought him out, for the pure pleasure of seeing his face, or of hearing his beautiful voice that could make a song of plain Gileni words.

"Why are you always guarded?" she asked him once as they rode in the sun. She glanced over her shoulder at the men who followed at a careful distance, unobtrusive as shadows, clad in shadow-black, who never spoke even when she spoke to them. She had never seen their faces: they went veiled, only their eyes visible, cold yellow falcon-eyes that saw everything and judged nothing. "Do they follow you even into the harem?"

For some little time she thought he would not answer. He did not glance at his twin shadows; he busied himself with a tangle in his stallion's mane. At last he said, "My guards are part of me. It is necessary."

"Who would dare to threaten you?"

He looked up, startled, almost laughing with it. "Why, lady, who would not? I am the heir of the Golden Throne."

She frowned. "No one would try to kill Mirain outside of battle. Or Hal; or Father."

"Some at least have ventured against the Sunborn."

"Years ago. People learn. The king is the king."

"The king is a mage. That matters, my lady. In

Asanion we are confined to our own poor wits, and to our guards' loyalty."

"Your court is very decadent, Father says. Death is a game. The subtler the poison, the greater the prize. Lives are taken as easily as we would pluck a blossom, and one's own life is a counter like any other, to be cast away when the game commands."

"It is not as simple as that," said Ilarios. "I for one must live, or all my game will come to nothing."

"Are you a pawn, then?"

His eyes sparked, but he smiled. "I like to think that I have a little power in the play. I will, after all, be emperor."

"How grim," she said, musing, "to live so.. And the poor women. Penned like cattle where no man can see them; veiled and bound and forbidden to walk under the sky. They must go mad with boredom."

"No more than do their lords. The emperor is kept as straitly as any concubine, for his life's safety and for the sanctity of his office. He must never leave his palace. He must never set foot on common earth. He must never speak to any save through his sacred Voice."

"What, not even his empress?"

"Perhaps," admitted Ilarios, "to her he might speak directly. And she may see his face. His people must not. They see him always enthroned, robed and masked in gold like a god."

"That is horrible," she said.

"No," he answered her. "It only sounds so. An emperor's body must be confined; it is holy, it is given to the gods. Yet he rules, and in ruling he is free. No man is freer than he."

"My father rules unmasked and unchained. Mirain is king incarnate, and his throne is the Mad One's saddle."

"Your father rules from Han-Gilen; he did not ride into the north. I would wager that he could not. And the Sunborn is the first of his line, a barbarian king, a soldier and a conqueror. The burden of empire has barely begun to fall upon him."

"How strange you look," she said, "when you speak

of empires. As if it terrifies you; and yet you revel in it. You will welcome the mask when it comes to you."

"It is what I was born for." He looked at her. "You are like me. You flee the cage which your lineage has raised about you, and yet what you flee to is a captivity no less potent, and far less easily escaped. You can comprehend the mind of the Golden Emperor."

She touched him, because she wanted to, because she could not help herself. He quivered under her hand, but did not pull away. "Am I transgressing?" she asked him.

"I give you leave," he said. Light; a little breathless. Smiling a sudden luminous smile. "You may touch me whenever you choose."

It was great daring, that, in an Asanian high prince. "I am corrupting you," she said. "See, your shadows are uneasy. What will they tell your father?"

"That I have gone barbarian." He laughed, and met touch with touch: a brush of fingertips from her cheek to her chin, tracing the path of her scars. It was like cool fire. Swift, and startling, and all too quickly gone.

She would have caught his hand; but his golden stallion had danced away, impatient, and the moment escaped. She did not try to pursue it. Her folly that she had even let it begin.

It did not come back. She told herself that it had never been; she made herself stop regretting it. Ilarios' presence was enough, and his beauty, and his golden voice. She needed no more.

ON A GREY MORNING WITH TOO MUCH IN IT OF WINTER, Elian wandered down a passage of the keep. She had meant to ride in the hills, but a driving rain had sent even the Mad One into the shelter of the castle. Mirain was closeted with Halenan and Vadin and the captains. She, having no more to do with her freedom than squander it in prowling the corridors, heard her name. Her ears pricked; she stopped. The speakers were Ianyn by their accents, men of the king's household playing at chance in a guardroom.

"Elian?" one mused, rattling the dice in the cup, in no hurry to throw. "Now there's a fine piece of womanflesh."

"How can you know?" his companion demanded. "She doesn't show any of it."

"Sure she does. It just takes a good eye."

"I've got a good eye. And all it sees is angles. If it's boys you like, why not take a boy and have done with it?"

"*She's* no boy," the first man declared. "Dress her up proper now, a little paint and a gewgaw or two, and you'll have something worth looking at."

"Not for my money. I like mine plump and tooth-some. Less sharp in the tongue, too. They say she can swear like a trooper."

"The king fancies her, for all of that. So do plenty of others. The boys down in the camp have got a wager on how long she'll last. I put a silver sun on it, with a side bet that he marries her before the year is out."

"You've lost your money, then. She's highborn, they say, sister to that southern general, the one who wears his beard like a man. Good in bed, too, if the king's kept her this long and this steady. But he won't make her queen. He can't. It's the law in Ianon, don't forget: No whore can share the throne." The soldier hawked and spat. "Here now. Are you going to throw those dice or hatch them?"

Elian stumbled away. Her feet felt huge, clumsy; she could not see.

She passed Ilarios without recognizing him. When he called to her, she stopped, losing the will to move. "Lady," he said. She could taste his concern. It was salt, like tears. "Lady, are you ill?"

"No," her voice replied. "No, I'm well."

His arm dared mightily. It circled her shoulders. She let him lead her; she did not care where. His own cham-ber, it turned out to be; he had been given one in the keep. There was no room in it for his guards, who per-force must stand without, with the door between, and solitude within, scented with flowers. Elian had found a tangle of briar roses, the last of summer, golden and

flame red; they had brought back a bowlful at great cost
to their fingers. But the heady scent was worth any pain.

It did not ease hers now. He made her sit in a nest of
cushions, and set a cup in her hand, filled with the yellow
wine of Asanion. "Drink," he bade her.

She obeyed him, hardly knowing what she did. The
wine was sharp to her taste, almost sour, yet strong. It
both dizzied and steadied her. Her eyes cleared; she
breathed deep. Lightly, calmly, she said, "It has finally
happened. A man has said what they all think. I have no
reputation left, my lord. Is that not amusing?"

"Who has dared it? Tell me!"

His intensity brought her eyes to him. His own were
burning, blazing. Hating the one who had hurt her. Loving her with all that was in him.

For a long while she could only stare at him, stupid
with shock. That it could matter so much to him. That
she could care, and caring, wake to truth. "It does no
good to run away," she said. "I have learned that. The
world is a circle; one always comes back to one's beginnings. I went to Mirain to escape Han-Gilen; now he
prepares to march there. I shall have to face my mother,
with what I have done and what I am supposed to have
done on the lips of every talespinner in this part of the
world. And the worst of it—the very worst—is that I have
not had the pleasure that goes with the tale. I doubt if
Mirain even realizes that I am a woman."

He said nothing.

She laughed, not too badly, she thought, although he
winced. "In truth I would not wish him to. He accepts
me. He lets me be what I choose to be. The tragedy is
this: His army is part of him also. And his army knows
what I am. I betrayed myself, do you know? So careful, I
was. So private, so well disguised. I even relieved myself
where none could see, though that is nothing to brag of.
Camp privies can be too utterly vile even for men. The
hardest thing was to watch people swimming, and to have
to pretend that I had duties; especially on the march,
with the heat and the dust and the flies. A basin is a very

poor substitute for a whole cool river, when even one's king is in it, fighting water battles like a half-grown boy."

"Tomorrow," he said carefully, "if the weather changes, you could go to the river, to one of the pools."

"What for?" she demanded, all contrary.

There was no banter in him; no mirth at all, and no comfort. He looked at her with wide eyes, all gold. "I see," he said. "One's king would not be in it."

She stared back at him. She was almost angry. Almost. That he could speak so: he too, of all who knew her.

His hair was as unruly a mane as Mirain's, and fully as splendid, left free in the custom of Asanian royalty though bound with a circlet about his brows. She stroked it. It was silken soft. "Gold should be cold to the touch," she said.

"And fire should burn." His hand ventured upon it, light, gentle, as if he feared to do her hurt. They were very close. She could feel the living warmth of him, and catch the scent he bore, faint yet distinct. Musk and saddle leather and briar roses. Their lips touched.

He was very beautiful and very strong, and his kiss was sweet. Warm and warming. He tasted of spices.

He drew back. His eyes had darkened to amber. "Lady," he said very softly. "Lady, you are a breaker of hearts."

She looked at him, not understanding, not wanting to understand.

He smiled as one in pain. "For every man who speaks ill of you, there are a thousand who would die for you. Remember that." He bowed low, as low as his royalty had ever permitted, and left her there.

With even Ilarios gone strange, she had thought that she had nothing left. But no blow ever falls alone. Toward evening Mirain summoned her, who had never had to do such a thing, close by him as she always was.

He was in the cell he used as a workroom. The clerks were gone; a brazier struggled to warm the chill air. Rolls and tablets heaped high about him, some sealed with his Sun-seal, some not. In his priest's robe, with a stylus in his hand, he looked like the boy who had taught her her letters. But he was frowning, if only slightly; his gaze was cool almost to coldness.

She stood in front of him with the worktable between them. Unconsciously she had drawn herself to attention. What sin had she committed, that he should look at her so? All her duties were done, and well done. She had given him nothing to complain of.

His eyes released her, but they had not softened. "In three days," he said, "we begin the march to Han-Gilen. It will be long, for I shall make of it a royal progress. I do not expect that we shall see the city very much before the opening of winter."

Her throat was locked. She swallowed to open a way for her voice. "The weather will be gentler as we go south. You will have no need to hasten because of it."

"Perhaps not." He turned the stylus in his hands. They were small for a man's, but the fingers were long and fine. A ring circled one, an intricate weaving of gold and ruby, flaming as it caught the light. She watched half-enspelled.

His soft voice lulled her, but his words shocked her fully awake. "As long as the riding will be, and with Han-Gilen at the end of it, I have given much thought to your place within it. My men know now who you are. They have accepted the knowledge well and without undue scandal, for you have proven yourself in the best of all ways, by your valor in battle. Yet there is scandal, and it will not grow less as we ride through the Hundred Realms. For your sake then and for that of your family, I have asked that your brother take you into his tent."

"And my oath?" she asked quietly. It sounded well, cool and steady, but she could muster nothing louder.

"I release you," he answered. "You have served me well. More than well. For that I would make you a knight, the first of my new empire."

Her lip curled. "So. It is no longer convenient for

your majesty to keep his esquire, now that men know he
is a she, and a princess of Han-Gilen at that. It is most
unpolitic. And, no doubt, it does not suit you to have
your chosen lady hear of it. Best and easiest then to be rid
of me, with a rich bribe to keep me quiet. Unfortunately,
my lord emperor, I am not to be bought."

He rose. Even in her anger she dreaded his wrath, but
he was fully masked. "I had thought to honor you, to
restore your good name. My own I have no care for; I am
a man, it does not matter. But in the way of this world,
yours is greatly endangered. I would not have it so.
Halenan is more than willing to share his lodgings with
you, and he has promised not to bind you, nor in any way
to restrict your freedom. He will even let you keep to
your boy's guise. You lose nothing by the change, and
gain much. A knight of my household is truly free to do
and to be what he chooses."

She shut her eyes against his logic. It was the core of
it that mattered, that fanned her temper into a blaze.
"Bribery. You rid yourself of a stain upon your majesty, a
ribald jest in every tavern. What is an emperor's econ-
omy? A squire who can serve him as well at night as in the
day. And what sort of squire is that? A squire who is also
a woman."

"No one says such things," he said. His voice deepened and lost its clarity. "No one would dare."

"Not in your presence, sire. I have long ears. I can
also read your mind, though you shield it with all your
father's power. I did not leave Han-Gilen and all I had
been and could be, to be sent into my brother's care like
an unruly child."

"What would you have, then?"

"Things as they were before," she answered swiftly.
She faced him. "Your good name does not matter, you
say. Let me look after my own. Or are you afraid of what
Mother will say to you?"

"I fear what she will say to you."

She could have hit him. "Damn you, I can take care

of myself! What does it take for me to prove that? A man's body as well as a man's clothes?"

In spite of his control, his lips twitched. "I would never wish for that, my lady. It is only . . . words can wound deep, far deeper than they ought. And you suffer most from them. Someday you may wish to be truly free, even to marry. I would not have you fear that no man will take you."

"I'm not afraid of that!" she snapped. And she added, because a demon was on her tongue, "Ziad-Ilarios would take me now, as I am, muddied name and all."

She had meant only to quell his arguments. She had not looked to drive him behind all his walls, with the gates barred and the banner of his kingship raised above the keep. "Very well," he said, "remain in my service. But do not expect me to ease your way with my subjects or with your family." He returned to his seat and opened a scroll. She was dismissed.

And she had won. But the victory held no sweetness. Almost she could wish that she had not won at all.

Thirteen

THE DAY BEFORE MIRAIN BEGAN HIS PROGRESS INTO THE south, a strong force departed under Vadin's command, turning back toward Ianon and the north. They would secure the tribes upon the borders of Asanion, and ascertain that all was well in Ianon.

"And I," said Vadin, "have a lady who objects to a cold bed."

Elian had gone to brood in solitude. The cavalry lines were quiet under the setting sun, the seneldi drowsing or grazing quietly, the grooms and the guards drawn off to a comfortable distance. She lay on her belly in the long grass, chewing a stem and watching Ilhari.

Voices startled her. Before she thought, she had flattened herself to invisibility. They nearly walked over her, too intent on one another to see her, striding together with a single woven shadow stretching long behind them. They stopped almost within her reach and stood side by side, not touching, not needing to touch.

Vadin swept his hand over the high plumes of grass, beheaded one, stripped it of its grains and offered it to the wind. Mirain turned his face to the setting sun. He

134

frowned at it, but it was to Vadin that he spoke. His voice was sharp with impatience. "I have no skill in the wooing of women."

Vadin snorted. "You have more than anyone. You've seduced whole kingdoms."

"Ah," said Mirain with a flick of his hand. "Kingdoms. Women are infinitely more complex. And that one ... whatever I do, she makes it clear that I should have done the opposite."

"Gods know what you see in her," Vadin said. Mirain glared; he grinned. "And I can guess. You like them difficult. Do you remember the little wildcat in Kurrikaz?"

Mirain grimaced. "My scars remember." He began to pace, a brief circuit. "She was dalliance. They all were."

"All three of them," Vadin muttered.

"Four." Mirain spun to face him. "This is truth, Vadin. This is the one who must be my queen: who always has been. And I know nothing of pursuit. All the rest have flung themselves at me, or been flung by fathers or brothers or procurers."

"Not that you've condescended to take any you didn't fancy."

"It's the curse of the mageborn. The body is never enough. Souls must meet; and so few even wish to. I tried once," said Mirain, "to take pleasure as a simple man would. It was like bathing in mire. She never saw me at all. Only my wealth and my title, and the use she could make of them."

"They're not all like that," said Vadin.

"I know it!" Mirain cried. "And the one I long for, the one I must have—she hardly knows I'm a man."

"Do you treat her like a woman?"

Mirain stopped short.

Vadin laid an arm about his shoulders, shaking him lightly. "I've seen how you are with her. Stiff and distant, and prim as a priestess. How is she to know you want her, if you persist in acting as if she were your youngest sister?"

"But she is—"

"She is royal and a beauty, and you want her so desperately you can hardly think. Let alone tell her the truth. She won't wait for you, Mirain; not unless she knows there's something to wait for."

"How can I tell her? She's as shy as a mountain lynx. She ran away from the last man who even began to court her."

"And he went after her, and now he's deathly close to winning her."

Mirain pulled free. His shoulders were knotted with tension. Suddenly he laughed, sharp and mirthless. "Here am I, new lord of the eastern world, fretting over a chit of a girl. An infant. A child who knows nothing of her own heart."

"Isn't it time you set about telling her?"

"I can't," Mirain said. "Call it pride. Call it stupidity."

"Cowardice," said Vadin.

Mirain bared his teeth. "That too. I can't conquer a woman as I would a city."

"Why not? Think of it as a siege. So you don't walk up to her and demand her hand in marriage. You can start hinting. Set up your siege engines: put on your best smile, give her a little of yourself, let her know she's beautiful." Mirain opened his mouth; Vadin overran him. "That's no more than the other man does. When she's warmed a little, then you can start beating down the gates. As," said Vadin, relentless, "he already has."

"Damn you, Vadin," growled Mirain. "I don't recall that you were so wise when you were the sufferer. Wasn't it I who made you start courting her? And didn't I have to give you a royal command before you'd marry her?"

"So," said Vadin, "I've learned how it's done. From you, O my brother."

"Did you, O my brother? Finish it, then. Win her for me."

"I can't," Vadin said. "I have to hold the north for you."

"Liar. It's your wife you have to hold."

"They're all one, aren't they? Beautiful, willful, and

determined not to come second in their lords' eyes. Go on, brother. Win your lady. It ought to be easier without me to get in the way."

"She's fonder of you than she knows."

"Hah," said Vadin. "Here now, stop glaring. Start your wooing, before she runs off with his royal Asanian highness."

Mirain paused, but suddenly he grinned. He aimed a blow at Vadin, which caught only air; he laughed, and went almost lightly, like the boy he still was. Vadin lingered, pondering the grass about his feet.

Elian's fingers clawed in it. She did not want to understand. She did not dare. That Mirain—might—want—

It was someone else. He had said it.

Had he?

It was a child's folly, to dream that every colloquy concerned oneself. And he had never—

He had said—

She scrambled to her feet. She never saw Vadin move. One instant he was frozen, startled. The next, his dagger pricked her throat. She met his hot glare, her own heat gone all cold. "You were talking about me," she said.

The blade dropped away. The sting of it lingered. Vadin eased, muscle by muscle, and began to laugh.

She waited. At long last he stopped. His brows went up. "You heard us?"

"Every word."

"Gods." He was almost appalled. Almost. A grin broke free. "So I won. You've found out. What will you do about it? Run away?"

"Where would I run to?"

"Asanion."

She closed her eyes. She was feeling nothing yet. Or too much. "I came for this," she said. "Because I promised. That I would—"

"Did you come for the promise, or for him?"

Her eyes snapped open. "I promised! I—" She bit her tongue. "If Mirain had not been Mirain, I would never have sworn my oath."

"Prettily said," drawled Vadin. He flung his long body to the ground at her feet. He was not wearing breeches under the kilt. She tore her eyes away. He propped himself on his elbow and regarded her from under level brows. "Sit," he said.

She did, with little grace. His amusement stung like the edge of his dagger.

"You're not a fool," he said, "well though you pretend to be. You know what you can do to a man simply by being yourself. It's diverting, isn't it? It's all a splendid game. Setting Han-Gilen on its ear, hoodwinking the army of the Sunborn, playing two imperial lovers against one another. Whet the Asanian's appetite with a long and perilous chase into the Sunborn's arms; prick the Sunborn to madness by falling into the Asanian's embrace. If you play your game cleverly enough, you can balance the two until the stars fall. Or," said Vadin, "until one loses patience and demands an accounting. What then, princess? Which heart will you break? One or both?"

"I think," she said, measuring each word in ice, "that I hate you."

"You hate the truth."

"It is *not* the truth!" She was on her feet, shaking, choking on murder. "I never meant this to be. From the very first that I can remember, I knew what I wanted. Mirain. He belonged to me. No one else could ever have him. Then—then he went away. Father tried to hold him back until he was grown and could muster an army for the claiming of Ianon. He obeyed as long as he could, but he fretted; his father was in him, burning, and time was running ever faster.

"In the night, in the spring, when he had won his torque but not yet had his fifteenth birth-feast, he covered himself in magery and slipped away.

"But I knew. He could never hide anything from me. I followed. I caught him; he almost killed me before he knew me, and came close enough after. I begged to go with him, though I knew I couldn't. He had to go alone; his father wanted it, and he needed it. He thought it was his persuasion that won me over. It was my power, and a glimmering of prophecy. 'Go,' I said. 'Be king. And when you are king, I will come to you.'

"He kissed me and set his face toward the northward road. And I stayed. I had to grow; I had to learn all I could, that would help me when I fulfilled my promise. It was never a grim duty, but the pleasure grew with me.

"Then I was a woman, and it was time, and it was never quite time. There was always some new art to learn, some new suitor to dispose of, some new hawk or hound or senel to tame. And I had kin who, though they could madden me, loved me deeply, and I them. *Tomorrow,* I kept saying. *Tomorrow I'll go.*

"I never stopped wanting Mirain. None of the men who came panting after me was ever his equal. Few of them came close to being mine.

"Until," she said, "until I saw Ziad-Ilarios." She stopped, staring a little wildly at the man who lay in the grass. The sun had lost itself somewhere. Vadin was a long shadow, kilted in scarlet, hung with copper and gold. She did not know him at all. Outlander, barbarian, soul-bound with Mirain whom she knew too deeply to know what she knew.

"Ziad-Ilarios," she said, like an incantation, or a curse. "I suppose to you he looks soft and small and daintily effeminate. To me he is all gold.

"Mirain is the other half of me," she said. "Ilarios is the man to my woman."

Vadin did not rise up to throttle her. Nor did he wither her with contempt. "I see," he said. "Mirain is too familiar to be interesting. The Asanian sets your body throbbing."

"The Asanian admits that he wants me."

Vadin sighed. "And you want both. A pity you're not a man, to keep two mates. Or a whore, to have as many as you please."

"That," she said levelly, "I have been called before."

His grin was white in the shadow of his face. "I married one, you know." Her silence troubled him not at all. He settled more comfortably and drew an easy breath, like a talespinner with his audience firm in his hand. "She was born to free farmfolk. One year when the crops failed, her father sold her to a procurer. She was good at her trade; she could have risen to a courtesan and bought her freedom, and no doubt set herself up in her own business. But I came along, and somehow I ended up being her favorite lover, which is no credit to my prowess: at that age I had none to speak of. I think she looked on me as a challenge; and Ledi loves challenges. Then Mirain set her free and gave her rank to match mine. Before I knew it we'd been maneuvered into the marriage bed."

Elian would not be shocked. He in his turn would not be disappointed. "So you see, I have to go and leave Mirain to his fate: or should I say, to you. Ledi has issued her ultimatum. I come home and inspect the tribe I've fathered, or they come after me. There are two I've hardly seen, the twins, they were beautiful when they were born but Mirain called me off to help him put down a nest of mages; and then, what with one thing and another, I never got back after. They're nigh a year old now."

"A tribe?" Elian asked, interested in spite of herself. "How many of them are there?"

"Two maids—that's the twins. And five lads. Seven in all." *Only* seven, his tone said; and there was no irony in it. "But then I've only the one lady, and somehow I've never had much of an eye for anyone else. She does her valiant best. She wants twins again this time, she says, and that will make nine, which is a good round number. She has a very strong will, does my Ledi-love."

"So," gritted Elian, "do I."

"Don't you? A pity it doesn't know what it wants."

She set her teeth until they ached, and was silent. His head tilted. "You don't like me, do you?"

"Am I supposed to answer that?"

He shrugged. It was fascinating to watch, for what it did to all his rings and necklaces and earrings. Three in one ear, copper and gold and one great carbuncle like a coal in the dusk. "Let me guess. You had Mirain first. Then he abandoned you. He attached himself to me, who didn't even have the good grace to appreciate the honor, and made me so much a part of him that now there's no dividing us. And you came and found us as we are, and Mirain persists in acting as if nothing has changed between you. And not only does that madden you; I don't even have the kindness to be jealous."

"That's not true."

"Give me credit for some intelligence." He sounded sharp but not angry. "I give you more than your fair share for not despising a gaudy barbarian. But you want me to hate you and to fight with Mirain over a love that's big enough for us all. Alas, I can't. I lost that degree of humanity when I took the lance in my vitals. It went both ways, that miracle. Mirain called me back, and I saw the full extent of what he was and is and always will be. He's mine, always, irrevocably. He's also Ianon's, and the north's, and the south's; he belongs to your father, he belongs to Hal, he belongs to you. It's no good to want to have all of him. Even Avaryan can't have that."

"What are you?" she cried through the tangle that was her mind.

"A prodigy," he answered, and his voice was bitter. "A monster. A dead man walking."

"No." She seized his hand. Its palm was hard with calluses, its back surprisingly silken, warm and strong and very much alive. "I didn't mean that. I'm not—you do surprise me. I'd hate you if you were I, sneaking little interloper that I am, and in trousers too."

That warmed him; his smile gleamed from the shadow of his face. "But," he said, "I never thought you were a boy."

Her jaw dropped. She picked it up with care. "You—"

"Oh yes, I would have resented a swaggering little cock-a-whoop who thought he could take my place. You only wanted your own back. You got it, and it was wonderfully amusing to watch you hoodwink the army. Stone blind, all of them. Even in a kilt you'd walk like a she-panther. And you've got breasts. Not much yet, and in all honesty you'll never match my lady, but breasts you've got. Didn't anyone ever tell you about strapping them flat?"

Her free hand flew to them, flew away. Her cheeks flamed. "I tried for a while. It was ghastly uncomfortable." Dark though it had grown, she glared at him. "You are presumptuous."

"Is that all?" Laughter rippled in his voice. "I'd say I was skirting the edge of the unforgivable. Or I would be, if I weren't so disgustingly close to being your kinsman. Has anyone told you lately that you're beautiful?"

"No!" she snapped. "Yes. I don't know."

She was still holding his hand. It gripped hers; it drew her to him. He was a shadow and a gleam, and a warmth as much of the mind as of the body. "Listen to me, Elian. I have to go away. There's no help for it; Mirain's god is leading him into the south, and someone has to keep the north strong behind him. I know we'll be part of one another wherever we go, and I know he'll never be alone while he has Hal to stand beside him. But he needs more. He doesn't know it; if he did, he wouldn't admit it. He's proud too, that one, and sometimes he's as blind as any ordinary idiot."

Elian was stiff in his grasp, breathing in the scent of him, the sheer foreignness of his presence. But his mind was not foreign at all; and that disturbed her more than any of the rest. One word, one flicker of the will, and they would be bound, brother, sister, kindred as he had named them: kindred in power.

"Look after him," said the outland voice in the outland tongue. "Take care of him. Don't let him be any more of a lunatic than you can help. And if you need me, send your power to me. I'll come. Because," he said, both solemn and wicked, "I also keep my promises."

Her eyes narrowed; her fists clenched. "After all you've said and done to me, you can ask me to take your place with him?"

"I'm asking you to choose as you have to choose, but

not to break him in doing it. You love him enough for that, I think. Even if you bind your body to the Asanian."

She could not speak. He rose, drew her into a swift inescapable embrace, let her go. He towered against the stars.

"What—" she whispered. Her voice rose. "What do I tell Mirain?"

"If you're wise," he answered, "everything. Or nothing." He bowed and set a kiss in her hand. "Avaryan's luck with you, Lady of Han-Gilen. We'll meet again."

Fourteen

VADIN WAS GONE. WELL GONE, ELIAN WANTED TO THINK. He knew too damnably much, and understood it all, and refused—adamantly refused—to despise her for it.

Mirain without him was no less Mirain. It was Elian who found herself looking for him. Missing his eternal and exasperating presence, and his scathing wit, and his talent for saying what no one else dared to say. However much she had resented his presence, she resented his absence more deeply still. It had nothing to do with liking him. It had everything to do with needing him.

She did not see him off. Would not. She had lain awake nightlong, watching Mirain sleep, as if suddenly he would wake and cry, "Choose me!"

And if he had, she would have fled. It had been so simple when she did not know: when he seemed content to be her brother, and she was content to be his squire. Now she must lie, or she must tell him what she knew, and lose her brother, and gain the burden of a lover.

Familiar, Vadin had said. Mirain was that. Too familiar. She could as easily lust after Halenan as after Mirain.

He had known her since she was born. He was part of her, blood and bone.

"Ziad-Ilarios," she whispered in the deeps of the night, and shivered. He was alien, and beautiful, and all desirable. She had seen all of Mirain that there was to see. Of Ilarios she had seen the face, and the hands, and a glimpse of comely feet. She could only guess what lay between. Beauty carved in ivory, with dust of gold.

Ebony slept oblivious, obstinate in its silence; and woke as if she had never been more to him than sister and servant. She was soul-glad; she hated him for it. She held her tongue and veiled her eyes and let him have his peace. In a blessedly little while, she had found a scrap of it for herself; she tended it, and schooled herself to think of naught beyond it.

When Mirain began his riding into the south, her joy in it could be almost as unalloyed as his own. The sun blazed upon him in all the splendor of autumn, the leaves of the woods as golden as the Sun on his banner; and he rode under both as light as a boy, with all his drudgeries packed away in the clerks' wagons far down the line. Men sang behind him, a marching song of the north that the southerners had taken a fancy to. The Mad One danced in time to it; and Mirain laughed with the simple joy of it, that he was alive, and king, and riding in the sun before the cream of his newborn empire.

His glance drew Elian into his delight. She could resist him, but not when all the earth seemed to conspire with him. She flashed him her brightest grin, and set Ilhari dancing likewise, matching the Mad One step for step.

They crossed Ilien and entered Poros with Prince Indrion in the van, guiding his emperor through his brother realm. It was indeed the royal progress Mirain had looked for; night found him in the heart of the princedom, feasting in its palace, surrounded by its people. Its women, Elian noticed, were enchanted with him. She noticed also that he betrayed no interest in any one in particular, although some were very beautiful, and some were very charming, and a few were both.

To her he had not changed at all. Not even when she surprised him with a glance or a smile, daring him to begin the siege. Not even when the demon in her sent her to Ilarios' side and kept her there, and made her bold and brazen, and brought her close to hating herself. Until Ilarios turned his golden eyes upon her and smiled, knowing what she did, forgiving her. She had kissed him before she knew it, there where everyone could see. She started back, blushing furiously. "I—" she began.

His finger silenced her, not quite touching her lips. "I know," he said. And began to speak of something else entirely.

When at last it struck her, it struck hard. Ilarios had won a victory. She had forgotten Mirain. She looked, and he was gone; and she had not seen him go.

He was in bed. Alone. Sleeping as a child sleeps, in blissful peace. She cursed him, but whispering, through gritted teeth. "*You* are no thwarted lover. He lied, that great lanky shadow of yours. Or I dreamed it all." He never stirred. She hissed at him. "Damn you, Mirain! How can I know if I want you, if you won't even ask?"

THE KING'S PROGRESS CONTINUED IN A SPLENDOR OF SUN-light. But the nights seemed doubly dark for the brightness between. Elian dreamed, and her dreams were fearful, but when she woke she could not remember them. She began to fight against sleep.

It was not her little tangle of lovers. This ran deeper, down to the heart of power, where prophecy had its lair. Fear was in it, and a darkness of the soul; and something terribly like yearning. Something wanted her. Something strove to draw her to it, if only she would lower her defenses, if only she would yield. Only a little. Only enough to know what summoned her.

She would not. And she dreamed; and there was a black and crooked comfort in it. Dreaming, dreading sleep, she had less leisure to fret over a man who would not admit that he wanted her, and over a man whom she wanted but not—quite yet—with all that was in her.

WHEN AUTUMN WAS WELL ADVANCED BUT THE TREES WORE still their scarlet and gold, Mirain paused near the border of Iban in the forests of Kurion. Having seen the army settled in a great field, almost a plain, within the wood, and his own household established in a forest manor of Kurion's prince, he rode out hunting. The air was like wine, the quarry both swift and crafty, the golden deer of the south. Elian, daring a long shot from Ilhari's saddle, brought down a splendid hart; its flesh made their supper, its hide she gave to Ilarios, who had lent her his bow for the shot. Its crown of ivory antlers she kept as a trophy.

The hunt had been good, but hers was the best kill; for that, as champion of the hunt, she had the place of honor at table. Mirain made her put aside his livery—"My scarlet does your hair no justice," he said—and he gave her a gift, a coat the color of an emerald, edged and embroidered and belted with gold. It was a man's coat, yet when she put it on over long fine tunic and silken trousers, there could be no doubt at all that she was a woman.

Her first instinct was to strip it all off and snatch for her livery. But he was watching, his eyes for a moment unguarded, and he said, "Sister, if I had only you to think of, I'd change my livery to green, and keep it so."

She waited. Her heart hammered. Now—now he would speak. But he only set a casket in her hands and went to his own dressing. She opened the casket. It was a royal gift, but not of necessity a lover's. A thin circlet of gold to bind her brows, and emeralds set in gold for her ears, and a collar of gold set with emeralds. She put them on with hands that wanted desperately to shake. Mirain was gone already. She made herself follow him.

Strange as her mood was, her entrance into the hall won all the stares she could have wished for. It was almost like old times: the hungry eyes, the smitten faces, leavened now with a large portion of startlement. Few might have guessed that livery could hide so much.

Mirain's face betrayed nothing. He smiled as she sat by him, no more or less warmly than he ever did, and greeted her with empty words. His nearness was like a fire on her skin.

It must be that, for the first time since she came to him, she both looked and felt a woman. And he was close, and he was a man; she had never thought before how very much a man he was. It made him all a stranger. It made him almost frightening.

He brushed against her in reaching for his winecup. She shivered. He wore scarlet tonight, but its fashion was the fashion of the south, very close indeed to her own, ruby to her emerald. His northerners were learning, slowly, not to be appalled when he put on trousers.

She tried to distract herself. He was not going to speak, now or ever. And she could not. She could not say, *Be my lover.* No more could she say, *You will never be more to me than a brother.*

His profile fascinated her. The purity of it; the fierce foreignness that yet was utterly familiar. The ruby in his ear glowed against his darkness, begging her to touch it.

She tore her eyes from him. She was beginning to comprehend the common lot of males: the prick of passion, sudden, urgent, bitter to refuse. There was no logic in it, and very little sanity; it knew nothing of times and seasons. Save that this was her time and this her season, springtide of her womanhood, when blood sang to blood, and fire to banked and shielded fire.

She took refuge in Halenan's face. He was splendid to see, but his beauty only warmed her; it did not burn. He sat oblivious, deep in speech with the Kurionin prince, smiling suddenly at a turn of wit. Beyond them at the table's end sat Ilarios. It might have been chance that set him so far from her. It might have been calculation. His eyes lifted, warming as they caught hers. She could not hold them. Her glance slid aside, restless, uneasy, alighting on comfort. Of a sort.

Cuthan had been her friend, or so she had thought, before the truth of her womanhood built its wall between them. Sensing her gaze, he looked up. Without its white grin his face was as haughty as any in Ianon. His eyes were black, like his brother's, like Mirain's, and steady, taking her in as if she were a stranger. She could not tell what he thought of her.

Suddenly both eyes and face were transformed. He grinned and saluted her as he had in the battle, offering for this little while all that she had lost.

Her throat was tight. But she did as she had done then: she returned his grin. Cobbled courage, but it bore her up. And it distracted her most admirably.

THIS DREAM SHE WOULD REMEMBER—MUST REMEMBER. DARK-ness and whirling, and a face, the face of the woman called Kiyali. Close, coming closer, drawn by her own desperate denial. The Exile's eyes in the dreamworld were not blind at all but terribly, bitterly keen, piercing Elian to the heart. Perceiving all her hidden places, her flaws and her secrets, her lies and her cruelties and her follies.

And understanding, and forgiving. *Kinswoman,* the low voice said. *Blood of my blood. Why do you fear me? Why do you flee?*

"No kin," Elian willed herself to say. It was a gasp. "Never. Enemy—"

I am not your enemy.

"You are Mirain's." Elian's voice was stronger, her resistance firmer. Because she must resist. Blood knew blood. Kin called to kin, however bitterly sundered.

I must oppose him. The law binds me, though its upholders sought to cast me out.

"What law? Temple law? It was never broken. The priestess never knew man. She bore a son to the god, as all the prophecies had foretold."

She lied. She was mageborn, and strong; and her lover was stronger yet.

"And the Sun in Mirain's hand? How do you deny that?"

Magery, the Exile said. Elian heard desperation in her simplicity. She shifted, coming closer yet. The furred collar about her shoulders opened eyes full of malice, and grinned a fanged grin. Elian's scars throbbed into pain.

It is the truth, said the Exile, here where no lie could be. *The Ianyn king is a monster of mages' making, a weapon of the light against the chains that bind the worlds. He will break them, and call it victory, and never know the true terror of what he has done. For the sun is splendid and much beloved, but its full force can blind and destroy. And your young king would loose it upon us all.*

"He will put down the dark."

Has it ever risen? It is necessary, kinswoman. It is the proper counter to the force of the light. Night after burning day; winter which bears the seeds of summer, as the summer begets the winter.

"No," said Elian.

The Exile stood silent. Her familiar had begun to purr.

"No," Elian said again. "Mirain is the god's son. I know it. My bones know it. Even—even if his body may not be—" Her tongue tangled in confusion. That was not what she had meant to say. "The god does as he wills. He is Mirain's father."

The Exile raised her chin. Age had gentled her manner, but never her pride. *You deny what you cannot accept. You toy with the thought of loving him. You cannot endure that he may be your father's son.*

The familiar hissed. It was laughing. It knew more than its mistress would tell. Brother and sister mated: what terror in that? Asanians were much given to it. In no way else could they have bred their emperors. Ziad-Ilarios himself . . .

Elian clapped her hands over her ears, little good as it did, crying out against it all. The lies which the outcast called truth, and the truth which was woven inextricably with lies.

Come, said the Exile. *Come to me. I can give you truth unalloyed. I can set you free of all your bonds. You need never marry, nor bow to kings, nor submit to the caprices of your father.*

Elian tossed, battling.

Free. Be free. Come with me to the world's aid. It must not fall to the sword of the light. Stand with me as your power bids you do. It is greater than you know, and wiser. Listen to it.

She could not hear it. The voice drowned it.

Come with me. Come.

Her hand stretched. Wanting—willing—

"*No!*"

She sprang awake, crying aloud. There were hands on her, arms about her, a voice in her ear. Not that voice. Not, by the god, that deadly voice. "Elian. Elian, wake; it was only a dream."

With agonizing slowness the dream retreated. She crouched trembling, gasping as if she had run long and far from a terror too great to bear, clutching at the warm strength that held her, only dimly aware that it was Mirain.

The awareness grew, calming her. He was the Sunborn. He would not let the darkness take her.

Her breathing quieted. Her head drooped upon his breast over the slow strong beating of his heart. He held her there without speaking, letting the silence heal her.

After a long while she said, "It was more than a dream. It was power."

He stroked her hair gently, saying nothing.

"Power," she repeated. "Prophecy. It has been haunting me; I have been fighting it. But power will not be denied. The enemy is arming against us. She is very, very strong. As she should be; for she is my kin, and trained in all the arts of power, both light and dark." She stiffened, straightening in his grasp. "We've been foolish, riding in the sunlight as if no cloud would ever come. She will make us pay."

"No," he said. "She will not. I have been on guard. She cannot enter my kingdom."

Elian looked long into his face. "She cannot, but she need not. She is in it already."

He did not deny it; and that frightened her as nothing else had. But he said, "She shall not touch you. By my father's hand I swear it."

It would be easy, so easy, to rest in the circle of his protection. Her body clung to him still, and found him strong. Yet her mind locked in resistance. "I'll fight my own battles, my lord."

"Is this your battle?"

She pulled away from him. "You can't protect me from prophecy. Only I can do that."

"By accepting it?"

"No!" she said quickly. But after a moment, very slowly, as if each word were dragged from her: "Yes. By—by letting it come. When we come to Han-Gilen . . . there are ways and rituals . . . O 'Varyan! Why did I have to be the one?"

He sat on his heels beside her pallet and reached again for her, this time to take her hands and hold them. "Elian, little sister, the god gives gifts where he chooses. You are rich in them, because in his reckoning you are strong enough to bear them. I'd bear them for you if I could, if either he or you would let me."

"We won't. I can't. Any more than I can be what you are."

He smiled faintly, painfully. "You wouldn't want that."

"Don't try to be me, then. And don't be so sure of yourself. Your enemy is mortal, but she is powerful, and she serves the dark. Are you strong enough to face her?"

His hands tightened upon hers. He could sense as strongly as she the current of seeing that ran through her, speaking in her voice. "Who knows?" he said. "Who can know, unless I try?"

"You can't. Not now. Not tonight."

"No," he agreed. "Not tonight." He raised her hands and kissed the palm of each. "Rest now. The vision is gone; it will let you have peace."

Whether he spoke the truth, or whether it was his own power that worked upon her, she slept almost at once, deeply, without dreams.

Fifteen

MIRAIN'S VANGUARD LOOKED DOWN FROM THE HILLS OF Han-Gilen. Below them spread the plain and the river and the white city. The sun, riding low, cast long shadows behind it of wall and turret and thin wind-whipped banner. Upon the tower of the temple the Sun-crystal flamed, brighter in the evening than the sun itself.

The king gazed at it for a long still while. He had been born there in that temple in the chanting and the incense. He had grown to young manhood under the care of its prince. This, more than Ianon, more than any other province of his empire, was the place his heart longed for.

Elian beside him, raw with homecoming, could not tell which pangs were his and which were her own. His were sharp with years of absence, but hers were still new, edged with fear of what she would find. He could expect a royal welcome. She . . .

Ilarios leaned from his saddle to touch the hand that clenched upon her thigh. "It will be well," he said.

She tossed her hair out of her face, fiercely. Mirain was already moving. He would be inside the walls by

153

night, with great ceremony, and up till dawn settling his
people. She sent Ilhari after him.

All the road to the city was rimmed with people, the
gates beyond them ablaze with light. Halenan and Mirain
rode side by side, the prince in a splendor of green and
gold, the king all in white that glowed in the dusk, with a
great mantle of white fur pouring over the Mad One's
flanks. Its scarlet lining shone in the flicker of torchlight,
now blood-bright, now blood-black.

Elian would have ridden as she had ridden to the
meeting at the ford, well back among the army. But Ilhari
knew her proper place: beside her sire. With no bit or
bridle to compel her, and neither the will nor the willing-
ness to overbear her with power, Elian had perforce to go
where she was taken.

The livery of the king was no shield here, where
every man and woman and child knew her face. They
cheered for Mirain, they cheered for Halenan, but they
cried out also for her, their lady, their bright-maned
princess. She greeted them with lifted hand and a fixed,
brilliant smile. But her eyes saw none of them.

Under the arch of the White Gate a mounted man
waited alone. His stallion was as white as milk, his coat
resplendent with gold; gold crowned his fiery hair. Dark
as his face was, black in the dusk, Elian could not discern
his expression, only the gleam of his eyes. They were
fixed upon the boy he had fostered, who had escaped his
care one deep night to gain a northern kingdom, whom
he had made an emperor. As the riders drew near, he
dismounted and waited, tall beside his tall senel.

Elian saw the glint of Mirain's eyes, the swirl of his
cloak as he left the saddle with the Mad One still advancing. He half strode, half ran up the last of the road;
caught Prince Orsan in the act of bowing to the ground;
drew him into a swift, jubilant embrace. "Foster-father,"
he said, clear in the sudden silence, "never bow to me,
you or your princess or your children. You are my heart's
kin; I owe you all that I have."

The prince's voice came deep and quiet, but touched with great joy. "Not all of it, my lord An-Sh'Endor."

"Enough." Mirain returned to the Mad One's back. When the prince also had mounted, the king held out his golden hand. "I shall never forget it; I, or all the sons of my sons."

CEREMONY WAS A MIGHTY PROTECTOR OF SINNERS. CAUGHT up in the welcoming of the emperor to the heart of his empire, neither prince nor princess could so far trespass upon dignity as to take official notice of the face above the squire's surcoat. But they were aware of her. Painfully. Excruciatingly, as the grand entry gave way to the presentation in the temple, the rite and the praises of the god, and at last to the feast of welcome.

Elian stood close enough to her father to touch; her mother's perfume was sweet and subtle in her nostrils, the princess clear to see on Mirain's left side, a flawless profile, a serene dark eye. Elian could have escaped with utmost ease, with but a word, a plea to be excused. There was enough and more than enough to do outside in the growing camp. Hal, having had an hour alone with Anaki, was there now, seeing that everything was ordered as Mirain wished it. Cuthan had gone with him. Even Ilarios had chosen to escape this lordly duty. She had no allies here.

She had known that before she committed herself to it. As she had known what a squire's place was: here, standing behind her lord's chair for every Gileni noble and servant to stare at. Wild though she had always been, none of them had ever thought to see her there.

The end was merciful, wine and graceful words, the departure of hosts and guests to their beds or to their duties. Prince Orsan had repaired and refurbished a whole wing of the palace for Mirain, at what expense she could hardly guess. He had stinted nothing.

Mirain stood in the center of the Asanian carpet as she labored patiently to undo the fastenings of his coat. He was silent: absorbed, she thought, in contemplation of the long night's work before him.

She herself had little to say. She slipped the coat from his shoulders and laid it in the clothing chest, careful of its jeweled splendor. When she turned back, he was still in his trousers and his fine linen shirt, watching her. She took up his working garb, a kilt as plain as any trooper's. "You should take a cloak," she said. "The nights are cold this close to solstice."

He accepted the kilt, but made no move to don it. "Elian," he said. "Why have you said no word to either your father or your mother?"

She stood still. His gaze was steady. She knew that if she reached, his mind would be open to her touch. Her shields closed and firmed. "There has been no occasion," she said, speaking High Gileni, distant and formal, with no warmth in it.

He met her coldness with a flare of heat and the patois of the city. "You spent a whole turn of the watch within their arms' reach."

"They made no effort to speak to me."

"They waited for you."

"Did they?" She began to unbind his hair.

He pulled free. How strange, she thought within her barriers. He was aflare with temper, and she was utterly cool, utterly in control.

"You are not!" he snapped. "Your obstinacy lies within you like an egg, hard and round and heavy, shelled in ice. Come away from it and look at yourself."

There was a mirror near the bed, polished silver. Because he held her in front of it, she regarded the stranger there. Whoever it was, it was not the child who had fled Han-Gilen in the night, this bright-haired person of ambiguous gender, lean and hard with long riding, with four thin parallel scars seaming one cheek. Its eyes had seen much and grown dark with it; its mouth tightened upon—what? Grief? Pain? Anger? Crippling shyness?

His hands held hers in a fierce grip. "You see? How can they speak to this? Easier to reason with the sword's edge."

"What could they say? That my beauty is ruined? That my value on the market has dropped to nothing?"

"They could say that they love you; that they grieved for your absence; that they are glad beyond words to have you back again."

"Let them say it then."

"They will." His eyes met her mirrored stare, his face beside hers, dark and eager. "Go to them. Now. They wait for you."

She turned her back on him and on her own face. "If they wish to see me, they may summon me." She pulled off her surcoat and reached for a coat as plain as the kilt he had abandoned. "Will my lord dress himself, or would he prefer that I aid him?"

Walled in the perfection of her coldness, she could not sense either his thought or his temper. She changed from state dress into common garb, in silence he made no move to break. When she passed him in search of her boots, her heart speeded a little in spite of itself. But he did not seize her. His face had hardened to match her own. "I have no further need of your services tonight," he said, cool and precise. "If you choose not to do as I bid you, then you had best confine yourself to quarters. I shall speak with you later."

Sitting on her pallet with her boots hanging limp and forgotten in her hands, she stared at the wall. Her eyes were dry to burning. He had sent her to bed like a wayward child; and for what? Because she would not abase herself before anyone, not even her father. Nor would she face her mother and listen to the long, gentle-voiced, relentless catalogue of her sins and shortcomings. Foremost of which was the stain with which she had defiled the reputation of her house. Not only had she shorn her hair and taken on the seeming of a boy; she had traveled alone and unattended through the north of the Hundred Realms, and slain men in battle, and shared the bed of a man neither wedded nor betrothed to her. She was a scandal from western Asanion to the Eastern Isles, utterly, irredeemably.

And she would not go to them and weep with them and beg to be forgiven. She could not. She was too proud; or too utterly craven.

"They can come to me," she said aloud. "They know where I am."

In Mirain's bed?

She laughed bitterly. "If only I were!"

With sharp, vicious movements she stripped off her garments, letting them lie where they fell. The mirror gleamed in the outer chamber. She faced it again.

She was too thin; but not everywhere. There could be no doubt at all now that this sullen-faced person was a woman. A gown, a daub or three of paint, and she would outshine any harlot on Lantern Street. Her hair was long enough now to tie back, even to twist into a short braid: the exact length prescribed for a woman of ill repute.

A small knife lay on a table. Mirain's, for cutting meat at feasts. Its hilt shone frostily, set with diamonds. Yet for all its beauty it was no toy. Its blade was deadly sharp.

She took it up. Carefully, deliberately, she cut her hair, cropping it well above the shoulders.

She let the knife fall. Her hands were shaking. The face in the mirror was green-pale under its cap of coppery hair; and yet it bared its sharp white teeth. "Now let them see how I mean to go on. Han-Gilen may house me, but it cannot hold me. I have freed myself."

Ah, but from what?

ELIAN SAT ALONE IN THE BARREN GARDEN, STARING AT nothing, thinking of nothing.

"Lady." She started, waking as from sleep. Cuthan stood over her, tall as a tree and vivid as a sunbird in the grey cloudlight. His face and his eyes and his bearing were at once bold and shy; she thought he might be blushing under the black velvet of his skin. "Lady," he repeated, "it will rain soon."

Elian looked at him and thought of hating him. "I am no lady."

The Ianyn captain sat on a low flat stone, clasping his knees, boylike, with a frown between his fine arched brows. "You refuse the name, but you can't change the truth. You're still what blood and training have made you."

"I have cut myself off from it."

"Have you ever tried to cut a jet of blood with a sword?"

"I have cloven flesh and bone, and taken the life within."

"It's less easy to sever oneself from one's kin."

Elian's anger flared white-hot. "Who set you on me? Mirain? Halenan? Or even"—her voice cracked, startling her, feeding her rage—"or even my father?"

"Your father," said Cuthan calmly, "is a very great prince. In Ianon we would call him a king. And he loves you."

"He let me go. I have come back, but not to his hand."

"I said love, not jesses and a lure."

Elian tensed to rise. She meant to strike with fierce words, and to flee his unwelcome presence, this mingling of youthful shyness and borrowed wisdom that pricked her almost to madness. But she heard herself say in a voice she hardly knew as her own, "I went to the mews. I thought it would be quiet there. Hawks and the Hawk-master have no care for the cut of one's hair. It was quiet, and the master did not care. But she was gone, my golden falcon. After I left, when I did not come back, they flew her, and she never returned. If I had been there, she would have come."

"Would she?"

Elian did rise then, fists clenched. "Yes. Yes! She was mine. I tamed her. I loved her. She would have come back."

"You," said Cuthan, "did not. Or will not."

"I am not a falcon!"

"But your father is a falconer?"

Elian willed herself to stalk away from this transparent subterfuge, this parroting of words learned by rote from the whole tribe of her kin. Of whom he seemed to count himself one, however tortuous the kinship: brother of her foster brother's oathbrother. Later she would laugh. Now she could not even move. Her body seemed rooted here on the winter grass, with the sky beginning to weep great cold tears. "You have no right to sit in judgment upon me."

"None at all," Cuthan agreed willingly, "except that of friendship. I thought we had that, you and I."

"Galan had it. Now you know he was a lie."

To her amazement, Cuthan laughed, light and free. "I knew all along." He spread his hands as if to sweep away all lies and disguises. "I only look like a brawn-brained fool; and I trained to be a singer for a while, till my master told me I had a fine voice, a fine mind, and no calling at all to the grey robe. But even with the little learning I had, I knew that Orsan of Han-Gilen would never have gotten a bastard—least of all a boy of exactly the same age, size, and looks as his famous daughter. A good part of whose fame lay in her ability to outride, outhunt, and outfight any man she met."

"Is there anyone who didn't know the truth?" Elian asked sourly.

His eyes were wide and dark and surprised. "Who else could have? Except Mirain, of course. And Vadin. Vadin always knows everything Mirain does. We didn't tell anyone. We didn't even tell each other till the secret got out."

"That explains a great deal. All your hanging about. Your fretting over me in the battle."

He had the grace to look sheepish and the gall to defend himself. "I wasn't hanging about. I was doing what any man would do for his friend. I never intended to humiliate you."

"No?" Her mouth twisted. "No, of course not. I'm a woman. Delicate. Fragile. Featherheaded. I can't be humiliated. Only protected to death."

"Lady," Cuthan said with heroic patience, "you wear defiance like a suit of armor. Won't you take off the helmet at least and look around you? The only one who's tormenting you is yourself."

Elian's hand lifted to strike him. With an effort of will she lowered it. "How much did my kinsmen pay you to say these things?"

The black eyes kindled, swift and terrible as a flame in a sunlit wood. "Barbarian I may be, and no king's son, but I'm no one's hireling. I saw pain in my king, and in his brother, and in a lord and a lady whom I've learned to admire. I saw it most of all in my friend, who simply happened to be a woman. Now I understand that I saw a friend where I had none. Unless that is friendship here in the south, to meet love with tooth and claw. In the north, even the lynx of the wood will not do that." He stood. His face was cold and hard. He bowed very slightly, very stiffly, as to a stranger. "I at least will go in out of the rain. Good day, lady."

The title was like a slap. Elian watched him go, unable to move, unable to speak, while the rain beat her with flails of ice.

She could have crawled into some dark corner and huddled there, and burned and shivered all alone. But deeper than rage or hate or even craven terror was the pride that had spawned them. Wet to the skin, steady by sheer force of will, she returned to Mirain's chamber.

He was there, as she had known he would be. He was alone, which she had not expected. A large and busy company she could have faced, effacing herself in it, but that solitary figure in a long robe lined with fur, seated by a brazier with a book in his lap, nearly undid her.

His eyes were lowered, but the book was closed, its spools bound together with golden cords. Deep in thought as he was, he did not hear her coming. She wavered in the door, dripping on the carpet, gathering herself to bolt. He looked like Cuthan. Damnably like. But the rain had washed her anger away, leaving only an echoing emptiness.

Something roused him: perhaps the chattering of her teeth. The sudden light of his eyes nearly felled her.

His hands were burning hot, drawing her into the room, setting her by the brazier, stripping her of her sopping clothes. He flung his own robe about her and fastened it high under her chin, and took her icy hands in his own and chafed them until the pain of life woke within them.

She should pull free. He was the king. It was not fitting that he should do squire service for his squire.

Gently he pressed her into his chair, drying her dripping hair with a cloth from his bath. She suffered it as she had suffered Cuthan's bitter words, with inward resistance, outward helplessness.

With the worst of the wet wiped away, he reached for the comb he had brought with the cloth. She blocked his hand. Her own had almost no strength, but he paused. "Say it," she gritted. "Say all of it."

"It has been said." He eluded her grasp and began to comb her cropped hair. He had more patience with its tangles than he ever had with his own.

"Of course," he said. "There's less of it." His palm rested against her cheek, warm now, but not to burning. Yet it was the right, which bore the god's fire, which had blinded his mother's murderer.

Elian swallowed round the knot in her throat. "Cuthan told the truth. The whole ugly truth. But I can't—can't—"

He was behind her; she could not see his face. His voice was soft. "Elian, my sister. Only the weak refuse to weep."

"I *won't!*" she cried, leaping up, facing him. "You have duties. We both do. And you in nothing but a loinguard. You could perish of a chill."

"Elian."

"No." She fumbled with the fastenings of the robe, pulling them free. "No. Not—not yet."

That minute concession was, in its way, as cruel as Cuthan's farewell. Yet Mirain accepted it with more grace than Elian could ever have mustered. Which in turn was its own, subtle, and well-deserved rebuke.

Sixteen

"HERE," SAID MIRAIN, "I SHALL BUILD MY CITY."
The wind was loud on the plain of the river, and knife-edged with cold, but Mirain's words came soft and clear beneath it. He stood with feet set well apart, head up and eyes alight, with his cloak whipping about him; his own fire warmed him, the fire of prophecy.

He spread his arms wide, taking in all the broad hilltop. Steep slopes bastioned it in the north and east; in the west rushed the deep flood of Suvien; southward it dipped gently into the levels of Han-Gilen, looking across the windswept land to the prince's white city.

"Easy to defend," said Cuthan. "With a good rampart all around and a good road up to your gate, you'll be as well served as any king alive."

"Better than most." Adjan paced off the edge of the hilltop. "There'll be water in any wells you sink; and there's space here for whole farmsteads."

"And the river to ride on and trade on," Cuthan said.

Mirain laughed as sometimes he did, for simple joy. "It will be the richest city in the world, and the greatest, and the most splendid. See: white walls, white towers;

163

Sun-gold upon the gates, and Sun's fire in its people, under the rule of the god."

Elian moved apart from the company about the king, through a city of shadows shaped out of power and sunlight for his servants to marvel at. She needed no such mummeries, who could see in truth as well as he. With a flicker of will she banished the image, leaving only the winter-dulled grass and the empty air and the fitful dazzle of sunlight.

Her feet had brought her to the bank of Suvien. The water ran black and cold, swirling about deep-rooted stones, eating away at the hillside. But the far bank rose sheer and implacable. There stood no wide welcoming hill, no seat of empire, but a jut of naked stone, black as the river, shunned even by the birds.

"Endros Avaryan," she said to herself. Avaryan's Throne. A curse lay on it. Curse, or fate, or prophecy. No man might walk there unless he be born of a god; and even he could not tarry lest he go mad and die.

No man but Mirain, who had been little more than a child when he ventured it: young and wild and armored in his lineage, and mad enough to dare even that great curse.

And Elian. He had not known that she was following him until he stood breathless on the summit. She, climbing to within a man-length of him, set her foot upon a stone which gave way beneath it, and fell with a sharp despairing cry.

She had not fallen far: another length down the sheer cliff to a sliver of ledge. But he, in rage that was half deadly fear, plunged down to catch her. Between her own fear and her own young, erratic magery, she shot out of his hands, up the last of the crag onto the bare cold stone. There she lay gasping until he dragged her up. "Fool!" he cried. "Idiot! Lunatic! You'll die here!"

His voice, which was breaking, cracked from a bellow into a shriek. She could not help it; she began to laugh. She roared with it, rolling on the top of Avaryan's throne, with the sun himself glaring down at her sacrilege.

Mirain snatched her up and shook her until at last she quieted. She looked up at him, blinking, hiccoughing. Somehow she managed to say, "I won't die."

"The curse—"

"I won't." She knew it as surely as she knew that the curse was real. It thrummed in the stone. "It can't touch me. I'm not a man."

Suddenly he was hardly taller than she, and changed: his free hair braided, his throat circled by the torque of his father's priesthood. She swayed for a moment in the throes of memory. So caught, timeless, she saw Mirain-then and Mirain-now, and beyond and about him a sweep of darkness shot with diamond light.

His hands gripped her, steadying her. "Look," she said. "The tower. But who would dare—"

"Tower?"

Was he blind? "Tower! There, on Endros. Someone's built a tower—on—" Her voice died. It was clear, so clear. Tall and terrible like the crag, black stone polished smooth as glass, wrought without door or window, and on its pinnacle a sun. Yet even as she gazed at it, it shimmered and shrank. There was only the rock and the wind and the empty sky.

Suddenly she was cold, bone-cold. Mirain said nothing, only spread his cloak about them both. Her will tensed to pull away; her body huddled into the warmth. Thoughts babbled about her, orderless and shieldless, bastard children of minds without power. Some were amused, and some were annoyed, and some were even envious, knowing only what mere eyes knew, dark head and bright one close together and one cloak between them.

"It's me they envy," said Mirain.

"And me they laugh at." Her shivering had stopped, her visions faded. Her body was her own again. Smoothly she slid away from him. He let her go; which, irrationally, roused her temper. She strode past him through the knot of guards and friends and hangers-on, daring them to stare. None did. They were all most carefully considering the city that would be.

Ilhari was grazing on the southern slope, eyed by a stallion or two: Ilarios' gold, Cuthan's tall blue dun. Halenan's grey, whom she rather favored, was not among them. With Anaki so close to her time, the prince did not like to ride far from her, nor would Mirain ask it.

Elian laid her cheek against the warm thick coat, breathing in the scent of wind and grass and senel-hide. "Oh, sister," she said, "you have all the blessings. No fates and prophecies, and no family to grieve you."

The mare raised her head, laying back her ears at the dun, who was venturing too close. Prudently he retreated. She returned to her grazing. Ah yes, seneldi had sense, though the stallions could be a nuisance. One came into heat, one mated, one carried a foal. One bore it, one nursed it, one weaned it, and that was that. No endless two-legged follies. But then, humans were cursed, were they not? Never fully weaned and always in heat.

Elian laughed unwillingly. "Straight to the mark, as always. And when you add power, it's worse than a curse. It's pure hell."

Ilhari snorted. Follies. A good gallop, that would cure them.

Or obscure them. Elian settled into the saddle; the mare sprang forward.

They ran abreast of the wind round the hill that would be the City of the Sunborn, out upon the open plain. Ilhari bucked; Elian whooped. This was senel-wisdom, beast-wisdom: fate and folly be damned, cities and kings and the hope of dynasties. Whoever ruled, the earth remained, and the wind, and the sun riding above them. Elian began to sing.

WHEN ILHARI BROUGHT ELIAN BACK TO THE HILLTOP, THE escort was gathered in a hollow out of the wind, clearing away the last of the daymeal. Adjan, whose skill in such things came close to wizardry, had kindled a fire; the wine which Mirain passed to Elian in his own silver traveling-cup was steaming hot and pungent with spices.

As she sipped it, Ilarios set beside her a napkinful of bread and meat. This was an ill day for her mind-shields. She caught a guardsman's vision of her fortune: to be waited on by emperors, when by right, for abandoning her post, she should have had nothing but a reprimand.

She smiled a little wryly, a little wickedly. Ziad-Ilarios smiled back. Mirain did not see; he had turned to speak to Cuthan.

Elian's fingers tightened round the figured surface of the cup. Her mood was as treacherous as a wind in spring. Perhaps her courses—

She drank deep of the cooling wine. No, she could not lay the blame on her body. She had been so since the army turned toward Han-Gilen, and worse since she came there.

"Yes," Mirain was saying to Cuthan, "it has begun. He knew it would be today."

The young lord laughed. "One would think he was the one who was birthing the child."

"I think he would if he could. But Anaki knows her business. She bears well and easily, and as serenely as she does all else."

"A very great lady, that one."

"Greater than most people know. She could be a queen if she chose."

"An empress?"

Mirain tossed back his heavy braid and laughed. "Her lord might allow it, under duress. But she never would."

Carefully Elian set down the empty cup. She could sense what Mirain spoke of, that the birthing had begun. It would not go on long, as such things went. With Anaki it never did. By the time the riders reached the city, the banners would be flying, green for a royal daughter.

The wine's warmth had faded. Elian was suddenly, freezingly cold.

*   *   *

As the last light of Avaryan touched the turrets of the city, no banners flew there, either princess green or princely gold. Ah well, thought Elian, it was early yet. And she was a fool for thinking so much of it. What did it matter to her how long Anaki lay in childbed? She was no part of it. She had sundered herself from her kin.

Neither prince nor princess took the nightmeal in hall. Mirain, alight still with the dream of his city, was inclined to tarry, spreading great rolls of parchment on a cleared table, bending over them with brush and stylus. When Elian withdrew, he was deep in colloquy with a small man in blue, her father's master builder.

"When he dreams," said Ilarios beside her, "he dreams to the purpose."

She walked with him down the lamplit corridor. "Mirain has no dreams. Only true visions. Even when he was a child, he never said *if*. He always said *when*."

"Superb in his confidence, that one." The high prince clasped his hands behind him, studying her. "Lady, are you troubled?"

Her brows knit. "Why should I be?"

He shrugged slightly.

She turned with the sharpness of temper, striding down a side passage. After a moment's hesitation he followed her. She did not look at him, but she saw him too clearly, a golden presence on the edge of vision. "Why do you always wear gold? Is it a law?"

"I thought it suited me."

"It does," she said.

"Should I try another color, for variety? Green, maybe? Scarlet?"

"Black. That would be striking."

He bowed, amused. "Black it shall be, then. An incognito. Have you ever marked this? If a man wears always one color or fashion, he has but to change it and no one will know him."

"Everyone knows you."

"Yes? I venture a wager, lady. Any stakes you name."

She stopped. He was laughing, delighted with himself. "What would you venture, my lord?"

"I, my lady—I would wager the topaz in my coronet, against . . ." He paused, eyes dancing. "Against a kiss."

Her lip curled. "Then you are a fool. If I win, I gain a great jewel; if I lose, I lose nothing by it."

"Well, two kisses, and a lock of your hair."

"And this knife to cut it with."

"Done, my lady." He bowed over her hand, half courtly, half mocking. "Shall I escort you to your chamber?"

"My thanks," she said, "but no."

He knew her well, now. He did not try to press her. She watched him go, turning then, letting her feet lead her as they pleased. Where she wished to go, she did not know. Some of the palace ways teemed with people; she sought those less frequented, winding through the labyrinth, yet with no fear of losing herself. No child of the Halenani could do that, not in this place which the Red Princes had built.

At last she paused. The door before her was different from the others, richly carved with beasts and birds. It opened easily at the touch of her hand.

Within, all was dark, with the hollowness of disuse. She made a witchlight in the palm of her hand and advanced slowly. Nothing had changed. There was the bed with its green hangings; the carpet like a flowery meadow; the table and the great silver mirror; and her armor on its frame like a guardsman in the gloom. Over it lay a silken veil, flung there she could not remember when, and left so because it suited her whimsy.

Setting the light to hover above her head, she took up the veil. Its fineness caught and rasped upon her callused fingers. She draped it, drawing it across her cheek. The mirror reflected a paradox: a royal squire with the head of a maiden. She laughed, an abrupt, harsh sound.

Her gowns lay all in their presses, scented with sweet herbs. Green, gold, blue, white. No scarlet. Red gowns and red hair made an ill match.

She drew out a glow of deep green, splendid yet simple, velvet of Asanion sewn with a shimmer of tiny firestones. Prince Orsan had had it made for her, the princess and her ladies stitched the myriad jewels, a gift for Elian's birth-feast.

It fit still. She had grown no taller and certainly no broader, though the bodice was somewhat more snug than she remembered. Now the strangeness was reversed: boy's shorn mane, maiden's ripening body. Her face hung between, more maid indeed than boy, with a drawn and discontented look. "Life," she said to it, "seems not to agree with you."

She sank down. The full skirt pooled about her. Unconsciously she smoothed it, as a bird will preen even in a cage, gazing beyond it at the heap of scarlet which was her livery. Here, exactly here, she had begun it all. And here in the end she had returned. To sneer at what she had been; to exult over her victory; to huddle on the floor, too bleak to weep, too empty to rage.

This then was her oath's fulfillment. A closed door and a dark room, and no one to care where she went. No one to ask, no one to tell—

She flung herself to her feet. "Gods damn them all!"

THE PRINCE WAS NOT IN HIS CHAMBER NOR THE PRINCESS IN her bower; the bed they shared was empty, their servants meeting Elian's fire with carefully bland faces. Having humbled herself so far, she could not bear to be so thwarted. "Where are they, then?" she snapped.

It was her father's body-servant who answered, perfect in his dignity; but when she was very small he had played at hunt-and-hide with her. His eyes upon her were warm and brimming, radiating welcome. "Surely my lady knows: they are with my lord Halenan."

Who was with his lady in his own great house, in a shell of silence. No royal child of Han-Gilen could be laid open at birth to the sorceries of an enemy; so was each born within the shield of its kinsfolk's power. In her preoccupation with her own troubles, she had forgotten.

She paused. Surely her errand could wait. Shame was creeping in, and shyness, and some of her old obstinacy. The morning would be a good time, a glad time, better and gladder than this. No one needed her now. She would only be in the way.

Somehow she had a mantle about her and a page before her with a lamp, and the gate-guards were letting her pass, bowing before her.

Halenan's house under the sun was high and fair, set in the lee of the temple, with gardens running down to the river. In this black night it loomed like the crag of Endros, its gate shut and barred, all within as silent to the mind as to the ear.

The guard was long in coming to her call, longer still in opening the gate. But he did not forbid her the entry, although he eyed her in what might have been suspicion.

There were shields within shields. This that caught her upon the threshold had a dark gleam, a hint of her father. She flared her own red-gold against it. Slowly it yielded. A moment only; firming behind her, on guard against any threat.

Even in her cloak of fur, she was cold. But was it not always so? She had never been outside it before, but in its heart, lending her own power to the rest. She gathered her skirts and pressed forward.

Twice more she was halted, twice more she proclaimed her right to pass. And a door was open before her with a woman on guard, and within, the birthing.

Her father sat on the ledge of a shuttered window, eyes closed, yet seeing all about him with the keenness of power. Her mother, lovely as always, elegant as always, rested beside him with a lamp above her and a bit of needlework in her hands. On the bed lay Anaki, Hal's bright head bent over her and the birthing-woman intent upon her. It was like a vision in water, silent but for the rasp of Anaki's breath; and in the mind, nothing.

The prince's eyes opened. The princess turned her head. Halenan looked up.

Elian stepped through the door, and staggered. Pain—there was always that. But this was worse—worse—

She never remembered crossing the room, but she was there, beside the bed. Anaki's sweet plain face was streaming wet, distorted with pain, yet she managed a smile, a word. "Sister. So glad—"

Halenan silenced her with a caress. His smile was less successful than hers, but his voice was stronger. "Yes, little sister, we are glad."

"What," Elian said. "What is—"

"Our daughter," he answered almost lightly, "takes after you. All contrary, and fighting us into the bargain."

Contrary indeed. Elian, unfolding a tendril of power, found the child head upward, feet braced. And being what she was, magebred, she fought not only with her body but with her infant power, struggling against this force that would compel her into the cruel light, striking at her mother in her blind and blinded terror. Anaki had power of her own, both strong and quiet, but this battle had sapped it; she could not both bear her body's pain and soothe her child.

"She needs greater healing than I can give," the Red Prince said. He had come to Elian's side and taken her hand, calmly, as if nothing had ever happened between them. She let her cold fingers rest in his warm strong ones. She felt dull, numbed, as if she had endured a long siege of weeping. Of course it would happen so. It must. Unless—

"Mirain," she said. "He has the power. He can—"

Her brother looked at her. Simply looked, without either pleading or condemnation.

Her eyes slid away. Anaki strained under the midwife's hands, twisting, crying out with effort and with agony. The lash of power from within, untrained, uncontrolled, turned the cry to a shriek.

Elian's own power reached without her willing it, in pure instinct, clasping, bending, *thus.* There were words in it. *Ah no, child. Would you kill your mother? Come with me. Come, so. . . .*

*   *   *

"ELIAN." SHE STARED AT WHAT HAL SET IN HER HANDS. Dark red, writhing feebly, and howling with all its strength. Above it hovered its father's broad white grin. "And Elian," he said in high glee. "What better name for your very image?"

"My very—" She drew her namesake close, and returned her brother's grin with one that wobbled before it steadied. "She is beautiful, isn't she?"

"Breathtakingly." Halenan reclaimed his offspring, to lay her in her mother's arms. Anaki was grey-pale and weary, but she smiled.

Elian's knees buckled. Hands caught her. Many. Her father's; her mother's. Mirain's. She blinked. "Where—how—"

"Rest first."

She fought free, glaring at Mirain. "You knew! You plotted this. You *made* me—"

"We did," Mirain agreed. "Later, if you like, you may continue in your cowardice. Today you will be civil. And that, madam, is a command."

His eyes flickered upon her. Half of it was laughter; half of it was not. She looked past him. She came of a proud family. They would never plead, would never even hint at it. Yet the eyes upon her were warm, offering, if only she would take. Only if she would take.

Her throat closed. She held out her hands. "Since," she choked out, "since my king commands . . . and since . . ."

They were there, all of them who could be, and Anaki in spirit, enfolding her. In that circle where she most longed to be strong, she broke and cried like a child.

Seventeen

FROM THE SCREENED GALLERY, ONE COULD LOOK DOWN into the hall and not be seen oneself. Which was why that narrow balcony was called the ladies' bower, and the sentry post.

Elian supposed that she was a little of both. Although she had returned to Mirain's livery, a gown or two had found its way among the coats and trousers in her clothing chest. Her mother had not even looked askance at her. The joy of reunion was still too fresh, and with it the fear of a new flight.

Not so long ago, she would have been glad to see her mother taking pains to voice no censure, to accept her as she was. But now that she had the upper hand, it did not matter. Victories were always so. Savorless, even a little shameful.

She shook herself hard. *That* victory deserved no sweetness. The best of it was the joy: that she had her family again; that her battle with them had been no battle at all, only her own craven stubbornness. Even now her father's mind brushed hers; she felt the warmth of his smile, although he seemed to be intent upon the petitioner before his throne. Her brother stood behind him. Mirain, though king and emperor, did not interfere in this business of the ruling prince, but effaced himself among the higher nobles. Or tried. Not a man there but knew where he was, he who without height or beauty or splendor of dress remained the Sunborn.

Elian peered down at the gathering. Today Ilarios meant to win his wager; restraining power, she left the search to her eyes. Who would have believed that there were so many fair-haired people in Han-Gilen? Or that so many of them would choose to wear dark colors on this day of all days?

Some of them were women. Some were too tall, some too broad or too narrow, most too dark of face: Gileni brown or bronze. One with a mane of the true bright gold—but no, it was a woman, and she wore deep blue.

There, at last. Near the somber-clad scribes, almost among them. That angle of the head was unmistakable. Somehow he had disposed of his shadows, or they had concealed themselves too perfectly even for her eyes' finding. He wore a scribe's fusty gown, and he carried a writing case; his hair was pulled back and knotted at the nape of his neck. Without that golden frame, his face seemed rounder, younger. Yet he still looked royal; imperial.

No one took the slightest notice of him.

A man approached him, a lord of the court. Knowing surely who he was, speaking to him. Ilarios bent his head in what he must have deemed to be humility. And the lord gestured, lordly-wise, and Asanion's high prince sat cross-legged at the end of the line of scribes and began to write to the nobleman's dictation.

Was that a smile in the corner of his mouth?

When Ilarios left the hall, Elian was waiting for him. He clutched his writing case to his breast and bowed, all servile; but when he straightened he was laughing for sheer delight.

She laughed with him, and kissed him. There was no

thought in it. It was very sweet, and he was startled, which made it sweeter still.

He took her hand. "Lady," he said breathlessly. "Oh, lady." But though he looked and sounded even younger than she, he remained Ilarios. "There are better places than this to collect the rest of my wager."

A lady passed with all her retinue. Seeing the scribe and the squire together in the passage, she beckoned imperiously. "Here, penman! I have need of you."

Elian stiffened. But Ilarios' eyes danced. Oh, people were blinder even than she had thought, if they reckoned him a meek commoner. "Yes, madam," he said. "At once, madam."

Elian caught his sleeve, slowing his retreat. "When you finish. The south tower."

His smile was his only response.

He was slow in coming to the tower. But it was a pleasant place, high up over the city, with her father's library at the bottom of it. Choosing a book at random, Elian mounted the long twisting stair.

The chamber at the top had been a schoolroom not so long ago, and would be again when Halenan's children were old enough to leave their nurse for a tutor. The furnishings were ancient and battered and exceedingly comfortable, laden with memories. The tallest chair had been hers, because she was the smallest, and because it had the only cushioned seat, though the cushion was stone-hard and full of lumps. Her behind, settling into it, remembered each hill and valley.

She leaned upon the heavy age-darkened table. Its top was much hacked and hewn, inscribed with the names of bored pupils. Royal names, most of them. *Halenan* was very common, carved in numerous hands. Nine, Hal had always insisted, although their firstfather could not possibly have learned his letters here, wild wanderer that he was, with nothing to his name when he came to Han-Gilen but a sword and a gift of wizardry. But Hal had carved the ancient name again, making it ten, and ruined his second-best dagger in doing it.

Her finger traced the letters, gliding from them across the ridged wood to the bright gleam of a wonder. It looked like a sunburst marvelously wrought of inlaid gold. But no goldsmith had set it there to gleam incongruously amid the childish scrawls. Mirain had done it by no will of his own, not long after his mother died, when power and temper roiled in him and made his grief a deadly thing. Pricked by some small slight—a sally from Halenan, or his tutor's reprimand—he had risen and braced himself, and his power had come roaring and flaming. Yet at the last instant he had mastered his rage; the power, thwarted, too potent to be contained, had left this mark of its passing.

With a swift movement Elian left chair and table. High narrow windows cleft the wall at intervals, letting in the cool sunlight. She knelt beside the hooded hearth, where a fire was laid neatly, as if there were daily need of it. Although flint and steel rested in their niche, she gathered a spark of power, held it a moment until its fierce heat began to sear her hand, and cast it upon the wood. Flames leaped up, red-gold like her hair, settling into their common red and yellow and burning blue.

Warmth laved her face. She had forgotten her book upon the table; she let it be, resting her eyes upon the dance of the fire. Shapes formed in it, images, past and present and to come. A corner of her mind struggled, protesting. The rest watched calmly. Peace-visions, these, with no taint of fear. Anaki and her si-Elian, small bright-downy head and smooth deep-brown one. Anaki was smiling a deep, secret smile, and her plainness was beautiful. Prince Orsan and his princess, all their royal dignity laid aside, laughing together, and after a time moving close, mirth forgotten, until body touched body. Ilhari with Hal's grey stallion in a green meadow, silver on fire gold.

Elian flushed with more than the heat of the fire.

Seeing, this certainly was, but all her teaching had told her that the seer could shape what she saw. Even unwitting.

Sharply, almost angrily, she banished the senel-shapes. The flames were flames, no more. No visions. No longings.

And what do you long for? Her inner voice was mocking. The fire rose and shaped itself. Once, and once again. Dark, gold. Emperor and emperor to be.

True child of the Halenani, she. Beset with maiden moods, she settled only upon the very highest. The one, she could have if she but said the word. The other . . .

The other vanished. Ilarios knelt by the fire, still in his scribe's gown. His face was as white as bleached bone; his eyes were the burning sulfur-yellow of a cat's. With tight-controlled savagery he ripped the bindings from his hair. It poured down his back, tumbled into his face.

Her teeth unclamped from her lip. She tasted blood. "My lord," she said. "Has someone offended you?" And when he did not answer: "Your wager is well won. Too well, maybe. If anyone has spoken ill to you, you should forgive him. He cannot have known—"

He flung back his hair. For all his leashed fury, his voice was mild. Alarmingly so. "No one has slighted me. Though to be a scribe and not the high prince . . . it is interesting. One sees so much. And one is never noticed. Until—" His breath came ragged. "Until one is forced to reveal oneself."

She waited.

He contemplated his fists clenched upon his thighs. His breathing quieted, but the tension did not leave him. "We have had an embassy. So many, there have been, since the Sunborn came to Han-Gilen. This one was small, plain, and to the point. And from my father." He looked up, a flash of burning gold. "With all due respect to his divine majesty, the Lord An-Sh'Endor has followers in plenty. He does not need the heir of Asanion."

"When?" She could barely speak; even the single word took all her strength.

His smile was bitter. "Oh, I need not take flight at

once. That would be unseemly. I am given three days to
order my affairs."

"And if you do not go?"

"I am to be reminded that, although I have no legiti-
mate brothers, I have fifteen who are sons of concubines.
All grown, ambitious, and eager to serve my royal father."

She sat still. After a long moment she said, "You
knew this would come."

"I knew it." He unclenched his fists, first the right,
then the left. "There are my half brothers. There are also
my full sisters. Four of them. Two, yet unwed, are priestesses of various of the thousand rapacious gods. Two are
wed to princes. Ambitious princes. One is rich, but not
fabulously rich; the other reckons himself poor. And
Asanion's throne is wrought all of pure gold."

Her hand went out. Living gold stirred under it; then
warm flesh. Panther-swift, panther-strong, he seized her.
"Lady," he said. "Elian. Come with me."

Never in all her life had she been so close to a man.
Body to body. Heart to thudding heart.

Her hands were crushed between. She worked them
free, linked them behind his neck. "Come with me," he
said again.

He was fire-warm, trembling, yet all his anger had
left him. She looked into his eyes, sun-gold now, both
burning and tender.

"By all the gods, by your own bright Avaryan: Elian,
Lady of Han-Gilen, I love you. I have always loved you.
Come with me and be my bride."

Her teeth set. Her body burned; there was an ache
between her thighs. Every line of him was distinct against
her.

"I will make you my empress," he said. "Or if you will
not have that, if a throne of gold seems too high and cold
for you, then I will abandon it." He laughed, brief and
wild. "You yearn for freedom; so too do I. Let us disguise
ourselves and flee, north or east or south, or even west
where my face is a common thing; and we can make our
way as we can, and live as we please, and love as the

simple folk love, for no fate or pride or dynasty, but only for ourselves." His arms tightened. "Oh, lady! Will you? Will you love me?"

His passion was like wind and fire; his beauty pierced her heart. And yet the cold corner of her mind observed, *How young he looks!*

He was nineteen. But the cool, controlled high prince had seemed a man grown. As old as Mirain, as Halenan, as—as her father.

He was no more than a boy.

A lovely, fiery, desperate boy. Her voice would not obey her and speak. Her body would not be silent.

This kiss was ages long and burning sweet.

At last they parted. Elian blinked, startled. Her eyes were brimming; her cheeks were wet. "I—" she began, and foundered, and began again. "I love you. But not—I am not worth a throne."

His joy blazed forth; he laughed with it, and yet he trembled. "A throne is worth nothing unless you share it with me."

"I love you," she repeated doggedly. "But—I am not—I must think!"

There was no quenching this new fire, although he tried. He did quell his face and his voice; but his eyes flamed. "Yes," he said in the gentlest of tones, "it is hard. You were away so long, and your quarrels are all so newly mended. But if you depart as my princess, will not your kin be glad?"

"Mother would be rather more than glad." She stiffened slightly; he released her, watching her with those hurting-bright eyes. "I have to think. Might you—could you—"

His smile was the one she remembered, child-sweet yet not a child's at all. "I shall leave you to your thoughts. You need not hasten them. I have three days yet."

"Not so long. I can think— Tonight. After the night-bell."

He gestured assent. "Here?"

Her eyes flicked about, flinched, closed. "No. Somewhere else. Somewhere—" She paused. "Somewhere for solitude. The temple. No one will come there so late."

"The temple," he said, "after the night-bell." He rose and stooped, brushing her lips with his. "Until then, beloved. May your god guide you."

Elian laughed wildly into the empty space; and then she wept; and then she laughed again. And squire service still to do. She straightened her livery and smoothed her hair and went down to it.

THERE WAS LITTLE ENOUGH TO DO, AND THAT LITTLE SHE did ill. Mirain, intent on some business for which she cared nothing, dismissed her early. Not in disgrace, to be sure. He hardly knew she was there, nor cared.

A bath calmed her a little. She performed her duties of the bedchamber: turned down the bed, filled the nightlamp, readied Mirain's bath. He liked a very little scent, for the freshness: leaves of the *ailith* tree mingled with sweet herbs. As she cast them into the steaming water, a darkness filled her mind; she began to shake.

"Fool," she cursed herself. "Idiot! A lovesick heifer has more grace."

Was it love, or was it fear? Of herself; of Ilarios; of—whatever one chose to name. Of falling after all into the trap which she had fled.

She had kept her oath. She had come to Mirain; she had fought for him. The other, older vow . . . need she keep it? Did she even wish to?

Voices sounded in the bedchamber. Mirain bidding goodnight to a lord or two, dismissing his servants.

She willed herself to rise, but her knees would not straighten. If she wedded Ilarios, she would not do this again. Servant's labor. Menial things: scenting Mirain's bath, braiding his hair, arranging his cloak. Cleaning his armor, grooming his senel, riding at his right hand. With Hal on his left and Ilhari under her and the wind in her face.

He stood in the doorway in his simple Ianyn kilt,

with his cloak flung over his shoulder. How dark he was, how deceptively slight; how deadly bright his eyes.

They saw nothing. She stood. "Your bath is ready. Shall I wait on you?"

Most often he refused. Tonight he said, "Yes. My hair needs washing."

He grimaced as he said it; in spite of herself she smiled. "You could cut it," she said.

He laughed a little. "That would be too easy. And," he added with a wicked glint, "I wouldn't need you to tend it for me."

Her throat closed. He never noticed; he was stripping off his kilt, laying it with his cloak beside the great basin. With his back turned to her, he took up a loinguard and began to put it on.

"Leave that," she said harshly. And when he glanced over his shoulder: "Am I any more delicate than your bath-maids in Ianon? I know what a man looks like."

He paused. After a moment he shrugged, dropped the loinguard, turned.

The heat raced from her soles to her crown and back again, stumbling between. But she made herself look at him. All of him.

With the suggestion of a smile he stepped into the bath. She began to loose his braid. Her fingers fumbled; silently she cursed herself.

Mirain lay in the water, eyes shut, utterly at ease. He looked like a great indolent cat. A panther, with a velvet hide and an air of tight-leashed power.

Her eyes slitted. A wildness unfolded within her. Even her shirt, soft and brief as it was, grated against her burning skin. She shed it. Mirain waited with the perfect, oblivious calm of royalty, for her to serve him.

She filled her hand with cleansing-foam. Still Mirain had not moved. But he was not asleep. His awareness hovered, flawless as a globe of crystal. Great mage and great king, god's son, child of the morning, he was warm and drowsy, and he smiled, drifting in the scented water.

She bent. He tasted of wine, and of honeycakes, and of fire.

The crystal flamed. Strength like a storm of wind bore her up, back. The world reeled.

Yet did not fall. Black eyes opened wide. She gasped, drowning.

Elian! It was silent; it filled her brain and washed it clean.

She lay on a heap of damp softness. Clothing, she realized; drying-cloths; a cloak lined with fur. And on her, all the length of her, a body as bare as her own: little taller, little broader save in the shoulder, and fully as male as she was female.

Mirain looked down at her. His eyes were veiled, and yet they glittered.

Say it, she willed him. *Say that you want me.*

He moved, half rising, to lie beside her. His face was calm. He was not going to speak. He was going to let her go, or stay, or do nothing at all.

Her demon sat up, prick-eared. No strength of hers could quell it. It said, "It was never like this with Ilarios."

He was still, like a stone king.

"He's very sweet. He warms my body. But this—no wonder you have so few women!"

"Am I so revolting?"

She had pierced a wall or two. His voice came deep and almost harsh; his face was frightening. Yet she bit down hard on laughter. "Dear heaven, no! Never. But if your kiss can drive your own sister mad, what if you give more? There must be very few who can bear the full fire of you."

"There is none," he said, still in that half-growl.

"None at all?" The laughter escaped, although she caught it swiftly and strangled it. "Not your lady regents? Not your nine beauties of the bath? Not—"

His hand stopped her mouth. "None." Her eyes danced disbelief. He glared. "There have been women in my bed. How not? Priest's vows can't hold a king. But the fire . . . is something else." He released her, pushing back his hair. Half wet, half dry, it covered his shoulders like a tattered cloak. "Though I fancy, from milord's dazed look of late, that you are stronger than I. Or hotter."

Her temper reared up and began to burn. "I've given him no whit more than I've given you."

"Ah," he said, drawing it out until she could have struck him. Then he laughed, painfully. "Poor prince! He has no power to shield him. Take care, lady; mere mortals are no match for the likes of us."

"I'm no god's get!" She scrambled to her knees. "He wants me to marry him. To go with him when he goes, and be his empress."

"And will you?"

Iron. Iron and adamant, and royal refusal to say a word, even one word of aught but what befit a brother. "I don't know!" she shouted at him.

And sank down upon her heels. For that was not what she had meant to say at all.

"I love him," she said. The mask never stirred. The lids had lowered over the black eyes. "I do love him," she repeated. "It's impossible not to. He's so splendid, strong and gentle, merry and wise, all royal and all beautiful. There's nothing in him that isn't perfect of its kind. And he loves me to distraction."

She looked at herself and at Mirain, and laughed until a sob broke it. "Here I sit like a whore with her client, telling over old lovers. But I told him I'd choose tonight, and I don't know. I can't even think. But I should!"

"Know? Or think?"

"Both!" Her fists clenched over her eyes. She saw a red darkness shot with stars. "Every scrap of sense I have, and most of my body, cries out to me to take him. But something stops me. It isn't fear. I could live as Empress of Asanion. I could make an empire in my image: even that one, with all its thousand years of queens." He said nothing. She let the light in. It hurt. Blessed, cursed pain. "Damn it, Mirain," she said. "Why don't you say it and get it over?"

"What am I to say?"

Cold, that. Kingly. She knew the pride of it. That same pride had held her apart from her kin until death's own shadow drove her back to them.

"I heard you," she said, not too unsteadily, "before Vadin left for Ianon."

Mirain's jaw clenched, eased. She wished that he would rage, or laugh, or turn away in shame. Anything but this damnable stillness. "What made you believe that we spoke of you?"

"Vadin told me. And," she said, "I knew."

"And?"

"And." She wanted to touch him. Her hand would not obey her. "It wasn't too late. Then. Maybe even now—" She could not look at him. She fixed her eyes on her feet. "The vow I meant to keep was to be your queen. If you would have me."

"Duty." His voice was soft. "Your given word. Your wildness is all illusion. You live by your princely honor. Else," he said, "else you would long since have fled us all, and gone to a place where none could bind you."

"I've . . . thought of it." She knotted her hands together until they began to hurt. "I would love you if you asked."

Her demon had said it. Mirain laughed with no mirth at all. "And if I refuse?"

"Damn you, Mirain. *Damn* you!" And herself, for asking that he ask.

He was as calm as ever, and as maddening in his stubbornness. "You want me to make your choice for you. I won't, Elian. Your heart is your own. Only you can follow it."

"Do you even have one?" He would not deign to answer that. "Yes, I went to you because I promised. And because I loved you. And because Ilarios could all too easily have taken your place; and that would have been a betrayal."

"Of what? Your leaden duty?"

Her eyes narrowed. Her lips drew back from her

teeth. "They're right, your enemies. You suffer slaves and vassals. But never an equal."

"My equal would never demand that I do her thinking for her."

Proud, proud, proud. They were too well matched, he and she; too damnably alike. Ilarios' pride was subtler. Saner. More sweetly reasonable. He would never cast back love because it was less perfect than his whim demanded.

She rose. Mirain watched her, and there was no yielding in him. "Your bath grows cold, my lord," she said, meeting stone with stone. "And I have a promise to keep."

AFTER ALL HER TARRYING, ELIAN WAS EARLY. THE NIGHT-bell rang even as she passed the gate of the temple.

Within, all was quiet. It was a very old temple, and very holy; shadows veiled the heavy pillars and lost themselves in the great vault of the dome. In its open center glittered a single, icy star.

Elian trod the worn stones, moving slowly. Patterns unfolded beneath her feet, broken and blurred with time: leaves and flowers, men and beasts, birds of the air and fishes of the sea. Some ran up the pillars, twining round them, glinting here and there with gold or a precious stone.

From all this faded splendor the altar stood apart, raised high upon a dais. It alone bore no ornament or jewel: a simple square of white stone, unadorned. But behind it upon the wall shone and flamed the only likeness of himself which the god would ever allow. Gold, pure and splendid, dazzling even in the light of the vigil lamp; yet in all but size, the image of the Sun in Mirain's hand.

Elian bowed low before it. There was no prayer in her. After a moment she turned from it.

Lesser altars stood in sheltered niches round the circle of pillars. Some were tombs of old princes. One held the body of the god's chosen, his bride, the priestess Sanelin. And one, very small, very ancient, drew her to itself. No high lord or lady rested there; no gold adorned it, no carving lightened it. Even its stone had not the pure beauty of the high altar: plain grey granite, rough-hewn and set into the floor. Its top was smoothed somewhat—that much one could see, and no more. For it was covered with darkness, cloth woven it seemed of the very shadows; yet that was no altar cloth but a hooded mantle. And beneath it, a hollow in the stone, and water that never fouled or shrank away, but remained ever the same, clear and pure as water fresh-drawn from a spring. The Water of Seeing, veiled in the mantle of the Prophet of Han-Gilen.

It knew her. It called to her. *Take my veil. Look at me. Master me. Prophet. Prophet of Han-Gilen.*

She had schooled herself to resist it. But power would never be denied. Had it bent her mind even in her father's palace, bidden her meet Ilarios here, to bring her to itself?

Look at me. You know not what course to choose. Look at me and see.

"I'll choose him," she whispered, "to escape from you."

Look at me, it chanted. *Master me.*

"No!"

She spun on her heel. She had put on a gown, for reasons she could not have explained even to herself; its heavy skirts swirled about her ankles. In the same movement, her cropped hair brushed her cheeks.

Would she ever be aught but a contradiction?

A shadow stirred among the shadows. Lamplight glimmered on gold. She leaped forward; stopped short; advanced more sedately, unsmiling.

Ilarios took her hands and kissed them. He wore his black robe still, with a dark cloak flung over it. But the hood lay on his shoulders, and his hair was free.

"My lord," she said very softly.

"My lady." It was not a question. Yet a question throbbed in it, an eagerness harshly curbed, a fear he dared not admit. He would be a courtier if she asked it, speak of small things, circle gracefully round his heart's desire.

She could not bear it. To play the courtier; to make her choice. His hands were warm and strong and trembling deep within. His face was pale. His gaze was level and very bright.

"My lord." She swallowed hard. "I— Forgive me. Oh, please forgive me."

She did not know what she meant. But the light drained from his eyes; his face lost its last glimmer of color.

And she cried, "I can't be what you need me to be! I can't be your empress or your wandering love. I can't love you that way. It isn't in me."

"It is," he said. His eyes were bitter. "But not for me."

She tossed her head, in protest, in pain. "Please understand. I want to accept you. I long to. But I can't. Han-Gilen holds me. My squire-oath binds me. I have to live out my fate here."

"I understand," he said. He was very calm. Too calm. "You are of your realm as I am of mine. And when the war comes, as it must come, for this world cannot sustain two empires—better for us both that we not be torn between the two enemies."

"There can still be an alliance. If—"

"There can be one. For a while. Perhaps for a long while: a year, a decade, a score of years. But in the end the conflict must come, and no union of ours may avert it. Empires take no account of lovers, even of lovers who are royal."

"No," she said. "No."

He smiled. It was sweet still, and sad, but there was nothing of innocence in it. There never had been, save in her foolish fancy. He was a royal Asanian, son of a thousand years of emperors. He said, "I can take you whether you give me yea or nay, whether it be wisdom or folly or plain blind insanity. Because you are my heart's love. Because without you I do not think that I can live."

He held her hands; she tensed to pull free, stilled. Shadows took shape: his guards in their eternal, unyielding black, cold-eyed, armed with Asanian steel. Her power could find no grip upon them.

"Yes," Ilarios said softly, "my bred warriors, my Olenyai. They are armed against magecraft. They are sworn to die for me, as you are sworn to die for your bandit king."

She stared at him. He was all new to her, his masks fallen, his gentleness no less for that it was not the simple whole of him. Mirain laughed as he slew, and wept for the wounded after. Ziad-Ilarios would weep in the slaying, and weep after, but his hand would be none the less implacable for that. As he would seize her, compel her, bear her away to be his bride.

She was not afraid. She was fascinated. How strange they grew, these royal males, in the face of a woman's intransigence. How wonderful to stand against them; how like the exhilaration of battle. She almost laughed. She was hemmed in, and she was free. She could choose one, both, neither. She could run away. She could die. She could do anything at all.

She looked at her hands held lightly in his, and up, into his pale taut face. Was this love, this sweet wildness? She wanted to kiss him. She wanted to strike him. She wanted to pull him down in the very temple, and have her will of him. She wanted to run far away, and cast aside all thought of him, and be as she had been before ever he came to beset her. Her mind cried out to him. *Yes! Yes, I will go. Damn my fates, damn my prophecies, damn my haughty king who will not, cannot speak.*

He could not hear her. He was no mage; only a mortal man. He would be emperor as he was born to be. He would age as all his kindred did, swiftly, cruelly, his gold all turned to grey, his beauty lost, his life burning to ash, as if his flesh could not endure the fire of his spirit.

She could make him live. She could be his strength, her flame suffice for both. And she could do it willingly, gladly, exultantly. If only her demon would yield up her tongue.

His finger traced her rigid cheek. His voice was infinitely tender, infinitely regretful. "I cannot do it. I cannot compel you. My grief; my fatal weakness. I love you far too much. You are a creature of the free air. In the Golden Palace you would wither and die. As must I. But I was born to it, and I have learned to accept it; even, a little, to overcome it. That much you have given me. For that alone may I thank the gods that I have known you." He bowed low and low. "I depart at dawn. May your god keep you."

She reached to catch him, to pull him back, to cry her protests. But he was gone. The night had taken him.

And she, utterly cold, utterly bereft, could not even weep.

Eighteen

ELIAN WANDERED FOR A VERY LONG WHILE, NOT CARING where she went, not caring where the hours fled. The tears would not come.

More than once she stopped short. She could still turn back. She could still run to him. Hold him. Tell him that she had lied, she had lost her wits, she had but tested him. Cruel, cruel testing. When had she ever been aught but cruel? Vadin had had the right of it. She had made it all a game. Played at love, played at loss. Held a man's heart as light as a pawn upon a board.

And she had dealt him a wound which might never heal.

She huddled in a cold and nameless corner, shivering, staring into the lightless dark. Now that she had lost him, she knew surely that she loved him. Her tongue and her cowardice had played her false. Her grief had reft her of will to do what she could do. Go back. Go with him. Be his empress. Raise strong children, bright-haired, with golden eyes. Bring him joy in the heart of his high cold empire.

Her head rose. There was a window before her; it looked out on darkness. The deep dark before dawn.

She was on her feet. She was running, blindly but with burning purpose. A door fell back before her. Chambers opened, rich, hung with Asanian silks, scented with Asanian unguents.

Empty.

Everywhere, empty. His guards, his servants, his belongings, gone. His presence darkened into bitter absence. But in the mound of cushions that had been his bed, something glittered. A topaz, filling her palm, rent from his coronet. It had no look of a trifle flung down and forgotten. It held a memory of his eyes. They gazed into her own, level, golden, loving her. Words drifted through her mind. "Alas, I am cursed with a constant nature. Where I take pleasure, there do I most prefer to love. And where I love, I love eternally."

She lay on her face in the alien silks, the jewel clenched in her fist, its edges sharpening to pain. She gripped it tighter. Waves of weeping rose within her, crested, poised and would not, could not fall. Higher, higher, higher. She gasped with the force of them.

Someone stood behind her. Had stood for a long while, waiting, watching. She dragged herself about.

Mirain looked at her and said nothing.

Her tongue had not yet had its fill of havoc. "He left me," it cried. "He left me before I could go to him. I *wanted* him!"

Still, silence. Mirain was a shadow, a gleam of eyes, a glimmer of gold in his ear, at his throat. She hated him with sudden, passionate intensity. "I don't want you!" she spat at him.

He sat on a heap of cushions, tucking his feet under him, tilting his head. He had always done that when she gave herself up to her temper. Studying it. Contemplating refinements of his own rages. Even in that, Mirain did not take kindly to a rival.

She raised her will against the spell. He was not her elder brother. She was not his small exasperating sister.

No more could he ever be her lover. He had refused to help her choose, and her choosing had gone all awry, and for that she had lost Ilarios.

"I am not yours," she said, soft and taut, "simply because I am not his. He has gone in despair, but I will follow him. You cannot stop me."

"I will not try."

"Then why are you here?"

His shoulder lifted. A shrug, northern-brief. But he was in trousers, his coat dark, plain, royal only in its quality. She was going mad, that she could notice it now, when all her mind was a roil of dark and gold, grief and rage and prophecy. "You need me," he said.

Arrogant; insufferable. "I need no one!"

"Not even your Asanian?"

"He needs me." She choked, gasped, tossed her throbbing head. Her hand hurt. She forced the fingers to open. The topaz glittered like gold and ice. "Let me go."

"Am I stopping you?"

She staggered up, fell against him. He caught her. She stood rigid. "I wish I had never been born."

"It might have spared us grief," he said.

She snapped erect. That was not even Mirain's art. That was her father's.

"But," he went on, "since you are here and all too much alive, you might consider that your choices are your own. You sent the high prince away. You, not I, not some nameless demon."

She tore free. His face was as calm as ever it could be. It was not even ugly. It was perfectly imperfect. Its cheek, unshaven, pricked her palm.

She recoiled. He had not moved. "I hate you," she said.

His head bowed, came up again. Accepting. "If you ride swiftly," he said, "you may catch him before the sun rises."

Her breath caught in her throat. Her eyes darted. Her heart was beating like a bird's: swift, shallow, frightening. Mirain was like an image of himself. "Cruel," her tongue whispered. "O cruel."

He smiled.

Her knees gave way. She sank down shaking. He stood over her, and his smile had faded to a memory, a glimmer at the corner of his mouth. She surged, pulled them down. He came without resistance; but his strength was potent in her hands, yielding of its free will, setting them face to glaring face. He blinked once, calmly. "Time passes," he pointed out.

She could not rise. She could hardly speak. The words that came were nothing of her own. "Do you love me?"

"That," he said, "is not what matters. Do *you* love *me?*"

"I love Ilarios!" Her demon seized her throat again, closing it. She bit down on her fist, hard. Mirain watched her. His chin had raised a degree. His eyes had hooded.

"No," she said hoarsely. "Not you too. I can't bear it. I can't lose you too!"

"Do you love me?"

There, her demon said. There was Ilarios' failing. He could not make himself be cruel to her. He was weak. Gentle. Compassionate. All fire and all sweetness, and a lover to the core of him.

Weak, the demon repeated. He had lost all his strength in words. He spoke of seizing her, binding her, bearing her away. He had not been strong enough to do it.

Mirain had let her go.

Because he knew what she would do. She belonged to him. She had always belonged to him.

And he to her.

She rocked from side to side. She did not want this. She did not want any of it. She wanted to go away, be free, be anyone but Elian of Han-Gilen.

"Do you love me?" Mirain, again. Pressing her. Driving her mad.

He seized her with bruising force. *"Do you love me?"*

"Not," she gritted, "while you are doing your best to break my arms."

He eased a fraction. Waited.

She looked at him. He did not look like a lover. He looked like a conqueror at the gates of a city. Waiting for it to surrender; or to defy him.

She gasped with the force of revelation. He was afraid. Mirain iVaryan, afraid.

And did she love him?

From her mother's womb. But as a woman loves a man . . . She studied him, carefully, thoroughly. And calmly. She had gone so far in her madness; she could be calm, she could think, she could ponder all her choices. And Ilarios was riding, fleeing the sunrise, setting the long leagues between himself and the woman he could never have. He had always known it. He had never thought to have her. But because he was Ilarios, he had done all that he might to win her.

He had lost her. She was of Han-Gilen; she would never be of Asanion. But in this much he had won. He had taught her that her fate was not fixed, that she could love another man than Mirain. That she could be free, if so she chose.

If so she chose.

She raised her chin to match Mirain's. "I give you leave," she said in High Gileni, "to sue for my hand."

His breath hissed. She could not tell if it was anger, or relief, or plain astonishment.

"You may court me," she said. "I do not promise to accept you."

He swallowed. Gaining courage? Restraining rage? Struggling not to laugh? "And what," he asked, "if I manage to discourage any other who should presume to seek your hand?"

"I can live unwed," she said, "my lord. The prospect does not frighten me."

His head tilted. "No; I can see that it does not." He rose and bowed, king to her queen. "I shall court you, my lady, by your gracious leave."

She inclined her head. And spoiled it all by bursting into laughter, and the laughter dissolved into tears, and

Mirain was holding her, rocking her, being for this last helpless moment her elder brother. She could not even hate him for it. He had taken all her hate, and shown her that it was only the other face of love.

"But not of a lover!" she cried, rebellious. "Only of a brother."

He said nothing. His silence was denial enough.

"IT SHOULDN'T MATTER SO MUCH," ELIAN SAID TO ILHARI. "I have my family back again, with Mirain and Sieli added to it. I have you. I have the whole of Han-Gilen, if it comes to that."

The mare shifted slightly under the brush. Her neck itched. Ah, there. She leaned into the rubbing.

"I miss him," Elian said through gritted teeth. "I miss him with every bone in my body. He filled so many emptinesses. He was friend, brother, lover. He was all that a woman could wish for. And I let him go. For what? For a man who won't even begin to court me."

Ilhari swiveled an ear at her. That came of two-legged stupidity. If she had let one of them mount her, then it all would have been settled. Her ache would be gone and so would they, painlessly.

Elian laughed with a catch at the end of it. "There are plenty of men who are like that, and women too; but neither of them is so minded. Nor I." She set down the brush. Even in the heaviness of her winter coat, Ilhari shone like polished copper. "Sometimes I wonder if I'm made wrong. Or maybe I'm mad. There's a wild streak in our family, that goes with the power. That one has it—the nameless one. She never settled on a man, either; and the god rejected her for an outlander. No wonder she did what she did."

She was a crawling on the skin. Ilhari twitched it off and investigated her manger. A grain or two lingered there; she lipped them up.

"I can't ever condone what she did. But I begin to understand her. She's still out there, you know. Hiding herself in shadows. Watching and listening. Waiting for me to break and go to her."

How could she watch? She was blind.

"Her power can see." Elian shivered. She had been a fool to say so much, even to Ilhari. The Exile had not beset her dreams since she came to Han-Gilen: her father's doing. No power for ill could enter his princedom. And she had been all tangled in her muddle of lovers.

But the Exile waited. Elian knew it beyond knowing. She would wait until Elian came, or until she died; or perhaps she had the power to wait beyond death, to ensnare her prey in bonds no living creature could break.

"Midwinter," Elian said, too quickly and too loudly. "Tomorrow is Midwinter. We'll sing the dark away this year with more power than we've ever had, with Mirain here to do the singing and dance the Dance. Do you know he won't be high priest? They've asked him three times, and the place has been empty this year and more, and they won't fill it, but no more will he. The world's throne is enough, he says. Let the temple choose someone more holy."

Thrones and temples meant nothing to the mare. She contemplated the heap of sweet hay which Elian spread for her, and began to nibble it.

"He'll take it in the end," Elian went on, mostly to herself. The Exile's presence was all but banished; but not quite. "It will be that, or leave the order without a leader. After all, they can't take a mere mortal, however wise and holy, with Avaryan's own son building his city half a day's ride away."

Cities were uncomfortable. So were stables. Open air was better, and an open plain.

"It's snowing."

The mare nudged her aside and trotted to the stable door. It swung open at a touch. Cold air swirled in, clothed in snow. Ilhari snorted at it and plunged into it, dancing and tossing her head.

Elian trudged in her wake, feeling irredeemably earthbound. The shouts of children rang in her ears. New though the storm was, they were all out in it, urchin and lordling alike. Nor were all of them so very small. She saw youths—men—in the garb of Mirain's army: southerners in particular, to whom a snowfall before Midwinter was a rare and precious thing, but great tall Ianyn soldiers too, fighting snow battles that began and ended in laughter.

White softness showered over her, blinding her. She gasped and wheeled. Mirain's grin was as wide and wicked as a child's. A bright-haired boychild clung to his legs and crowed at her: Halenan's eldest, Korhalion.

As she spluttered and glared, Mirain swung the child onto his shoulders and filled his hands with snow. "Throw it!" Korhalion cried. "Throw it!"

The last assault was melting into icy runnels down her back. With a smothered cry, half of wrath, half of mirth, she wheeled and bolted. She was as swift as a golden deer, darting through the great court. But Mirain was a panther, ridden by a laughing demon.

Everyone was cheering, some in Mirain's name, some in her own. Shapes flew past her: faces, bodies, a bright gleam of eyes. The cold and the race and the shouting came together like strong wine, filling her with a sweet wild delight. She eeled round a man like a tall pillar— Cuthan's white grin atop it—and stopped short behind, and laughed in Mirain's startled face; and slid beneath his snatching hands. Snatching herself great glistening armfuls, and wheeling, and flinging them upon him. Revenge had a taste like wild honey. She danced about him, taunting, showering him with snow.

He lunged. Korhalion's weight overbalanced him; he slipped and fell, bearing her down in a tangle of limbs, full into a drift of snow.

He lay winded, trying to laugh. Elian, whose fierce twist had brought her down between child and king, set Korhalion on his feet and brushed the snow from his face. His tongue quested after it; his eyes danced upon her. "Do it again?" he begged.

Mirain struggled up and cuffed him lightly. "Not

quite yet, imp. Every racer needs a brief rest between courses."

Korhalion's face fell, but brightened again in an instant. "So then, I don't need you. I've got my new pony. Lia, did you see him? Mirain gave him to me. He's black, just like the Mad One."

"His grandsire was my first pony," Mirain added. "Do you remember him?"

"I should," said Elian. "I inherited him."

Mirain's hair was full of snow, his brows and his thick lashes starred with it. Swallowing new and perilous mirth, she brushed it away. He laughed unabashed and reached to serve her likewise. His hand was light and deft and fire-warm.

Korhalion danced between them, sparking with impatience. "Come and see!"

THE PONY OCCUPIED A STALL IN THE CORNER OF HALENAN'S stable. It was black indeed, clean-limbed as a stag beneath its heavy coat, with a mad green eye and a swift slash of horns.

"He's Demon's get," Elian said with assurance as the black head snaked over the stall door, lips rolled back, teeth gleaming. Deftly she evaded the snap of them to seize the woolly ear. "Nurse must be appalled."

"Nurse doesn't know about him yet," said Korhalion. "Mirain's going to teach me to ride. He said you'd help. He says you can ride anything he can. Can you, Lia?"

"Yes," she answered swiftly, with a glance at Mirain. He was all innocence, feeding a bit of fruit to Anaki's placid gelding. "I can do better than he can. Demon never bucked *me* off."

"I calmed him down before I passed him on to you," Mirain said.

"Calmed him? Passed him on? He was as wild as he ever was when I got away from Nurse and the grooms and put a saddle on him. But I taught him to mind me. He was like the Mad One. All bluster." She smiled at Mirain, sweetly. "As they say: Like master, like mount."

He laughed aloud. "As they also say: Was never a woman born but yearned to rule her man. And all his chattels."

"Her man?" She tossed her head. Her heart was leaping strangely. "Not quite yet, brother."

"Perhaps not, little sister. And," added Mirain, "perhaps so." He cocked an eye at Korhalion. "Shall we give her her gift now? Or make her wait for it?"

"Now!" cried Korhalion.

They were bursting with a great secret, the man as much as the child. But neither would be his own betrayer. Elian let herself be led unresisting, with Korhalion tugging eagerly at her hand. In the quiet of her mind, she tested Mirain's mood. Strong though his shields always were, more than eagerness crept through: a thrumming tension, strong almost as fear.

They left Halenan's house, passing through the snow-clad streets to the palace. In the wing which Mirain had taken was a wide-roofed court. He had filled the chambers about it with his own picked men. Already they called themselves the Chosen of An-Sh'Endor, the Company of the Sun. The open space served them as gathering hall and training ground, full always with men and voices and the clash of weapons.

But on this day of snow it was unwontedly quiet. The men of the company stood round the edges, drawn up in loose ranks, armed as for inspection. In the center by the winter-dry fountain, ten waited alone. Their cloaks were somber green; they bore no device. One was Cuthan, head up, wearing a torque of greened bronze. Five were women. Tall or short, plump or reed-slender, every one looked strong and capable, and held herself like one trained to arms.

The scarlet company saluted their king with a great clash of spear on shield. But those in green stood erect and still.

Elian turned on Mirain. "I never knew there were warrior women in your army."

"I have a few," he answered her in the ringing silence, and smiled. "The whole company would have been of women, but I reckoned without my men. They protested vehemently; they came close to rioting. You see their ringleader yonder: the one I've punished with the captain's torque. For him I had to give way, and settle it with a mixed company, half of each. For both of us I cry your pardon that there are only ten to greet you; we've not had time to raise the full hundred."

"A thousand would vie for the honor, my lady," Cuthan said, clear and proud. His eye was steady, laughing a little, but grave too. It seemed that he had forgiven her for lacking the sense to come out of the rain.

She looked at him and at his command. It was a careful scrutiny, missing no small detail: the excellence of their arms and armor, the pride in their faces. One of the women was as lovely as a flower of bronze. Another must surely have been born of the red earth of Han-Gilen, a broad, sturdy, strong-handed peasant woman. She had a level eye and a touch of a smile, as if to mock all this display.

Last of all, Elian looked at the giver of the gift. Very quietly, very carefully, she said, "My lord forgets. I am not to be pensioned off. If he will dismiss me, then let him do so outright, without pretense."

Equally quietly he responded, "It is not a dismissal."

"Shall a squire boast her own Guard? And one of them a high nobleman?"

"A squire, no. But a queen well may."

It did not strike her all at once. Her tongue spoke of its own accord. "I am no queen. I am but a princess."

"A queen is one who weds a king," he said as patiently as to a child.

"But the only king here is—" At last, mind and mouth met. Her limbs went cold. Her voice went high and wild. "You *can't!*"

"Why not?" he asked reasonably.

How could he be reasonable? He had trapped her. No word at all but what she had beaten out of him, and suddenly this, in front of his whole household. Where she could not refuse. When she could not accept.

He reached. If he had not been Mirain, she might have said that he moved with diffidence. But he was Mirain, and his eyes were steady, black-brilliant. "You are my queen," he said.

Her hands rested cold and limp in his burning-strong ones. Her mind was a hundredfold. It laughed, or wept, or howled in rage, or gibbered in stark terror. How dared he trap her? How dared he be so sure of her? She was no man's possession. She was herself. She did not want him. She did. She did not. She *did*.

"My lady." He spoke to mind and ears alike, a murmur as soft as sleep. "My queen. My heart's love."

She struggled in blind panic. It was not that he had said it. It was not that he had said it here, for his army to hear. The worst of it, the very worst, was her own inner singing. It mattered nothing that he was king and emperor, that the god's blood flamed in his veins, that he had chosen her of all living women, that he had half the world to lay at her feet. It mattered only that he was himself. Mirain.

She had lost Ilarios for her tongue's slowness, and he was gone. Mirain would go nowhere until he had made her his own. As if she had no choice but that; as if she could have none. Fate. Prophecy. Inevitability.

She tore her hands from his. "My thanks to my lord king," she said with venomous softness, "but I am not the stuff of which queens are made."

He said nothing, made no move. She remembered with a stab of pain how he had looked when she spoke of loving Ilarios. Precisely the same. Cold and still and royal, offering nothing, taking nothing.

Her teeth bared. "This company I will take, because it is a free gift, theirs as much as yours. I think I can command a force of ten in my king's service. The rest"— she swallowed round bile—"O son of the Sun, do you keep for your proper empress."

"There can be none but you."

Had they been alone, she would have struck him. She bit down on her fist until her tongue tasted the iron sweetness of blood. "Oh, you men! Why do you always fix upon the worst?"

"That," he asked gently, "always being you?"

"Yes, damn you! You hound me, you haunt me. You moon after my so-called beauty, make allowances for my notorious wildness, and calculate my lineage and my dowry down to the last half-cousin and quarter-star. Can't you understand that I want none of you? None!"

His tension had turned to amusement. He even had the gall to smile. Worse—he dared to say nothing of all he might have said, of the true and of the cruel and of what was both together. It was the smile of a great king or of a carven god: calm, assured, and infinitely wise. And giving not a hair's breadth to her will.

She did the worst thing, the craven thing, the thing she always did. She ran away from him.

SHE DID NOT RUN FAR. THAT GREAT IMPULSE WHICH HAD sent her northward had long since faded. But she gathered her belongings upon the bed she still kept near Mirain's own: an untidy heap, surprisingly high. And there was her armor, and her trophies. She would need a servant to help her with it all.

Even in moving to summon one, she sank to the floor. Where could she go? Her old chambers—he knew all the ways to them, both open and secret. Nor would he hesitate to use them. She knew this mood of his. Mirain An-Sh'Endor would have what he meant to have.

Ilarios' topaz had found its way into her hand. She stared at it, only half seeing it. She stared for a very long time. Her mind was utterly empty.

A shadow crossed it. Her eyes turned slowly. Even yet they could widen.

The perfect lady was never to be seen afoot, only seated upon a throne or in her bower, or for the greatest festivals, in a curtained litter. If indeed she deigned to touch her delicate sole to the ground, it was to be cush-

ioned with carpets and shod in the most elegant of san-
dals. Nor was she ever to be seen unattended.

The Lady Eleni was alone. Her gown was as practical
as a servant's; there were boots on her feet. Boots of the
finest leather, with inlaid heels, but boots. They looked as
if they had been in snow, and even, wonder of wonders,
in stable mire. The heavy coils of her hair were glistening
with melting snow; if she had had a veil, she had lost it.

"Mother," said Elian. "Where are your maids? What
are you doing here?"

The princess sat in the one chair the room afforded,
and settled her skirts. "My maids are in their proper
places. I have been searching for you."

"Anyone could have told you where I was."

"Anyone could not. Your father and your brother
have other troubles."

"And the Sunborn would not."

"The Sunborn was occupied." The princess frowned
slightly. "I made a vow that I would let you be. I intend
still to keep it. But I will remind you that our guest is no
longer merely our foster kin. He is the king."

"He's still Mirain."

"He is Mirain An-Sh'Endor."

The words, so close to Elian's own thoughts, cut at
old wounds. "I know who he is! I wait on him day and
night. Day," she repeated, "and night."

Her mother betrayed not the least disturbance. "I
have not come to plead for your reputation. I do not even
beg you to accept his suit, mighty though that match
would be, the mightiest in our world. I only wish to know:
Why?"

Elian would not answer.

"It may be the Asanian prince," Eleni mused. "I
think not. Is it then some youth of low degree, a servant
or a farmholder, or a soldier in Mirain's army? You should
not shrink from telling us. Helenani have wedded with
outlanders before. They have even wedded with com-
moners. Though you have no look of one who loves

without hope. Why then, Elian? Why do you do battle against every man who asks for you?"

Still, silence, with a hint of obduracy.

"Is it perhaps that you are afraid? You are fiercer than is maidens' wont, and you have always been free. You have never met a man as strong as yourself, or as sure in his strength. Unless it be Mirain." The princess folded her hands. "Yet in the end, however feeble the man, his lady must give of herself. Her body certainly, perhaps her heart if she is fortunate. The giving is frightening, and the more so the stronger one is. Is that your reason, daughter? Are you afraid to face your womanhood?"

"No!" It burst out of her with no grace at all. "I know what men do with women. I've seen it in the army." For all her bravado, Elian's cheeks flushed hotly; her tongue was thick, unwieldy. "It is not fear. Believe me, Mother, it is not. I've always expected that I would marry. One day. When it was time. I meant my husband to be Mirain. Because it had to be. Because there could never be another.

"Then I saw Ilarios. And nothing *had* to be; there was no such thing as destiny, and if there was, how dared it bind me? My world was rocking on its foundations. I fled in search of safety.

"To Mirain. Who acted as if I were no more than his sister. And I found that I was glad of it. I began to think that maybe, after all, my vows and my destinies had been mere childish fancies: the infatuation of a very young maid for her splendid elder brother.

"And Ilarios came after me. When at last Mirain admitted that he wanted me, he spoke too late and not to me; and my heart was shifting, turning toward its new freedom. My life was not foreordained. I could choose. To wed, or not. To wed with any man I fancied, or with none. Ilarios paid court to me, and I began to think that, yes, I could be his lover, and he mine. Mirain did nothing to stop us. Maybe I wanted him to do nothing. I think I wanted him to do something. Claim me. Tell me I belonged to him. And he would not. And now," said Elian, "he has, and I don't know what to do. He says he loves me. I know—I know—" Her voice broke. Incredulous. Frightened. "I know I love him. After all, I know . . . I love him. I turned Ilarios away because of him." Elian's fists clenched; her voice rose. "Mother, I *can't!* He's the king. The Sunborn. The god's son."

"He is still Mirain."

Again, her own words. She flung back her mother's. "He is An-Sh'Endor!" Her hair was in her eyes. She scraped it back. "He's not a tyrant to be afraid of. But he's king. Great king. Emperor. How in all the world did I ever hope to stand beside him?"

"It seems to me," said the princess, "that you have been doing just that. Do you know what the army has begun to call you? Kalirien. Lady who is swift and valiant. I note that, daughter. Lady, and valiant. When Mirain set out to choose a Guard for you, a thousand men, hearing but the rumor of it, clamored to be chosen; a thousand more thronged after them. He had to set a difficult test, and then another more difficult still, and then a third; and in the end, to ask that each one submit to the probing of his power. The five who were taken are now the envy of the army, ranked as high as princes."

"Oh aye, for having an easy path to my famous bed."

"Such thoughts demean yourself and your Guard. Where is the truth which we raised you to see? An-Sh'Endor's soldiers have chosen you for their lady. So too have the common folk."

"And the high ones?" Elian rose. "What of them?"

"The high ones know what they see. Some can even understand it."

"No," Elian said. That had been her second word.

The first had been spoken clearly and firmly to the center of her world. Not the name of mother or father, or even of the nurse who had raised her. No. From the very first, she had known who mattered most.

Mirain.

"I'm afraid," she said. "I'm not valiant at all. I'm

terrified. After all I've sworn and done and plotted—I can't be his queen."

Very gently the princess said, "You can be his lover. All the rest will follow."

It was even more shocking than that she should be here, alone, speaking freely and even knowing what soldiers thought: that she could say such a word to her maiden daughter. *Lover.* And with such tenderness.

Elian looked at her hands and at the bed. Both were empty. While she spoke, while her mind paid no heed, she had returned each possession to its place. Save the jewel. It lay in her hand and glittered, and the light of it was cruel. She thrust it into her coat.

She could have wept. She could have screamed. She huddled on the bed, knees to chin, eyes burning dry, and said, "I can't understand him. What if he only wants me for my face? And my dowry, and my father's goodwill. He never acted like a lover. He hardly seemed to notice me. Was he so sure of me? Or is it that he didn't care? He wasn't even jealous of Ilarios."

"Was he not?"

"No!" she snapped. With an effort she softened her voice. "Ilarios wanted me to go away with him. When I told Mirain, he wouldn't decide for me. He didn't try to make me stay."

"He did not counsel you to leave." The princess smiled. "Ah, child, if you saw nothing, still there were others who could see. He would watch you when you were together with the prince, watch you steadily and constantly. Or if you were gone, riding or walking, his mind would wander; he would snap for no reason. Ah, yes, he was jealous. Bitterly so."

"Then why didn't he—"

"He was too proud."

Of course he was too proud. A man had to be humble, to woo a woman properly. "He can't love *me!*" cried Elian.

Her mother laughed softly. "But, daughter, he always has." She sobered, though only a little. "I can understand your fear. He is dear to us all, and he is most human, but he remains Avaryan's son. And yet, being man as much as god, he is very easily hurt. Take care lest you wound him too deeply for any healing."

"I would never—" Elian broke off. "Oh, Mother, why does it have to be me?"

"If I knew," the princess answered, "I would be a goddess myself." She slid from her chair to her knees, unwonted as all she had done in the past hour, and circled her daughter with her arms. "When I bore you, I knew the god intended great things for you. He has given you many and wondrous blessings. Now he asks for his payment. You are strong enough to give it. Believe me, child," she said, measuring each word, "you are strong enough."

Nineteen

THE NIGHT BEFORE MIDWINTER WAS THE DARK OF THE Year. In old days it had been the great festival of the goddess; when Avaryan rose to full and sole power in Han-Gilen, her rites were forbidden, her festival diminished before the feast of Sunreturn. But the old ways lingered. At the Dark of the Year, all fires were extinguished. The temple was dark, the priests silent. Folk huddled together and shivered, and thought on death and dying and on the cold of the grave.

The palace nourished warmth in its old bones; but as the sunless day passed, the chill crept closer. With music and song forbidden and laughter quenched, the halls seemed darker still.

Elian passed a warm delicious time with Anaki, who as a new mother need not endure the fireless cold. But both guilt and duty drove her forth. The sky had begun to loose its burden of snow.

She left its grey weight for the icy air of the palace. Mirain was in the workroom with his clerks; they, needing lamps for their work, warmed their hands at the small flames. They had no need of her; no more did he, although he smiled at her, a swift preoccupied smile. She went to polish his armor. It was a hideous task, but it warmed her blood wonderfully.

The gold-washed plates gleamed, splendid even in the gloom. As she rubbed at his helmet, pursing her lips over a dent which the smith had failed to smooth completely, soft darkness fell over her.

She struggled out of it. It was a cloak, a wonderful thing, deep green velvet lined with fur as fiery vivid as her hair, light and soft and warm as down, as beautiful to the touch as to the eye. Her fingers lost themselves in it; her breath caught in wonder. *"Hazia,"* she said. "This must be *hazia.*"

Mirain sat at her feet, smiling. "Yes, it is."

"But it's as precious as rubies. More precious."

He gestured assent. "The beast is little larger than a mouse, and elusive, and shy besides. It took, said the merchant, the better part of twenty years to gather enough for your cloak." He tilted his head. "Do you like it?"

"Don't be a fool!" The heat flooded to her face; she scowled. "You can't buy me, Mirain."

"May I not give you a Midwinter gift?"

"I have one already. My Guard."

"And this is another," he said. His finger stroked the fur lightly, almost absently. "I'm appallingly wealthy, you know. The tribes of the north are richer than you would ever believe; and their richest kings have paid me tribute, every one. After a while it begins to seem like sea-sand. Worthless with surfeit. Except to give away."

"Don't give it *all* away!" she cried, stung to practicality.

He laughed. "No fear of that, my lady. Even if I were so minded, my clerks would bring me to my senses. Armies have to be paid; and there's my city." His eyes kindled as they always did when he spoke of that. "When the spring comes, we'll begin the building. You'll help us with it. There are things you'll be wanting in the palace and in the city."

"How can it matter what I want?" she asked. She was cold in her splendid cloak.

"You matter," he said. And added very calmly, "I should like to be wedded after the snows pass. On your birth-feast, in the spring; or on mine if you would prefer, at High Summer. Or anywhere between."

She hated him. She hated his cool assurance; she hated his steady regard. She hated her own heart, that had turned traitor and begun to beat hard, and her voice, that was weak, half strangled. "What if I won't choose?"

He touched her hand, the merest brush of a finger-tip, yet she felt it as a line of flame. "There's time yet for deciding. And"—he followed the burning touch with a white-fire kiss—"for loving."

She choked on bile. Treacherous, treacherous body. It sang with his nearness. It yearned to be nearer still.

But he moved a little away, and her anger was swift, fierce, and utterly reasonless. His voice had lost its softness, turned crisp: his brother-voice, with a hint of the king. "Meanwhile, there is the winter. After tomorrow's feast I'll send the bulk of my allies home to rule their lands for me. The summer will see us on the march again."

She shuddered.

He clasped her hand. No fire now, only warmth and strength. "Asanion, if not our ally, is not yet our enemy. For a time. That much Ziad-Ilarios won from me. But the east is rising. The Nine Cities encroach on the princedoms of the farthest south, at the desert's edge. I hear of horrors committed and of armies strengthened. The Syndics are testing my flanks for weaknesses."

The cold in her was sudden and soul-deep. "Sooner," she said very low. "Cold. North."

His grasp tightened. "The north is firm, and mine."

"The north holds the dark."

He frowned. "It's Midwinter, sister-love. It chills us all."

"No," she said with swift heat. "I can feel it."

She had touched his pride. "My realm is like my body to me. It lies at rest, deep in winter's grip. Save only for the uneasiness in the south. And," he added more slowly, "a little in the north. A very little. A raid or two. The tribes thrive on them; without them, all the young men would go mad and turn on one another."

"Tribes? In the Hundred Realms?"

"It is not—"

IT WAS ASHAN. THE MESSENGER CAME IN LATE AND CHILLED to the bone, his mare all but foundered. With wine in his belly and a warm robe about him, he told his tale. "Men of Asan-Eridan began it," he said. "A girl of theirs, a favorite of the lord's favorite bastard, caught the eye of a visitor. He was a man of little enough account, but he had kin in Asan-Sheian. He accosted the girl and raped her; her man caught him at it, and quite legally and rightly, if somewhat precipitously, saw to it that the outlander would never enjoy another woman. The culprit, turned loose, made his way back to Sheian; and his kin by then were weary of winter and eager for a diversion.

"That would have been little enough, sire, and easily dealt with. But my lord Omian is marriage-kin to Sheian's lady, and he was there when the wounded man returned. He bound his own men to Sheian's cause.

"Now Eridan lies near Ebros' border, and has close ties of alliance and of kinship with a handful of its Ebran neighbors. Faced with Luian's own troops, Eridan's lord called on his friends. And now we have the beginnings of a healthy war." He left his seat to kneel before Mirain. "We would not trouble you, Sunborn. But my lord is old and his heir is not minded to make peace, and of the rest of the sons, most have arrayed themselves with the younger lord to rouse war against Ebros. Before the end, Ashan may well turn upon Ashan, and fight as fiercely within as without." The man clasped his hands in formal pleading. "Majesty, if this small fragment of your great empire is of any worth to you, we beg you, aid us in our trouble."

Mirain looked down at the messenger. Elian knew that look: dark, level, and utterly unreadable. She had seen high lords flinch before it.

This man was no lord, of blood or of spirit. He crouched upon the floor, shielding his head with his hands. But he had the strength to cry, "Sunborn! By your father's name, give us your aid."

The words rang in silence. In the heart of it a note sang, faint yet clear: the chiming of a bell. Mirain raised his head to it. "Avaryan sets," he said. "The temple waits for me."

The envoy clutched his knees, great daring and great desperation. "*Sire!*"

"After the rite," said Mirain, "you will have my answer." He seemed to do nothing, but he was free and striding through the hall, the messenger kneeling still, gripping air.

THOUGH CROWDED WITH THE FOLK OF THE CITY, AVARYAN'S temple held within it a black and ancient cold. The high ones felt it in their places near the altar, prince and princess seated side by side, their son and their daughter standing close behind them. Although no fire lightened the darkness, a glow clung to them, a faint red-golden shimmer: the mage-light, that was always strongest in the heart of Han-Gilen. It shone even through Elian's cloak.

She barely heeded it. The cold within her had deepened to burning. Her mind was brittle, clear and bright and fragile as ice. The thoughts of the gathered people rang upon it. But stronger than they was the call of the darkened altar, the mantle and the water of prophecy. All her will scarcely sufficed to hold her in her place. *It is time,* sang the water. *Time and time and time. Come, seer. Come and rule me.*

Her jaw set, aching-hard. There was no one to cling to, even if she could. Orsan and his lady were just out of her reach. Hal supported Anaki, who would come to this ritual, even though she came in a chair. Mated, all of them, and centered upon one another.

Light flared blinding-bright in the gloom. A child's voice, high and piercingly pure, rent the murmuring silence.

Every priest and priestess in Han-Gilen walked in that endless procession, a stream of white robes, golden torques, fine-honed voices. Before them trod the novices in saffron gold, bearing tall candles. Behind them came a great light.

The Halenani shone with power. But this was Avaryan's own child, in Avaryan's greatest temple: robe and torque like all the rest, voice as pure as a sacred singer's, yet all of it but a veil over light. Elian's eyes blurred and flinched before its brilliance.

If he will not be called high priest now, her cold self said, *then the name is nothing. He is only what he is. The god's son, greatest of the priests of the Sun.*

He mounted to the high altar and bowed as a flame will bow in a high wind. She never heard what words he sang, nor saw the movements of his dance, the dance of the binding of the goddess. For the darkness' binding loosed other powers, Elian's own far from the least of them. With no memory of movement, she stood no longer beside her brother, but shivered in deep shadow. Perilously close, close enough to touch, lay the Altar of Seeing. No mind but hers focused upon it, no eyes turned toward it. She was as much alone there as if the temple had been empty.

Her hand stretched out. The mantle was thick and startlingly soft, pouring over her hand like water. Black water, glistening in its hollow in the stone, stirring and kindling. She should fight—fight—

Come, it whispered. *Rule. Be strong and see.*

Strength lay in surrender. Strength was to open wide the mind, to let the water pour into it with all its burden of dreams and nightmares and true sight, to master the visions; to gather, and shape, and rule.

Rule. Her brain was a dazzle of images. Yet her eyes saw, her mind knew where she stood: by the altar of prophecy, with the black mantle cast over Mirain's gift of green velvet and *hazia.* She was no longer cold. All the temple flared with the Sun's fire: while she bound her visions, Mirain had kindled the light of Sunreturn. Priests and Sunborn sang the great antiphon, deep voices shot with the silver brilliance of the novices and the priestesses. *And the god came forth*, they sang, *and clove to his bride*. And he alone: *And the darkness was cast down, and the light rose up: sun in triumph, conqueror unconquered, king forever.* . . .

King forever, a single voice echoed him. With a shock she knew her own, though higher and purer and fiercer than she had ever known it could be. The ranks of priests wavered. The people turned, staring. Their eyes smote her. Yet the voice ran on of its own accord, like a bell that, once struck, continues to sound, untouched by any hand: "King forever or king never, son of the Sun! Look; even as you stand here binding the dark with chains of light and song, it moves against you. And you sing, and you dance the Dance, and you ponder this small trouble in the north. You are restless with winter—you will go yourself to settle it, to cow your rebellious people with your own mighty presence. Ill pondered and ill chosen, Sunborn. North waits the full power of ancient Night. North lies your death."

Mirain stood unmoving behind the high altar. His light had faded to a shimmer, barely perceptible in the splendor of the full-lit temple. He wore no mark of rank, only the vestments of a priest in the rite, white without adornment, and his torque. His face blurred through the flocking visions: Mirain the boy atop Endros; Mirain the youth on his throne in Ianon; Mirain but little older, locked in deadly combat with a giant of the north; Mirain come to manhood, riding to claim his empire. Mirain lying on cold stone, eyes open to the sky, all light fled from them; and over him a shape of shadow, mantled in night. It stretched forth a long gaunt hand, and bent, and reft his heart from his breast.

"Send another," Elian said quite calmly, quite clearly. "Send one who will be strong at need, ruthless at need; and tarry here. Then indeed shall you be king forever, you and all the heirs of your body. All the worlds shall bow before you."

It was strange how clear her mind was. She could see through Mirain as through a glass; the others, the lesser ones, were like bright water babbling unheeded on the edge of perception. But he was still, clear-eyed, and completely unafraid. "How may I send another," he asked, "if I dare not send myself?"

"It is not a matter of daring or of cowardice. It is a matter of the world that hereafter shall be. You are the sword of Avaryan against the dark. If you are broken before the time appointed, what hope then has any child of the light?"

"You are the seer," he said. "See for your king. Is my death inescapable?"

"If you go not into the north, you may escape it."

"And if I go? Is all hope lost?"

She shivered. But the sight knew neither mercy nor human fear. It spoke through her, cold and distinct. "Your death waits in Ashan. Yet on one thread of time's tapestry—one thread only, of all the myriads—there is hope. Hope for your life. What that life shall be, whether prisoned in deep dungeons or hounded into exile or even—pray the god it be so—set again upon your throne, I cannot see. A shadow lies upon my sight."

"But I shall live."

"You may. If you pursue that one course of the many, make the one proper choice, speak the word and make the gesture and face the danger as the seeing demands. But the word and the gesture I cannot see."

"No. You would not. My enemy is strong enough to darken even prophecy. Yet hope cannot be hidden." His voice rang out, clear and strong. "I shall venture it. I shall go forth and crush this serpent in the grass of my kingdom, and my father will defend me. No mortal can conquer me."

"But a goddess may," said Elian.

No one heard her. They were all crying his name. And he—he chose not to listen. He even smiled; and he turned back to the rite, singing more splendidly than ever, with all the power of the god in his voice and in his eyes.

Twenty

"WILL YOU GO?"

Mirain was clad for the feasting in full Ianyn splendor, but Elian wore still the gown and the cloak she had had in the temple, with the prophet's mantle cast haphazardly over them. No one had touched her or spoken to her. She was a figure of awe now, the seer of Han-Gilen.

She hardly heeded it, or the servants who moved about Mirain, settling his broad collar of gold, braiding gold and pearls into his hair, painting the sunburst of his father between his brows. "Will you go?" she demanded again.

He left his servants to approach her. He was not like the rest; he dared to slip black mantle and green from her shoulders, to touch the lacings of her dark plain gown. "I will go," he said. He beckoned. One of his dressers came forward with a cascade of gold and white, the robe of a princess, a queen.

They dressed her as if she had been a carven image, women who came from she knew not where, with faces she might have known. They suppressed sighs over her cropped hair, though that had grown out a little, binding it with a jeweled fillet, painting her eyes and her cheeks and her cold lips. When they were done they held up a silver mirror, but she did not need it. Her beauty shone in Mirain's still face. He bowed over her hands, and kissed the palms one by one. "You are the fairest lady in the world," he said.

She was empty of words. Over his royal finery, death lay like a cloak. Yet his touch was warm and living, his arm strong, his smile luminous. The small child in her wanted to cling to him and never let him go. The newborn prophet held herself aloof, suffering him to lead her, but offering nothing of speech or of gesture.

They walked from his chambers, maids and manservants falling in behind. Two guards stood at the door: one of his men in scarlet, one of her women in green. Mirain smiled at them. Elian could muster nothing but a bare inclination of the head.

Haughty lady, her mind mocked her. *How can they endure you?*

"Because they love you," Mirain said softly, for her alone to hear.

A deep shudder racked her. The coldness fled. She stopped short, tangling the retinue behind her. "You will go," she said. "So be it. But first you shall make me your queen."

He glanced at their followers, who were careful to be oblivious. His brow, raised, conceded the justice of her assault now, all unlooked for, in front of a full company of servants. But she had had no thought at all of revenge.

"Is that your seeing?" he asked her.

"It is my will."

He looked hard at her. She stared back. His lips tightened. "Why? Why now, after so much resistance?"

"Because," she said. Fire came and went in her face; her fists knotted. "Because—after all—I see—I love you."

"Because your power tells you I will die." That was brutal, but he struck harder still. "I will not marry for pity, Elian."

She stiffened at the blow, yet she answered calm with flawless calm. "Even for the sake of the dynasty that will be?"

His breath hissed between his teeth. "When I return from Ashan," he said with great precision, "then we shall be wedded. If that is still your will."

She tossed her head, her fear bursting forth in a flare of temper. "No! I want it now. Tonight. The feast is ready. We're both arrayed for it. And afterward . . ."

"Child," said Mirain with utmost gentleness, "whatever you wish for, you wish for with all that is in you."

"You want it as much as I."

"Not this way. When I take you, I shall take you as a queen, not as a battle-bride. Without haste, and without regret."

"I would never regret it."

"No?" He smiled and set her hand upon his, and began again to walk. "After Ashan," he promised her.

He was immovable. He would have her, but not until it suited his whim. She could not even touch his mind, let alone sway it to her will.

It was a wondrous feast, the most magnificent she could remember. Half the royalty of the Hundred Realms adorned the hall: princes and close kin of princes, high lords and their ladies, chieftains of the north in kilts and mountain copper, even the ambassador of Asanion with his perpetually pained expression, as if it irked him to be cast among all these savages.

Mirain sat not as lord but as high-honored guest, and she beside him, stared at and wondered at. That, she had been born to, and she had made herself a legend beyond her lineage. Many of the songs sung that night were of her, or spoke of her.

For the third time her cup was empty. A page came forward to fill it. But Mirain's hand stopped his. "Eat first," he said to her.

"Are you my nursemaid?" she flared at him.

He laughed, lifted a morsel from his plate, proffered it with a flourish. For all his merriment, he knew well

what he did. Should she accept, she would accept his suit:
the first movement of the formal betrothal. She considered it minutely, through a haze of wine. Considered him
more minutely still. "Tonight?" she asked.

"After Ashan."

Her eyes narrowed. Slowly she took what he offered.
A bit of honeycake, heavy with sweetness. From her own
plate she took another. He was not as slow as she.

When he had taken it, he rose. The singers faltered.
Scattered voices cheered him. But he turned away from
them to the prince and the princess, and bowed the bow
of king to king. "My lord," he said clearly, "my lady. You
have given me gifts beyond the desire of emperors. Yet in
my great presumption I ask you for yet another. It shall
be the last, I promise you."

The prince stood to face him. How young he looked,
thought Elian. Scarcely older than Halenan, whose smile
flashed white beyond him. Prince Orsan seldom smiled,
and did not smile now, but his eyes upon Mirain were
warm, his voice likewise. "You who are my lord and my
foster son know that all I have to give is too paltry a gift for
you. Only ask what you desire and it shall be yours."

Mirain's eyes glinted. "Take care, my lord! I may
seek no less than the greatest jewel in all your princedom."

"It is yours," Orsan said unwavering, "with all else
that is mine."

"Even your daughter?"

A murmur ran through the hall. Prince Orsan looked
down from his great height at the man who was his king.
"Even my daughter," he replied. "If she is willing."

"She is," said Elian. "She asks that you bless the
union, now, tonight." She paused, and added with tight-
leashed passion, "No, she does not ask. She begs."

Mirain turned, outflanked but unsurprised. It was
not easy to surprise Mirain. Nor was it easy to face him as
she faced him now, before the cream of the Hundred
Realms. She smiled her sweetest smile and rose, only to
sink down in a deep curtsey. Softly, demurely, she said,
"The choice lies with the lady, my lords. And the lady,

having tarried so long for her folly, would wed without delay. Will you say the words, Father?"

"*I* will not," gritted Mirain, but not for all to hear.

She met his glare and laughed. "I shall be your luck and your talisman. Am I not fair to see?"

"You are wondrous fair." His voice deepened with warning. "Elian—"

"Father," she said, pressing.

The prince regarded them for a long moment. One could never tell what moved him, whether mirth or grim anger.

Suddenly the mask cracked. He smiled, he grinned, he laughed aloud. His people gaped. His peers and his allies stared nonplussed. He stretched out his hands. "Come, my son, my daughter. Be wedded with my blessing."

The hall cleared for them, the joy of festival turned to something brighter and stronger. There could be no garlands in winter; for flower-clad maidens there were the women of Elian's Guard; and the feast was consumed, its remnants swept away to make room for the rite. It was never the wedding Elian had looked to have; yet she would have chosen no other.

She stood in the circle of her guards, and tried not to tremble. Not all was fear. Some was wine, and much was plain weariness.

Her mother's perfume sweetened the air; the firm gentle touch startled her. For a moment she rested upon it.

"Child," said the princess. "Ah, child, how would the singers live without you?"

Elian stood straight and lifted her chin. "This may be precipitous, Mother, but I think it is wise."

The Lady Eleni glanced across the hall, where a knot of young men marked Mirain's place. The king himself was not to be seen, but Halenan's hair was like a beacon; Cuthan towered over him, flashing with copper and gold. From the sound of it, they were more than pleased with the turn the feast had taken.

"It is wise," the lady said, "and utterly like you."

Elian laughed shakily. "Oh, no, I know what a fool I am. But this folly is so extreme that it can only be wisdom."

Her mother stroked her hair smooth, settling the fillet more becomingly over it. "You have always followed your heart, even when you seemed most to oppose it. Follow it now, and be strong. Has it not chosen the greatest of all kings to be its lord?"

"It has. I have." Elian drew a shuddering breath. "I don't know whether to be glad or terrified."

"Both," said the princess. She kissed Elian's brow and turned her about. "Come. The men are ready."

The tables were gone, the folk in the hall arrayed in twin ranks with a passage between. A single pure voice soared up in the silence, the song of the bride brought to her wedding. The circle of young men tightened to a wedge and began to advance. Elian's women faced outward.

Wedge met half-circle. By custom the maids should shriek and scatter and leave their lady undefended. But these were warriors, and Elian's warriors at that. Each laughing man found himself confronting a cold-eyed woman. The advance halted in confusion.

Halenan, at the point of the wedge, swept a deep bow. "Greetings, fair ladies," he said with perfect courtesy. "We come in search of your queen. Will you help us to bring her to our king?"

"I shall," said the princess, coming forward to take her son's hand. "Come, ladies. Let the king look on our queen."

Glances flickered round the circle. Smiles followed it. Hand met hand; men and maids linked in a ring.

Elian stood in its center, face to face with Mirain. He had his grim and royal look. A corner of her mouth curved upward. His eye answered it with a brief, reluctant spark. She sank down in a pool of shimmering skirts, bowing to the floor.

He raised her. Beyond that first glance he would give her nothing. His eyes fixed upon the dais and the prince; his mind walled against her.

Anger warred with amusement. The hunter hunted, the pursuer pursued. *It's a mercy for us all that you always win your battles,* she said to the fortress of his mind: *even this small loss is too much for you.*

He stiffened but did not turn or respond. Side by side, pace and pace, they approached the prince. Their followers spread behind them. Drums joined the lone marvelous voice, beating in time to their hearts; harps and pipes wove through them. The lamps blazed sun-bright, dazzling.

"Lady of Han-Gilen," intoned the prince beneath the complex melody, "son of the Sun. Elian and Mirain, child of my body and child of my heart, before Avaryan and before the people of this empire he has forged, I bring you together, body and body, soul and soul, matched and mated in the god's name. Is it your will that I speak the words of binding?"

"Yes," said Elian with only the slightest quaver, and that not for herself. Mirain could still refuse. Could still shame her. He was fully as proud as she, and he could be no less perfect an idiot.

"Yes," he said distinctly, without a moment's hesitation. "I so will it."

The tension fled from her body. Almost her knees buckled. She stiffened them; his hands clasped hers, holding fast. Her father's settled over them. "Hear then and take heed. On this night of the goddess' binding, between two who stand so high in the world's ways, we forge not only a bond of earthly marriage but one of mighty magic. As the goddess is bound below, let these two be bound above; as the god strides free through the heavens, so shall they be free within their loving: two who are one, greater together than ever alone." He raised his arms and his voice. "Sing now, people of the Sun. Sing the binding that is their freeing."

MIRAIN SHUT THE DOOR OF HIS CHAMBER UPON THE THRONG of revelers, and shot the bolts. Their shouts and laughter echoed dimly through the panel, punctuated with snatches of song and the drumming of fists and feet.

Elian sat where her attendants had left her, in a chair made into a wedding throne. Cloth of gold covered it; rare spices scented it, lingering in the air about her. She herself wore a white gown, simple to starkness, clasped at the throat with a single green jewel.

The king turned his back to the door and the tumult, and folded his arms. "Well, my lady? Shall we let them in?"

The shouts had come together into a song reckoned bawdy even in Prince Orsan's guardrooms. Elian, who had been known to sing it without a tremor, felt the blood rise to scald her face. Mirain seemed quite frankly amused, as if he had surrendered wholeheartedly to her will; but however complete her triumph might be, she had never known him to yield without a battle. And Mirain was one who laughed as he fought.

She swallowed. Her mouth was dry. "It is for my lord to choose," she said.

Since my lady has chosen all the rest of it? He smiled with a wry twist. "By custom we should let them look on you and sing to you, and in the end put you to bed with me. In Ianon a chosen pair, man and woman, would remain to see that the rite was performed in full."

Her blush fled.

"But," he added after a pause, "neither of us is a great follower of custom."

He left the door. Involuntarily she stiffened. He passed her with scarcely a glance, stripping off his ornaments, casting them into their casket. His cloak followed, flung over a chest. Again he passed her, again with eyes forward, striding toward the bathing-room. He loosened his braids as he went.

She hissed in sudden, furious comprehension, and sprang to bar his way, forgetting the peculiarity of the bridal robe. Its clasp gave way; the heavy fabric fell free. She wore nothing beneath it but a chain of gold and emeralds, riding just above the swell of her hips.

Mirain halted as if he had struck a wall. Had she been less angry, she might have laughed.

His face disciplined itself. His eyes hooded. "You may bathe first," he said, "and take my bed. I shall sleep well enough in your old one."

Elian did laugh then, sharp and high. "Oh, no, Mirain. You wanted me; now that you have me, you can't cast me off."

"I wanted you in the full and proper time."

"Don't be afraid," she said acidly. "My father has no intention of withholding my dowry."

"I don't *want* your damned—" He broke off and spun away from her, tearing at his plaits. A cord snapped; pearls flew wide.

"You're angry," she said. "You wanted me on your terms, and yours only. So then, I tricked you. I trapped you. I admit it. Can you forgive me? Or have you been king too long to remember how?"

He wheeled with blazing eyes. "You self-centered little fool! You see what will be; have you no comprehension of what is? I will go to Ashan. I will not be encumbered with a wife—one who is all too likely to be carrying my child."

"All the more reason for us to be wedded now. Then, if you—die—"

"If I die, the world is well rid of me. If I live, I swear by my father's power that I shall give you such a wedding night as never a woman knew before."

She approached him, stepping softly, to lay her hands upon his shoulders. "Give it to me now."

"A choice," he said, "and a bargain. I shall give you what you ask for. More: the full three days of the wedding festival. Afterward I shall go to Ashan. You will remain here in safety."

"Or?"

"Or I ride to Ashan in the morning, and you ride with me, wedded in name only."

"I would go with you no matter which you made me choose."

"Not if I laid a binding on you."

"Could you?"

Under her hands his shoulders flexed; he breathed deep. Power sang in her mind's ears.

She smiled. Like an eel, like a golden fish, she slipped through all his shields, deep into the bright waters of his mind. They roared; they seethed. She rode at her ease in the depths where no storms could come, in halls of pearl and fire, wrapped about in the protection of his inmost will. *Bind me,* she said. *I welcome it. For if you do it, you too will be bound; and that will keep you from Ashan.*

Nothing will keep me from Ashan. His voice was a distant booming, like waves upon stone.

And nothing will keep me apart from you, she said.

Not even this surety? Our union will bring forth an heir. And our enemies will know it. They will strike at you then, at the life new-kindled within you, and through you both they will destroy me.

Or be destroyed, said Elian.

No. I will not allow it.

I will do it whether you allow it or no. Elian drifted closer to his voice, swelling with her own strong power. *Listen to me, Sunborn. Alone you may defeat your mortal enemies, but never the dark that stands behind them. It is too strong, and too well aware of your strength. But with me you may have hope. More than hope. Victory.*

Waves of denial bore her back. She struggled against them, twisting, leaping, up and out.

His braids had unraveled, falling over his shoulder. There in the hollow where bone met bone lay a deep and pitted scar, mark of a northern dart. It had been poisoned; he had almost died. She set her lips to it.

"I know that I am mortal!" he cried.

Her hands slid between his hair and his skin, stroking, kneading the knotted muscles. They hardened against her. He stared stonily ahead, his nostrils pinched tight, his mouth a thin line.

"Is that what I've been looking like?" she asked, bemused. "No wonder I made everyone so angry."

He pulled free, leaving his kilt in her hands, and spun away. But she saw enough to blush hotly, and to smile in spite of herself. "You're not all in agreement, are you?"

He opened the inner door. She let the garment fall and came after him. The bathing-room was warm, walls and floor both, from the hypocaust beneath; water steamed in the great gilded basin. That too was custom. The viewing of the bride; the singing; the disrobing and the bathing. Men and maids would try to keep the lovers apart while taunting each with the other's manifold beauties. Sometimes the guardianship would fail and the marriage be consummated then and there.

Mirain halted on the far side of the basin and faced her across it. "Yes," he said, "I want you. But if you come to me, you must swear that you will remain in Han-Gilen."

"You know I won't."

"Then my body will school itself to wait. It's most skilled in that."

"I'm not, and I won't." She stepped into the water, wading through it, ready to leap if he moved. "I could swear your oath, take my three days, and do as I please. But I'm honorable; I tell you the truth. Whether you give me three nights or none, when you go to Ashan I go with you. I'm your hope, Mirain. Your hope and your queen."

Her voice quivered on the title. She cursed herself for it, for the doubt it betrayed. That the certainty of her knowledge might be not of the light but of the mocking dark.

Mirain stood motionless, face of a royal stranger, body of an eager lover. But the eagerness was fading, yielding to his will.

She closed her eyes. The hope that had borne her up, the power of prophecy that had moved within her, ebbed away, leaving behind an utter weariness. She let her knees yield, her body sink into the warm scented water.

Strong arms lifted her. She looked into Mirain's face. Seeking for no yielding, she found none.

All damp and dripping as she was, he laid her in his bed. His arms were very gentle; his expression was cold, almost angry. "Woman," he said, low and rough, "you would tax the patience of a god."

"I know." It was a sigh. "You've always said it: I don't think. I just am. I love you, Mirain."

"And I . . ." He stroked the hair from her brow, tender hand, grim mouth. "There's never been anyone for me but you. Women—lovers—friends, some of them; but only one of you. Though I never knew how very much I wanted you until I saw you there in the wineseller's stall, so obviously and exquisitely you that I wondered how anyone could possibly take you for a boy. Do you know what it cost me, then and after, to keep my distance?"

"No more than it costs you now. And that is remarkably little."

"No," he said. "Oh, no. It costs the world."

She clasped her arms about his neck. There was no calculation in it. He was stone-stiff, stone-hard. Her lips touched his. Cold, so cold, with no yielding in them. She opened lips and mind, both at once, offering all she had to give.

Fire burst from him. Light and heat and sudden, fierce, uncontrollable joy.

Twenty-One

ELIAN OPENED HER EYES. MORNING LIGHT MET THEM. SHE lay in it, warm, languid, every muscle loosed.

Warmth stirred against her, and memory flooded. She was a maid no longer. She was a woman and a queen.

Dark eyes caught hers. "Regrets?" Mirain asked softly.

She touched his cheek, following the line of it down his jaw to his neck to the plane of his chest. A slow smile rose and bloomed. But she said, "Yes." His eyes stretched wide; she laughed. "Yes, that it took me so long to know my own mind. And," she added with the beginnings of a blush, "your body."

He laughed, deep and joyous, and rose above her. "Would you know it better still, my lady?"

She kindled; but she held him back, palms flat upon his breast. "Are *you* sorry, Mirain? You could have had any woman in the world. There are many more beautiful, and some more witty, and a few of higher birth; and any one of them would be more sweetly submissive than I."

"How excruciatingly dull," he said.

"Am I interesting?" she asked, all wide eyes and astonishment.

He leaped. Her laughter broke into a gasp, half of startlement, half of piercing pleasure.

When it was past, Mirain was very quiet. Not sad; but his high delight had faded, his mind withdrawn into some realm of its own. She, seeking, met a wall. Not a high one nor very strong, but she respected it, turning her will to the suppression of a sudden and utterly ridiculous jealousy.

Her head rested on his breast; his arms circled her, one hand tangled in her hair. Its fire fascinated him. "And fire even . . . there," he had marveled in the night, laughing at her fierce blush and taking her by storm.

A memory flitted past. Ziad-Ilarios in the temple, all gold and all lost. She clung to Mirain with sudden fierceness, startling him out of his reverie. "I won't let them kill you!" she cried. "I won't!"

"Nor shall they," he said with royal confidence. He sat up, drawing her with him, and smiled as he smoothed her hair out of her face. "Now, ladylove. How shall we receive the waking party?"

IT FOUND THEM MOST DECENTLY CLAD, HE IN A WHITE KILT and she robed in green, playing at kings-and-cities beside the glowing brazier. Even the most uproarious young lord stood still before their calm. But the women smiled, the maids in admiration mingled with envy, the wedded ladies with approval; and the eldest folded back the bed's coverlet. There was the maiden-chain, and the marriage stain.

With a roar of delight the young men fell upon the lovers. Two, the youngest, bore garlands of winter green; with these they crowned both, while others brought forth cloaks of fur to wrap them, and lifted them up, singing the morning song.

For that was the wedding of a great lady in the southlands: three evenings and three nights alone with her lord, but three mornings of festival. On the first, they must be carried in procession through the keep, and break their fast with their closest kin; on the second, all the palace would see them and feast with them; and on

the third, they would be borne through the city and
presented in the temple, and brought forth to bestow
their blessing and their largesse upon their people.

Elian clung to every moment. Even in the depths of
his mind Mirain betrayed no impatience, but she knew:
the fourth morning would begin the ride to Ashan. With
but a word or two, to Adjan the commander of his armies
in Vadin's absence, to Halenan the general of the southern legions, he had seen to it that all would be ready. And
having so settled his fate, he laid it aside, becoming wholly
the young lover.

She tried. But she was a woman and a seer. She could
not make herself forget.

The third day fled like the dove before the hawk. She
had dreaded the ordeal in the temple, the long ritual so
close to the Altar of Seeing. Yet the altar was silent, the
water unclouded by visions; and soon she was spun away
from it. The blessing, which she barely heard even as she
uttered it; the feasting, of which she partook almost nothing, so that the old dames and the young bucks ex-
changed wicked, knowing looks; and she was alone again,
the doors bolted, and Mirain sinking to the bed with a
sigh.

She perched beside him, stiff in her jeweled skirts,
and regarded him without speaking. His quick hand found
the lacing of her bodice; it came free all at once and
somewhat to his surprise. His hand closed over her bared
breast.

She shivered convulsively. He found the fastenings
of her skirts and loosed them one by one, letting them fall
where they would, and wrapped her in a furred robe.

Even that could not take away the chill. He drew her
close and held her. "I know," she said through chattering
teeth. "I know what it is. It's seeing. It's—knowing, and
trying not to know. Mirain, I hoped this would be the
saving of you. I prayed it would be. But—I don't—know.
It's so cold."

"And dark."

She clutched at him. "You know. You know too!"

"Yes." His lips brushed her hair; his fingers kneaded the knotted muscles of her back. "We have enemies who would rob us of all hope. And now there are two of us for them to strike."

"Three," she whispered.

His arms tightened until she gasped. But, "Three," he said steadily. "We may be deadly weak. Or—as the god is my father—we may be stronger than ever we were alone. The dark would never let us see that. But we can believe it. We must."

"I want to." Her voice was stronger; she was a little warmer. A very little. "I will. If only—" She pulled back to see his face. "You can't make me stay behind."

His brows knit. "Distance is nothing to power. You can aid me just as well from here. Better, maybe, with no hardships of travel to—"

She cut him off with a flare of anger. "Don't be an idiot! By your own logic, I can be killed as easily here as in Ashan. More easily, what with fretting for you and pacing in a cage."

"The child—"

"The child is the merest spark of life, but it won't go out for a little riding in the wind. On the contrary. We'll both thrive on it."

He laid a light hand on her belly. "You see why I wanted to wait for you. Now I'll be doubly afraid."

"And doubly dangerous to anyone you meet," she countered swiftly. "We'll make you strong, the little one and I. We'll make you conquer. Because if you won't, my dearest lord, we'll do it ourselves."

Suddenly he laughed. "Why, you've already done it! You believe now. You're warm again."

She was, to burning. She bore him back and down, and pinned him there. "Do you love me?" she demanded of him.

"Desperately. Madly. Eternally."

For all his lightness, his mind bore not a grain of mockery. She searched it, piercing deep through all his open barriers, knowing that he saw likewise into her own soul. No one else had ever gone down so far. It was like nakedness—worse than nakedness, for her body had nothing to hide. Even its womanhood; had he not possessed all of it already?

Gently, and in the same moment, they withdrew. Mirain brushed her lips with his fingertip. "Lady," he said, "you are as wondrous fair within as without."

"And you," she said, "are splendid. Within, and without."

For once he did not try to deny her.

LAMPLIGHT ILLUMINED SERENITY: THE PRINCE OF HAN-Gilen stretched out upon a low couch, half in a dream. His princess sat beside him with a lute, playing softly, singing in her low sweet voice. His hand moved idly among the freed masses of her hair.

Elian hesitated in the curtained doorway. She had looked on this scene, or on scenes like it, more often than she could remember. It was a fact of the world's existence, like the rising of Avaryan or the running of Suvien, certain, immutable: that she was the child of two who were lovers. She knew how very rare it was, and how very precious.

But her own new joy made her the more keenly aware of it, an awareness close to pain. She had this, and oh, it was sweet. Yet would she have it when the child within her was grown? Would it even live to be born?

The prince stirred. The song ended; he turned his head a little, smiling, holding out his hand.

She came to it as a drowning man to a lifeline. There in the warmth between the two of them, for a little while she rested. They did not press her with speech. Her mother returned to the lute, a melody like spring rain, note by limpid note.

Elian stared at her father's fingers that held her own. A mage's fingers, a warrior's, long and fine but very strong. A thin scar ran across the knuckles, mark of one of his first battles.

Their family lived long and aged late. But he was no

longer young. Odd uncomfortable thought to have when he was so strong and so sure in his power: no grey in the fire of his hair, no weakening of the long lean body, and his daughter newly wedded to the man whom he had made an emperor. He alone, by the working of his will upon the princes of the Hundred Realms.

Mortality preyed upon her mind. It saw Mirain as she had left him, asleep and smiling, looking hardly more than a boy. He was young by any reckoning; and before the moons waned again, he could be dead.

She did not even know why her eyes blurred, until her father brushed a tear from her cheek. "I love him so much," she said. "And I'm close—so close—to losing him."

The lutestrings stilled. "Sometimes," the princess said, "a prophecy is its own fulfillment."

"Which it need not be." The prince drew his daughter close. "Elian, if you despair, all that you fear may come to pass. But if you are strong—we are not gods, daughter. But we can oppose fate. Sometimes we can even defeat it."

Elian blinked the tears away, scowling. "I know that. You taught it to me in the cradle. It's only . . . he knows it too. Too well. He doesn't even care that he might die!"

"That is why he is what he is. The art of kings and of gods: to venture all on a glimmer of hope, and to waste no strength in anguish."

"Then a queen's art—a woman's, at least—must be to feel the anguish for him. Especially if she's cursed with the sight."

They gave her no pity, and less compassion than she had looked for. "Yes," her mother said, "there is balance in all things. The king dares; the queen bears. And stands ready to be his prop and his shield."

"An ill one I make," muttered Elian. "He still calls me *child* and *little sister*. And I am."

"And you are not," the prince said.

She took the lute from her mother's lap, plucked a formless tune. Her fingers were stiff, out of practice. "Everyone is so strong and so sure, so certain that he has the right to work his will on the world. I was; when I

made Mirain take me in my good time, and not in his . . .
I was. I'll never forget it. But I'm no longer—I don't
know—" Her voice was breaking. She stopped, mended
it. "Nothing will keep him here, short of the god's own
bonds. Not when he knows the danger. It's a madness in
him. Part of his pride. He's been challenged; he can't
retreat. He won't. Not even for me."

Her fingers stumbled, steadied. She lowered her head
over the lute, aware of their eyes, concentrating very hard
upon the halting music. No longer quite so halting. She
was remembering her skill.

A touch like wind brushed her hair. Her father's
hand, her mother's kiss.

With a sudden, convulsive movement she flung the
lute away. Her face was tight, her throat sore. "I'm going
to be strong. I'll be his strength when all of his is gone.
And I'll save him. I'll give him life. He'll never die while I
live to defend him."

Twenty-Two

THE DAYS OF THE WEDDING HAD SEEN A BREAK IN THE cold, a melting of the snow, a baring of startlingly bright green. Here on winter's threshold, spring made a brief and precarious entry.

The air was soft even in the early morning, the sun rising in mist, casting a silvered light upon armor and spearpoints. A hundred of Mirain's best gathered in the paved square before the palace: the chosen of his Chosen; picked men of the Green Company of Han-Gilen, honor guard of the prince-heir and under his command; and the ten men and women of the Queen's Guard. They were a fine brave sight in the morning, raising a shout as their king came forth with his foster brother and his queen.

Others of the army who stood by, watched with envy. Those who had not already returned to guard their own realms, or who would not be returning in due time, would garrison Han-Gilen under the regency of the prince. It was a proud duty, but none so proud as this, to ride with that small striking-force into Ashan.

"Small," Mirain had said, "for speed, and for a message. I will ride swiftly, I will settle this quarrel, I will return. I will not dignify it with the full strength of my empire." To which he had added to the Halenani alone, "If a hundred picked troops cannot end this treachery, twenty thousand will not. And will cost me a kingdom's wealth besides in stores and in time."

He seemed fresh and joyous now in scarlet and gold. His Chosen laughed and whooped; one called out, "Aiee, Sunborn! Married life becomes you."

Elian swung into Ilhari's saddle in a shimmer of armor, a swirl of green cloak. "So it should," she called back, "when it's me he's married to."

They roared at that, all of them, and Ilhari reared and belled. *Yes,* thought Elian fiercely, *laugh. Laugh at death, and watch her shrivel!* She knew she was fey; it was blackly wonderful.

The Mad One whirled close to her. Mirain had something in his hands. Copper-gold helmet, proud green plume, and circling it a golden coronet. Her old bronze helmet he tossed away, setting the new and royal one on her head, smiling his brilliant smile. "Now we match," he said. He kissed her, to loud and prolonged applause, and spun his stallion away again, gathering the company.

They left the white city by the north road, as they had come in; as Elian had gone—was it only half a year past? The road was mud and melting snow, the air was luminous; the men sang as they rode. Elian's women sang the descant; one, burly and black-browed as many a man, had a voice like shaken silver. Elian raised her own to match it, and Ilhari danced, weaving through the ranks, out to the fore and the Mad One's side.

THE WEATHER HELD. AND HELD, THROUGH IBAN, THROUGH Kurion, through Sarios and Baian and Shaiar. Sun like spring, moons and stars in a merciful sky. They camped in comfort as often as they lodged with the highborn, finding the former to be wiser. A lord, faced with An-Sh'Endor himself, would flutter and scurry; assured that the army would take care of itself, still he would insist that the king and the queen accept his full hospitality. And inevitably, once morning came, he would beg the high ones to linger for the merest moment, an hour only; there was a case, a judgment, a quarrel which only the Sunborn's wisdom could resolve. And there would go a morning, a noon, a full day of marching time without a furlong's advance toward Ashan; and another night to endure his lordship's entertainment. By then the cream of the local talent would have gathered, and all the gentry who could crowd themselves into the hall, for a feast that would leave the countryside to face a lean and hungry winter.

The camps were best. A tent no bigger than a trooper's, with a cot in it and a stool and one small chest for two; field rations and firelight, and music better than anything in hall.

This was Mirain's element. Even as a boy he had fretted within walls; the man, who had learned to be a king, still took to the march and the camp like a hawk to the air. Elian had not even known how cramped he was until she saw him free.

At first she dreaded the nights and the dreams they would bring. But the power, having wielded her, lay now at rest; and the Exile seemed to have given up the battle, or else to have drawn back beyond the edge of perception. For whole days Elian even forgot to what she rode. The forgetting turned the long advance into a wedding journey.

As for the nights . . .

"So it's true," she said in the midst of one, fitting her body to Mirain's on the narrow bed, "the best lovers are . . . small men."

"*Small?*" It came from the depths of his chest.

"Well, middling," she conceded wickedly, twining her legs with his. "How nicely we fit. If you were as big as Cuthan, or even Hal, we'd never get both of us into this bed."

"Have you been proving it?"

Her laughter lost itself in his hair.

Deftly, and with no effort at all, he tossed her out of bed. She grunted in surprise, and a little in pain. Even carpeted, the ground was hard.

He stood over her with fists on hips, brows knit over the arch of his nose. Her mirth flooded through the tent. "Oh, you *are* a fine figure of a man!"

"A small man."

"A very well endowed, just tall enough, perfect, wonderful—"

"Don't strain your ingenuity," he said dryly.

She hooked his ankles and overset him, perching on his chest. "—splendid, beautiful, royal husband," she finished triumphantly.

He raised a brow. After a moment the other went up to join it. He weighed her breast in his hand. "They're growing," he said. "You're growing all over."

She looked down at herself in real dismay. "I am not!" she cried. "I won't even start to show for—I wouldn't even know, if I weren't—" His eyes mocked her. She pulled his hair until he yelped; and they rolled on the carpets in battle that was all love.

The tent wall brought them up short. Elian tossed back her hair, breathing hard. "The whole camp can hear us," she said.

"And who began it?" He ran his fingers down her side. "In Ianon the kingdom lives by the manhood of its king. I caused my people no end of worry, so few lovers as I took, and so seldom. And not a single bastard to prove my strength."

"I should hope not!"

He laughed softly. "Lady, you have fire enough for three. For you, for me, and for him." His hand rested on her belly. It was as flat and firm as ever, the life within waxing invisibly yet surely. "When he grows big enough to see, he'll have to have a name."

"What if he's a she?"

"Is he?"

Elian looked at his hand, suddenly finding it fascinating. And a little, a very little, frightening: as any miracle can frighten, for its simple strangeness. She shook herself. "It's . . . he. Maybe. Or she. Does it matter?"

"It's ours. Our firstborn. My heir."

"Even if it's a daughter?"

He hesitated only a fraction. "Even then."

Her joy leaped, startling a grin out of him. She laughed and kissed the corner of his mouth. "It will be dark like you."

"And red-haired like you."

"With your Ianyn nose."

"Ah, poor child. And your Halenani height, and your beauty, and a Sun in his hand. Or hers."

"Imagine," she said softly. "We made this, you and I. Son or daughter, it will be a child even the god can be proud of."

"It will be." Mirain kissed the place where his hand had been lying. "Truly and certainly, it will be."

ON THE MARCHES OF EBROS AT LAST THE WEATHER BROKE, and with a vengeance. They waded into Ashan through torrents of icy rain, in a wind that howled straight out of the north. Even in armor, even in oiled leather, the riders were wet to the skin. Their mounts plodded with heads down, ears plastered back. The Mad One was vicious in misery; not even Ilhari dared to come within reach of his heels.

Where the rain turned to sleet, the hills turned to mountains: the steep cruel ridges of Ashan. There the northerners might have burst into song, for this was a shadow of their own country; but even they trudged and cursed, forced afoot by the icy paths.

The southerners were long since emptied of oaths. Elian, struggling up and down the line, heard little more than harsh breathing, and the clatter and slide of hoofs on ice, and the wailing of the wind. Wrapped in the leather coat of a trooper, with a scarf wound about her head, she was blessedly anonymous; men who would never accept aid from a woman, and least of all from their queen, availed themselves willingly enough of her steadying hand.

Some, young Gileni dandies, suffered cruelly in their handsome boots, narrow and high of heel as those were, and never meant for walking, let alone for scrambling over mountain passes in the sleet.

Mirain's tribesmen sneered at them, making no secret of their scorn. "Fancy-boy have hurtings in his little feet?" they sang in mincing voices. "Oh, be careful, sweetling; don't tear your pretty trousers." One, with the aid of liberal swallows from his belt flask, mocked the Gileni's painful gait with much swaying of his hips and a comical display of not quite losing his balance.

Elian's temper flared. She sprang; and as he laughed, thinking her one of the sufferers, she kicked his feet from under him. He toppled like a tree. She set her foot upon his throat, with the merest hint of pressure. "One more move," she said, her voice hoarse with damp, "only one more, and I'll pitch you into the next valley."

He gasped and gaped. With a snort of disgust she hauled him up. "Here. You dance so lightly over these mountains; lend the rest of us a hand."

Ilhari appeared out of the storm to snap wicked teeth in his face. It went slack; he dropped to his knees and pressed his forehead to Elian's sodden boot. A moment later, with conspicuous enthusiasm if with little grace, he offered his shoulder to a stumbling Gileni.

A shout rang out ahead. Elian clawed the ice from her eyelids and strained to see. The mare nudged her. The way was not too hard for the Mad One's daughter, whatever the foolish two-legs might think.

Elian peeled away the saddle's covering and swung astride. Ilhari strode forth, sure-footed as a cat, and proud with it. Even half-frozen as she was, Elian managed to smile.

The vanguard had halted above, just below the summit of the pass. But its numbers had doubled; beside the dripping Sun-banner flapped one of water-darkened yellow, its staff wound with the grey streamers of a messenger.

Mirain was on the ground under a canopy of leather, a tent upheld by a handful of his Chosen. Halenan shared the shelter with him, and a stranger, a man of middle years with a cough that woke Elian's anger. What right had anyone, even a prince, to send a man so ill on an errand so grueling, in such a storm?

His glance caught her as she slid between the king and the prince, but he did not break off his speech. It was hoarse and painful, yet clear enough. "Yes, sire, my lord prince has left Han-Ashan, hoping by his living presence to restrain the combatants. He left word that, should you deign to come to his aid, I should ride to meet you, and direct you to him."

"Where is he now?" asked Halenan.

"He rode first to sojourn with his kin in Asan-Sheian, though I fear that by this time his son will have led the young bloods to attack Eridan. I am bidden to conduct you to Sheian, and thence, if my lord is gone, to Eridan."

The prince's glance met Elian's. *He's telling the truth,* she said in her mind. *Or the truth as he's been allowed to see it.* She addressed the messenger herself, a little sharply. "How far is Sheian from here?"

She watched his courteous efforts to place her, muffled she was, her voice gone sexless with the cold. But, though dizzy with fever, he was no fool. He could guess who would be here between these two men, and speaking as freely as they. "Two days' ride in good weather," he answered her, "my lady. Longer in this; but there is a castle in the valley yonder, and its lord is loyal to my prince. He begs you to accept his hospitality."

Elian ran her tongue over her cracked lips. She did not like the feel of this. Yet the man was honest. Transparently so; and so feeble that, for all his strength of will, he could barely keep his feet.

Her eyes flicked to Mirain. He had his king-look: weighing, pondering. He could press on with those of his company who could manage, leaving the rest behind; and if there was a trap, spring it before it was well set. Or was that the trap itself, to separate him from the main body of his men? Or was there after all no trap and no treachery? The messenger had no falsehood in him. Conflict rumbled in the earth of Ashan: troops gathering, fear mounting. Mirain knew the taste of civil war. It burst upon Elian's tongue, hot and foul; she gagged on it.

The messenger swayed. She caught him, to his surprise, not least at her strength. But though he was tall, he had no more flesh than a bird. "I think," she said, "that we should try to sleep dry tonight at least. And the men need rest, and some will need healing. It's been a cruel march."

Yet, having spoken, she felt no better. There was a wrongness in it. But if Mirain tried to go on . . .

The king's chin lifted; his brows met. "It has been bitter," he said, "and I for one would welcome dry feet. Lord Casien, will yonder castle hold my full company?"

The man coughed, deep and racking, battling to master himself. Elian's power uncoiled. His voice, freed, came almost clear. "I fear not, majesty. But there is a place on the mountain's knees close to the pass, an arm of the vale and a great cavern. Your men would be at ease there, and out of the rain."

And neatly closed in like rats in a trap.

So would they be if they were shut up within a castle wall. Elian set her teeth. She was letting her fears master her.

Briskly Mirain gestured: assent, command. "Very well. Lead us, then; and send a man ahead to the lord of—?"

"Asan-Garin, sire."

"I shall accept his offer, with thanks. My men have food, but would be glad of fuel, and any other aid he may provide."

"It shall be done, majesty."

As ELIAN MOUNTED TO THE TOP OF THE PASS, THE LASHING of sleet eased. The clouds boiled and broke, laying bare a deep cleft of valley amid mountain walls. Beyond the pass it divided like a stream flowing past a stone, one arm thrusting deep into the east, the other, shorter and higher, slanting into a treeless upland and a steep loom of cliff. But the east way was the way to Asan-Garin, the Fortress of the Wolf: black trees and black stones, and at its head where the mountains met, a spur of the peaks. Men had built upon it, erecting walls and keep far above the floor of the vale.

"Impressive," Hal muttered beside her. "But what's the use of a castle there if there's none here, where anyone can come in?"

Elian worked her numb fingers within her gloves, and settled deeper into the saddle. "Maybe people are supposed to come in. Have you ever seen a spider's parlor?"

"Cheerful child." He grinned through the ice in his beard. "Race you down."

"In *this?*"

He laughed and sent his grey over the edge at a pace just short of lethal. After an instant's gathering pause, Ilhari launched herself after him.

Twenty-Three

"*THERE'S* WHY HIS LORDSHIP DOESN'T NEED A CASTLE here," Elian said when she had got her breath back. She had won the race, plunging ahead even of the Mad One, skidding to a halt at the edge of the western meadow. It was high, and sloped higher, almost to the level of the pass; there the mountains opened. Man's hand had touched it, or perhaps the hands of giants; for as she drew closer she saw the vast stone gates open wide, seeming almost to be a part of the peak, save that no mountain wall boasted hinges of grey and rustless metal.

The cavern was both broad and deep, smooth-floored, with hearths built at intervals along its walls and its center; from the air's movement she thought there would be vents far above. There was ample room here for a hundred men, indeed for ten times as many.

Hoofs clattered behind her; voices woke echoes. "Magnificent," breathed Mirain, halting by her side, springing from the Mad One's back. "Look, there were lamps here once, set in the stone. And a stair—there. I wonder where—"

245

"Sire!"

He turned. Elian realized that the company could not see them. They were lost in the darkness beyond the cavern's center, seeing with witch-eyes where mortal sight was useless.

Light blazed. Mirain had stripped the glove from his right hand. The shadows fled from a mighty vault of smoothed stone, a hall of giants.

And giants there were, marching upon the far wall. An army, deep carven: men like the tribesmen of the north, tall and high-nosed and proud; chariots drawn by strange beasts, cats and broad-horned bulls and winged direwolves; women riding upon huge birds. Above them all rode a man in armor in a burning chariot, and drawing it yoked lions, their manes fanning like flames.

Mirain's mirth was light and free. "See! Even the giants of the old time knew my father."

Elian tilted her head back to study the carven god. His armor was strange, ornate, covering his whole body like a skin of jointed metal; over it he wore a long loose surcoat and a flowing cloak. But his head was bare, the hair blown into rays about it. "He has your face," she said to Mirain.

To the life; even to the slight curl at the corner of the mouth. Mirain had it now, examining this his portrait that had been made long ages before he was born. "What an eagle's beak I have!"

"You," she said severely, "are unspeakably vain."

"Isn't he, now?"

Elian almost laughed. As she leaped to set herself between Mirain and the voice, Mirain leaped to set himself before her. They ended shoulder to shoulder, swords drawn, points meeting at a throat some few handbreaths above their own. Their captive grinned white in a face as dark as any in Ianon, and lounged against the cavern's wall. Torches, kindled, struck fire in all his northern finery.

"Vadin!" Mirain's sword flashed into its sheath; his joy leaped with him into his oathbrother's embrace. And died, thrusting him back, chilling his voice. "I sent you to hold the north. I remember no word of your meeting me here."

Vadin glanced at Elian. She stared back, refusing to flinch. Mirain looked from one to the other. His brows drew together. "Elian," he said, soft and still.

She sheathed her sword, taking her time about it. She did not think either of them could see her hand shake. She inclined her head to Vadin. "My lord. I trust you had a pleasant journey."

"Pleasant enough," he answered, "considering. And you?"

"The same."

"I see he finally got up the nerve to declare himself to you."

She tossed her head. "Nerve! He had nerve. He did it in front of his whole household. And even then I had to trick him into marrying me."

"That's Mirain," Vadin said, sighing. "With armies and kingdoms he puts an Asanian courtesan to shame. With women he goes all tongue-tied."

"Only at the beginning," said Elian. "Once he had warmed to it . . ."

"Elian." Mirain's tone was ominous in its gentleness. "What have you done?"

She faced him. He was not angry. He was determined not to be. Because if he let go, even for a moment, he would flay her alive.

She lifted her chin to its most maddening angle. "What do you think I've done?"

There were words for it. One or two might have been acceptable outside of a guardroom. Vadin spared Mirain the trouble of uttering them. "I had a summons from my lady empress. It was concise. She had need of me. Would I meet her in Ashan?"

Mirain's breath left him in a hiss. His eyes glittered upon Elian. "You don't even like him."

"What does that have to do with it? My power says we

need him. Therefore we have him. If nothing else," she said, "he can give us a proper burial."

"They burn Ianyn kings," Vadin informed her. And as they both glared: "Now see here, children. This is a very clever trap, very enticingly baited. I've had a day or two to sniff around it." He stepped aside. His shadow bred men: great bearded Ianyn warriors who poured out of the mountain to overwhelm their king, drowning what more Vadin would have said, sweeping them all toward the hall's hearth.

Mirain's own company was in and dismounted, settled well within where wind and sleet could not reach, tending their seneldi, freeing the packbeasts of their burdens. Adjan had found fuel, only he knew where or how, and kindled a fire in the central hearthpit. They all leaped up from it in the face of the invasion.

"Peace," said Mirain. "These are friends."

They settled slowly. Vadin's barbarians eyed the southerners in open contempt, and took care to crouch well away from them, but as close to their king as they might come.

Mirain's barbarians, Elian noticed, had taken umbrage. They mingled conspicuously with their trousered comrades; they glowered at their kinsmen.

She swallowed a smile as she sat between Mirain and Vadin. It boded well for the empire, that mingling and that outrage.

And now they were three tight circles: the warriors of Ianon, and the soldiers of the empire, and the followers of the Lord Casien. The last of them huddled apart, surrounding their lord. Here in the mountain, with a hundred king's men hemming them in, lounging about with hands never far from hilts, they had a taut and wary look. One, though shivering convulsively, tried to press a steaming cup on his master.

Mirain beckoned to Halenan and Cuthan and a captain or two. They withdrew somewhat from the rest, leaning forward as Vadin finished what he had begun. "Yes," he said, "this is a trap. The whole of Ashan is a trap, for the matter of that. The center of it is here."

"How do you know that?" Mirain asked. Curious; completely unafraid.

"I feel it in my bones." Vadin grinned, a baring of sharp teeth. "And I've been exploring. This cavern is only an antechamber. The mountain behind it is a maze of tunnels. Most of them lead to nothing but blank walls. Some are traps; I lost a man in learning it. One winds up to the Wolf's castle. Its side ways are . . . interesting. And rather well guarded.

"It's true what you've been told, that there's no room in Garin for you," Vadin said. "It's large enough to hold an army; and an army fills it."

"Ashani?" asked Halenan.

"Ashani," Vadin answered. "They've turned on you, Mirain."

Mirain smiled. It was not comfortable to see. "Have they?" he asked, almost purring. "Luian alone? Or do his sons have a part in it?"

"Luian and his heir. The rest run at their heels. I found them marching up from Han-Ashan; I tracked them here. I saw them send out their bait." Vadin glanced at Casien. The lord slumped against one of his escort: a kinsman, perhaps. His eyes were closed. If he was not unconscious, he was perilously close to it. "He's an innocent; they know that much of hoodwinking mages. And they rely on your famous clemency to keep you from inquiring too deeply into his memories and finding any hint that might betray their plotting."

"They think I'm soft." Mirain laughed at the sudden rash of denials. "Of course they do. Look at me. I'm young, I'm a priest, I'm famous for sparing my enemies. And I'm arrogant to idiocy. Even if I caught wind of Luian's ambush, I'd throw myself into it, because he sent a messenger near death from sickness, and because I am the god's son; I am not for any man's slaying."

They stared at him. "You wouldn't," Elian said.

"Why not? It's a pity to waste so lovely a trap."

Even Vadin was appalled. Unsurprised, but appalled. "That's insane even for you."

"What's mad about it? I know what Luian intends. I have my best men with me. And I have you, who know the hidden ways to the castle. I'll ambush the ambush."

"Ah," said Halenan. "An attack from the rear. For a moment I thought you were going to spring the trap."

"I am." Mirain was on his feet, beating down the outcry. "I must! Else they'll know that I suspect something."

Elian left the protesting to the men. They could as easily have moved the mountain as persuaded Mirain to see sense. More easily. Mere stone would yield to a mage's will.

When the flood had ebbed a little, she said, "There's always an alternative. A ruse. A soldier spelled to look like Mirain."

The king rounded on her. "I will not command a man of mine to die in my place."

"In your name, often. But never in your place." She stood, the better to bear the brunt of his anger. "If you go, I go."

"You will not."

"I will." She smiled sweetly. "By your hand I swear it."

For a mad instant she knew that he would strike her down with that same glittering hand. But it rose only as high as his breast, and fell, trembling. It could not clench. The white agony of it pierced her shields. She caught it, held it to her heart, taking the pain as she had taken it since she was a young child.

He drew himself up. He was as well aware as she of the life that sparked below his hand. "Take back your oath."

"You know I can't."

"I must go." He had forgotten the others; he was all centered on her, his hand shifting of itself, cupping the breast beneath the sodden leather of her coat. "No one else can do what I can do: blind Luian, convince him that

I come in all ignorance, ensure that the castle lies open to my army."

"You could retreat. Luian will hang himself soon enough, or be hanged, when his allies turn against him. As they will if you come riding with all Ebros at your back."

"But," he said, "that would take time; and my enemies would call it flight, and proclaim that a clever man can betray me and live."

"When have you ever cared what your enemies say of you?"

"I care that an ally has betrayed me. I mean to win him back; or to have his head."

Vadin spoke behind her. He sounded both weary and furious. "A valiant effort, my lady. But useless. He's bent on killing himself, and on playing the just king while he goes about it."

"Have I died yet?" Mirain asked sharply.

"No," Vadin replied. "But I have. Who will call you back? I'm no god's son, to win battles with milady death."

"And therefore you need me." Elian met Mirain's hot stare. "Unless you have the wits to desist. We can take Garin from the tunnels; we've no need to risk our necks by riding in the front gate."

"Luian needs it," Mirain said, obstinate. "If I can win him, there will be no need to fight at all."

She sighed deeply. She was not afraid; she was too utterly exasperated. "Very well then. We'd best go, before our enemies become suspicious."

"Elian—"

Her eyes held his; her hand gripped his own. "I keep my promises, Mirain."

He pulled free, hand, eyes. He would yield. He must. She set all her will upon him.

He turned his back on her, raised his voice. "Lord Casien," he said, "I leave you here in the care of my Chosen." As the man moved to speak, Mirain held up a hand. "You should be abed and under a healer's care. My company can provide the beginnings of both."

"Sire, my prince has commanded me—I am to accompany you wherever—"

"You will not endanger your life by riding farther tonight. Surely your prince will understand that." Mirain crooked a finger at the man with the cup. "You, sir. See that your master has all he needs. My men will give you whatever you ask for."

The servant bowed, still shivering. Not all of it was cold. Elian marked the way his eyes kept sliding round the cavern to the carven wall, and back in a nervous skitter to Mirain's face.

If the king saw, he took no notice of it. His eyes ran over his company. Swiftly he named names: twenty altogether, gathering before him, grinning like the valiant idiots they were. None of them was Halenan.

The prince's face was dangerously still. "My lord king. It is my right as your general—"

"It is your duty as my general to command the army in my absence."

"The Lord of Geitan is perfectly capable of commanding your troops by himself. And," said Halenan, "he knows the secret ways to Garin."

"You will share the command." Mirain was immovable; but he held out his hand. "Brother, I need you here, with your wits and your power and a guard on the pass. Whom else may I trust so?"

Elian suppressed an urge out of childhood, to vanish into a corner. Halenan's hot eye flashed to her; Mirain's had no need. "My lady has sworn to come with me," he said with a touch of irony. "What power has any of us to prevent her?"

"That's idiocy!" snapped Halenan. "I have two sons and a daughter, all safe in my city. What have you?"

Elian started forward, but Mirain's hand caught her, steel-strong and unyielding. Quietly he said, "My brothers, you know what you must do. If by tomorrow's nooning I have sent you no signal, nor any word of my victory over Luian, mount the attack."

Halenan opened his mouth. Vadin silenced him with

a firm hand. The Ianyn lord looked long at Mirain, and pulled him into a swift embrace. "Try to come out of this alive," he said.

Mirain grinned up at him. "I'll do more than try. I'll be victorious."

"Arrogant." Vadin let him go. He turned, facing Halenan. The prince was stiff, angry. Mirain tilted his head, brows up.

"Farewell," said Halenan coldly, "sire."

"Farewell," said Mirain, "brother."

Halenan unbent a very little. He suffered Mirain's embrace, and Elian's after it. He returned the latter somewhat more warmly than he might have, and stepped back, nursing his temper.

Elian faced Vadin. They did not speak, nor did they touch, save glance to glance. She groped for resentment, even for dislike. Neither would come to her hand. He was necessary. He was part of the world as it must be; part of Mirain. *Protect him,* he willed her, *until I come.*

Always, she answered. And: *If your bones tell you to come, don't linger. Come quickly, and come with all your strength. Else . . . else we lose him.*

He bowed. It was a promise.

THE LAST ELIAN SAW OF EITHER OF THEM, THEY STOOD IN the arch of the great gate. Vadin stood still, arms folded, both haughty and patient. Halenan's head was bare in the bitter wind; his eyes burned even at the full length of the meadow.

She faced forward. If there was worse misery than riding from dawn to dusk in a storm of sleet, it was pausing by a fire; beginning to remember warmth and dry feet; and riding out again.

The escort was silent. Ten of Mirain's best in scarlet darkened by the wet to the color of drying blood; her own ten in moldy black that had begun as green. It was little mercy that the sleet had thinned almost to nothing: the wind had risen, knife-keen.

From the vale of the cavern the land fell down into

the deep wooded coomb of Garin. The road was narrow, following a stony stream; where trees overhung the track, careful hands had cut back the branches to the height of a rider's head.

"That's not bandits' custom," Elian said. Her teeth were chattering; she bit down hard.

Mirain's knee brushed hers. With a startling-swift movement he swept her into his own saddle, settling on the crupper, wrapping his cloak about them both. The Mad One was steady beneath them, tolerant of their follies, even amused.

Warmth crept through Elian's body. She basked in it, although she knew that there were grins behind her. The army took an unholy delight in watching their lord and their lady at love-play, however innocent.

"Of course," Mirain said in her ear. "It proves we're actively pursuing our dynastic duty."

"Not in this saddle," she muttered.

He laughed and kissed the back of her neck. "Later, then. Shall we be scandalous? Bathe together, dispose of our supper and our enemies as quickly as we can, and go to bed sinfully early."

"And sin all night." She leaned back against the living warmth of him, hands laced with his at her waist. He was choosing to forgive her; accepting the inevitable. She was choosing to allow it. "Sometimes I think I'm too happy. Even here, even with what waits for us in Garin ... it almost isn't fair."

"Of course it's fair. Eminently so. It's love, you see; and we're riding to a war."

She smiled a little. "The Grey Monks say that love is the worse of the two. A man can go his life long without once dreaming of battles, but even eunuchs dream of love."

"Do they?"

"I knew one once. He'd been a slave in Asanion. He said he never even thought of women; but I know he dreamed of men."

Mirain considered that in his inimitable fashion, both

swiftly and thoroughly. She liked to watch the turning of his mind; to fit herself into it, turning with it, losing for a little while her shallow, flighty self.

She looked out of his eyes. Aware of the differences: the angles of his body, the joining of hip and shoulder, the fullness where she had none; and no need to balance the soft heaviness of breasts. And the sparking awareness of warm woman-body against him—desire as keen as a sword, and half-mirthful suppression, and a wonderfully gratifying rush of blood to his cheeks.

She was herself, odd-familiar, laughing softly. And he reached, and he was there, sharing her body, searching out its curves and crevices. How strange it was, how marvelous, with its secret places where he was all open to the world; its softness where he was hard, and its deep-rooted strength.

Through her eyes he saw the road's sharp curve; through her ears he heard what made the Mad One pause, head up, nostrils flared. Metal on metal; hoofs on stone.

Ilhari ventured ahead alone. At the bend of the road, she halted. Mirain, enclosed within his own body once more, sent the stallion to join her.

From the curve the road ran almost straight into a grey light and the loom of mountain wall. A small company rode there: mounted men surrounding a laden wain, and foremost, the man whom Lord Casien had sent, spurring his weary mount forward, bowing over his pommel. "Lord Garin of Garin, your majesty—he comes himself to greet you."

The Wolf fit his name well. He was not an old man, but his hair was iron grey, cut thick and short like a wolf's mane. The face under it was narrow, long-nosed, and yellow-pale, with eyes narrow and tilted and the same amber-gold as a wolf's. They glinted, bright and mocking, taking in the man, and the woman in man's dress, and the small plain-clad escort. "Your majesty," he said, bowing low in the saddle, baring long yellow teeth. "My lady—Kalirien, is it not?"

Even with her back to it, Elian felt the cold brilliance of Mirain's smile. "Kalirien indeed; and Elian ilOrsan of Han-Gilen; and my queen."

"Majesty," said the Lord Garin, unruffled. "You honor us." He indicated the wagon with a flick of his hand. "Here I have fuel, and food and drink, and blankets against the cold. Your men will not suffer in your absence."

"My lord is generous," Mirain said.

"I am a loyal man, your majesty."

"You do seem so, my lord Garin," said Elian, sliding smoothly from the Mad One's saddle to Ilhari's. The mare stamped; Elian smiled a slight, edged smile. "Shall we go up to your castle?"

Twenty-Four

THE ROAD, THOUGH STEEP, WAS SMOOTH, THE CASTLE
much larger than distance had made it. As large
within its grey walls as Han-Ashan itself; and that
was no small stronghold.

But Han-Ashan pretended to grace: fine carvings,
fine tapestries, and even the slaves well and often ele-
gantly clad. Asan-Garin feigned nothing. It was a fortress,
a strong holding. Its men walked in leather or in well-
worn armor. Its women kept to their houses or flitted in
shadows, heavily veiled. Its barefoot, bare-bodied children
stared solemnly at the newcomers and made no sound.

The silence was eerie. Every other holding—every
one—had rung with acclaim for the king. Grudging, some
of it, but clearly audible. These people did not cheer, did
not call out his name or his titles. They simply stood in the
courtyards and in the corridors, and watched.

There were too few of them for an army. Elian,
seeking with power, found none beyond them; and no
love for Mirain, but no hate. He was nothing to them.

Had Vadin lied? Or had he been deceived? Perhaps
he had tricked Mirain into a place of safety, so that he

might dispose of his king's enemies without danger to his king. Perhaps Luian had repented and withdrawn to Sheian. Perhaps—

The grey walls closed in about her. Instinct struggled and shrieked. Brutally she beat it down. She had bound herself to this. She made herself walk coolly onward, now beside Mirain, now ahead or behind as the way narrowed, warded always by their escort. They were calm, these chosen of their king, eyes watchful, hands resting lightly on swordhilts.

Cuthan walked just behind Elian, close as her shadow, relaxed but wary. "Rather like home, this," he observed pleasantly.

Lord Garin did not choose to notice him. Nobleman or no, he was a mere guard, and speaking out of turn. But Mirain said, "It does have an air of the north. The stern walls; the stern faces. No southern fripperies here."

The lord paused before a guarded door. The sentry opened it crisply but without haste. "I hope this will be to your satisfaction, sire," Lord Garin said. His eyes were full of wolf-laughter.

In spite of her determination to be unmoved, Elian stared. It was as if all the luxury of the south and west had drained from the castle into this one tower. A broad chamber with the proportions of a guardroom and the furnishings of a seraglio; an inner room dominated by a huge bed hung and draped with velvet, lush with furs and Asanian carpets; and a bath of lapis and silver, deep enough and wide enough to swim in.

Mirain took it all in and laughed, the free and joyous laughter of a boy. "Why, my lord! You're a voluptuary in disguise."

"Not I, sire. My late father." Lord Garin showed his sharp teeth. "A reiver of repute, was my lord Garin the elder."

"Indeed," said Mirain unabashed, "that's clear to see. Not I myself could have done better."

That caught the Wolf off guard; for a moment his glance betrayed a hint of admiration. "You flatter my father, sire. No doubt his bones are warmed by it, cold as they have been all these years, naked under the gallows tree."

"Ah! Who hanged him?"

"Why, sire, I did. I am a respectable man, you see."

WITH THE DOOR SHUT AND BARRED FROM WITHIN AND HIS own men warding it, Mirain laughed again, long and deeply. He spun still laughing, and spread his arms. "Come now, my friends! This is no time for grim faces."

"Isn't it?" Elian muttered. But her lips twitched. "You're quite mad, you know."

"Oh, quite! Milord is more his father's son than ever he would wish us to dream; but I find I like him for it. He has wit; he has subtlety. And he has no fear of me at all."

"Neither do I," Elian pointed out.

"So. But you I do not like." His eyes danced. "You, I love." He swept her up, heedless of her struggles, and carried her past the grinning guards, and kicked open the door of the inner chamber, and dropped her onto the bed.

She struggled out of the tangle of bedclothes. He was stripped already and striding toward the bath.

She plunged in after him. The water was a wonder, a marvel, a long delight: warm, sweet-scented, and swirling gently, bearing all her travel stains away.

With a shock she realized that the doors were open, the guardroom clear to see. The women had arranged a curtain between themselves and the men, but both could look straight into the pool.

Mirain's white grin surfaced beside her. "Ho, guards!" he called. "There's room here for us all. Quick now, while the water's hot!"

The full score of them came in a mob, whooping. The men were shyer than the women; the Ianyn, too dark to show their blushes, looked everywhere but where their minds were. Elian laughed at them, and needled them until they laughed back. But Cuthan led them in a gloriously wet revenge.

Mirain was first off the field as he had been the first
on it, leaping out of the battle and snatching the least
sodden of the drying-cloths. " 'Varyan!" he said. "I'm
dying of your foolishness. Go on then, drown yourselves in
mere water. I'm for mine host's good wine."

As Elian watched him saunter away with his cloth
flung over his shoulder, Cuthan spoke beside her, half
amused, half somber. "He's always like that: looking for a
better way to die." He bent, took up a cloth, wrapped it
calmly and boldly and quite firmly about her. The others
had quieted and begun to scatter, drying one another,
sorting out the tangle of clothing.

Elian looked up. She had to crane her neck a little.
Cuthan's face was unwontedly still; he looked more than
ever like his brother. Quietly, rather slowly, he said, "I
have no wizardry, but my nose is keen enough; and
there's that in the air which I don't like. This trap is not as
it should be."

Elian hugged the cloth to her, trying not to shiver. "I
know. I can't find the army Vadin spoke of. If it's gone, I
yearn to know where, and why. But if it is not . . . My
power is strong, Cuthan. Any mage who can hide an
army from me may prove too much even for Mirain."

"Maybe there is no army after all," Cuthan said.
"Maybe Lord Garin is no more than he seems."

"Maybe." Elian sat on the pool's edge, running her
fingers through her hair, wrestling out the tangles. "This
is a very strange place. Every mind is clear enough to me,
down to a certain point. Then nothing. Nothing at all. It's
uncanny. Like looking at a crowd and realizing all at once
that none of them is real; they're only masks set up on
spears."

"Even the lord?"

"He's the worst of all. And yet he's no sorcerer. He
has no power."

"A lord may be without magic but employ a mage.
There are all too many such in the north: court wizards
and tame enchanters, and shamans of the wilder tribes.

Most are foreign-trained, mages from the Nine Cities or followers of one or several of Asanion's thousand gods."

The name of the Nine Cities rang in Elian's head like a gong, dizzying her, catching her breath in her throat. And it was in Ashan that the Exile had found her; into the wilds of Ashan that she had vanished. If she was here, if it was she who raised these walls of nothingness, then Elian had need of more than fear. She needed all the strength she had, and all the resistance.

She made herself face Cuthan steadily, speak coolly, calmly. "I've heard the songs," she said. "Mirain and the Insh'u Master; the Sunborn and the Mage of Arriman; the Ballad of An-Sh'Endor and the Thirty Sorcerers."

"There were only six," said Cuthan with a surprising touch of severity, "and four were apprentices." He grinned suddenly, and that was more surprising still. "But what's a song if it cleaves to the truth? I'm composing one now. A very good one, I'm so presumptuous as to think: the tale of the Sunborn and the Lady Kalirien."

But for once Elian could not return his lightness. Her power had been stretching itself, of itself, with no will to compel it. And her fear was mounting. "Cuthan," she said very low, "this strangeness has another face. It hems my power in. I can't mindspeak to anyone outside of these walls; I dare not force the barriers. Whoever, whatever wields power here"—*Not the Exile,* her inward self keened, *O Avaryan, may it not be she*—"must not know what our brothers will do. Which means—"

"Which means," he said, and she loved him for that quickness of wit, "that my lord cannot give the signal to attack. And morning may be too late."

"Morning will be too late," she whispered. It was dark behind her eyes. In the dark was light, grey-cold like a winter dawn; and Mirain fallen upon cold stone.

Cuthan's hands were warm, gripping her. She let them hold her to the world of life and love and hope of victory. "I'll go if I can," he said, "as soon as I can. I'll bring the army to you."

She smiled. It was not as hard as she had feared it

would be. Cuthan was very easy to smile at. "To me, my captain? Not to your king?"

He looked down abashed, but he looked up again swiftly, with lordly pride. "I am *your* captain, my lady."

"Gallant knight." She rose. "Come. Let us gird our-selves for the slaughter."

WITH THE WINE, WHICH WAS THE SWEET GOLDEN VINTAGE of Anshan-i-Ormal, Lord Garin had sent robes of honor. White Asanian silk for Mirain; and for Elian a gown the color of flame, and a golden veil. The gown might have been made to her measure. The veil she almost cast away; but she paused. It was a lovely thing, cloud-soft, cloud-fragile. If it was meant for an insult to the notorious Lady Kalirien, why then, let it become a badge of honor.

She draped it carefully. Nimble hands aided her: Igani, the beauty of her Guard. The warrior woman was as deft as a lady's maid, but no maid ever wore such a wicked smile, or said as she settled the golden fillet, "Give 'em hell, my lady."

Elian met her own mirrored eyes and smiled slowly. Paint and perfumes she had none, and no jewels but the fillet, yet she was—fair. More than fair. She would not shame her king.

Nor did he put his own legend to shame. Despite his words, he had drunk but a sip of wine; the glitter in his eyes was his own, and the sheen that lay upon him, of danger and daring and of high royalty. She, meeting that splendid gaze, for a moment was blinded.

He bowed low and kissed her fingertips; her palms; her throbbing wrists. Whispering with each: "Lady. Queen. Beloved."

She looked down at his bent head, bent her own, and kissed it.

He straightened. Her eyes, freed, flicked round. The guards had drawn together about them, a living shieldwall. Beyond them the door stood open, with Lord Garin in it.

The ruler of Garin had put off his riding leathers for a plain brown coat. No jewels, no precious metals; only a

belt with a simple clasp, and a knife hanging sheathed
from it, both hilt and clasp of hammered bronze. Like his
people, like all his castle save this tower, he affected no
elegance.

That in itself, perhaps, was an affectation. He regarded the king and the queen with a careful scrutiny
and a bow that conceded very little. And yet, veiled though
his mind was, Elian sensed strong stirrings beneath.
Tension, tight-reined fear, and—elation?

The gloating of the wolf before it pulls down its prey. Yet,
Mirain said in her mind, *this victim is armed and ready. It
will not fall as easily as he may hope.* He offered his hand.
Elian laid hers upon it. With a smooth concerted movement, the wall of guards parted. King and queen paced
forth. The guards followed them, save only those who
warded the chambers behind them.

WHATEVER SPLENDORS THE ELDER GARIN HAD BROUGHT TO
his hall, his son had long since stripped away. The
chamber was long, its grey stone bare, with no softening
of trophy or tapestry. Torches illumined the walls, thrust
into brackets of iron. Its center was a hearth where roared
and smoked a great blaze.

Just within the cavernous door, Elian stopped. The
folk of Asan-Garin stood along the walls, or sat on benches,
or crouched upon the rushes. Faces, eyes—tens, hun-
dreds. Men in brown, men in grey, men in yellow, men in
mottled green.

With all her power she mastered her face. She could
have cried aloud for purest relief, and for purest, most
exhilarating terror. An army, after all. An enemy to face
and, the god willing, to overcome.

As if some will had worked upon it, the hearthfire
leaped up and died abruptly. Beyond it spread a dais and
a high board. People sat there in state: men, a veiled
woman or two. Elian's eyes, blurred with smoke and sudden dimness, would not come clear.

They had no need. She knew those handsome black-
bronze faces, those affable smiles. They were all there as

they should have been: Luian of Ashan, the Prince-Heir Omian foremost and on his feet, and in the tall canopied chair of the lord, the Prince of Ashan himself.

But those faded and paled before the one who sat at Luian's right hand. Tall, gaunt, clad in black, with eyes like flawed pearls. Her familiar purred in her arms.

Four thin lines of fire seared Elian's cheek; but she hardly felt the pain. Prophecy was a keener fire, and cleaner. It burned away her fear, left her calm, almost content. *So,* her mind observed, *it has come at last.* And the sooner come, the sooner gone, for good or for ill.

Behind her the doors boomed shut. Shouts sounded dim beyond, the outrage of the guards, the mockery of Garin's men. One only had outrun the closing of the gates: Cuthan, swift to see and swift to move, and closest to his lady.

Mirain stood at his royal ease, almost smiling. As Cuthan halted behind him, he said to the man who had guided him here, "There is no need of that, my lord Garin. I shall not attempt to escape." Coolly he moved forward, Elian at his side, the Ianyn lord a bulwark behind, down the length of the hall, skirting the fire. His smile was quite visible and quite amused. "Prince Luian; Prince Omian. This is a pleasant meeting. Have you then settled the matter of Eridan?"

The prince examined him minutely, as if he had been a stranger. Elian, watching him, for the moment unregarded, reeled with vertigo. He was not *there*. He could be seen, he could be heard; he could even be smelt, a faint musty odor like old rooms long untenanted. But to the mind there was nothing.

Her power unfolded. All her outward senses cried out to her of crowding bodies: Luian's men, Garin's people, the followers of the woman called Kiyali. Her mind met only void. Even Mirain—even he—

Wrath drove back her panic. The Exile sat as a queen of mages, smiling at Elian. Without a word of mind or tongue, she beckoned. She invited. She offered strength that was infinite beside Mirain's haughty weakness, and power that knew no bonds of light or dark. Elian raised all her barriers and huddled within them. Immovable, by the god; unassailable. Though bolts of seduction battered the gates, and temptation sang its sweet song, beckoning her into the deadly air.

Luian spoke, dry and cold. She took refuge in his insolence. "Eridan shall be dealt with in its proper time. Meanwhile I have other and more immediate concerns."

"Such as myself." Mirain tilted his head to one side, all bright interest. "You were rather clever, prince. I would have expected you to trap me in Sheian, or even to wait until we came to Eridan. But this is much more convenient. A spacious and isolated prison for my army; a strong castle to lock me in, with ample room for all your forces; a lord who is, by his own admission, a loyal man. You have even managed to tame a sorceress to oppose my famous wizardry; and that one of all sorceresses . . . has she ever told you why she is blind?"

The Exile's smile gained an edge. "I have told him, King of Ianon. All of it. You took me once by surprise; you can never do so again."

"No," said Mirain willingly, "I cannot. You have grown strong since you betrayed my mother."

"I executed her by the law of her order. The order you claim, priestess' child, no-man's-son. You have risen high on the strength of her lies. But every falsehood must be uncovered at last; and the greater the lie, the more terrible is its revealing."

Mirain looked about him. "They believe you, I see. Your skill in mind-twisting is impressive. But then, you build on strong foundations. My lord Garin, the loyal man; Prince Omian, whom I forced into close and constant commerce with his ancestral enemy; my royal lord of Ashan, displaced from first and greatest ally to scarce-regarded vassal. Men were content with their wars and their petty thieveries before I came to disturb them, I with my mad conviction that the world is mine to rule."

"By your own words are you condemned."

"And quite cheerfully, kinswoman; for some vices

make excellent substitutes for virtue. You know that well, who slew the bride of Avaryan. I regret that I took such vengeance as I did. I should have killed you cleanly, or let you go wholly free."

"You had no such power. You were a child then, untaught, unrestrained. You are a child still. Else you would never be here before me."

"I might. I might have decided, kingly-wise, that it is time you were disposed of. You subvert my people; you disrupt my kingdom. You are, in short, a nuisance."

The Exile laughed softly. "Am I not? We are always troublesome, we defenders of the truth."

"Can you even tell what is truth and what is a lie?" Mirain mounted the dais, moving with that swift grace which made him so deadly in battle. The Ashani princes drew back from him, their smiles long gone. Luian, trapped by the proud bulk of the throne, held his ground, although Mirain leaned upon the table and fixed him with a steady, glittering stare. "So, prince. I have obliged you; I have fallen into your web. I admire art, even in treachery. But this I cannot forgive: your cruel misuse of your messenger. Kingslaying may have its excuses. The murder of an ill and innocent man has none."

The prince's eyes hooded; his face was unmoved. "Lord Casien is an utterly honest man and an utter fool. As for his illness, the songs give you great powers of healing. Are they lies then?"

"Prince," said Mirain softly, "you cannot have two truths. If the tales of me are true, then I am indeed the king, and you are a traitor. If the tales are false, you are something less foul, perhaps, but more despicable: a murderer of his own good servants." He leaned forward slightly, resting on his hands. "Whichever you are, Luian of Ashan, and whichever I am, mind you this: You have me. You do not have my empire. And it will avenge me."

"Will it, King of Ianon?" murmured the sorceress. "Are you so greatly beloved? With arms and songs you won the north. The Hundred Realms came to you by gift of the man who fostered you. Fathered you, it might be thought. But for his power, you could never have come so far; never, with all your pride and your vaunted wizardry, have laid claim to an empire. It is Orsan of Han-Gilen who rules in the world's heart, and who has always ruled there, whomever he raises as his figurehead."

Mirain stood straight, still at his ease, unruffled. "That may well be. You who were of the Halenani know well their greatest pride. Kings they are not and will not be. They are princes among the princes of the Hundred Realms; they claim no greater title, and no less. And they accept no king over them save one of their own choosing."

"A puppet king. An illusion of power, a pretense of royalty." The blind eyes opened wide, fixed upon him as if indeed they could see. Elian's nape prickled. Power gathered like summer thunder, swelling in the smoke-dimmed air, filling the emptiness where minds should be.

"Puppet," whispered the Exile, wind-soft, wind-cold. "Little bantam cock, dressed to seem a king. Men are slaves to their eyes and to a clever song. Let them see and hear the truth. You are nothing. You are an empty thing, a counterfeit, a shape of air and darkness. Long ago I knew you; long have I suffered for that knowing." She raised her hand. Shadow filled it. She cast it outward. "Down, liar, child of lies, begotten in falsehood. Down, and know your master."

That voice froze Elian where she stood: low, vibrant, thrumming with power. Her knees had locked, else she would have fallen. Her eyes swam with darkness.

Mirain swayed in the heart of it, wrapped in it, helpless, powerless, lost. It buffeted him; he reeled to his knees. All his splendid sheen was gone, leaving him stripped bare, a smallish unhandsome man in an extravagance of gold and silk, his face drawn taut with anguish. The little power he had, had been enough to blind simple folk, to erect a semblance of kingship. But against true magery he had nothing: no strength, no magic, no god-born splendor.

His head fell back, as if he had lost control even of his body. The skin stretched tight over the proud bones of his face, grey-pale where they thrust forth, blue-pallid about the lips. A great tremor shook him. His teeth bared, white and sharp and strangely feral.

With an effort so mighty that it seemed to shake the very stones of the hall, he lurched to his feet. His hands worked convulsively, the right clawed, trembling in spasms. Light dripped from it, slowly, like blood.

It snapped shut.

The darkness shattered. The sorceress cried out, sharp and high.

Elian nearly collapsed in the sudden, mind-numbing clamor. All shields had fallen. The hall thronged with thoughts as with men, throbbed with astonishment, quivered with hostility. Only at her back was there a refuge, the strong fierce loyalty of her captain who was her friend, warmed to burning with the love he bore his king.

Mirain stood upon the dais in a cloak of light, head high, strong voice ringing from end to end of the long hall. "Now I see. Now I see it all. As I am called Prince Orsan's puppet, so does Prince Luian dance to your piping. I was most skillfully deceived: I looked for naught beyond mere mortal treachery."

"Not all men are blind to the truth," the Exile said.

Mirain's lips stretched, baring teeth. It was not a smile. "How easily you mouth the words. Truth; falsehood. What would you now? A simple slaughter? A refinement or ten of torment?"

"Neither," the Exile answered him. "I am neither murderer nor torturer." His lip curled; she sensed it. "Nor," she added, "executioner. No longer. You who were a half-mad child have become a king; you are renowned for your honor. I would face you in fair combat. Power against power; mage against mage. Have you the will to face me?"

Elian could say no word; could not even move. Nor was it the sorceress who held her. It was Mirain. Mirain kindling with something appallingly like delight. "I have the will," he said. "I have will and to spare. I have fought body to body against a slave of the dark; I have waged the duel arcane with demon-masters in the lands of the north. But never have I faced an equal in wizardry, servant of the goddess as am I of the god. Formal combat by the ancient laws: To the victor, my empire. To the vanquished, death."

The Exile turned her eyes toward him, as if to search his face. "You would set the stakes so high?"

"You have trapped me. I know that I cannot persuade you, of all women in this world, to let me go; nor will you ever be my ally. I can work free by painful degrees while my people wage war to win me back, or I can risk all on a single cast of the dice." His grin flashed, wide and white and fearless. "I have never been noted for my prudence."

Prince Omian jerked forward. "Treachery!" he cried. "I know the songs. No prison can hold him. He will lull us with false bargains, go quietly to his chamber, and walk out in the night, to bring all his armies down upon us."

The nameless one smiled, undismayed. "Set yourself at ease, my lord. He knows as well as I that he cannot escape the bonds which I have set. Only through battle may he win free; and that, have no doubt, only into death." She turned her voice and her face upon Mirain. "So let it be. The battle of true power, by the laws of the masters. We meet at dawn according to their dictates. Gird yourself well, King of Ianon."

Twenty-Five

ELIAN SAT ON THE BED IN THE STATE CHAMBER. ITS SPLENdor dripped with irony, as bitter a symbol as chains of gold. Even, she thought, without the knowledge that its first master had been hanged by his own son.

Mirain was in the outer room, sharing a late meal with the guards. Whatever his intent toward his guests, Lord Garin was not minded to starve them. The food was plain but plentiful and, from the evident relish with which they consumed it, not ill to the taste.

She had no appetite for it. They were all so calm, and Mirain calmest of all, passing round the ale and laughing at a jest. She too was calm, for the matter of that, but it was the quiet of numbness. Her body was leaden, unwieldy, strange to itself.

She stretched out, pulling veil and fillet from her head, letting them fall to the floor. Of their own accord her hands went to her belly. The life there was a Brightmoon-cycle old this very night. Had she been without power, she would have begun to wonder if indeed she had conceived.

Her fingers tensed. She wanted to rip it away, to cast

off all of it, to be her own self again: Elian, Han-Gilen's wild lady; Galan, esquire of the Sunborn. She wanted to cradle it, to brood over it like a great bird, to rend any who dared to threaten it.

She lay on her face. Laughing, a strangled gasp, for when she began to swell she would not be able to lie so; choking on tears. And laughing again, because every tale of bearing women trumpeted their mad shifts of mood; but she had always been as wild as a weathercock.

A light hand traced the path of her spine. She raised her head. Mirain sat on the bed's edge, balancing cup and bowl. "Here," he said, "eat."

Her stomach heaved, and settled abruptly as she turned about. There was meat in savory stew; warm bread dripping with honey; strong brown ale. All at once she was hungry.

He watched her eat, smiling, approving.

She brushed crumbs from her rumpled gown and drew up her knees, turning the heavy ale-cup in her hands. "Mirain," she asked after a little, "are you afraid?"

He studied his hands. The one that was like any man's; the one that cast a golden light in his face. "Yes," he answered her, "I am afraid. I'm terrified."

"But will you do it?"

His eyes flashed up. "Do I have a choice?"

"Would it matter if you did?"

He followed the curve of her cheek with his finger-tip, lightly but carefully, as if he needed to remember it. "If I fall, my enemy wins my empire; and I mean you to get it back again. Whatever becomes of me, our child will rule. It must." She opened her mouth to speak; he silenced her. "The nameless one is very, very strong. I too have great power, but wizardry, unlike the body's strength, grows with age. And in the duties of kingship, in the forging of my empire, I have had little leisure for the training of my power. She has spent long years under the tutelage of masters, to one sole end: my destruction. I mean to defeat her; but it is very likely that I shall not."

"If you die," she said calmly, "I'll die too."

He caught her hands in a sudden, fierce grip. The ale-cup, empty, flew wide. "You must not! What I said to you before you made me wed you, that if I fell the world was well rid of me—that was folly, and cruelty too. That woman has all darkness behind her. She will take my empire and all my people, only to rend them asunder. You must stand against her. You must do as she did: hide, gather your forces and raise our son, and perfect your power until you are strong enough to cast her down. Promise me, Elian. Swear that you will do it."

Her chin set. "Oh, no, my lord king. You can't take the easy road and leave me to finish what you started. Either you win tomorrow, or your whole dynasty dies with you."

He shook her hard. She laughed in his face. "Yes, rage at me. The wilder the better. I warned you that your death was waiting; you rode straight for it. Vadin warned you of the trap; you threw yourself into the heart of it. Now you have to choose. You win and save all you fought for, or you lose it all. There are no half wagers in this game."

His eyes blazed; his teeth bared. "I command you."

"Do you?" She tossed her hair out of her eyes, lightly, almost gaily. "We women are different, you know. Even little fools like me, who try to forget, and play at being boys. Thrones and empires, great matters of state, the wars of men and gods—they don't matter. I'd gladly die for you, and I probably will, if you're so determined to get yourself killed. But I won't fight your battles for you."

"I can fight my own damned battles!"

With a quick deft twist she freed her hands, to take his burning face between them. "In that case," she said, "you had better win this one."

His glare was sun-hot, sun-fierce. She met it steadily. With perfect, suspicious coolness he said, "This is deliberate. You're provoking me, to make me fight harder."

"I am," she agreed. "I'm also telling the truth. Your death is my death. If you want your heir to inherit your empire, you'll have to live to see the birth."

"That is—"

"Murder and suicide, all in one. Or your salvation; and the child's, and mine, and your empire's. Until," she added after a moment, "the next time."

His hand flew up. She braced herself for the blow; with a convulsive movement he struck his own thigh. "Avaryan and Uveryen, woman! Won't you let me get through this one first?"

She smiled. "Get through it," she advised him. "Win it. With luck, your army will come to stand behind you. I've bidden Cuthan to take word to the army. He might elude both men and magery. And I think—I almost think—our enemy doesn't know of Vadin. She knows only what she wishes to know. It's part of her madness. It may save us yet."

Muscle by muscle, with skill he had labored long to learn, Mirain relaxed his body. His eyes smoldered still, but his face was quiet, his voice calm. "It may. I'm gambling on it."

"Good," said Elian. Her hands left his face to travel downward, working into the hollows of his robe, finding its fastenings.

"You," he said roughly, "have the instincts of a harlot."

She laughed, half at his words, half at his garments, which came apart in a most interesting fashion. He snatched at them; she twitched them away. "I used to think I should become one. Shall I think of it again? I'll be a wonder; men will come from the ends of the earth for a glimpse of my face. I'll amass the wealth of empires, and pour it all away. All the world will fall at my feet."

"Not while I rule this half of it."

Her fingers found his most sensitive places and woke the pleasure there, while her eyes danced upon his rigid face. "What will you do? Lock me in your harem? Chain me naked to a pillar? Flog me thrice a day to keep me docile?"

"If you touch any other man—if you even look at him—"

Her hands stilled. Her eyes narrowed. "Will you try to stop me?"

He surged against her, bearing her down. She lay motionless under him, laughing silently, but with a flicker of warning. He disdained to heed it. "You are my wife. By law you are my chattel. I can keep you in any manner I please; I can cast you away. Your very life is mine to take."

"Would you dare?"

His eyes were very dark. Deep within, a spark leaped. "Would you dare to test me?"

"Yes."

He laughed suddenly, glittering-fierce. "I could do worse than that. I could find another woman."

"Don't—you—dare!"

"Someone soft. Sweet. Obedient. Living only to please me. Dark, I think, like me. And her hair—"

"I'll kill her!"

His laughter this time was warm, rich, and direly infectious. She fought it. She struggled; she glared. Her lips twitched, her eyes danced, her mirth burst forth. It swept her up, scattering her garments, twining her body with his.

On the bright edge of passion, he paused. "Would you truly dare?"

She set her lips upon his and pulled him down.

HE SLEPT AS A CHILD SLEEPS, DEEPLY AND PEACEFULLY, ALL the knots of care and kingship smoothed away. That was part of his legend: that he never lay tossing before a battle. Often he had to be awakened lest he be late to the field.

Gently Elian loosed his braid, combing it with careful fingers, smoothing the heavy mass of it upon the coverlet. She never had given him his answer.

As if he needed it. Born wanton she might be, but as a harlot she had this fatal flaw: all her desire turned upon one man. It had been so since she was too young even to know what desire was.

A small smile touched her mouth. Now that she was an ancient crone, she was lost completely. Such a man to be lost for: an utter lunatic who fancied himself the son of a god. His golden hand lay between her breasts, half curled about one, burning even as he slept: a pain he had never known the lack of. He insisted that she eased it. Maybe; maybe he needed to think so.

Those two, the pain and its lessening in her presence, helped to set a limit on his pride. He could not exult inordinately in his lineage when it tormented him lifelong with a living fire. Nor could he wield his power in a tyrant's peace, not with a sun blazing in his sensitive palm. Sword or scepter he could grip, but only if he wielded them with care. And for what easing the god would grant, he must rely upon a snippet of a child-woman, a maddening tangle of love and resistance and red-headed temper.

Except that the love seemed to have swallowed the resistance. The temper, unfortunately, showed no signs of abating. She could still wish that she had never heard of Mirain An-Sh'Endor, while her heart threatened to burst and her body to melt with love of him.

She traced the whorl of his ear, pausing where it was pierced for a ring, an infinitesimal interruption in the curve of it. He murmured something and smiled, and tried to burrow into her side. She buried her face in his thick curling hair. *Avaryan,* she said in her mind, shaping each word in red-golden fire, *if truly you came to this man's mother, if you played any part at all in his begetting, listen to me. He needs you now, and he needs you tomorrow. Stand with him. Make him strong. Help me to make him live.*

There was no answer. No voice; no sudden light. And yet, having prayed, she felt the better for it. Perhaps even, after all, she might sleep; and no dreams would beset her.

AFTER ALL HER WAKEFULNESS, IT WAS ELIAN WHO WOKE late in a great tangle of bedclothes. She struggled out of them to find herself alone, the chamber empty. For a moment her heart stopped. No. Oh, no. He could not have.

Voices brought her to her feet. Snatching what was nearest—Mirain's riding cloak, voluminous and almost dry—she opened the door.

They were all in the guardroom, all but Cuthan who was gone, all fully clad, most looking as if they had not slept. A grey pallor sat on their faces; their eyes were sunken, their mouths set tight. Elian did not need to ask. The army had not come. They must face this alone. Win alone, or die alone.

The king stood among them. He had bathed; he was fresh-shaven; he wore a kilt and nothing else, and his hair, drying, seemed thicker and more unruly than ever. As a guardswoman struggled with its tangles, he directed one of his own men in the unrolling of an oblong bundle.

Deftly Elian took Igani's place. The bundle, she saw, was a length of leather as pale as fine ivory, tanned to the softness of silk. In the center of it someone had cut a hole.

Her hands faltered. "So," she said as steadily as she could, "you'll do it the old way."

His thought caressed her although his body held still. "The oldest way of all. The shield-circle; the ordered combat."

The first order of which was that the combatants bear about them no binding. No knot or fastening, no seam, no woven garment, only the long tunic of leather, unbelted and unsewn, its sides open to the wind. Thus there could be no aids to enchantment hidden in one's clothing, no spells braided into one's hair. The victory must come through the purity of power.

Elian laughed shakily. "If that's so, my love, you'd better crop your head as close as a desert rover's, or you'll be called down for all your tangles."

"I'll chance it," he said, light and unconcerned. " 'Varyan! I'm hungry. I've been wallowing in luxury too long; I've lost the knack of fasting."

"Think about all you'll feast on when it's over." Igani

lifted the long strange garment. Mirain shed his kilt, pausing a moment, drawing a deep breath. She slipped the length of leather over his head.

It settled smoothly, its paleness catching the dark sheen of his skin, its weight falling straight before and behind. For a moment Elian could not breathe. He was going to fight. He was going to die.

She remembered her mother's words, the voice low and sweet in her mind. *A prophecy can be its own fulfillment.* It need not be. It must not be.

They were too somber, all of them; subdued, afraid. Even Mirain. Someone had brought the torque of his priesthood from beside his bed; he held it for a stretching moment, grey-knuckled, eyes too wide and too fixed.

She snatched it from him, and grinned her whitest, fiercest grin. "Yes, Sunborn, put it on. Show them who your master is."

"I am not—" He shut his mouth with a snap. "Put it on me, then."

Slowly she did as he bade. It was pure gold, soft and leaden heavy. Yet he wore it always, putting it off only to sleep, and sometimes not even then; had worn it so since he was a very young man. Even more than Asanion's golden mask or the coronet of a prince in the Hundred Realms, it marked his kingship. The splendor, and the crushing burden.

And my service to the god. He kissed her hands. *Every priest of Avaryan bears this same burden. No lighter and no heavier.*

"Except that they are plain servants of Avaryan, and you are the king."

"Is there a difference?"

She looked at him. He was smiling very faintly. Strong again, sure again, whatever terrors stirred in the hidden heart of him. "You make me strong," he said softly.

They were nearly of a height. They could stand eye to eye with a palm's width between them, bend forward in the same instant, touch.

She clung with sudden desperate strength, yet no

stronger than he, as if he could crush her body into his own, make it a part of him. They said nothing with mind or voice. There was too much to say, and too little.

Elian drew back. Conscious of herself again; aware with a rush of heat that she had lost her covering. No one stared; no one ventured it. With what dignity she could muster, she gathered up the fallen cloak and retreated to the bath.

IT WAS THE LORD OF GARIN WHO CAME FOR THE KING. AND only the king. Elian, scoured clean, dressed again in coat and trousers and boots, was briefly speechless.

The Wolf spoke to Mirain quietly, reasonably. "You are to come alone, sire. I swear on my honor that there shall be no treachery."

Elian's voice broke free, lashing him. "That is not the law! Each combatant is allowed one witness."

He looked her up and down without haste and without judgment. "So it shall be. I am to attend him."

"You!"

Mirain stepped between them. "The law also allows a choice of witnesses. I choose the Lady Elian. And," he added, "the Lord Garin."

The lord paused. Clearly he had not been so instructed. But he smiled and bowed. "As your majesty wishes. Will it please you to follow me?"

Mirain walked lightly beside the Lord of Garin. If it wrenched at him to leave his escort behind, he did not show it. They watched him go with eyes like wounds, open and bleeding. Elian tried to meet them, to heal them a little, to smile and breathe forth confidence. She doubted that they even saw her.

IN THE DARK BEFORE DAWN THE CASTLE WAS VERY STILL, grimmer and greyer than ever, and bone-cold. Elian shivered in all her riding gear. Mirain, barefoot and nearly naked, might have been swathed in furs. But he was never cold; he had the Sun's fire in his veins.

Lord Garin led them through a maze of passages.

Down out of the tower, through the keep, up and round by twisting torchlit ways. Even where the torches failed, he did not falter. Perhaps, like the Halenani or like the wolf of his name, he could see in the dark.

Mirain's hand found Elian's. His grasp was light, fire-warm, and perfectly steady. She could feel the strength in it, quiescent now, awaiting its time.

The passage narrowed and spiraled upward. Elian fell behind Mirain, but his hand kept its grip. Even for her eyes the way was dark, Mirain's tunic a pale blur ahead. The air was cold in her face like the touch of the dead, and dank, heavy with age and darkness.

Mirain stopped so abruptly that she collided with him. Metal grated harshly upon stone. Hinges protested. A gate swung open with rusted slowness.

Dawn was still unbroken, the night at its deepest. Yet Elian blinked, half blinded. All the clouds of storm had blown away. Silver Brightmoon, just past the full, hung low in the west. The great half-orb of Greatmoon rode high above, trailing pallid fire; about it flamed the stars in all their myriads.

Old tales gave Greatmoon to the powers of the dark and Brightmoon to those of the light, calling the huge blue-pale moon the Throne of Uveryen, its god her lover; and singing of the love of the silver goddess for her lord the sun. Some people of late had begun a new naming, and called the brighter moon Sanelin, and set the priestess there, sharing the heavens with the father of her son.

Elian dragged her eyes and her mind from the vault of the sky. There was myth. Here was living legend.

She stood on sere grass in a deep bowl rimmed by mountain walls. In its center glimmered a lake, a pool of ice under Greatmoon, and in the lake a dark curve of islet, a tall shape of shadow: a standing stone.

Lord Garin led them round the lake. Its water lapped upon the shore, infinitely lonely, infinitely sad. Shadow rose upon the far side. As Elian drew closer it grew clearer, taking shape in the moonlight. A building, it had been once; ruined now, no more than a ring of roofless pillars, some tall and straight, some half-fallen like broken teeth. Framed within them lay a pavement of stone.

There waited the Exile. To the eye she was a darkness on darkness, one of three cloaked and hooded shapes. To the power she stood forth in utter and terrible clarity.

As Mirain set his foot upon the level stones, his power stirred and woke. A shimmer of pale light ran upward from sole to crown, and outward through the broken pavement. Elian's gasp was loud in the silence. The stone seemed not stone at all, but sky in the waking dawn, silver flushing to rose and palest gold.

Before the light reached the Exile, it stopped, sharp and clean as if cleft with a knife. That beyond seemed darker still for the brightness so close, a darkness as limitless as the void between stars.

Mirain smiled in the strange light. "Dawnstone," he said with a touch of wonder, a touch of delight. "My keep in Ianon is made of it. And this—would it perhaps be nightstone, that holds the night as dawnstone keeps the glow of morning? I have heard of it in old tales, but I have never seen it."

"It is nightstone," the Exile answered him. "And this is a place older than legend, fane of a people whose works are all vanished from the earth: older than Han-Ianon, older than the Cavern of the God, older even than gods, though not those we serve. Can you perceive the power in these stones?"

It throbbed in Elian's brain, immense, slumbering, yet stirring uneasily in the presence of these small intruders.

"A place of power," said Mirain. "I have never come upon one so mighty."

"Nor shall you or any man, unless you come to the Heart of the World where lie the chains that bind the gods. There are no chains here. Only power. It will not aid us in our battle; it will seek to hinder, and even to destroy, if in disturbing it one of us lacks the strength to soothe it. Do you think still to challenge me, priestess' child?"

"How not?" He advanced a step. "Shall we begin?"

Twenty-Six

IRAIN SPOKE FREELY, EVEN EAGERLY, WELCOMING whatever must come. His enemy stood tall and let fall her cloak. Beneath it she was clad as was he, white hair falling long and free over the shoulders of a tunic as dark as his was pale. Her familiar was gone: fled, hidden, subsumed into her power. For she was strong. She had never pretended to weakness, but her strength now was greater than ever Elian remembered, filling her, mantling her in a shimmer of mingled darkness and light.

The witnesses faded back, retreating from the pillared circle. Well before the shadows took them, Elian had forgotten their existence. She too retreated, but only to the joining of earth and stone. There lay the remnant of a column half-buried in earth and grass and the dead brittleness of a vine. She sank down upon it, her toes almost touching the edge of the dawnstone. Its gleam caught at her eyes; its power sparked her own. In its pale depths she saw the circle shrunken to the breadth of her hand, and two figures upon it, one erect and triumphant, the other fallen utterly. But the image shifted, blurred; now white hair spread across the stone, now raven-dark.

She tore her eyes away. The greater circle opened wide before her, dawn and deepest night. Over it the moons wheeled. Brightmoon sank beneath the mountain wall; Greatmoon thinned and paled. The sky's darkness greyed. Avaryan was coming.

Power gathered. The air hummed and sang. Mage in white, mage in black, both spread their arms. Mirain's voice rang upon the first note of binding. The nameless one took up the second, a high eerie keening. The two notes quivered, distinct and dissonant; eased; softened, drawing together, meeting, merging into a terrible harmony.

At once and as one they broke off. Slowly Mirain's hands met, palm to palm. The Exile's mirrored them. As her palms touched, the circle blazed up, white light and black fire, and dimmed again. But a shimmer lingered, a wall of power, and within it nothingness. Not until one of them fell might that wall fall; nor could any open it, man or mage, god or demon. They were alone, utterly.

Elian reeled upon her cold perch. She was alone, sundered, torn.

She had eyes. And power, though forbidden to pass the barrier, could see all within.

At first there was little to see. They stood motionless, facing one another. Although nothing with mind or power could pierce the wall, a thin wind slipped through the emptiness. It stirred their long tunics; it made witchlocks of the Exile's hair; it blew Mirain's mane into his face. He shook back the heavy mass, to little effect; shrugged; let it be.

The Exile raised her hands. A tendril of darkness uncoiled, reaching, groping for the light.

Sparks leaped. The darkness whipped back.

Mirain stood unmoved. His face was lost in the tangles of his hair. The wind, strengthening, danced about him. Playful fingers caught his tunic, tossing it away from his body, whipping it round and round, binding, tightening.

His swift hands caught and gathered the wildness of

his mane, twisted it back from his calm face, knotted it behind him.

The wind fled. His tunic fell loosely to his feet. The knot, which should never have held, kept its place unaltered.

Elian's stiff lips bent in the beginnings of a smile. The first round, it seemed, had gone to Mirain.

He was in no haste to press his advantage. He forsook his rigid stillness, wandering a little in his half of the circle, setting down his feet with feline delicacy. Round, sidewise, back, step and step and step, with a cat's precision, a dancer's grace.

And with each step a glimmer of light grew in the nightstone, a tangled skein of pale fire circling the Exile's feet, weaving among them, drawing together, closing.

Her clawed fingers swept down, rending the web.

He laughed and whirled like a devil-dancer, lithe dark body in a circle of pale leather. The web, torn, spun up the Exile's lank form, knee-high, hip-high, breast-high.

She tossed her head. He spun faster, faster, faster. The web shredded and tattered. A blur of black hummed within a blur of white.

With a vicious, whip-sharp crack, he stopped. His eyes flamed. His hair was free again, witch-wild, his garment a tatter. His breath came hard. And yet he smiled.

The web had melted into the night. His enemy inclined her head very slightly. "You have the beginnings of art," she conceded. "Will you play further? Or shall we do battle at last?"

Mirain fought with light and fire and with his supple voice. The nameless one opposed him with darkness visible, in a wall of living silence. Against his spear of levinfire she raised a shield of night; against his weaving of subtle melody, a stillness that swallowed all sound. The rising dawn illumined his half of the circle, but in the other, deep night reigned.

At first Elian did not credit her eyes. Mirain's half of the circle was smaller. No—he had moved; her eyes were weary; the growing daylight deceived her, dulling the shimmer of the dawnstone.

He stood as he had stood since the battle began in earnest, and the line of darkness crept toward him. His body swayed; his voice sang three lines of an ancient cantrip. The advance halted.

Elian's hands knotted; her breath caught. The darkness in the circle was a handspan less. But Mirain's face glistened damply; his eyes were squeezed shut, his body rigid. All his strength bent upon the holding of that line.

Slowly, inexorably, the darkness advanced. He trembled visibly with the effort of resistance. His enemy was as still as a standing stone, utterly without expression save for the thin grey line of her lips.

The mark of her power approached his feet. Step by step he retreated. Step by step the dawnstone dulled and blackened. And the line began to bend. Before and beside him, to the full stretch of his arms, the light lingered. But night held the rest. His back touched a pillar. Beyond it he could not go; the shield walled him in. All about him, save only where he stood, was darkness. Slowly he sank to one knee, bowed as if beneath a mighty burden. The light beneath him had lost all its brilliance, flickering greyly, pallid as winter fog.

His enemy came toward him without haste and stood over him, blind eyes bent upon him. She had him, and she knew it. His breath rattled in his throat. Her hand rose, swept sidewise, cast him helpless to the ground.

And she turned her back on him. She faced outward. The circle wavered, stretching. About Elian's feet wove a small furred cat-creature, singing a yowling song. The Exile's power yearned toward it.

Elian snatched it up. It came as if it were pleased to come, warm and solid, supple. It nestled in the hollow of her shoulder. And she, tensed to leap back, to cast up her shields, to sunder witch and familiar, could move no muscle of her body. Her scarred cheek throbbed. The beast ended its song and began to purr.

"Yes," said the Exile. "She knows you, my swift one,

my dancer in the grasses. We are kin; we are sisters in power."

A shudder racked Elian: deep, pulsing, black-red denial. With terror in it. Because she set all her will to refuse the truth.

The Exile gestured behind her, not in scorn, not without respect. "He was strong, as befit his heritage. But he had not the strength which I have. He will have no part of the dark; he who is born of the burning noon, denies the night with all that is in him. Look now. See. Know what he would make of the world."

Sunlight. Green places. Water falling, and white cities rising, and fields rich with the harvest.

Sunlight. No night. No relief of the cool dark, no light of stars. Green withered, blackened, burned. Water shrank into dust. White walls cast back the light in blinding splendor, in carrion stench. White bone lay bare beneath fire-ravaged flesh; the land itself was stripped, seared, destroyed by the merciless light.

And armies rode through the shattered country. As they rode, they sang a hymn to the Sun; and cursed the dark; and saw only beauty in all that desolation. Faintly within it, something moved: a human figure, gaunt, scorched, staggering with hands held out in supplication. The army fell upon it. It shrieked once, suddenly cut off. The army passed. The dust was dark, dampened with blood; but in a moment the sun had drunk the last of its wetness.

"No," said Elian. A shaft of agony pierced her center. She clutched it, doubling. *"No."*

"Indeed," said the Exile, "no. He has seen the light and the white city. He has not seen its price."

"Not our child. *Not*—"

"Your child?" The woman was astonished. "We do not take the lives of the unborn. That is for the gods alone; or for men who fancy themselves better than gods. Your king's price is for the world's paying. The price of fire, and of the balance's breaking."

The pain was passing, draggingly slow. Elian drew herself up. The familiar had not even shifted its grip. It had solidity but no weight; strength, but very little bulk to house it. She could not force her hands to tear it away. They flattened over her belly. "You will not have our child. I will die before I surrender him."

"Or her," said the Exile. "Or can you not endure the prospect of a daughter?"

"I can endure either, if only it lives to be born."

"Can you?" The woman approached the circle's edge. "You may gather your power to stand against me. You are strong enough; you can will yourself to be blind enough. Or you may stand with me. You bear in your womb both weapon and healing: seal of the balance, seal of the Sun's dominion. What your brother and lover has been, this seed of his shall be a thousandfold."

Elian reeled. Needle-claws brought her snapping erect. The cat mewed softly. Warning. Imparting strength.

It was evil. *Evil.*

It was a cat. Small, swift, quick-tempered, centered on itself. Yet when it chose, as it chose, it could bestow its affection. It did not regret its marring of her face; it did not begrudge her battering of its body. It was power, and its purpose was simply to be.

"And," said her kinswoman, "to bolster waning power, of body or of mind."

Elian's eyes squeezed shut against the vision. It blazed within, unconquerable. Traps within traps within traps. Danger and daring and a spice of treachery, to lure Mirain. Mirain, to lure his lifelong shadow. Mirain was to die. She was to suffer it, or to accomplish it. To be seduced. To give her soul to neither light nor dark, but to this thing called balance, that was no god she had ever known.

Mirain was the greater mage, perhaps. She was the greater power. Because of what she was, mage's daughter, royal seed, child of night and fire; and woman, and bearer of a child. This child. Sunborn, mageborn, ruler of the world.

If it lived. Her eyes opened, blinded with vision; met

blind eyes which could see beyond sight. The Exile loved her, because she was blood kin; hated her, envied her, but loved her. And would take her life without the slightest qualm, if she chose awry.

"There is no choice," gritted Elian. "There is only the light and the dark. I was born in the light. I cannot embrace its enemy."

The Exile's hand shaped potent denial: a sign in the air, red-gold, gleaming in the waxing morning. "They are not enemies. They are one. Stand with me, sister. Defend them against their sundering."

She pleaded: she, who was as proud as Elian had ever been. She begged. She all but wept for the world that would lie beneath the hammer of the Sun. The wars, the souls cast down into death, the blood poured out in rivers in Avaryan's name. And in Mirain's.

Elian's heart clenched with love of him. And yet . . . and yet . . .

Follow your heart, they all bade her. *Listen to your power. They know. They see what cannot but be.*

Almost she laughed. She had writhed in agony over a pair of lovers, each perfect of his kind. She had not known what agony was.

The cat settled in her arms. She rubbed its soft ears. It purred. It lay against the spark of her child. Defending. Strengthening.

All her understandings swayed and unbalanced and fell. Good, evil. Dark, light. Friend, enemy. Hate, love, peace, wrath—all one, all mingled, all lost in a mad tangle of changes. She could not endure it. She would lose her poor wits; she would die. She could—not—

The Exile raised her hand. Offering. Beckoning. Elian's hand moved of its own will. The cat sang its joy.

White fire reared up above the shadow that was the Exile, and swooped down. The world shattered in an explosion of light.

IT WAS VERY QUIET.

Elian swayed in emptiness. She was still afoot; she

could not understand why. Nor, for a long while, could she understand why she should not be. The cat was gone. Perhaps she had dreamed the whole of it.

Abruptly and violently her stomach overturned itself. She crouched, gasping and retching; and some of it was hysteria, laughter well past the border of madness, for long shafts of sunlight dazzled her streaming eyes. Morning sun. Avaryan had found his way at last into the mountain's crown.

Sick, half blind, she crawled in a ragged circle. Her hand jarred against an obstacle. A hand, long and bone-thin; an arm; the charred ruin of a face. The eyes had escaped, blind now within as without, opened wide upon nothingness. There was no horror in them, and no surprise at all. Only peace, and something very like triumph.

Elian's breath caught. This was the shape of her vision: white hair spread upon pale stone.

And black beside it. Mirain lay where the last great surge of his power had cast him, limbs asprawl, golden hand flung up beside his face. His eyes were closed, seemly; no mark of burning stained him.

His tunic had fallen awry. Carefully she smoothed it, covering his nakedness. Her hand shrank a little, briefly, from touching him: as if he could loose his fire upon her. Sun's fire.

He had made her choice for her. Or she had, as she always did, in tarrying until it made itself.

She looked at him. She saw a man whom she loved, whom she would gladly die for. She saw . . .

Her mind's eye closed. Her choice was made. She would not seek to unmake it. His truth, the Exile's truth—here and now, it made no difference. All that mattered was Mirain.

"Sweet merciful gods."

Elian looked up. She had heard nothing, seen nothing. Yet it surprised her not at all to hear her brother's voice, to see him there with the Lord Vadin beside him, armored and helmeted and bearing each a sword. The blades, she noticed, had seen use.

Men thronged at their backs. She saw Lord Garin between two grim women of her own Guard, and Prince Omian grey-faced and staggering, and a flocking of men of both Ianon and the Hundred Realms. Cuthan stood in front of them all with his smooth braids fallen in a tangle, and blood on his cheek, and a red blade dripping on the grass.

Elian rose slowly. "You took your time," she said. And cursed her tongue. He stared at her, mute, his eyes dark with misery. She tried to comfort him, but no words would come. She could only touch him. His arm was rigid, but he did not pull away. He had stopped seeing her.

Halenan had sunk to his knees beside Mirain. Somewhere in the ranks, someone cried aloud. Ashan's heir shouted and struggled and suddenly broke free. A dozen swords flashed up. Blood sprayed wide.

Elian turned. She faced Lord Garin. Steel glittered a hair's breadth from his throat, but no closer. "Where is your prince?" she asked him.

The Wolf's eye was steady and fearless and very much amused. "Dead," he answered her, "majesty. It seemed fair enough, upon consideration. A life for a royal life."

She tilted her head, studying him. "Why?"

"Because, your majesty, I am a loyal man."

"Loyal to nothing but his treachery!" Cuthan's voice was raw with hate. "Through him was our king betrayed. Through him was our king destroyed. On his head be it. Murder. Murder of the Sunborn."

A deep snarl ran through the ranks, a snarl that turned to a howl.

Elian ignored it, meeting the despair in Cuthan's eyes. "But," she said, "Mirain is not dead."

Hope made him beautiful again. He looked so young, so easily moved, like a child. Even in her numbness she found the ghost of a smile for him. He turned, stumbling, blinded with tears, but his voice was as splendid as ever it had been. Soft at first, full of wondering joy. "Did you hear?" Louder then, clear and free and glad, ringing in the morning. "Men of the Sun, did you hear? The king is not dead. He lives. An-Sh'Endor lives!"

Twenty-Seven

MIRAIN LIVED. HE BREATHED; HE SEEMED TO SLEEP. But he did not wake.

Elian sat by the great bed in the chamber of Garin the elder. People came and went. They tried to be quiet, a sickroom stillness, muting the thud of booted feet, lowering battle-roughened voices. It mattered little to her and less to Mirain whether they whispered or shouted. There were wounded to settle, prisoners to guard, watches to set; and it kept coming back to her. She was the queen. It was her place to rule.

Sometimes her brother sat with her. More often it was Vadin. He was not like the rest; he was quiet, he did not intrude. She could forget that he was there.

Halenan could not efface himself so perfectly. He was restless, like fire. He persisted in chattering. "I have his lordship under guard," he said. He had been drinking ale, from the scent that came in with him; he lowered himself to the floor at her feet. It was not all weariness. He had taken a slight wound in the side, and it had begun to stiffen.

She touched it with hand and healing; he sighed. "Ah,

that's better." He swallowed a yawn. "Lord Garin is under
guard, but free to go where he likes. The guard is mostly
for his sake; the men don't love him. Not in the least."

"Mirain rather likes him." She laid her hand on the
still brow. With the women of her Guard, she had bathed
and tended him and combed out his many tangles. His
braid lay tamed upon his shoulder.

Halenan leaned back against her knee and yawned
outright. "I feel as if I haven't slept for a Greatmoon-
cycle, what with settling the men in that infernal cave and
fretting over you in this infernal castle, and all that's
come after. You vanished from power's sight, you know.
One moment I looked and you were there, passing Garin's
gate. The next, you were gone. I went a little wild. More
than a little." Vadin looked at him, brows up. He grimaced. "Very much more than a little. Yonder savage had
to knock me down and sit on me, or I'd have sent the
whole troop against Garin, then and there. 'Wait,' he said,
as if he weren't twitching himself, and starting at shadows. 'Give it time.' I had to: he wouldn't let me up, else.

"We waited till sundown. Just barely. Then we divided our forces. Half we left to guard the cave and Lord
Casien's company, and to face any force that might come
through the valley. They put on a brave show of numbers, with fires and tents and a wall of tethered seneldi.
The rest of us went under the mountain.

"We paused in a cavern only a little smaller than the
outer hall, with a deep pool in it. Vadin's people had
penned their seneldi there, under guard. We gathered all
but a few of the sentries and went on.

"We went carefully, and slowly enough to madden
me. But for all of that, we kept going astray, ending in a
blind passage or a sudden chasm; or hearing the clatter of
armed men, and scrambling for hiding places, and hearing the noises fade away among the tunnels.

"An eon after we began, we saw a light. The rest ran
for cover yet again, but I'd had my fill of prudence. I
flattened myself into a fold of the wall and tried not to
breathe. The light came toward us. It was moving fast,

and it was quiet; I could just hear footsteps, booted but running very light. When it passed me, I pounced." He rubbed his side. "I got this for my pains. He was a big lad, that one, and vicious as a cornered ul-cat. We rolled on the floor, snapping and snarling and doing our utmost to throttle one another.

"Until Vadin swooped over us and thrust a torch in our faces. We kept up the fight for a bit, for the fighting's sake, but in the end we stopped and burst out laughing. It was that or howl. I'd been getting the worst of it; Cuthan picked me up and dusted me off and was most apologetic.

" 'Never mind that,' said Vadin. 'What news from Garin?'

"Cuthan sobered all at once. It was bad, I'd known it already; I hadn't known how bad. He'd been lost as we were, and he'd had a guide, a rat of Garin's whom he'd caught and tamed at sword's point. They'd managed to pass the first windings of the maze, which were full of armed men: we'd been hearing them as they mustered, through a trick of the tunnels. We were fortunate they hadn't heard us; or maybe they'd taken us for more of their own.

"Cuthan's rat was killed in a pitfall that nearly took Cuthan with it; he went on by instinct and what power he had. It was enough to take him to us. It just barely sufficed to lead us all on the right path, armies be damned.

"That was a wild march," said Halenan. "The way was steep in places, and it was infernally dark. I prayed to every god I knew, and to Avaryan over them all, that the sorceress wasn't looking for a blaze of power under the earth; because Vadin and I had left off trusting our mortal senses. It was a labyrinth we were racing through, with no way out but the castle, and no time to spare, and precious little light; and enemies all around us." He shuddered. "Avaryan grant I never see such a devil's lair again!

"We met the first of the enemy somewhat closer to the castle than to the cave. They weren't looking for us.

We took them by surprise, but they were no fools. No tyros, either. If Lord Garin hasn't tried a little reiving in his father's line, then he has a liking for drilling his troops in mazes.

"He certainly keeps his loot there—and the loot of the past dozen generations with it. If we can haul even half of it out of here, every man of us will be as rich as a lord."

"You always were greedy," said Elian.

He snarled in mock warning; she ruffled his hair and tried to smile.

"Ah well," he said, smiling back, "we weren't paying much attention to the treasure trove while we were in it. We were too busy trying to get out. I was desperate; I could feel morning coming, and I knew when the duel began. I think I lost what little wits I had left. I know Vadin did. We left most of the company to mop up behind us and flamed our way through, clear to the castle.

"Your guards were ready and willing and at least as wild as we were. We had hell's own time to find the way up to the mountain, and a castleful of people in our way, but they weren't quarreling with power. Much.

"We found the door and the tunnel, and we found the open air. And there you were at battle's end. I thought"—he faltered, which was utterly unlike him—"I thought Mirain was dead."

"He . . . almost . . . was."

Halenan caught her hands. "Lia. Little sister. It's over now."

She looked at him. She was very calm; it was he who was shaking. "It's not, really," she said.

His head tossed from side to side. His grip was painfully tight. "It's only exhaustion, and power stretched as far as it will go. He'll sleep the sun around and wake up ravenous and growling, like a cave bear in the spring."

"He'll sleep." Her glance strayed to the bed. "I caused it, you know. The end. She almost had him, but she let him go too soon. She broke the law and the shield and all honor, and turned to me, and tried to make me fight with her. Maybe her mind was breaking. Maybe she thought Mirain was too weak to trouble with; or too strong to stand against alone. Maybe—maybe she knew what she was doing. To him, to me, and to herself. He had power left; she could not but have known it. Enough to wake what slept in the stone, and to aim it when it woke. It carried him with it. It drained him dry, and dropped him when it was done." She freed her hands from her brother's, to take Mirain's slack one. "If he wakes—if he even wants to wake—he'll have nothing left. No power, and very little consciousness. You know how it is when the body uses itself up . . . it dies. Or its life is only a shadow of what it was before."

"No," said Halenan.

"She said he was a danger," Elian said. "To all the world. She showed me what he would do to it. She wanted me to stop him. Because I could. And maybe I did. By listening. By coming so close to betraying him."

She caught Mirain's hand, anchoring herself to it. It was warm, but no strength lingered in it. His life flickered low and slow.

Halenan lurched to his feet, all long limbs and coppery hair, awkward as he had not been since he was a boy. But it was a man who flung down his sheathed sword and swore in a soft deadly voice, the most terrible oaths he knew.

His grief woke something in her. Something she had striven to suppress. Awareness; understanding. Feeling.

She could not feel. She dared not. She had to be strong; to smile; to be queen. They needed her, all these men, these few women, this empire. And this stranger within her, who drifted quiescent, invisible, all but imperceptible, yet mighty in what it would become.

Oh, clever, Mirain, even at the end of all he was. He sat on death's threshold but advanced no farther, nor retreated, binding her to her own flesh, to the child he had begotten and the empire he had won.

Rage she could allow; could welcome. She regarded

the still and lifeless face, the lips curved in the shadow of a smile. He thought he had won. He thought he could trick her, bind her, leave her to bear all his burdens.

Better the harem. There at least the chains were visible, the guards solid before the bolted gates.

Her brother was gone, fled. Poor Hal. He loved Mirain almost as much as she. But he could go and weep, and hammer down a wall or two, and whip the castle into order. He was not saddled with an empire and its heir.

She looked up. Eyes rested upon her, dark as Mirain's, deep and quiet. They did not condescend to judge her.

She spoke with great care. "Only once," she said, "has Mirain ever argued me down. That was when he ran after his fate into Ianon, and I knew well enough that mine was in Han-Gilen. He doesn't even have that defense now."

Vadin sat back in his chair. It was a little small for him; he looked extraordinarily long and lean and angular. He was thinner than she remembered; he seemed older. Amid the copper braided into his beard, she glimpsed a thread of silver. He could not have had an easy time of it, abandoning his lordship and his lady and his people on a moment's notice, in the jaws of winter, at the command of a haughty girlchild; with Mirain's death to face if he failed, or even if he did not.

He mustered a smile, although it fled swiftly. "You've looked after Mirain rather thoroughly, haven't you? I didn't say you had to marry him."

"If you had, I wouldn't have done it."

He actually laughed. But again, not for long. Mirain weighted them both like a stone, breathing just visibly, alive and no more.

Elian spoke to him, not caring that Vadin heard. "Ziad-Ilarios loves me still. He'll be emperor in his time, and he'll wed as his duty commands. He'll grow and he'll change, and the change will be bitter, a chilling and a darkening. All his gold will turn to grey.

"But I can go to him. I can tell him I love him. He will believe me, because he longs to, and it will be true. And he won't grow old in bitterness. I won't let him. I can do that, Mirain. I can even make him accept your child, for my sake. Your empire won't last, but I'll see to it that your seed rules in Asanion. And I'll have a man, not a corpse, to share my bed."

No consciousness stirred behind the mask of his face; no power glimmered about it.

"Your empire is dead already. Father will try to keep it alive; Vadin will want to, and Hal. I could, maybe, if I would. Except that I'll be in Asanion and not wanting any rivals. It's rather a pity. There was so much we were going to do. Your city, that would be the most beautiful in the world. Your throne in it, and your tower atop Endros, built with songs and with power. Your priesthood—now you'll never be browbeaten into taking the high seat, and priestesses will go on in their useless fidelity to the god, and the order will fade and crumble, all its promises and all its prophecies come to nothing. I'll never have my company, not only my Guard but a whole fighting force of women, the Queen's Own, that was going to set a few more of us free. You'll never break the slave trade out of Asanion; we'll never climb Mount Avaryan or look on the sea. The Exile will have won after all. We'll never prove that her vision of fire and death was a lie. All because you're too cowardly feeble to face the world again."

Her eyes bled tears. She dashed them away, but they would not stop for that. "Damn you! If you don't come to, I'll kill myself!"

He was far beyond either hearing or heeding.

She seized him, shaking him. His head rolled slackly. His eyelids never flickered. She sobbed, half in fury, half in burning, tearing grief, clutching him, rocking him, blind and mad.

The blindness passed, eternally slow. The madness hovered. Her eyes ached and burned; her throat was raw. She was cold, as cold as death.

Her mind was very clear, her power bright and keen and deadly. To its eyes she was a dark glass full of lightnings, and in its center a pearl of white fire. Mirain was glass only. Empty. Life without mind, without thought, without will. The grass of the winter field shone more brightly than he.

She made a shield of will, glass round burning glass. Stretched it, rounded it, enfolding the emptied other. He who had blazed like a sun in the world of living light—

No grieving. Grieving weakened the shield. She firmed her will, pure guard, pure strength. Joy woke all unlooked for, a pure cold delight. She was young, she was but half trained, but she was strong. Time would make her stronger still, great mage and great queen, equal even to the Sunborn.

Time closed in about her, weighted with death. Her body laid itself down beside the shell of Mirain. Her power slipped free, bright fish in the sea of light. There below swirled the maelstrom, great whirling emptiness, spinning down and down and down. She hovered above it, holding herself still with her power. Pausing, gathering.

Another came to hover beside her, brightness flecked with coppery dark. She arched her supple body; she bared her myriad teeth. This storm was hers to ride. *Hers.* How dared he trespass?

He darted; he twined himself about her. He gripped her fast, and he had hands, a face, a human voice speaking in her human ears. "I go with you. You need me."

She struggled, but he had mastered this seeming; he was himself, great tall Ianyn warlord, mage of Mirain's making, oathbrother, soul-bound. She seared him with hate. He shook it off. He smiled, damn him to all the hells. "You need me," he said again. "I need you. Mirain needs us both."

"He needs none but me!" She tore free. She wrought her fish-shape; she poised once more and leaped.

Dark. Dark without sound, without scent, without touch. Void without end, death without life, no light, no air, no strength. Only memory, scattering in a soundless scream.

Remember. *Remember.*

Elian, Orsan's daughter of Eleni's bearing, Mirain's bride: Elian ilOrsan Kileni li'Mirain. Elian who was herself and of herself, free and apart, her own. Longlimb, firehair, fire-tempered and all contrary. Elian.

She stood alone in a dim corridor. It was very plain, floor, walls, ceiling: black stone without sheen, smoothed but unpolished. She wore a long tunic like that which Mirain had worn in the shield-circle, dyed deep green. Her hair poured free and heavy to her knees, a flood of molten copper.

She ventured forward. The passage sloped gently downward. Sometimes it curved; sometimes a door opened upon shadow. She did not turn aside, could not. Some force of will, whether her own or another's, drew her onward.

A wall rose before her, a door in it, opening to her touch. The light beyond was somewhat less dim, like twilight on a day of rain. Before her spread a wide rolling country under a lowering sky. In sunlight it might have been very fair: field and wood, hill and green valley, rising into a wall of mountains. So must Ianon be, where first Mirain was king.

Her body shifted and changed. She spread wide green wings. A sudden wind caught and lifted them; she arrowed upward, pouring forth a liquid stream of song.

The grey land fled beneath her. She outflew the wind; she outflew her own song. The mountains loomed like the world's wall. Singing, she hurtled upon them. Clapped wings to her sides. Soared over them, the bleak stony peaks all but clipping the feathers of her fiery breast.

She swooped down on an endless slide of air into a green bowl lit with dawn: a lake and an islet, a ruined hall, a pavement half of dawn and half of night.

Bare human feet touched the grass. The green tunic settled upon them. In the circle lay a lone figure, black hair spreading upon pale stone.

Slowly she approached him. As she set her foot upon the pavement, it blazed up with heatless fire. Out of it swelled a shape. A woman all of night in a robe woven of dawn, barring the way.

Elian stood still. The woman was beautiful, yet it was not a human beauty. It was too high and too cold and too terrible. The voice was as cold as wind upon ice, as bloodless-pure as the notes of a harp. "If you have wisdom, come no closer."

Elian knew neither wisdom nor fear. She essayed a step. The woman did not move, but said, "You seek what is mine. He woke me; he wielded me. Now he pays. All that was his, I have taken. All that was power, I have made my own."

"But," said Elian, "he woke you for my sake. Only give him back, all as he was, and you may have me in his stead."

"I do not bargain," said the woman of night.

Elian's body drooped, but stiffened anew. "So then. Give him to me."

"Why?"

"Because he is mine."

"He is mine now."

Elian stepped swiftly sidewise. The woman did not seem to move, but she was there, inescapable. With the courage of desperation, Elian flung herself upon her.

And staggered and fell to the stones. She had met only air. Mirain lay lifeless. Elian gathered him up, holding him to her breast, rocking him.

A shape loomed over her. A woman of dawn, clothed in night. Elian looked upon her in neither surprise nor awe, only weariness.

This beauty was high and terrible yet not cold, this voice achingly pure yet warm, like a deep-toned flute. And yet it was the same. They were the same, dawn and night: two faces of one power.

Elian turned her mind away. It was temptation. In this place it could be her death, and through her, Mirain's. Her arms tightened about his body.

"He is mine," said the woman of dawn, "and he shall remain mine. Unless . . ."

Elian's breath caught with the agony of hope.

"Unless," said the woman of dawn, "you pay your own price."

"Anything!" cried Elian.

"Slowly, child of earth. I do not bargain. This is the price which the gods set, and not I: the price of one man's salvation. If you will pay it."

"Only name it and it is yours."

The woman of dawn regarded her in what might have been pity. "The name of it is very simple. Your self."

Elian blinked stupidly. "My—"

"Your self. That which makes you Elian, alone of all the children of earth. That which makes you dream that you are free."

Her self. The very power which had snatched her from madness, and flung aside Vadin's strong aid, and brought her to this place. Her strength; her obstinacy. Her reckless temper. Herself.

Mirain lay in her arms. He had never been closer to beauty, or farther from it.

She loved him. Her heart ached with it; ached to see him standing again before her, moving with grace which few men could match, warming her with his rare and brilliant smile.

And yet. To pay so much. Had she not paid enough and more than enough? Other women had lost their loves and gone on. Other women had borne children, served regencies, held fiefs and kingdoms until the heirs could claim them. She could rule Mirain's empire; she had the strength, and the people's love, and her father and her brother to stand behind her. Even Vadin, even he would bow to her for her child's sake.

Or she could simply kill herself as she had threatened to do, and end all her wavering.

Save that life was sweet, and hers had barely begun. And love was the sweetest thing in it, not of the body only, but all the wonder of being two who were one: separate, distinct, yet joined, like gold twined with copper in a fillet for a queen.

If she paid this price, she would lose it all. And

Mirain—what would it do to him to wake and find her as she was now? Or worse. Awake and aware, but no longer Elian. Meek and pliant, as the world believed a woman should be, with no thought or word that was her own.

Maybe he would not mind. Maybe he would even prefer it.

Maybe she would not know what she had done to herself.

She trembled, shaking with sickness that was all of the soul. What virtues she had were warrior virtues: courage, high heart, and lethal honesty, and loyalty that could set all the rest at naught. She could be generous with possessions or with power; she had plenty of both. But that great virtue of the priests, that which with bitter irony they called selflessness, of that she had none at all.

"I'm a soldier," she said. "A queen. I was never made to be a martyr."

The woman of dawn stood tall and silent above her.

She bent her head over Mirain's body. She could die. He could die. They both could die. The world would go on without them. Maybe it would be better so. Maybe the Exile had had the right of it, and evil was not only dark alone but light alone, and the world's peace lay in the delicacy of their balance.

His arm slipped from his side and fell, palm up. The Sun shone with none of its sometime brilliance, none of its god-born power. It seemed no more than a folly, a dandy's fashion, an ornament set in the most improbable of places: awkward, impractical, and faintly absurd.

She raised her eyes from it and set her chin. "I'll pay," she said.

Twenty-Eight

THE WOMAN OF DAWN BOWED HER HIGH HEAD. ALL PRIDE was in that gesture, yet it was a gesture of respect.

Elian's sudden selflessness, though soul-deep, had no patience in it. "Well. Why do you wait? Take my mind away from me."

"That," said the woman, "was not the price. Nor can I take what you give. You must give it of your own accord."

"But I don't know how!"

That, perhaps, was a smile. The woman of dawn raised her hand. "Look yonder."

Elian looked, thinking to see the woman of night, or some greater wonder still. Seeing—

"You." Vadin said nothing. He was the same here as ever, tall, tired, detested, inevitable. "Of course it would be you. How did you get here?"

"I was always here."

"You were not!" she cried, stung. "I was one with Mirain. You were never there. Never!"

"You didn't want to see me."

The blood flooded to her cheeks. But she had no

cheeks here. No blood. No flesh at all. This was but a
vision of her mind, a shape she had given to the workings
of her power. She was a naked will in the void that had
been Mirain's mind, set against the power that dwelt in
the mountain. Vadin trespassed, invading where he had
no need and no purpose, betraying at last his jealousy of
her who had taken his place in his oathbrother's soul. She
willed him away.

He stood unmoving and unmoved. If anything, he
was more solid than ever. "Don't be more of a fool than
you can help. Mirain is trapped, that much at least you
have the wits to see. If you want to set him free, you have
to give up your stubbornness; banish this illusion; plunge
into his mind, and find him, and lead him back to the
light."

At last, and terribly, she understood. When she was
very young, she had learned: Every mind descended
through many levels. The greater one's power, the deeper
one could go. Yet even the mightiest of mages, the master
enchanters, the great wizards of the songs, had never
dared to plunge to the bottom. For beyond a certain
level—Sigan's Wall, her father had called it—there was no
returning. One was trapped in the black deeps below all
consciousness, beneath even dreams. One's self, indeed,
was lost.

And the one gate, the only gate . . .

There was no escaping him. Not through hate, or
contempt, or simple refusal to acknowledge his existence.
He made it worse; his eyes asked her pardon, but they
would not forsake their pride by begging for it. That he
was here, deeper even than she had ever gone. That she
could not pass save through him and with him. That she
must do worse than sacrifice her self for her lover's sake;
she must sacrifice it to him whom she could not even like,
much less love.

She rounded upon the woman of dawn. "Is there no
other way?"

Night flickered over the luminous face. The deep
eyes were cold. "None," said the power.

She looked at Mirain, so still upon the stone. She looked at Vadin, whose gaze likewise had settled upon the Sunborn. He knelt; he touched the lifeless brow; he smoothed the hair away from it, as if Mirain had been one of his children.

Hatred roared through her, flaming. And passed, and left her empty. He wept, that haughty lord of warriors. He wept, but he would not plead with her intransigence.

He was the gate, but she was the key. Without him she could not pass. Without her he could not open the way.

His eyes lifted, brimming. Her own were burning dry. "He told me," she said. "Mirain told me—if any man so much as touched me—"

"When did you ever do as you were told?"

She lurched forward a step. Her hands wanted to strike him; to stroke him. Invader, interloper; she hated him. Sharer in Mirain's soul, brother, kinsman; she—almost, she could force herself to—if he were Hal—if it were necessary—

She touched him. Mirain breathed between them, but slowly, slowly, cooling into death. Her breath caught, sharp with pain. "For him," she said. "Only for him."

Vadin rose. Before he could reach for her, she had seized him. Body to body. Mind to mind. Weaving, interweaving, warp, woof, the flash of the shuttle between. He was bright; he was strong. He was Mirain, but he was not. Kinsman. Brother. He shaped himself for her: a strong hand clasping hers, a strong will bolstering her own. Even—even a touch of joy, the delight of a master who has met his master in power.

With joy then, and with Vadin both her armor and her gate, she faced Sigan's high Wall. Which in truth was not a wall at all, but a growing awareness, a swelling of fear. *Back, turn back, or be forever lost.*

The fear rose to a crescendo and shattered. She fell into the void.

Eternity ticked off its ages.

Light.

She thought she was mad. No; she knew it. There was light below. The merest glimmer. Like a candle, pale gold, burning low. Like a star at the end of night, growing larger by infinite degrees. Swelling. Blooming. Enfolding her. With the suddenness of all endings, she struck the heart of it.

Earth. Grass. She stood naked on it, under a sky that was all light. Someone gripped her hand. Vadin. But if she shifted her eyes, she was he; they were one.

They looked down. Mirain looked up. Mirain at his ease, open-eyed yet drowsy, smiling. He beckoned. "Come," he said. "Rest. You look worn to the bone."

Elian was speechless. It was Vadin who snapped, "Of course we are! A fine chase you've led us, down through all the levels of your mind, looking for something resembling intelligence. I should have known we wouldn't find any."

"Ah now," said Mirain unruffled, "there's no need to yell at me. Won't you sit down at least? It's comfortable here."

"Comfortable!"

Elian silenced Vadin with a finger on his lips. "It's a trap, brother," she said, using the word with care; but Vadin was in no mood to notice it. "That's Mirain, but it's not."

The Ianyn's eyes widened, then narrowed. "What are you saying?"

"It's Mirain, but Mirain in part only, walled in his own cowardice. He'd keep us here in this comfort of his; before we knew it, we'd all be comfortably dead."

Vadin shook himself, and laughed almost freely. "I must be turning foolish in my old age. Of course this is a trap. I've seen the other side of death. It was even more comfortable than this; I hated to go back. But he made me.

"You made me," he said to Mirain, who yawned and stretched, sensuous as a cat, and smiled indulgently at his

vehemence. "You made me, damn you. It's well past time I repaid the debt."

"Debt?" Mirain asked. "I owe you nothing. I have to linger here for a while. There was something . . ." His brow creased very slightly, as if he sought a memory that eluded him. "It doesn't matter. It's a very pleasant place, don't you think? It will do until the time is past. Whatever it must pass for."

Vadin drew himself up to his full height. Once more Elian stilled him. She yearned to scream, to strike, to run, to do anything but face this travesty of the Sunborn. "It is not Mirain," she told Vadin, and herself. "It is *not*." She freed her hand, aware that her mind wove still with Vadin's, an awareness as distinct as the warmth of flesh against flesh. She knelt in the grass, and clasped this vapid smiling Mirain-creature, and held it tightly. "Now," she snapped over her shoulder, surging to her feet. "Out!"

Mirain roused. Began to fight. Serpent-supple, serpent-strong. He was too much for her. He was too strong.

She clung. She mustered all her strength. She clutched at Vadin's power; she seized it; she became it. He and she, long powerful man-body, arms hardened by a lifetime of wielding sword and lance and bow, power honed to a bitter edge under the greatest of masters: under Prince Orsan; under Mirain himself.

"Outward!" she cried. "To the light!"

The serpent flared into fire, flowed into water, scattered into air. She flung her power about it, netted it, flasked it, englobed it in crystal. It sprang into an edged blade. The crystal shattered; her hands closed about shards and steel. Pain mounted into agony. She thrust it down. She battled toward the light.

The wall loomed. She cried in despair. No gate. No passage. She must strike, fall, die.

"No." Vadin's voice, strong and quiet, though it shook a little. He led her now, drawing her upward, and in her bleeding hands the thing that had been Mirain. Writhing, snapping, steel-toothed creature, no shape to it at all, only struggle. She clasped it to her breast.

They struck the wall. Faltered. Slipped. Mirain bolted; she caught him. "Help," gasped Vadin. "Help—"

She flung them all forward.

The darkness burst. Stars sang in pure cold voices. Men wept; women laughed aloud. Grass whispered as it grew.

Elian opened her eyes. The world was a blur with a shadow in the middle of it. She blinked.

They smiled down at her. Vadin, his cheeks more hollow than ever, his grin white enough to blind her. And Mirain.

Mirain.

She clutched at him. He was warm and solid and as naked as he was born.

With a mighty effort she unclamped her fingers. They were whole, unscarred, no mark of tooth or claw. "I dreamed," she said. "I dreamed—"

"No dream." She had forgotten how beautiful his voice was. He kissed her brow, and then her lips. She shifted as easily as breathing, and stared at her own bewildered face. And again, from farther away, seeing herself and Mirain together. She wore no more than he. How wanton; how lovely to the eyes of this body. The eyes under the bright brows were Mirain's, laughing, raising a hand to run it down the strangeness in which she dwelt.

She inhaled sharply, and the breath completed itself in her own lungs. Vadin was Vadin, Mirain his unmistakable self. No languor, no madness. "This," she said, "could be confusing."

Mirain laughed. Vadin drew back. At last she saw his proud eyes lowered, and the part of her which was he, knew that he blushed. Why, she thought, he had no more sense than she when it came to considering consequences. Now that it was far too late for any remedy, he was beginning to regret what he had made her do.

"What I did for myself." She took his hand, though he tried to escape; she kissed it. "I was a fool, brother. But not for letting this happen. For letting it take so long." Her lips twitched. "Hal is going to be hideously jealous."

Vadin's eyes went a little wild. "You wouldn't!"

"No," Mirain said. "It's enough that we aren't three anymore; or two. Four in one would be unwieldy. Although," he added, "I can't bring myself to be sorry that you two did what you did."

Elian's thoughts wound through the twinned bright skein of theirs. Hers, Mirain's, Vadin's, all mingled. It was very beautiful.

One skein unraveled. "But I'm still *me*," she protested.

"And I am I, and he is he, but we are one." Through the splendor of his gladness, Mirain let slip a note of gravity. "It is very unorthodox."

"It's heretical." But Vadin was quieter now, more like the haughty prince whom Elian had thought she knew. He grimaced. "Though I fancy that's not the word most people will like to use. 'Immoral' will sound much more apt to the rumormongers. Not," he said, "that I intend to go so far. Some things are best kept in the inner room where they belong."

He sounded almost prim; Elian laughed, and kissed his hand again. Mirain's eyes glinted, but not with anger, and not ever with jealousy. Her free hand caught his and brought it to her cheek; her eyes flicked from his long-loved face to the one which she was learning only now to love. She smiled at them both.

Yet her brows had drawn together. "The powers in the circle, all the teachings I've ever known . . . they said that if I did this, I'd lose everything. But all I've lost is my stupidity. I've gained a whole world."

"I think," said Mirain, "that none of the masters knew what would happen. None has ever tried this; none has dared. Only you." His hand curved about her cheek, caressing it. "You gave all you had to give. While I . . ."

"I haven't given anything."

"You'll never be free of me again."

She glared at him. "When was I ever free of you?" Sudden laughter shook her. "The day I was born, I decided that you belonged to me. And I to you, although I'd never have admitted it."

"And Ziad-Ilarios?"

"Shall I reckon up all your lovers, O priest of the Sun?" She sat up so abruptly that her head spun. "Look at me, Mirain."

He could do very little else. Rumpled, blear-eyed, and torn between a grin and a snarl, she was the most beautiful creature in all the world.

"Except for Ledi," Vadin said, mischievous.

Her grin won the battle. Beauty she could not judge. But she knew her own fortune. Warrior, mage, and queen; she was all three. Yet greater than those . . .

They waited.

"And greater than those," she said, "I am the sister of Vadin alVadin who came back from the dead. And I am the lover of Mirain who is An-Sh'Endor, who has but to lift his hand to bring all the world to his feet." She paused. Vadin was smiling his white smile. But Mirain waited still. His head had come up, his eyes kindled. Oh, he was vain—as vain as a sunbird, and as beautiful, and as kingly proud.

"But not and never," she added wickedly as she pulled him down, "the Lady of Han-Gilen."